'Livvy Davis?'

She stared blankly at the woman who spoke.

'We are going to carry out a strip search . . . Could you stand up, please?'

The arresting officer walked towards the door and quietly disappeared. The women moved forward and Livvy stood as she'd been asked to do. She saw the blank gaze of one of them and realised then what she had to do. She began to shake.

'Could you remove each item of clothing separately and hand it across to me. I will tell you when to remove the next item.'

Livvy looked down at the ground for a few moments, then she pulled her sweatshirt over her head and handed it to the officer. She stood awkwardly and waited while it was carefully examined, folded and placed on the table. She unfastened her shirt and took that off next.

Several minutes later, standing naked, she put her arms up across her chest and tried to control her shivering. She couldn't look at the women. She stared down at the ground, the tears thick and painful in her throat. After what seemed like ages one of the officers said, 'OK, you can get dressed now.' And she nodded, reached for her bra, then finally began to cry.

FOR W.B.

(AND THE ETERNAL HOPE OF
A FULL NIGHT'S SLEEP)

ACKNOWLEDGEMENTS

I would like to thank the following people:

Jules' parents, June and Pat, for helping us to buy the house we live and work in, and my own parents, Maureen and Ted, for helping us to furnish it, the staff at the Princess Mary SCU for their wonderful care of our son, my dear friend Jo Francis for her knowledge of Lloyd's, Martin O'Collins at the BBC and Pam Royle at Tyne Tees TV, James Mulholland and Simon Waley for some very precise legal advice, HM Customs and Excise, particularly Joe Lyons and David Chester OBE, Barbara Waite at the *Newcastle Chronicle*, Mum and June for looking after William and me when we needed it and, as always, J.B.

Oxford, July 1984

'Livvy! Livvy! Oi! Over here!' Lucy Deacon screamed across the noise of the square. She waved her arm so frantically that she knocked her cap flying.

'Lucy, please!' Her mother bent and picked it up. 'Show a little decorum, this is your graduation!' But her words were lost as Olivia Davis flew into vision, all five foot eight of her, long tanned legs under her gown covered only to the top of her thigh by a tiny piece of black velvet skirt.

'Luce!' she shrieked, darting through the crowd of black-gowned graduates milling around like a flock of crows, and they flung their arms around each other theatrically, kissing on the lips in the provocative manner that had earned them such a reputation in college. Then they stood back and laughed.

'My God! You look bloody marvellous!' Lucy said enviously. 'What a tan!' Livvy licked her finger and rubbed it over her cheek. 'Doesn't wash off either!' Lucy's mother turned away in embarrassment at their performance and tried to distract her husband's attention from Olivia's legs.

'How was it then?' Lucy's smile faded to a frown. 'A whole

six months you've been away in the Far East with James and only two postcards!'

Livvy hooked her arm through her friend's affectionately. 'I'm sorry, Lucy, really I am. Forgive me?'

Lucy looked sidelong and saw the genuine regret on her friend's face. Livvy was very hard to resist. She yielded. 'Yes, all right then. But tell me how it was. You haven't answered my question yet. Was it tons of heat and passion?'

'It was . . .' Livvy paused, 'simply marvellous!' Actually that was a lie. The trip had been far from passionate, the heat of her affair with James fading very quickly to a safe familiarity. But Livvy had her pride and James was perfect in every other way.

Changing the subject then, she looked across at Mr and Mrs Deacon and said politely, 'You don't mind if I borrow Lucy for a few minutes, do you?' She smiled. 'It's just that David's here with my mother and he's promised to take some photos of us all.'

Daphne Deacon smiled back for the first time. Perhaps, with all Olivia's media connections, it was David Bailey?

'Er . . . David . . .?' she probed.

But Livvy didn't answer. She just threw Daphne a look that implied it was very probably who she thought it was and Daphne nodded at her daughter eagerly.

'Go on, Lucy dear! Don't keep Olivia's party waiting!'

So it *was* David Bailey, she thought triumphantly. Now that really was something to show off at the Bridge Club! 'Lucy dearest, go on! Hurry up, dear!'

Lucy stared blankly at her mother as Livvy steered her away from her parents.

'He's fearfully busy, you know!' Livvy called over her shoulder and Daphne nodded, an excited gleam in her eye.

'So we really must dash. How he's managed to find the time to get here, I don't know!'

Daphne started to follow and Livvy upped the pace. 'I shan't keep Lucy for long, Mrs D, I promise!' They were walking, half running across the square towards the main entrance of the Sheldonian Theatre. 'He does take such lovely pics!' she shouted behind her, waving. 'I'll send you some.'

'It's not really Dav . . .' Lucy began. Livvy cut her short. 'Yes, of course it is,' she said, and then laughed gaily. 'David Schneider, my mother's agent! He's just bought himself a Pentax.'

'Oh, Livvy!'

'Livvy, what? Do you want a commemorative photograph of the three best years of your life or not?'

'Yes, but . . .'

'But nothing! It's taken me twenty-five minutes to get our little group in the same place at the same time, so just be quiet and follow me.'

Lucy glanced sidelong at Livvy's perfect profile and saw that it would be useless to protest. It always was. Since the first day they had met in college, she had never known Olivia Davis not to get what she wanted; in the nicest possible way, of course. Livvy's life seemed charmed at times and the only thing to do, Lucy had decided very early on, was just to go along with it and enjoy the brilliance of the light that shone around her friend.

Hugh Howard stood very slightly apart from the small, elite group that was Livvy's clique and looked away from the camera for a moment at the shining faces gathered for the photograph, all smiling and laughing in the afternoon sun. Even the grand beauty of the Sheldonian Theatre behind them could not detract from the radiance of the little group, Oxford's best, the hand-chosen few, all picked by Olivia Davis for inclusion in her dazzling sphere of existence.

His shoulders tensed as he felt the familiar stab of envy and dislike of her and glancing across at James, he saw the same, smug look of satisfaction on his face and it sickened him. He had been used, he had foolishly given himself up, naively and passionately in love, and he had been dumped, dropped, for what? Hugh swallowed hard and turned to the camera as the photographer called for a smile.

He had hung on, of course, gone to all the parties, been part of 'the' group, but he had never fitted in, never felt comfortable. He had never forgiven any of them.

All money and no brains, he thought, hearing Jack Wilcox shout something silly and rude in reply to an instruction from the chap with the camera. And he wished that just for one moment James would look across at him and smile, sharing that feeling of conspiracy once again, the knowledge that regardless of where they both came from, they were far, far superior to all the rest.

'Hugh! For God's sake, smile, will you?' James was grinning across at him and Hugh realised that he'd been scowling. 'I think he's still trying to translate the Latin ceremony!' James said and Livvy laughed. 'I shouldn't bother, Hugh,' he continued. 'The only thing you need to remember are those two magic initials MA and the wonderful word "Oxon"!' Everyone laughed now, including Hugh, but Jack Wilcox laughed loudest; he was already drunk.

'Forget everything you learned during your time here except how to slip the name of your college into the first few sentences of a conversation and the world will be yours!' James, holding Livvy's hand, put it to his lips and kissed it affectionately. Fraser Stewart flinched. 'Oh, and keep a note of who you slept with, because if they did anything perverse at all, you can guarantee that they'll end up in the House of Commons!' Hugh flushed but no one noticed.

'James, stop it!' Livvy cried, delighted. 'The only thing we'll have on film is everyone's fillings!'

'OK, OK, stop laughing, everybody, now, please!' James dropped Livvy's hand and put his arm around her, pulling her in close. They looked joyous and golden in the warm July sun, both tanned from their trip to the Far East and both clever and beautiful. The perfect couple.

Fraser Stewart looked away and wondered how it was that Livvy had no idea. He turned back as David Schneider called out for the final few shots and tried to smile, not thinking about Livvy, or James, not thinking about the past two years of hoping and waiting. He thought instead about Aberdeen, not with any joy or excitement, but with a heavy feeling of duty and an aching disappointment at having to give up his place at Bar School. He tried to put it from his mind and smiled tightly on the count of three.

He had things to do, a mess to sort out, and perhaps Scotland was the distance he needed. A year from now he wouldn't feel like he did today, not once he'd settled properly. Maybe he would ring her from time to time, see how she was, but nothing more. He had to let go, he had to face up to his responsibilities with the paper. Besides, she had James now. Fraser clenched his fists by his side at the idea of that and made one final attempt to smile. He held it for twenty seconds, ignoring the senseless remarks that Jack

Wilcox kept making, and finally the photographs of the year of '83 were over.

Seconds later, the small group of friends broke up, made their farewells, and, each carrying his or her own memories, went in search of their families and their own separate ways.

PART 1

Chapter One

Oxford, October 1992

Hugh Howard followed the small crowd of tourists towards the Sheldonian Theatre, half listening to their guide and wanting to correct several of the points she made. She irritated him with her sharp nasal tone and the way she kept jabbing her umbrella in the air to command them all forward. Poor bastards, he thought, trudging round the city in her wake and missing all the beauty of it for the sake of getting it all done in an hour.

He left them in the square outside the theatre. He smiled as, turning away, he briefly glimpsed the bored face of an adolescent, nodding relentlessly to the beat from the speakers of his walkman while the guide droned on.

Hugh wandered alone in the shadow of the buildings, letting the magic of Oxford fill his senses and the memories flood back, for the first time in over eight years.

Hugh had never returned. Not once. He had left Oxford with nothing but bitterness, anger and hurt; the romance of the place had sickened him for years afterwards. He remembered it all, so clearly that it seemed like yesterday, every emotion he had felt, every word said, every kiss. He stood, away from the cold stone façade of the building, in the centre of the Square, and let the weak October sunshine warm his face. All that was over now. It had been over for years and Hugh had forgotten it.

Almost.

Only now, standing here and imagining the echo of Livvy's voice in the wind, he felt a small stab of triumph. He allowed himself a tiny moment of gratification as he thought of all the hard work of the past few months. It was about to pay off. He was about to seal his plans for the future and, in the midst of all this, he would have his delicious vengeance. The sweet, sweet taste of revenge.

Turning to leave, he glanced back at the exact place he had had his photograph taken with all the rest on graduation, a photograph he had sent to his parents as consolation because he had been too embarrassed to invite them on the day. He had hated it anyway. He had far outgrown the awkward, gauche young man in the picture. He knew who he was now, he knew where he was going, and this time it was his turn to use whoever came his way.

Hearing the clock chime eleven, Hugh checked his watch and then pulled the starched white linen of his cuff down a fraction below the sleeves of his morning coat so that the black enamelled pattern of his art nouveau cufflinks was just visible. He straightened his waistcoat, Italian silk brocade from a Florentine business trip, and turned towards the High. Eliza and Henry's wedding was at twelve-thirty in the church at Duns Tew fifteen miles away, so he had over an hour to spare. Just enough time for a visit to the blushing bride, he thought, smiling as he caught the faint reflection of his own image in one of the shop windows. He would take her a gift for her honeymoon, something very chic and sexy to wear, something from Viva. After all, he mused, in a year or so's time he would have a great deal to thank Eliza for. The invitation to her wedding could not have been better timed.

Hugh parked his bright red Porsche 911 in the drive of Chard House, alongside the family Bentley, which was decked out in white ribbon, ready to take the bride to the church. As he climbed out, he saw a young man gazing out eagerly from inside the porch. Hugh smiled. The bride's brother, he guessed, and walked on confidently towards the house.

'Hello. You must be . . .?'

'Phillip. Liza's brother.' The young man flicked back a fringe of long blond hair rather affectedly and looked past Hugh to his car. Hugh slipped his hand inside his trouser pocket.

'Phillip, I'd like to see Eliza for a few moments. Which is her room?'

Phillip looked at Hugh, sizing him up for a couple of seconds, and remained silent. Hugh took the tenner he had ready in the palm of his hand and placed it neatly in the breast pocket of Phillip's morning coat, just underneath his silk handkerchief. Phillip flicked his fringe back again and nodded up the stairs.

'Fourth on the right,' he said. 'At the end of the corridor. If you go through the kitchen you can use the back staircase.'

'Thanks.'

Phillip shrugged and slipped in a quick put-down as Hugh went to walk past him. 'Henry's got a Saab Turbo soft top.'

'Poor Henry.' Hugh carried on into the kitchen. He went

up the stairs, found the fourth door on the right and quietly turned the handle, walking in without knocking. He stood silently for several moments and watched Eliza at work.

Eliza Nash squirted a little more cream into the palm of her hand and delicately rubbed it over the full roundness of her breasts. She then picked up her scent bottle, took the stopper out and dabbed at each nipple with it, leaving a smear of perfume behind. She replaced the stopper, pulled up the thin ribbon straps of her silk chemise and bent to adjust her suspenders. She turned, ready to take her dress off its hanger, and jumped as she saw Hugh Howard, as good-looking as ever, leaning nonchalantly against the door of her bedroom and watching her every movement with a small, smug smile on his lips.

'You bastard, Hugh!'

His smile widened to a grin and from behind his back he produced a glossy white carrier bag with distinctive green writing and held it out for her.

'Forgive me?'

She smiled and crossed to him, taking the bag from his hand. 'I see you twice after sending you a wedding invitation, the only times in the past nine years since we went down, I might add, and then you suddenly appear in my room to watch me dress for my wedding! You've got a bloody nerve, Hugh Howard!'

Hugh pulled her towards him and kissed her mouth briefly. 'But you're not cross.' He let her go. 'I know.'

Eliza suddenly laughed. 'Of course I'm not cross.' She turned back to her dressing table and placed the bag next to her perfume. 'The thought of it is rather erotic actually.'

Hugh rolled his eyes. 'You're getting married in an hour,

Eliza my darling. What would Henry think if he heard you saying things like that?'

'Not much. Henry doesn't think, that's why I'm marrying him.'

Now it was Hugh's turn to laugh. He walked across the room to the chaise and sat down, still smiling. 'Carry on as you were, sweetie. Don't let me stop you.'

Eliza raised an eyebrow. She came and stood before him, slipping the strap of her chemise down and revealing a round, pink breast. 'Why not?'

Hugh leaned forward and gently licked her nipple. Hearing her sigh, he sat up and eased the strap back into place. 'Nice scent, Eliza.'

She looked down, disappointed. 'You always were an odd one, Hugh.'

'Not odd, just different.'

She shrugged. 'Oh, well, I suppose seeing as it's my wedding night the perfume won't go to waste.' She glanced down at her nipples – still erect – and smiled.

'What's dear old Henry like, by the way?'

Eliza shrugged again and turned away. 'The equipment's all there, he's just not very good at operating it.'

Hugh laughed. 'Oh, poor Eliza!'

'Not poor Eliza at all.' She glanced round. 'Henry has more money and less sense than any other man I know. Who needs sex with that combination?' She picked up her lipstick from the dressing table and, turning back to the mirror, opened her mouth slightly to apply it. 'Now,' she said, lips parted, 'what did you come here for if it wasn't to send me to church with a smile on my face?' She looked at Hugh's reflection over her shoulder. 'Oh God! Not James Ward and Livvy Davis again?'

Hugh grinned. 'No, not them. You told me everything I wanted to know last time, you wicked gossip!'

Eliza laughed and smudged her lipstick. 'Shit!' She reached for a tissue.

'Jack Wilcox,' Hugh said. 'Didn't you do some invest-ment work for him at Cazenoves?' If he was going to use him, Hugh needed to know how much Jack was worth.

Eliza, happy with her second application of Charles of the Ritz pink, turned and shook her head at Hugh. 'If I wasn't leaving the city and if you hadn't bought me such an extravagant gift last time, Hugh my love, I probably wouldn't answer that question.'

'But . . .?'

'But I'd recognise that expensive carrier bag anywhere. It's from that wonderful shop Viva, isn't it?'

He nodded and she laughed. 'Oh well, I never really liked Jack very much anyway!' And, taking her dress off its hanger, Eliza began to relay the Wilcox investment portfolio to Hugh in all its glorious and infinite detail.

Just after one-thirty, Hugh drove up to Chard House for the second time that day. He turned into the field that had been opened up for parking, swung the Porsche into a space between a Range Rover and a Mercedes and climbed out, careful of his highly polished shoes on the muddy grass. He smoothed down the tails of his morning coat, adjusted his tie and made his way across to the huge marquee at the back of the house. He had sat the service out in the pub, unable to stand the sound of choirs, and had given the receiving queue a good forty minutes to go down. The one thing Hugh Howard hated about weddings was the bloody wait in that queue for a drink!

Walking through an awning and into a long tented passage hung with white silk lining, Hugh followed the noise of the crowd towards the marquee, joining the last of the receiving queue and smiling politely at the couple in front of him. Within minutes they had edged forward and into the huge white marquee adorned with big floral displays of lilies and roses and packed tight with an impressive array of hats and morning dress. He glimpsed Eliza kissing an aged aunt and Henry next to her, the nervous groom looking rather dazed by the whole thing and certainly as stupid as Eliza had made out. Hugh smiled and looked away across the marquee. It was then that he saw James.

James Ward stood next to Livvy Davis, who looked as stunning as ever, listening to the conversation of a short and rather ugly blonde woman with an impassive look on his face. He elegantly smoked a long thin cigar and nodded every now and then, all the time still managing to keep his attention focused on the rest of the party. He was immaculately, and expensively dressed, his morning coat expertly cut and his waistcoat an extravagant silk of red, green and silver stripe. He was every inch the aspiring diplomat, the type of person Hugh had always thought he would be. And yet his face was completely unchanged.

Looking at him now, Hugh realised he could have been the same boy that he had met that first registration day in college, the same, elusive, charming boy, unsure of himself but confident enough to lead the shy and awkward Hugh Howard through the minefield of the first few days. Looking at him now, Hugh knew he hadn't forgotten. No matter what he had planned, what he had thought, just the sight of James Ward bought back all the pain and confusion and the same deep, powerful ache he had felt from the first moment they met.

Hugh stood where he was and simply looked across at James, and for one fleeting moment he didn't know what to do next. But he had schemed for too long, he had worked too hard for this deal and hunted too many months for the right man to finish it for him. There was too much at stake to throw it all away on a moment of weakness. He could handle James Ward. That was part of the thrill, wasn't it? Part of the sweetness of revenge, getting what he wanted this time round, grabbing all the power for himself. He moved forward a pace into the marquee and kept his eyes on James. He watched the ugly blonde drift away and waited for James to turn. Seconds later their eyes met.

James Ward had been thoroughly bored by the woman just departed. He had feigned a modicum of interest for as long as he could and then yawned, rather loudly, and sent her scurrying away. He glanced round at the entrance to the marquee, to see if anyone of interest had come in and instantly he saw Hugh Howard. He stood still, looking at the cool grey of the other man's eyes and his whole body shivered, shivered in a way it hadn't done for ten years. He held his gaze for a moment longer, unable to look away, and then suddenly the magic was shattered.

Livvy saw Hugh and her face broke into a broad, excited grin. She called out. 'Hugh? I don't believe it!'

Immediately she began walking across to the entrance, not noticing that James had flushed a deep crimson behind her, and Hugh smiled in greeting. He had not forgotten the warmth of the glow from Olivia Davis, the feeling of being enveloped in her special aura, and as she approached, he saw the same beautiful woman, overwhelmingly confident in her femininity, the pale pink silk of her Giorgio Armani suit perfectly matched with the straw of her Herbert Johnson hat, its chiffon veil drawn down to just below her eyes. She reached him, held her hat with one hand to keep it steady and kissed his cheek, the rich scent of her perfume filling the air between them.

'Hugh! You look absolutely marvellous! It's been ages – no, more than that – aeons since we saw you last!' She stepped back and looked him up and down admiringly, then she laughed.

God, she was lovely, Hugh thought, and then hated himself for weakening to her charm. 'Livvy, you haven't changed a bit!' He took her hands and kissed them both. An expert now in deceit, he made it look as if he were totally surprised and delighted by this unexpected encounter. 'I had no idea you and James would be here, I . . .' He stopped as James joined them. 'James! How nice to see you.' He held out his hand and saw the briefest look of irony pass across James's face. The same look, a look that took him back ten years and made him want to laugh out loud as it always had.

He turned back to Livvy. 'So what about the others? Fraser Stewart, Lucy Deacon? Are they lurking in the undergrowth anywhere around?'

Livvy frowned. 'No, sadly not. Lucy will be furious when she knows she missed you! She's off doing some kind of promotional work in the States for a new fund she's managing. She's pretty high up in that bank of hers.'

'What about Fraser?'

'Surly bastard!' James interjected.

'*James!*'

'Well, he *is*. He rings the flat and can hardly be bothered to give me the time of day.'

'Fraser isn't here either,' Livvy said, throwing James a

look, half in jest, half in warning. 'He runs a small paper up in Aberdeen and couldn't get the time off, apparently.'

Hugh saw James smirk.

'James always finds the idea of Fraser running a paper incredibly funny,' she said, sounding exasperated. 'I've no idea why!'

But Hugh had. He knew damn well how much Fraser Stewart used to annoy James – he was far too brilliant for James ever to like him. He smiled and Livvy smiled back.

'And Jack Wilcox?'

Both Livvy and James pulled the same face at the same time.

'Oh, Jack's here all right!' James said and Livvy laughed. 'In about an hour you should be able to hear him from across the marquee.'

'Or maybe an hour and a half, James,' Livvy interrupted. 'It all depends on how often they go round with the champagne.' They both laughed and Hugh smiled, a wide, satisfied smile.

So Wilcox is still as senseless as he always was, he thought. He lit up a cigarette, took another glass of champagne from a passing waiter and decided that the afternoon was really going to be rather enjoyable.

Chapter Two

The alarm clock beeped piercingly and Livvy rolled over in bed, dragged her mind from a strange and wonderful dream and reached out an arm to touch James and make sure he was awake. She felt an empty space.

Opening her eyes, she peered blearily at the clock, sighed heavily and forced herself awake. She could smell fresh coffee from the kitchen and saw that the blind had been half drawn to let a little of the November light into the room. James was obviously up and about. She sat up, eased her long, slim legs over the side of the bed and then stood, pulling on her robe and crossing the bedroom. She walked out through the open, light sitting room and into the kitchen where James sat reading *The Times*.

'Morning, darling.'

He didn't look up or reply but Livvy bent to kiss the top of his head anyway. She helped herself to coffee, added milk and sugar and waited for him to realise she was in the room. Several minutes later, he turned the page and, still without looking at her, said, 'D'you want coffee?'

'I have some,' she answered coolly.

Now he glanced up. 'Oh yes, so you do.' He smiled, one

of his charming, half-apologetic smiles, and shrugged.

Despite her irritation, Livvy smiled back. She always did. 'You're up early.'

He had folded the paper and was skimming the back page. 'Hmmm.'

'Is there something going down at the office?'

James finally abandoned the paper, stood up and looked at her fully for the first time since she'd walked in. 'You know nothing ever goes down at the Foreign Office, Livvy,' he said patiently.

'Yes, of course.' She had meant it as a joke. 'So why are you up so early?'

'I have a bit of work to do,' he lied. He crossed to the sink and placed his breakfast things on the side, avoiding her eye. 'Now if you'll excuse me, Mrs Nosey, I must get dressed.' He turned towards the door and offered a smile. 'Have you seen my new Trumpers shaving soap?'

'Yes, I put it away. It's . . .' Livvy stopped mid-sentence. God, their conversations were boring these days! She hardly ever saw him and when she did it was all domesticity and work. 'It's in the bathroom cupboard,' she finished.

Picking up *The Times*, she took it with her coffee through to the sitting room and flopped down on to one of the long, cream leather sofas. She put her feet up on to the low table and stared out of the window for a few moments. She could just make out the figures of the dedicated, running on the machines in front of the huge bank of glass at the Peak Health Club across Cadogan Square, and she shuddered at the thought of such effort. Taking a large gulp of creamy, sweet coffee, she settled back against the cushions, opened up the paper and began to read.

*

Twenty minutes later, Livvy stood in the doorway of the bedroom and watched James as he finished dressing in front of the mirror. He tucked the fine cotton striped shirt into the trousers of his dark grey pinstripe suit and fastened his tie, long thin fingers elegantly threading the piece of silk to form a perfect knot. He drew it up to his collar and smoothed it, making sure it was exactly the right length before reaching for his jacket from its hanger. He pulled it on, double-checked that the tie went with the silk lining and then took up one of his brushes from the chest to smooth back his hair.

Livvy came into the room and picked up a discarded shirt and tie from the bed, taking them over to James's wardrobe. 'What was wrong with this one?' she asked.

'Hmmm?' He looked round. 'Oh, it didn't go.'

'I see.' Actually she didn't. Livvy possessed a natural elegance and something a journalist had once called 'throwaway chic'. She never cared particularly about what she wore, perhaps because she didn't have to; she could have worn a pair of old curtains and still looked fantastic.

'So what time are you off, Livvy darling?' James was rifling in the drawer for a handkerchief as he spoke.

'Oh, I don't know, some time this afternoon. I'm going into the office for an hour or so this morning to run through some rushes of the interview I did last week and Lucy said she might meet me for lunch at Ziani's if she can get away.' Livvy turned to look at him. 'You know, you could still come this weekend if you wanted to – we could drive down together this evening.'

'Livvy.' James tucked the handkerchief into his pocket. 'We've been through this loads of times. You know I don't like family weekends.'

'Nor do I particularly.'

'Yes, but the difference is that I don't have to go.'

'You'd come if there was going to be someone interesting there for the weekend, wouldn't you?'

'Yes. But there won't be, will there?'

Livvy shook her head. Only her mother, Peter and her young half-brother Giles would be at the house in Sussex. She hated going down almost as much as James did, but if she didn't go her mother would make a huge fuss. He crossed the room to her and placed his arms around her waist, laying his head on her shoulder.

'We spend too much time apart,' she said quietly.

'The price of success,' he answered, lifting his head. 'An up-and-coming star in the world of television presenting such as yourself, Livvy my love, has to make sacrifices.' He slipped his hands down to her bottom. 'You have to earn that staggering salary of yours, you know. It's more than just a cute ass nowadays!' She smiled and he bent to brush her lips with a kiss. Suddenly she reached up and caught her fingers in his hair, pulling his mouth down on to her own. She felt the heat of his tongue and then instinctively he pulled away.

'You'll make me late,' he whispered, easing his body apart from hers. He removed her fingers and smiled, the same easy, apologetic smile she had seen earlier. He kissed them and said, 'Tempting, but . . .'

She nodded. 'Duty calls.'

Within seconds he had moved to the door, smoothing his jacket and straightening his tie. He blew her a kiss. 'Have a wonderful weekend, my darling.' She nodded again. 'Love to Moira and Peter, and a smack on the head for Giles.'

'*James*!'

'Only kidding! Bye, darling.'

She went to blow him a kiss back but he had gone. She heard the front door slam and realised he had left the flat before she had even had time to call goodbye. She shrugged and turned towards the bathroom. The lack of passion between her and James was nothing new; in fact it had been going on for years.

In the grey marble bathroom, Livvy flipped the switches by the door and the large, elegant space was suddenly illuminated by a bank of light. She stood in front of the huge mirror above the sink and looked at her reflection lit by two high-intensity spots on either side of the glass. Letting her robe drop to the floor, she inspected every inch of her long, lean body, tanned even down to the small triangle of blonde hair between her legs, and then trailed a finger down from her collarbone, over her full, round breasts to the small swell of stomach and finally the sleek line of her thigh.

'Not bad for a woman your age,' she said aloud. 'Well worth the investment of seven hundred quid a year at Holmes Place.' She smiled at herself but the smile was a little jaded. Somehow she couldn't help feeling that it was all beginning to be a bit of a waste. The last time she and James had made love was . . . She paused mid-thought and tried to remember back. What with her trip to Prague, which had taken nearly a month, and then working all hours to get the programme finished, and with James going to Paris . . . She sighed and shook her head. Well, whenever it was, it was too bloody long ago!

She reached behind her for a thick white towel off the hot rail and pulled open the door to the shower cubicle. Turning on the tap, she gave the torrent of water several seconds to warm up and then, hanging her towel by the door, she stepped under the jet of steaming water and stretched for her Clarins Eau Dynamisse shower mousse. As was her habit, she quickly put the problem of James from her mind.

Half a mile away, at much the same time, James stepped inside a phone booth in Sloane Square, took a slip of paper from the top pocket of his overcoat, and dialled the number. He was nervous and his hand was damp with sweat as he held the receiver up to his ear. He waited for the line to connect and wondered for the umpteenth time that morning why the hell he was doing this. He heard a ringing tone, then a pause and finally the voice he had been dying to hear for days.

'Hello, Hugh? It's James,' he said, and in that one moment he knew exactly why he was doing it. He laughed, his whole spirit alive with an excitement he hadn't felt for years and went on, 'Hugh, it appears that I am free for lunch today, after all. Sorry to leave it so late but can you still make it?'

Hugh replaced the receiver after James's call and smiled, a small triumphant smile. He was on his way.

'Do I take it the smile means you know already?'

Hugh looked up as Paul Robson, a senior underwriter he'd just made junior partner, strode confidently into his office.

'Know what?' Hugh was instantly wary. Robson was good but he was too damn involved in everything.

'IMACO!'

Hugh relaxed slightly. 'Of course I bloody well know!' he

snapped. Then he smiled quickly. 'I know you're a junior partner, but who still runs this company?'

Robson put two files down on the desk. He took no notice of Hugh's manner; he didn't get paid a massive salary to worry about Hugh being nice to him.

'Well, here it all is,' he said. 'IMACO want a bigger line, and after all the small lines we've taken, I reckon we could go for a more substantial chunk of their insurance this time.' He smiled. 'It's all in the file.'

Hugh picked up the files and flicked through the top one. 'It's already been discussed,' he said.

'Oh, really?' Robson was surprised. He dealt largely with the IMACO business, took care of most of their insurance. It was his deft reinsurance that had made Howard Underwriting a good deal of money in the past year. Hugh going behind his back like that made him look small and, though he didn't show it, he was angry. 'What portion of the business have you decided to take?'

'I've taken it all.'

Robson smiled, thinking Hugh was joking, but moments later his face fell. 'You're not serious?'

Hugh raised an eyebrow.

'Fifteen million quid's worth of insurance?'

'Yes. Any problem with that?'

Robson shook his head. 'Yes, there's a problem,' he said. 'It's a hell of a lot of reinsurance to find, that's the problem! We take a small line each time, two to three million, then all of a sudden we're taking fifteen million! Isn't that a bit of a leap?'

Hugh shrugged. 'It's the way to make money,' he said coolly.

'And what about me? Where am I supposed to find that kind of reinsurance . . .?'

'You don't have to!' Hugh interrupted. 'I've got it covered already.'

Robson looked at Hugh. 'You have?'

'Yes, it was one of the conditions of me taking the business.'

'Who with?'

Hugh sighed, suddenly irritated. 'With as many small underwriters as I could find.' He picked up the files and handed them back across the desk. 'I don't mean to be rude, Paul, but I am free to make any decision I like in this company. You understand that?'

Robson took up the files. He had to get out of the office before he said anything he regretted. 'Yes, Hugh,' he answered, 'I understand.' And without another word, he turned on his heel and left.

Hugh leaned back in his chair and took a deep breath.

He'd known he'd have trouble with Robson; that had been his only real concern. The accountants did as he asked, he paid them enough to, and no one else was involved. It was just Robson, he was the only one who might cause a problem, the only one who could possibly find out that Hugh hadn't reinsured the IMACO business. He hadn't even touched it.

If he really was going to get this deal in South America off the ground then he needed a massive boost to the books of Howard Underwriting, and IMACO's business was too good an offer to refuse. He needed to prove to Manuello that he was in the big league now, that he had the Midas touch. He needed to prove that he could be trusted. Besides, petro-chemicals was a safe industry, it wasn't high risk. Any other company and he might have been wary about such a big leap in their insurance, but not IMACO. Fertilisers, for

God's sake, he thought, taking his cigarettes out of his drawer and lighting one up. He took a long pull on the Marlboro and relaxed. Fertilisers, he mused, where was the risk in that?

'Morning, Ron!' Livvy strode into the glossy black and chrome Reception of City Television and called out to the security guard on the desk as she went past.

'Morning, Livvy. Beautiful one it is too!'

'Absolutely!' She started up the stairs and Ron watched her go. Bloody nice pair of pins on 'er, he thought, waiting for the heart-warming sight of her lovely bottom, encased in the black Lycra leggings she wore under her cropped red jacket. His eyes followed her up the stairs, fixed firmly on the round, pert cheeks until she turned, nearly at the top and said, 'I think I ought to get a longer jacket, to cover me bum, don't you, Ron?' And smiling at his look of embarrassment, she carried on round the corner and out of sight.

'Morning, Livvy!'

'Hi, Bill! Morning, Sam!' Livvy threw her bag down on to the desk and made for the coffee machine. 'Wow, Sam! Love the specs!'

Sam, the production assistant, lifted the pair of pink plastic and shimmering diamanté glasses from her eyes for a moment and grinned. 'They're a present from you know who!' She winked and Livvy laughed.

'Will he lend you one of his frocks and a bunch of gladioli too?'

'Not unless I give good head.'

'Samantha!'

'Ha, only kidding. I shocked Livvy Davis! Did you get that, Bill? I shocked Livvy Davis!'

'Oh, Sam, please!' Livvy stuck out her tongue and indecently rolled it around for a few seconds until Bill looked up. She left Sam convulsed and carried on towards the machine. 'Can I get my producer a coffee, Bill?'

'Yes, great, thanks.'

'And Sam? White or black, large or small?'

Sam almost recovered, shook her head and sniggered again.

'Livvy, are you here for any particular reason?' Bill asked. 'I thought you were taking the day off.'

'I'm supposed to be off home to Sussex for the weekend but I thought I might go through the rushes of that Mick and Vic interview before I go. They might be artists but they can't string a bloody sentence together! Also I'm meeting a friend for lunch and . . .'

'Oh, Livvy, that's not Lucy Deacon, is it?' Sam interrupted.

'Yes, it is. Why?'

Sam reached for a yellow Post-it stuck on to the side of her PC. 'Lucy Deacon rang this morning at eight-thirty, and er . . .' Sam read out her shorthand. '. . . she's had to go up to Sheffield for a meeting this afternoon and she's sorry but she can't make it for lunch. She says she'll ring you at home this weekend. OK?'

'Oh damn! Never mind, thanks, Sam.'

'And the rushes of that interview are at home in my sitting room, Livvy.' Bill pulled a face and shrugged his shoulders apologetically. 'I started them last night and thought I'd go over them this weekend. Sorry.'

Livvy added hot water to the contents of the small foil sachet and tried not to feel peeved. The aroma of nearly fresh coffee was released and she took a sip out of her cup before adding milk to Bill's. Her whole morning had suddenly disintegrated and she'd have to go down to Sussex early as a result. She carried the cups back across the office and delivered Bill's before sitting down at her desk.

'There's always the post,' she said irritably, and then decided to ring James to see if he was free for lunch. They rarely met up during the day but maybe he'd make an exception. Anything was better than a whole afternoon in the garden with her mother talking about Peter and Giles as if her own father had never even existed. She picked up the phone and punched in James's number. The line was answered after just two rings and she smiled at the smooth, dark timbre of his voice.

'James, it's me.'

'Hi, Livvy. What have you forgotten?'

She noticed his patronising tone of voice but ignored it. 'I wondered if you wanted to have lunch.'

'What, today?'

'Yes, today.' She kept her irritation down.

'Can't, I'm afraid. I've already made arrangements.'

'Oh.' She waited for him to expand on that but he said nothing. After several moments of silence she said, 'Never mind, then, I'll just have to set off earlier than planned.'

'OK.'

Livvy thought James sounded odd but she didn't want to comment on that in the office with Sam only feet away. 'Well, I'll see you Sunday night.'

'Yup, see you then.' A short pause, then: 'Oh, and have a good time, darling.'

'Thanks.'

'Bye.' The line went dead.

Livvy sat and stared at the receiver for a minute or so before replacing it and then said, 'Well, that's that then!'

She picked up a pile of post and some photographs of the previous week's public appearances and shoved them into her bag. 'I'll be off,' she called across to Bill. 'I'll see you Monday morning.' She stood and noticed Sam's puzzled look but was too irked by her conversation with James to pass it off with a joke. She turned away and fiddled with the catch on her Armani rucksack, then slung it over her shoulder and moved past her desk towards the door. 'See you Monday, Sam. Don't do anything I wouldn't do!'

Sam snorted. 'Leaves the field wide open, Livvy!'

Livvy couldn't help but smile. 'Bye,' she said, and disappeared through the door.

Sam looked over at Bill. 'James or the weekend in Sussex?' she asked.

Bill rolled his eyes. 'That jerk of a boyfriend first and foremost and then memories of Bryan, I'd say.'

Sam nodded. Both of them knew that weekends at home reminded Livvy of her father and that even after twelve years it was still painful. Bill shrugged and Sam nodded again in reply. Both of them also knew that Livvy was too much on her own and that James was a waste of space. But neither of them had the courage to say so.

Down in the car park, Livvy pressed the alarm pad on her key ring and the BMW central locking system clicked open as she approached her car. She pulled open the passenger door, threw her bag on the seat and then went round to the driver's side and slid in behind the wheel. She started the engine and it purred to life, the stereo coming on at the same time. The sound of Dina Carroll echoed through the speakers. Livvy put the car into reverse, swung the wheel round and looked over her shoulder behind her. She glimpsed the slash in the vinyl of the soft-top roof and stopped for a moment, smiling at the memory of her conversation with Fraser Stewart some months back when she was buying the car. 'Bloody soft top, Livvy?' he'd exploded. 'Bloody soft in the head if you ask me! How long d'you suppose that's going to last in London?'

'About sixteen hours, Fraser!' Livvy said aloud to the empty car and then grinned. The roof had been slashed the first night she'd got the car and then twice after that. Not that she'd ever admit it to Fraser, though – a girl had to have her pride, bloody know-it-all! She reversed out of her space in the car park, drove down to the security gate and flashed her red pass at the guard in the booth. The barrier lifted and she pulled off. Maybe I'll ring him tonight, she thought, turning up the music. It was ages since they'd spoken. Then she remembered that she was never comfortable using the phone at her mother and Peter's, so she put the idea from her head.

She turned up the music a fraction more and accelerated up to the lights; she couldn't wait to get the car out on to the open motorway. Maybe going home did have its compensations, just.

Chapter Three

James crossed the road at the corner of Fortnum's and turned down Duke Street towards Jermyn Street, glancing at his reflection in the plate-glass window as he went. He put his hand up to his hair to smooth a stray strand back into place and straightened his jacket. He was slightly nervous, on edge. He had no idea what to expect. Eight years was a long time, he thought, people changed. Perhaps it wasn't such a good idea after all.

But crossing the road again at Simpson's he saw the sign for Roley's up ahead and knew, with a sudden jolt of pleasure, that he was really looking forward to the next few hours. It was the first time in years he had experienced anything like this and the heady danger of it all made him feel really alive.

He quickened his pace and stopped outside the restaurant at ten minutes past midday, checking the time just before he went inside. He could see several early lunchers through the window but Roley's was only a quarter full. He pulled open the door, was met by the rich aroma of garlic and steak, and stepped inside. He glanced round, saw he was the first to arrive, then gave his name to the head waiter and followed him to the table he had requested at the back. He ordered a drink, sat down with the *Economist* and waited, the pulse of excitement and deceit heavy in his veins.

Hugh Howard watched James from just inside the doorway of Fortnum's, saw him stop at Roley's after checking his watch and enter the restaurant a few seconds later. This lunch had taken weeks of careful manipulation: the accidental meeting after Eliza's wedding, the supposed business call, the unwanted invitation to a private view at the Nicholas Thorpe Gallery in Fulham. Hugh had been meticulous in his planning but it had been necessary that James call him for lunch today; that was an intrinsic part of the strategy.

He stood where he was and waited long enough to give James time to seat himself, then he headed after him, the heels of his Lobbs handmade brogues clicking smartly on the pavement as he went, the silk of his Hermès tie spotted with the few drops of rain that had just started to fall. He reached the restaurant a few minutes later, glanced through the window to locate James before opening the door and then walked inside, nodding to the waiter and striding to the back, where James sat.

He stopped several paces away from the table and for a few seconds stood looking across at James as he read, at the slick, groomed hair, the narrow, square features that fitted together so perfectly, the immaculate clothes and the long, thin fingers of his hand as he turned the page of the journal; fingers Hugh remembered so well. Then he stepped forward, a casual, well-formed smile on his lips and said, 'Hello, James. I'm glad you could make it.'

James glanced up with a start; the waiting was over. He stood, held out his hand and looked directly at Hugh. 'Yes,' he answered, 'so am I.' And the two men shook, the feel of James's hand exactly as Hugh recalled it. Then James smiled. One of his hauntingly familiar smiles, private and intimate, it needed no other communication, and despite his hardened heart, Hugh felt the same involuntary spasm in his stomach, a deep, exquisite pain.

'It's been too long, Hugh,' James said. 'Far too long.'

Livvy swung the BMW on to the hard shoulder off the dual carriage way and gently slowed the car. She stopped just in front of the flower stall and climbed out, nodding to the young man. It was twelve-thirty and she was about fifteen miles from home.

'Afternoon!'

Livvy smiled. 'Hi! Can I have a couple of bunches of the carnations, please?'

The young man pulled the flowers dripping from their buckets and expertly wrapped them in paper. He kept his head down as he sellotaped the edge and said, 'You're Livvy Davis, aren't you?'

'Yes.'

Still with his head down, he handed the flowers over. 'Can I have your autograph?' He glanced up, blushing slightly. 'For my sister, that is?'

'Of course!' Livvy took the flowers and dug in her bag for some cash and a pen. She handed over the money while the young man cleared a small space for her on the stall to lean on. He gave her a bit of paper and she paused, about to sign. 'What name shall I put?'

'Mal . . . Oh!' The young man glanced away, embarrassed.

'Er . . . could you put . . . er . . . all my love, or something like that?'

Livvy held back a smile. She caught sight of a large, gold initialled signet ring on the young man's right hand and wrote: Dearest MJ, all my love, Livvy Davis, and signed several large scrawly kisses at the end. She stood straight.

'Oh, er . . .' The young man read the inscription and then grinned broadly. 'Great! Thanks a lot, Livvy!'

Livvy smiled. 'My pleasure.' She headed back to the car and put the flowers in the boot along with her weekend bag. It had been spitting for the past half hour and now it began to rain, heavy icy drops against a background of dark grey sky. The light almost instantly disappeared. Livvy waved briefly at the young man and slid inside the dry warmth of her car, switching on the engine and warming her hands over the hot air vent. She looked out at the weather and hoped it wouldn't last all weekend. The last thing she wanted was to be cooped up in the house from Friday to Sunday: there were too many memories of her father at The Old Rectory for her ever to feel comfortable or relaxed there.

'Livvy!' Moira, Livvy's mother, was waiting just inside the entrance porch as Livvy climbed out of the car. It was still raining hard so she hadn't ventured out to greet her daughter for fear of spoiling her hair. A semi-retired actress, her looks were still essential to her. 'Come on in, darling. Quickly!' she called, in her beautifully modulated RADA voice. 'Peter will get your bags later.'

Livvy made a dash for the house and dived into the porch, banging the door behind her and shaking the rain from her hair. Once inside, she kissed her mother's expertly made-up face and followed her into the warmth of the house, breathing in the smell of faded potpourri and beeswax polish; the smell of home. She took off her smart red jacket and reached for one of the tatty old cardigans from the porch, pulling it on and buttoning it up.

'Come on through, darling,' Moira said, automatically hanging the jacket up after her daughter. 'I've made a huge pot of soup for lunch.' She went to the stairs and shouted up, 'Giles! Tear yourself away from the telly for five minutes, please. It's lunch time!' Then she hooked her arm through Livvy's and led her through to what Livvy always thought was the best room in the house – the large, untidy, warm and comforting kitchen.

Lunch was eaten at the scrubbed pine refectory table with Willy the labrador curled up by Livvy's feet, mouth open and drooling all over the stone floor, and Giles, Livvy's spotty twelve-year-old half-brother, on half-term from Winchester, stuffing himself moodily, his walkman on and a *Viz* magazine spread out before him. Moira chattered endlessly about Peter's court cases and Giles's progress in school, just as Livvy had known she would, and the phone rang three times but was ignored. Livvy couldn't wait to get away up to her room.

At two-thirty Moira got up from the table and put the kettle on. 'Your grandmother will be here in a couple of minutes,' she said. 'She's taken to calling every other afternoon for tea.'

Livvy stood and began to clear the plates away. She could hear the note of irritation in her mother's voice and noticed a look pass between her and Giles.

'How's Granny been?'

'As bloody cantankerous as ever!' Giles said through a

mouthful of bread and cheese. He was in the process of changing the tape over. 'I don't know why Mum puts up with her, she's so rude and every time she . . .'

'Giles!' Moira cut him short. 'That's enough!' She turned to Livvy. 'She's beginning to show her age,' she said.

'No she isn't! She's always been like it, ever since you and Dad . . .'

'Enough, I said!' Moira very nearly lost her temper and Giles shut up immediately. Livvy kept her thoughts to herself. Her father's mother blamed Moira for Bryan's death and in a way Livvy understood that; she herself had certainly blamed Peter enough in the past. It wasn't such a bitter pill to swallow, was it, Eadie calling round, even if she was a bit tricky to handle? Not after all the grief her mother's affair with Peter had caused.

Livvy said, 'We're probably all going to lose our marbles at some time, Giles, if we keep living to such ripe old ages. It's a fact of life.'

'Not for me it isn't!' Giles answered. 'I'm going to tell my wife to put me down immediately if I start getting like that. I'd rather . . .'

'Moira! Moira!'

Giles stopped mid-sentence and glanced at his mother. He stood quickly and picked up his walkman, turning towards the door.

'Moira! Are you in the kitchen?' Eadie's high, gravelly voice was sharp and irritable and Moira called out, 'Yes, Eadie, in here.' Giles made a hasty dash for the door just as Eadie swung it open and strode in. He leaned back against the wall to let her pass and tried to pretend he wasn't there.

'Well, you might bloody well have answered me the first

time!' Eadie said, dumping her Tesco's carrier bag down on the table. 'I see the bastard's on half-term, then?'

Livvy saw Moira's nostrils flare but she said nothing; Giles had slipped silently through the door and out of the kitchen as a strong smell of mothballs began to overpower the room.

'Gosh, Livvy, it's warm in here,' Moira said. 'Could you open a window?'

'What do you mean, warm?' Eadie snapped. 'I've never known that husband of yours to have this house warm! It's not the house it was when . . .'

'I don't think that's really fair, Granny!' Livvy tried to interrupt. 'I . . .'

'Did I ask for your thoughts on the subject, Olivia? Did I?'

Livvy stood speechless and shook her head. Eadie was no more difficult than usual but Livvy never quite remembered how awful she was until she saw her again.

'Anyway,' Eadie suddenly smiled. 'Come and give your grandmother a kiss.' She opened her arms and Livvy stepped forward into her embrace, holding her breath.

'Still living with that slick upstart of a boyfriend, are you? Hmm, thought so.' Eadie snorted with derision. ' 'Bout time you got shot of him and found yourself someone with real class, Olivia, not a jumped-up grammar school boy who has to pretend all the time.' Eadie sat herself down. 'Moira! Have you put the kettle on yet?'

Moira nodded, refusing to be taunted by the old woman. She turned away and fussed with the tea things while Eadie scratched at a hairy mole on her face.

'Olivia, I've bought you a present by the way,' Eadie said without warmth. 'It's in the bag.' She leaned back and looked at her granddaughter. 'Well, don't just stand there like a gormless idiot, I went to a lot of trouble with that present! Go and get it!' Her voice was sharp and irritated and Livvy immediately crossed to the table.

'She's too skinny,' Eadie commented over her shoulder to Moira, as if Livvy wasn't there. 'Maybe you could give her a bit of your excess flesh and then you two would even out.' She began to cackle but it turned into a cough and she spluttered, pulling a grubby old handkerchief from inside the sleeve of her cardigan to blow her nose noisily.

'It's lovely, Granny,' Livvy called out, holding up a shiny red nylon shirt with a big floppy bow at the neck.

'Good! I thought you'd like it; I said to the lady in the shop that you'd like it.'

Livvy suppressed a smile and exchanged glances with Moira. 'Thanks, Granny,' she said. 'It's great, really!'

'Of course it is, Olivia,' Eadie said, reaching for the chunk of Cheddar and cutting herself off a slice. 'And I shall look forward to you wearing it on the next programme.'

Later that evening, before supper, Livvy stood in the centre of the faded rose-coloured sitting room and tried to remember what it had looked like when her father was alive. She recalled certain pieces of furniture, like the Georgian mahogany bookcase and the walnut sofa table, but the rest she had no memory of. Everything had changed; slowly but surely, nearly everything had been replaced. Her father had been erased.

She looked up as Moira came into the room and held the door open for Peter to follow behind with the drinks tray. She smiled at her mother who looked tired and strained and felt a rare moment of love for her. Moira crossed to the fireplace to warm herself and Livvy went to join her. They stood silently together, waiting for Peter to pour the drinks.

'So how was your afternoon, you two?' Peter asked, handing them both a whisky soda.

Moira shrugged and Livvy smiled. 'Pretty awful,' Livvy answered, 'due to Eadie's untimely appearance.'

'Oh, not again!' Peter turned and looked at Moira but she ignored the look and said nothing.

'What's wrong with Granny coming round?' Livvy asked tartly.

'It's just not on!' Peter exploded. 'It really isn't, coming round here every other day, it's not fair on Moira. She's so bloody rude, calling Giles the bastard and bullying Moira . . .'

Livvy noticed her mother threw Peter a look and he shut up immediately, took a gulp of his drink and then said, 'But your mother and I agree to disagree on this one.'

Livvy looked down at the fire for a few moments. 'I know she's pretty objectionable but Eadie is the only link we have with my father,' she said. Again she saw an unspoken communication pass between Moira and Peter. 'It's important to stay in touch, I think . . .'

'I know,' Peter said, cutting the conversation short. 'Moira told me what you think.'

'So she comes and goes as she pleases,' Moira said, finishing the subject.

Both Peter and Livvy kept quiet and several seconds of silence ensued.

'Is Giles going to grace us with his company this evening, do you think?' Peter eventually asked. He said it as light-heartedly as he could manage but there was an edge to his voice and it came out sarcastically. Talk about Eadie and seeing the rotten effect she had on Moira really pissed him off.

'I'll call him,' Moira said. She went to the door and called out into the hall, 'Giles, I have a packet of Walkers cheese and onion crisps down here for you!' Then she came back and sat down next to Peter on the sofa. She smiled, one of her charming, easy smiles, and Peter realised, as he some-times did, suddenly and with an acute feeling of joy, just how much he loved her.

'He'll be down in a minute,' she said, then, looking at Livvy, explained. 'I keep a store of them in the larder to lure him down whenever he's needed. We don't eat crisps and I've always found bribery and corruption, particularly with adolescents, very useful tools.'

Livvy and Peter both laughed; it cleared the air.

'Where're the crisps then, Mum?' Giles's face peered round the door.

'In the larder, second shelf down. One packet only, please.'

'Right!'

He could be heard dashing across the hall and through the kitchen to the larder. Minutes later he was back.

'Great!' He munched noisily.

'You smell nice, Giles.' Livvy breathed in the fresh smell of his aftershave and Giles blushed.

''I, er, I had a shower.' He glanced down at the floor. 'And I used some of that Clarins dynamite of yours.' He looked up again at Livvy, somewhat sheepishly. 'I hope you don't mind?'

'Of course not!' Livvy held down a smile. 'The Eau Dynamisse, you mean?'

'Yes, that's it. Oh, and I used some of the shower stuff as

well, Liv,' he continued, more confident now, 'only I couldn't get much of a lather. I practically had to use half the tube!'

'What shower stuff?' Livvy tried to remember what she'd brought with her.

'The cleansing gel one, in the white tube?'

'Oh, thanks a lot, Giles!' Livvy shook her head, unsure of whether to laugh or take an almighty bloody swipe at him. 'That's my blooming face cleanser,' she wailed. 'It costs fourteen quid a tube!'

It was after midnight, and Livvy sat in the room at the top of the house that was hers, with only a small bedside lamp on and the chill night wind whipping against the old glass window panes. She was buried under a heavily quilted counterpane and wore one of her mother's old cotton nightdresses, a white, long-sleeved affair that covered her from the neck to her ankles, but she was still cold.

This room has always been cold, she thought, despite Peter's attempts at heating and insulation. She remembered how Peter had insisted that she have her own space when he moved into The Old Rectory, nearly a year after her father's death. And she remembered, as though it were yesterday, how much she had resented his presence, and how obviously she had made that resentment known. He had tried, in his rather clumsy bachelor's way, to befriend her but she had rejected him, along with her mother, too griefstricken and confused by what had happened to be able to forgive or love.

She needed to blame someone for her father's suicide, so she blamed Peter. Her mother had had an affair with Peter Marshall and so he was responsible. Bryan Davis, Livvy's father, had found out, discovered that Moira was pregnant, walked out on her and Livvy and a year later had killed himself. To a bereft seventeen-year-old it was all so painfully simple.

Livvy glanced up at the row of broadcasting awards that she kept on the mantelpiece, her father's achievements, and she knew in her heart that she had never really forgiven Peter. She hadn't ever truly known Bryan Davis. She had been away at school for much of the time and when she wasn't, he seemed to be always off somewhere, travelling the world with his news team. But he was such a charismatic man, such a vibrant, loving, generous man. When she saw him he would shower her with affection, bombard her with interest, listening to her every word, treating her like a grown-up. He made her feel as if no one in the world meant as much to him as she did and even today she felt the loss, perhaps more acutely because she had seen so little of the man she worshipped.

Looking down at her watch, Livvy wondered if it was too late to call James. Thinking about her father always saddened her and she felt as if she could do with a chat. Reaching over to the phone, she picked up the receiver and dialled her London number, listening to the ringing tone and waiting for James to answer. She checked her watch again – it was twelve-thirty – but the phone went unanswered. She left it a minute longer and then replaced the handset and snuggled down under the quilt. James must be out, she thought, wondering briefly where and who with. Not that it bothered her particularly; they were too independent to worry about trust. Without that independence, they couldn't have survived.

I'll ring again in the morning, she decided, switching off

the light and plumping up her pillows. Hopefully if the rain has cleared I can get up early and go for a long walk, I'll ring before I go. She closed her eyes and listened to the wonderful old creak of the house as it settled down for the night. And within minutes, she was fast asleep.

Chapter Four

It was nine-fifteen and James rolled over in bed, luxuriating in having the big warm space all to himself. He pulled the duvet in a little tighter around him and opened his eyes just as the telephone began to ring. He sighed, went to sit up and then thought better of it. The only person who would call at this hour on a Saturday was Livvy and he really couldn't be bothered to get up and answer the phone to her. He listened to it ring for a couple of minutes or more and then it stopped. He smiled, turned over on to his side again and eased himself pleasantly back to sleep.

An hour later, he woke properly. The rain had stopped and the sun was breaking through the clouds, lighting the sodden grey London landscape with its pale wintry rays and creeping into the bedroom through the gap in the blinds. It made the yellow and white of the interior glow and, sitting up, James thought, as he so often did, what a truly wonderful room this was that Livvy had designed for them.

He let his eyes adjust to the morning for a short while and then he climbed out of bed, crossed to the window and carefully pulled up the heavy yellow and white striped silk Roman blinds, making sure the folds in the fabric fell evenly and in a straight line. He opened the window to let in some air, took his towelling robe off the brass hook on the back of the door and glanced at himself briefly in the huge antique pine mirror that took up most of one wall. He tied his robe and wandered lazily through the sitting room to the kitchen.

Making the coffee, James thought about the previous night, about how lunch with Hugh had slipped into mid-afternoon, then calling his office to say he'd not be back. The walk over in Richmond along the river as the rain stopped and the sun dropped down behind the trees in the park, taking the light of the day with it, and talking, talking in the dark night air, all the time talking, in a way he had forgotten existed, in a way that made him feel young again and full of hope. They had talked about everything, they had laughed and remembered, and the early evening led into dinner and then a late-night drink in Soho and finally a taxi ride home with all the exciting, dangerous feelings of being close to Hugh and looking out at the world from inside a cab as if none of it existed, except just the two of them.

James poured himself a cup of coffee and carried the cafetière over to the table. He added some sugar and sat down, looking across at the nineteenth-century fruit and vine prints Livvy had collected for the kitchen. He loved the kitchen, the way Livvy had fitted the whole look together, with old oak cabinets, antique prints, the wooden pole with its hanging copper pans, strings of onions and garlic and huge aromatic bunches of herbs. Actually, James loved the entire flat, its smart W1 address, the surprise of going up to the top floor of the Victorian mansion block and finding this huge, wide open-plan penthouse, all cream and beige and the palest yellow and white.

Livvy had exquisite taste, he had to give her that, and the income to match it. James knew only too well that he would never have been able to afford the lifestyle he enjoyed now on his income alone and he was certainly under no illusions as to what advantages sharing his life with Livvy Davis had brought him personally. The only problem was that his reasons for staying had become somewhat blurred over the years and today he just wasn't sure what mattered to him most. But James never asked himself that question; as far as he was concerned, truthful living was for people with a hang-up about religion.

Pouring himself a second cup, James took his coffee through to the sitting room, drew the blinds and then fetched his briefcase for the *Economist*. He saw his suit jacket hanging over the back of the dining chair and remembered Hugh slipping his home number into the breast pocket, then taking out James's silk handkerchief in exchange and laughingly tucking it away in his coat as a souvenir.

James walked up to the jacket and picked out the scrap of paper, unfolding it to read the number. He would probably never ring Hugh. He had flirted with him last night and as far as he was concerned, that was all there was to it. Yet holding the number in his hands, he suddenly felt the same sharp excitement that had pulsed through him the whole of yesterday. Its intensity shocked him.

Crumpling the paper into a tight ball, James stuffed it into the pocket of his dressing gown and attempted to put it out of his mind. Trifling with danger was one thing, he thought, courting it was another. Leaving his coffee where it was, he strode into the bathroom and turned on the shower. A good hot shower always eased the body and soul.

Twenty minutes later, drying himself on a big warm towel, relaxed and refreshed, James cursed as the telephone rang for the second time that morning. It was probably Livvy, he thought, knotting the towel round his waist and padding barefoot through to the sitting room. If he didn't answer it, she would wonder where the hell he'd got to. He picked up the receiver and leaned his bottom against the warmth of the radiator.

'Hello?'

'James?'

He felt a moment of panic and then a quick sharp thrill of excitement.

'Hugh! How did you get this number?' James had been so careful last night, had not given anything away.

'Jack Wilcox. You don't mind, do you?'

'No! No, of course not.' He relaxed back against the wall. The sound of Hugh's voice made him suddenly feel really good and that feeling dominated all others. 'I'm glad you rang,' he said.

'You mentioned Livvy was away. I wondered if you wanted to come to an exhibition?' Hugh was careful, he knew an invitation in broad daylight would be considered safe, practically harmless.

'I don't know.' James smiled. He wanted to tease. 'What sort of exhibition?'

But Hugh knew him better than he remembered. 'Does it matter?' he answered and James laughed.

'No, not really.' No need to be overly cautious, he

thought, it was only an afternoon out and he could certainly do with one.

'Shall we meet up for lunch first?'

James hesitated. 'I can't do lunch, Hugh,' he answered. He needed a bit of space after yesterday. 'I can meet you at say, two? Two-thirty?'

Hugh knew exactly what James was playing at, he'd always done it; two steps forward, one step back. Their affair in those first few months at college had been a constant source of bewilderment to Hugh, never knowing where he stood. It didn't bother him now though; he was quite prepared to wait, to play all the games James needed to. Hugh wanted revenge and for that he knew he had to be patient.

'Two-thirty's fine,' he said. 'How about the Tate?'

'OK. I'll see you just inside the main entrance.' Hugh made a note of it and went to hang up.

'Oh, and Hugh?'

'Yes?'

'I'll be wearing a red carnation and carrying a copy of *The Times*. The codeword's . . .' James paused and thought about it for a moment. 'The codeword is ATIC!' He began to laugh.

'Jesus!'

'I knew you'd remember it!'

'How could I forget it?' Hugh suddenly thought back to all the times James used to say the word at the most inappropriate moments, making Hugh's heart hammer so loudly in his chest that he thought it would explode. No one knew what it meant, of course – any time I'll come – with all its double meanings, and no one knew about them, but James had gone pretty close to the edge at times, he'd really scared

Hugh once or twice. That was in the beginning, though, in the days before Livvy Davis, before the great social whirl that took James way up into the dizzy heights of notoriety and miles away from Hugh Howard. That was in the days when Hugh felt happier than he had ever felt in his life before.

'Hugh? You still there?'

Hugh came angrily back to the present. 'Yes. Don't say that word, James. It belongs in the past.'

'OK, I'm sorry.' One of James's great skills was his diplomacy. He knew exactly what to say and when to say it. He backed down easily. 'You're right. It was just a bit of a joke, that's all.'

'Yes. Look, I'll see you later, all right?' Hugh was placated by the apology; it gave him a slight advantage.

'OK. Two-thirty at the Tate.'

'Two-thirty, then.' Without another word, Hugh hung up.

James stopped in front of one of the late works in the Clore Gallery and marvelled at Turner's use of colour. The painting seemed to have a life of its own, an almost mystic life that touched anyone who looked at it, and he could feel the strong pulse of his blood as he stood there, a vibrant, excited pulse. He sensed Hugh behind him but he didn't turn, he wanted the sensation of Hugh's body close to his own for a moment longer. He could smell Hugh's aftershave, sharp and citrus, and it mingled with the colour, heightening the intensity of what he was experiencing, making his head swim. It wasn't real, none of it was real, just colours and soaring emotions. He glanced sidelong at the huge empty space of the gallery and then, just as he knew he would, Hugh put his hand on James's hip and his fingers spread to his groin.

'Let's go,' Hugh said quietly. James said nothing. In an instant Hugh had turned and walked out of the gallery, through the glass doors, down the steps and out into the dark, cold November afternoon. James followed him, unable to stop himself, walking as if in a trance. In the silent shadow of the building Hugh stopped and moved towards James. James closed his eyes, seeing the painting again, the burning fire of red and gold, and then he felt the hard, dry lips of Hugh's mouth on his own and the strong, sexual line of his body. He was lost. Nothing else mattered but this. Nothing.

Later, when James woke, he was alone. It took him a few moments to work out where he was and then he sat up, a feeling of panic tight in his chest. He pulled the sheet off him and stood up grabbing his shirt. He walked out of the bedroom pulling it hastily on and saw Hugh reading in the large, immaculate sitting room, sprawled out over the sofa and half listening to the Brahms Violin Concerto. He stood in the doorway and wondered what the hell to do. He was confused, frightened by the reality that had just hit him, and he felt the overwhelming burden of guilt.

Suddenly, Hugh started, as if he knew someone was there and he glanced round. He saw James, met his gaze briefly and sensed his tension. He let his eyes slowly travel the length of the long lean body in the door and then brought them back to James's face.

'I thought I'd let you sleep,' he said. 'Come and sit down.' James hesitated for a moment, then came into the room. He picked up a packet of cigarettes from the table and took one out, lighting it with Hugh's Dunhill lighter, his fingers trembling slightly. He glanced nervously out of the window at the lights of Chelsea Harbour.

'It's all right, no one can see us up here,' Hugh said. He stood anyway and crossed to the window, pulling the string to close the slats in the black Italian blind.

He moved towards James and stood a few inches away from him. 'James,' he said quietly. 'No one can see us, no one can hear us, no one will ever know about us. All this is . . . is you and me.' He shrugged. 'A fantasy. It has nothing to do with reality. You do understand that, don't you?'

James nodded and Hugh took the cigarette from James's fingers, inhaling deeply and then placing it back between James's lips. He blew the smoke out of the side of his mouth and reached up to trace the strong line of James's jaw with his finger. He let it trail down over James's chest to the opening of his shirt. 'Now,' he said, 'do you want a drink?'

James stood for a moment, aware of the intense excitement in his groin. He flicked the ash of his cigarette into the palm of his hand and glanced down as he began to harden. He saw Hugh follow his eyes and they both knew there was no controlling what he felt. It had been too long, he needed it too much.

'Yes,' he answered. 'I'd like a drink.'

Hugh smiled. 'Good.' He leaned in a little closer so that his warm breath touched the skin of James's cheek. 'Why don't you go back to bed?' he said softly. 'I'll bring you one there.'

No longer really aware of what he was doing or why, James nodded and turned towards the bedroom. He still felt the pressure of guilt, right down in the pit of his stomach, but for the moment he decided to ignore it. It had been replaced by something else, by something that overwhelmed him, consumed him, and left him weak with a longing he'd had no idea he still possessed.

Chapter Five

The black cab drew up outside the City Television offices in W1 and Livvy climbed out, shivering in the freezing January morning and carrying a large bag from Harvey Nichols. It was eight a.m. and her interview was at nine.

Striding into her office, she waved across the other side of the room at Bill taking his daily fix of caffeine, and walked up to her desk. She opened the carrier bag, took out the new bright pink Nicole Farhi jacket and hung it up, smoothing out the perfect folds of the wool. She smiled at it nervously and then crossed to join Bill at the coffee machine.

'Black, no sugar,' he said.

'No, white, two sugars this morning, please. I haven't eaten since yesterday lunchtime.'

Bill reached for the milk and sugar and added a liberal amount of each to Livvy's polystyrene cup.

'Nervous?'

She shrugged, took a gulp of the scalding liquid and then said, 'Scared to death actually.'

'Why's that?' Sam had just appeared, the bright pink plastic frames of her glasses perched on top of her head and an angry scarlet mark around her nose where they pinched. She was squinting. 'Oops! God yes! Sorry, Livvy, I forgot.'

Bill turned and cuffed her on the top of her head. 'Samantha! How could you forget Livvy's interview with The Controller this morning? Call yourself a researcher? This is the sort of information you should have at your fingertips!'

Sam pulled a face and saw that Livvy wasn't smiling. 'You'll stun 'em, Livvy! Don't worry.'

But Livvy merely nodded and wandered off back to her desk; she was far too nervous even to notice the banter. Sitting down, she stared out of the window and went over her prepared answers for the fifth time that morning. She tried to think again what the odds were of being offered the job but she really had no idea. Her confidence was high, though, despite what she was up against. Livvy knew that this was her big chance, a series of arts programmes on the national network with a prime-time slot that would absolutely make her career. It was what she had always wanted, to be really successful, it was what she had striven for since the first day she walked through the door of the BBC that summer after Oxford. For as long as she could remember, Livvy Davis had wanted to be the best, to be her father's daughter. And so far, without much problem, she had succeeded.

The sharp bleep of the telephone rang by her side and Livvy started. She picked up the receiver and flicked on the Reuters screen up on the wall to skim through the headlines as she talked.

'Livvy Davis.'

'Hello, Livvy? It's Hugh Howard.'

Livvy swivelled her chair round, away from the screen.

'Hugh! My goodness!' It had been months. 'How nice to hear from you.' She reached for her coffee. 'How did you enjoy Eliza's wedding?'

'As weddings go, it wasn't too bad!' He laughed lightly. 'But it was good to catch up with James again, it's been good to see him.'

'Yes,' Livvy wasn't sure what he meant. 'I'm sure.'

Hugh immediately sensed her puzzlement. He had guessed right; James hadn't said a word. It was about time she knew, though; it was important that James understood who was in control. He picked up *The Times* and glanced down at the show he had circled in red pen. In the most subtle of ways, Hugh was about to invite himself for dinner. That would certainly put the wind up James.

'Livvy,' he said, 'I'm sorry to ring you at work but I just wanted to check whether you wanted me to pick you up tonight or if we should meet at the theatre.' He lied so easily; it was becoming second nature.

Livvy was confused. 'Sorry, Hugh? I don't quite understand what you mean.' James had organised a dinner party tonight for some of his Foreign Office cronies. 'Theatre?'

Hugh held down a smile on his end of the line. 'Oh no! Don't tell me James forgot to say.'

'Say what?'

'That I've booked to take you both to *Miss Saigon* tonight, as a way of celebrating our renewed friendship.'

Livvy was instantly angry. 'You're joking! Oh, Hugh, I *am* sorry! Bloody James, I could kill him!' She shook her head. 'He's gone and organised a dinner party for some colleagues at home . . . Oh God, I really am awfully sorry!' She felt terrible. How could James forget?

Hugh was silent for a few moments. He knew that Livvy

and James were giving a dinner party, he knew everything that James did. He waited a couple of seconds longer for Livvy to think it through and then said, 'Oh well, I suppose I can give the tickets to one of my staff; it'll always improve goodwill.' He was pretty certain of Livvy's reaction and almost right on cue, she suddenly had an idea.

'Hugh? Can you really do that? I mean pass the tickets on to someone else? If you did that, then you could join us for dinner. What d'you think? It'd at least help to make up for James's awful behaviour!' She was thinking quickly; if she rang Lucy then that would make up the numbers and she could order extra food. 'Oh, do say yes, Hugh!' she pleaded. 'I know it's short notice, but we'd love it if you came.'

Hugh hesitated. This was exactly as he'd planned but he didn't want to sound too eager. Finally, he said, 'Well . . . if you're sure it's not too much bother?'

'Don't be daft! Of course it's not. And James will be delighted.'

Will he heck, Hugh thought, James will be livid. 'OK then, Livvy,' he answered, smiling, 'I'd love to!'

'Excellent!' She sighed, relieved to have sorted out the mess with the tickets. 'Now, let me give you the address. Everyone's coming about eight, eight-thirty . . .' And she gave him all the details as she made a list on her pad of the extras she'd need for two more people and thought again how stupid it was of James to have forgotten to tell her about the theatre date, let alone even mention that he'd met up with Hugh again.

A couple of minutes later, Livvy hung up and instantly redialled Lucy Deacon.

'Hi Luce, it's me!'

'Livvy! How are you?'

'Well . . .' Livvy wondered whether to tell her about Hugh's meetings with James and the tickets and how cross she was, but she saw Sam looking over at her and simply said, 'Sort of all right, but I need a favour. Can you come to dinner tonight? To make up the numbers? I've just asked Hugh Howard.'

Lucy hesitated for a moment. She was tired and didn't really want to go out but Livvy was difficult to refuse. 'All right,' she answered, 'I'd love to. What time shall I come?'

Livvy was doodling on a piece of paper, thinking that James's silence about Hugh was really rather symptomatic of their whole relationship, when Lucy called loudly down the line.

'Livvy! Are you still there?'

'Oh God, yes, sorry. Come at eight, Luce.' Livvy always told Lucy half an hour earlier than any of the other guests as she was always half an hour late.

'OK. I'll be there at eight—' she paused and smiled, knowing Livvy too well, '—thirty,' she finished and Livvy laughed.

'Anyway,' she went on, 'I'm glad you rang because you beat me to it! I was going to call to wish you luck with your interview this morning.'

'Oh, thanks, Lucy. I really appreciate that.' Livvy didn't add that James had completely forgotten and that she was furious about that as well. 'I confess that I'm nervous.'

'Don't be daft! You, nervous?' Lucy laughed. 'What are your chances, do you think?'

'Fair, I'd say, nothing stronger. Apparently Jeff Ridge is also up for the programme and he's far more experienced, much better known than me.'

'You can only do your best, Livvy. You've done incredibly

well already so try not to worry too much.' Lucy listened to the brief silence on the other end of the line and knew that this sort of wisdom didn't suit Livvy Davis. Livvy set out to win, anything else simply wasn't good enough. 'Look, I'd better go,' Lucy said, 'someone's on the other line. I'll be thinking of you.'

'Thanks, Lucy, thanks a lot.'

'Good luck, then. See you tonight at eight-thirty.'

'Yes, see you tonight.' Livvy hung up. She swivelled her chair round and suddenly looked at the pink jacket with trepidation. 'Sam?' she called, taking her make-up bag out of her briefcase and putting it on the desk. 'Sam?'

'Yup!' Sam looked up from her screen and peered through her preposterous pink glasses.

'What do you think of this jacket?' Livvy asked, needing reassurance. 'Is it too much? The colour, I mean?'

'No! It's terrific! Just right, super, lovely, wonderful!' Sam stood up and walked across to Livvy's desk. 'The jacket's fine, it's not a problem. Now if only your boobs were three sizes bigger, I seriously think you would be in with a chance!'

Livvy ran up the steps of the mansion block and buzzed her flat, then she went back to the mini cab and began unloading the boot with the help of the driver. They piled the carrier bags up on the pavement, propping them against each other until the car was empty and an impressive stack of shopping sat waiting in the drizzle.

'How much do I owe you?' She rummaged in her bag for her purse.

'Two fifty, love.'

'Oh, James. Thank goodness!'

James left the main door open, smiled tersely at Livvy and bent to pick up some of the shopping as the driver climbed back into his car. 'Is that the lot, Livvy?' His voice was abrupt and he didn't look at her. 'God knows why you had to invite bloody Hugh Howard,' he muttered as he carried the first lot into the hall and dropped it by the lift. As he glanced up, Livvy shot him an angry look and he realised he had to be careful. She would have no idea why the thought of Hugh for dinner infuriated him. 'It's just that you're always changing plans at the last minute,' he added sulkily.

'Changing plans at the last minute!' she exploded. 'Christ you've got a nerve, James!' She threw a bag of shopping on to the ground and marched outside for another. James followed lamely.

'If you hadn't forgotten the damn arrangement to go to the theatre,' she continued angrily, 'then I wouldn't have had to invite him, would I?' James said nothing. What frigging arrangement? he thought as he lifted the last two bags. He was absolutely furious about the whole thing and had said as much to Hugh this lunch time on the phone. But Hugh had simply laughed and called him paranoid. Maybe he was. But he didn't like it, this business of involving Livvy, he didn't like it one little bit. And this afternoon, thinking about how dangerous it could be, he had realised for the first time that perhaps he was in deeper than he'd imagined. He didn't know what the hell Hugh was playing at but he did know that a friendship between him and Livvy was too bloody close for anyone's comfort!

'Is that everything?' Livvy asked. She held the lift as James dumped the remaining bags down by her feet.

'Yes.' He stood straight and she released the doors just as

he slipped inside the elevator. He moodily watched the ground drop away through the open ironwork of the lift cage and stayed silent.

'James?'

The lift juddered to a halt on the top floor and James looked up. 'Yes?'

'You know, if there is anyone who should be behaving badly about tonight, it's me.' Livvy kept her voice even but James sensed the edge of anger in it. He felt a small chill of fear start in the base of his spine.

'What do you mean?'

'I mean that talking to Hugh made me realise something.' They stood inside the lift, eleven floors up, a small iron cage suspended in the air. 'How little I know you.'

James stood motionless and held his breath.

'Is there something that perhaps you might have had the sensitivity to mention to me this past week?' Now her voice was openly harsh and he could hear the tears in the back of her throat.

He turned his face away from her for a moment so that she wouldn't see the terrible guilt and fear in his eyes.

'Like?' He could hardly breathe, waiting for her answer.

'Oh for Christ's sake!' she cried, attempting to yank open the iron door with all her strength. It was jammed and as she heaved she felt all the disappointment of the forty-minute interview on the fifth floor well up inside and suddenly overwhelm her. Finally she freed the handle of the door, pulled back the iron gates and burst into floods of tears. She stormed out of the lift.

'You haven't even mentioned it to me!' she cried, turning back to him. 'Not once, not even good luck!' She fumbled with the key and James, relief washing over him, realised in an instant what she was talking about. He rushed out of the lift after her.

'Oh, Livvy, my darling, I'm so sorry. Your interview, of course. How could I have forgotten?' He had never even given it a thought, so preoccupied was he with Hugh. 'Oh God!' He put his arms out and pulled her towards him. He had begun to hate physical contact with her the past few weeks but at this moment he was so desperately relieved that he didn't think twice about reaching out for her. He stroked her hair, as much a comfort to himself as to her and then, when she stopped crying, he opened the front door and led her inside the flat.

'Sit down there and I'll get you a drink,' he said. The initial panic over, he wasn't sure how to cope with this outburst; Livvy was so rarely irrational and never emotional. He went through to the kitchen to open a bottle of wine. 'So what happened this morning?' he called over his shoulder. He popped the cork, fetched two long-stemmed glasses from the cupboard and poured a measure of dark red wine into each one. He carried them back to the sitting room and stood for a moment watching Livvy from the door.

The truth was, Livvy thought, lacing her fingers together as she tried to answer James's question, that she didn't really know what had happened that morning. For the first time in her life, things had not gone exactly the way she had wanted them to. All through her career in television, Livvy Davis had graduated so easily through the ranks and with so little effort that she had almost taken it for granted. From the BBC she had moved into commercial television and to a salary twice what she had previously earned and once there she had done a succession of jobs ever increasing in profile and remuneration. Whatever she set her mind to, Livvy

Davis achieved and this morning, despite her nerves and her reservations, her confidence was high. She had no real reason to suspect that this job would be any different.

Glancing up at James as he passed her the wine, Livvy said, 'I don't really know. They didn't say anything.'

'So?' James sat opposite her and surreptitiously glanced at his watch; he wanted to catch the six o'clock news.

'So, usually one can get some kind of idea of what they think.'

'Oh, Livvy!' James couldn't help but smile. ' "One" means you, presumably? And every other interview I've ever known you to have has been a sure thing from the moment you walked in the door! Is that what you mean?'

'Yes. Well, no. I . . .'

'Livvy, this job is big, it's a top job and it's three times what you've ever done in the past. Don't be so easily put off.'

'Yes, but . . .'

'But what?' He shook his head. 'But you may have to work for it, it may not fall into your lap as other things have had a habit of doing. Is that the but?'

Livvy looked away and James felt a moment of pure envy. He had no right to, of course – he'd done very well off Livvy's success over the years – but he couldn't help it. It all came so effortlessly it made him sick. He wondered briefly if Livvy would ever have to grow up to live in the real world like everyone else but he put the thought from his mind. He at least had the intelligence to realise that if she did, she would see through him straight away.

'Come on, Livvy,' he said. 'Get yourself in the shower and try not to think about this morning. I'm sorry I forgot, OK?'

Livvy nodded and sat where she was for a while to calm down. He stood and crossed to her, putting her glass down and taking both of her hands in his. 'Livvy, I really am sorry, OK?'

Again she nodded and looked up at his face. His smile was so charismatic that she couldn't help but respond. Swallowing down the last of her wine, she stood up. 'Perhaps I am being a little oversensitive,' she said. How could she tell him how much her success meant to her? At times it was all that really mattered.

'You know, I'm really looking forward to seeing Hugh again tonight,' she said, crossing the room. She stopped in the doorway. 'I can't believe that you forgot to tell me you'd met up with him after Eliza's wedding!' She smiled. 'If he hadn't rung this morning, I might never have known.'

James shrugged.

'Chance meetings can lead to so much,' she said, going through to the bedroom. 'They can change lives,' she called out. She came back to the door. 'Don't you think?'

Again James shrugged. He didn't even have the courage to look her in the eye.

'Game, set and match!' Hugh called across the net to Jack Wilcox and, grinning, walked towards his opponent to shake hands. 'Well played, Jack!'

'Not well enough, though,' Jack laughed and bent to pick up a ball. He stuffed it into the pocket of his scruffy old white shorts and Hugh watched him with a sudden jolt of envy. Old money, he thought, a gentleman, even in his grubby, sweaty kit.

'Bloody nice courts, these,' Jack said, following Hugh off the indoor arena. 'Shame the club's a bit of a way out of

London,' he continued. 'Wouldn't mind joining myself otherwise.'

Hugh shrugged and handed him an ice-cold Lucozade Sport from the drinks machine, slotting the money in for his own.

'What's the membership fee like?'

'Expensive,' Hugh answered. 'You can either just join the David Lloyd Tennis part or you can do the whole thing. Gym, pool, saunas, whatever. I did the whole thing on a corporate membership scheme. Several of my people live in the Wimbledon, Raynes Park area so I offered membership as a perk.'

'Bloody good idea! I have to confess I'm a bit pissed off with Queen's myself, there's nothing like this there.'

Hugh looked away and smiled cynically. The most exclusive tennis club in the country and Jack was pissed off with it! They wouldn't even look at Hugh – he didn't have the right ties in his wardrobe.

'Drink up, Jack, we've got time for a sauna, if you like?'

'Yup, love one!' Jack crunched his can up and aimed it at the bin just as a tall, leggy blonde came off court with her tennis instructor. She sat and crossed her long, tanned legs while the coach bought her a drink and Jack's eye was drawn to the split in her short white skirt, revealing a less than discreet amount of firm and rounded upper thigh.

'I say, Hugh,' he whispered as they passed her en route to the changing rooms. 'You don't get that quality at Queen's, I can tell you!' He glanced back over his shoulder for one last look. 'All buck teeth and thunder thighs there,' he said, 'too much riding and too many hunting falls!'

In the bar upstairs, Hugh sat and waited for Jack to bring the drinks over. He glanced at his watch and reckoned on forty minutes from the club back into central London; he was due at Livvy and James's at eight-thirty. He smiled as Jack handed him a bottle of Sol and said, 'What time are you meeting Nel?'

Jack pulled a face. 'You know I'm still not sure if this is such a good idea, Hugh.' He took a swig of his beer and placed the bottle on the table. 'I think I'm a little old for blind dates.'

'Nonsense!' Hugh grinned. 'You'll love Nel, she's great fun.' That was an understatement, he thought briefly, but she was well paid for what she did. 'Anyway, how else are you going to meet eligible young women unless your friends introduce you? I don't suppose your chambers are overfull of bimbos, are they?'

Jack laughed. 'No, apart from Laura Meissen. Thirty-five, American tan tights and sensible shoes. A real stunner with a great line in Council Planning law!'

'Oh nice! Listen, where are you taking Nel?'

'Chutney Mary's. Is that all right, d'you think?'

'Perfect.' Nel went anywhere. 'She loves curry!'

'Tell me how you know her again?' Jack looked suddenly nervous. 'Just so I've got something to say when we meet.'

'She's the cousin of one of my brokers. But relax, Jack! She's a lovely girl, you won't need to scrabble round for conversation, I promise you.' Hugh smiled. Jack wouldn't need conversation at all, but he'd find that out for himself soon enough. 'Look, I'm sorry, mate, but I've got to go.' He drank the last half of the Sol and stood up.

'Where're you off to tonight?'

'I'm going to Livvy Davis and James Ward for supper.'

'Oh, very nice! Have you been to their place before?'

'No.' Hugh took his keys out of his pocket.

'Well, it's fabulous. Livvy redid it herself.' Jack stood up as well and both men walked out of the bar, collecting their bags on the way out.

'Next time we must play at Queen's,' Jack said. 'How about midweek sometime if I can get a court?'

'Great!' Hugh held the door and followed Jack out into the car park. When he reached the red Porsche he turned to shake hands. 'Have a good time tonight with Nel,' he said, smiling.

'What's so funny?' Jack asked.

Hugh shrugged.

'I'll fucking kill you, Howard, if she's an old dog!' Jack said, grinning back.

'Trust me, Jack. Quite the contrary, she's amazing!'

'Yeah, yeah, yeah,' Jack held up his hand and continued on down the car park to his BMW.

'Just don't eat too much,' Hugh called as he slowed the car to pass Jack. 'Indigestion plays havoc with one's performance!'

Jack laughed. 'I should be so lucky!' he shouted back.

Oh, you will be, Hugh thought, not without malice, you will be. But he said nothing. He waved, put the window up and beeped the horn. 'I paid good money for that luck,' he commented to himself. 'You'll get more than lucky!'

Thinking about the devious Nel, he accelerated off, turned out on to the dual carriage way and headed back for Chelsea.

James walked out of the bedroom and looked across at Livvy as she arranged a large glass bowl of white lilies in the centre of the table. She was deep in concentration and picked each stem carefully from the pile to place it artistically in the arrangement. He glanced at her selection of flowers and thought for a moment that Livvy must spend almost as much on flowers as most people spent on an entire dinner party. He carried on into the kitchen.

Taking his corkscrew over to the refectory table, he sat down and began to uncork the four bottles of Barolo '85. He picked a grape off the fruit bowl and peered under the muslin to see what cheeses Livvy had bought.

'Don't touch!' Livvy carried the remains of the flowers and folded them inside the paper, stuffing them into the bin.

'Are they all Italian?'

'No, there's a Welsh goat's cheese as well.'

'Yeach!'

'Well, some of us with more cultured tastes love it,' she said, bending double to take a long plate of Parma ham from the fridge. 'Throw me the bag of figs over, will you?'

James put the bottle down and lifted the bag of fruit. He reached out and handed it to Livvy. 'So what's on the menu, then?'

'Parma ham with fig puree, and then . . .'

'From?'

She turned and frowned. 'Why do you always assume that I've bought in?'

'From?' he repeated.

She sighed. 'From Mario's Italian on the King's Road.' She turned back to the fruit. 'Don't make me feel any more guilty than I do already!'

'Why should you feel guilty, Livvy? The food is wonderful and you always manage to make it look as if you've done it yourself anyway.'

'Cheek!'

He finished the last bottle and laid the corks in a row. 'Not cheek, just the truth.'

'Now there's a word!'

James looked up quickly and saw that Livvy was smiling. He smiled back, one of his careful, practised smiles, and then stood, taking two of the bottles through to the sitting room. He placed them on the sideboard to breathe and looked out at the lights of Cadogan Square through floor-to-ceiling glass. He was dreading tonight, he was as nervous as hell about Hugh and yet at the same time he could feel the familiar sharp ache of excitement in his groin.

'Does it look OK?'

He started and looked round. Livvy was watching him and she nodded to the flowers and candles in the room.

'It looks great.'

'Well cheer up then, our guests should be here any minute.' Suddenly she smiled as the main door buzzer went. 'I told you!' she said. 'Perfect timing.' She headed out into the hall to release the door. 'Blimey! Luce, you're early, I don't believe it! Yes, come on up.'

She waited out on the landing with the front door open and James heard her call down to Lucy. He poured himself a glass of wine and took a large gulp just as the two of them came in.

'Lucy!' He crossed and kissed Livvy's best friend on both cheeks.

'Hello, James,' she answered. She didn't smile particularly warmly but then she hadn't ever really liked James that much. 'How exciting to see Hugh after all this time,' she said. 'It must be wonderful for you. You were great friends at college, weren't you?'

James nodded and felt a rush of blood to his face. He

turned away quickly to hide it. 'Great friends,' he mumbled. 'Now, what can I get you to drink, Lucy?' He wondered how the hell he was going to get through the evening.

Hugh finally parked his car after several drives round the block, locked it and pressed his alarm. He held two bottles of 1986 Côte de Lechet Premier Cru Chablis, which the man in Berry Bros had ensured him was a quite acceptable wine to take and he carried a box of Leonidas chocolates. It wasn't that he wanted to impress, more that he wanted it to be known he had, at last, fitted in, that he knew how to do things properly.

There were four people he didn't recognise when he walked into the flat. He was briefly introduced but he didn't take much in. Jack had been right, the sheer size and elegance of the room he had just entered stunned him for a moment – the bank of windows overlooking Cadogan Square, the luxury of cream and white and dark natural wood, the highly scented lilies – it all took his breath away.

'My God! What a marvellous room,' he said, having learned over the years that compliments showed a natural acceptance of a situation rather than an ignorance of it as he had previously thought.

'Thank you.' Livvy smiled and Hugh knew instantly that she had hardly changed at all. Compliments were a matter of course to someone as lovely and talented as Livvy Davis, they always had been.

'Here.' He handed over the wine to her as James came up.

'Hello, Hugh!' He held out his hand and they shook, James letting go almost instantly.

'Oh, and these,' Hugh said, turning back to Livvy and remembering the chocolates.

'Oh, lovely! We'll have them later.' Livvy turned towards the kitchen. 'James, I don't want you to hog Hugh all night, take him over to Lucy!' She laughed. 'Lucy has been dying to see you all week, Hugh, she wants to bore you stiff with all her city talk!'

'Oi! I heard that, Davis.' Lucy appeared from across the room and kissed Hugh warmly on each cheek. 'Mmwah, mmwah! Hugh, my love, you look absolutely wonderful.'

Hugh grinned and for a split second his gaze met James's. The private joke that had existed between them all those years ago was suddenly resurrected and despite the sharp suit from Gieves and Hawkes, the account at Berry Bros, the handmade brogues and membership to Annabel's, Hugh knew he didn't really fit in. Only nowadays, he couldn't give a shit about it. He wasn't here to compete; he was here on business. It was all part of his meticulous and careful planning.

'Now, Hugh, James tells me you underwrite an awful lot of business in Brazil. Is that right?' Lucy lit her cigarette from the gold lighter that Hugh held out for her.

'A fair amount. We've a number of good premiums coming from over there.' He never said much about Brazil; it wasn't wise. South America was a hell of a risk, illegal, immoral but so lucrative that Hugh would have been mad to turn the business away. He saw Lucy's immediate interest and swiftly moved the conversation on to safer ground. 'Our biggest business in the UK though is IMACO.'

'Blimey!' Lucy didn't deal in Industrials but everyone in the City knew IMACO; they were huge. 'How much of their business do you underwrite?'

'Don't get overexcited!' Hugh laughed. 'I can see the dollar signs in your eyes, Lucy. I've only got a very small

71

portion of their business. But,' he shrugged modestly, 'it's worth a good deal of revenue to me.'

'I bet it is!' Lucy laughed. 'There's no need to be coy, Hugh. You don't get your own box at Lloyd's at the tender age of twenty-nine without a hell of a lot of work and more than a touch of brilliance.'

'Brilliance? Who's brilliant?' Livvy refilled Lucy's glass.

'Why Hugh, of course!' Lucy took a gulp of the cold, dry Sancerre and said, 'I have this terrible feeling that Hugh here is on his way right to the top and that he'll leave us all behind him, confused and shivering in the wake of his success.'

'Oh, Lucy!' Livvy burst out laughing and turned to Hugh with the wine. 'Is that right, Hugh? Are you on the way to the top?'

Hugh smiled. Lucy Deacon had always had an uncanny knack of hitting the mark exactly and yet remaining completely oblivious to it. 'I don't really know yet, Livvy, a lot depends on the next few months.' He spoke truthfully but only he knew the real meaning of what he said.

'Well, you'll tell us what the view is like, from up there, won't you?'

'I hardly need to tell you, Livvy.' Hugh smiled. 'You've been way above most of us for as long as I can remember.'

Again Livvy laughed, missing the note of malice in Hugh's voice. 'I hardly think you're right, but thanks anyway.'

Hugh raised an eyebrow.

'Normally Livvy would agree with you, Hugh, but tonight she's sulking,' Lucy said, having spent a good hour on the phone to Livvy that afternoon after her interview. 'She went for a job today and wasn't offered it the moment she sat down. It's come as a bit of a surprise.'

Deceived

Livvy pulled a face at Lucy. They both knew that Lucy could get away with this kind of comment because of their friendship and because it was said with warmth and humour.

'What sort of job was it?' Hugh asked.

'To front a series of six new arts programmes going out on the national network. A sort of "South Bank" type of thing.'

Hugh let out a low whistle. 'Do you think you got it?'

'I don't know. They said they wanted some really innovative ideas and that my own personal input was essential. I don't know whether they liked my proposals or not, they didn't say. I kind of felt they wanted someone or something to really stun them and I just didn't do it.' She shrugged.

'You could have done the interview naked!' Lucy interjected.

'Lucy, please!'

Hugh laughed.

'Anyway, that's quite enough of me,' Livvy said, conscious that Hugh's attention had wandered to the other side of the room. 'Tell me all about South America, Hugh, I'm fascinated by the whole continent. Do you travel there much?'

Hugh flicked his eyes away from James and nodded in answer to Livvy's question. 'I've seen quite a bit of Brazil over the years,' he said. 'But then so has James. I won't bore you with my tales of Rio, I'm sure you've heard them all before. I have seen something of Bolivia, Peru and Argentina, though.' He carefully left out Colombia. 'The whole continent is one of extremes, fantastic but appalling.'

'Well, tell me more,' Livvy demanded. 'I want to hear all about it.'

Hugh held down a smile. It was typical of Livvy to want

73

to dominate his conversation. 'Where shall I start?' he asked.

'Anywhere you like,' Livvy replied, placing the bottle of wine on the table, the task of handing it round completely forgotten. 'You've got all night if you want!'

The candles had burned low and the conversation was intense and spirited around the table, people talking in twos and threes. Port, cheese, red wine and fruit had been consumed and the cafetière had been refilled for the third time. The Leonidas chocolates were open and every now and then one of the guests would lean over and pick a rich, fresh-cream truffle from the box, rustling the gold paper and leaving a small trail of chocolate crumbs on the table. Livvy sat back and looked across at Hugh as he finished his story, her eyes bright with excitement. She was oblivious to the rest of the room, to the hum of voices, the odd burst of laughter. Her conversation with Hugh had been private, just the two of them and all she could think of now was what he had just said.

She leaned forward. 'And you actually saw him?' Her voice was thick with amazement.

Hugh nodded. He was staggered by her reaction and he couldn't stop playing on it now. A dark, intricate idea was forming in his head and he wanted to see just how far he could push her.

'But no one has seen or heard of Lenny Duce for nearly ten years!' She stopped, the full weight of what she had just said heavy in the air between them. Lenny Duce was one of the most brilliant and highly paid modern artists of the past three decades, or at least he was until he had disappeared ten years ago. 'How the hell did they do it? Find him, I mean.'

Hugh took a long drag of his cigarette. 'He wanted to negotiate with one of the companies I deal with. He felt passionately about the area of rainforest the government had sold to them; he wanted to buy it back.' It had all been a very corrupt affair, with Manuello heading up the whole thing and making a large amount of money from the deal but Hugh didn't mention any of that.

'Jesus! You must be talking . . .'

'About sixty million dollars. He's worth an absolute fortune, Livvy, that was nothing to him.'

'So he just came forward to talk to the company lawyers?'

Hugh smiled. 'It wasn't quite as simple as that. He's a very reclusive person, you know. Totally paranoid about being found by the world.'

'I can't believe that you actually met him!' Livvy took one of Hugh's cigarettes and lit it. She hardly ever smoked but what she was hearing absorbed her so deeply that she was barely aware of what she was doing. 'So what was he like, Hugh? Was there any evidence of the rumours about AIDS?'

'No. Duce was perfectly fit and healthy, very laid-back but very eloquent about his cause. He seemed like a pretty nice chap to me.'

'Did you speak to him personally?'

'Livvy! What is this? Twenty questions?' Hugh leaned back in his chair, fascinated by the change in the person opposite him. He saw something in her eyes that he recognised and it both shocked and thrilled him. He had never thought of Livvy Davis as fiercely ambitious but he could see it now; it blazed around her, hot and intense, giving her an air of aggression that he found faintly attractive.

He smiled as his idea took shape and he began to realise

just how he could use her. He lit himself a cigarette using the tip of hers in a slow and intimate gesture, then he looked across at her and said, 'You know, there is a chance that I might be able to find Duce again, if I needed to.' He turned away to flick his ash but from the corner of his eye he watched Livvy's face closely. He saw a fleeting look of triumph and then an expression of such brazen ambition that he knew in an instant that he'd got her. He knew that hunger so well there was no mistaking it and the whole basis for his plan took on a completely new dimension. He would use James, there was no doubt about that, but if he could use Livvy as well, then how much sweeter the taste of revenge would be. It was a flash of inspiration, to catch the spider in her own web, a pure and fleeting moment of genius.

Livvy's heart beat so hard that she had to put her hand up to her breast for a moment to try to calm it. She thought about the interview that morning, about the job and about a media coup that could make her a worldwide celebrity. A meeting with Lenny Duce, the only person in ten years to get through to him – it was the chance of a lifetime! It would secure the job, she thought, but it would also secure much, much more than just a series of arts programmes with City TV.

'Hugh, could you . . .?'

Hugh interrupted her. 'Really find Duce? For someone else, you mean?'

Livvy looked up earnestly. 'For me. For a special programme on him.'

'Livvy, that's a hell of a tall order!'

'Well, put me in touch with the company he spoke to then?'

Hugh glanced surreptitiously across at Lucy Deacon on the far side of the table; she was talking quite earnestly to the man on her right. As she was the only person who might know that IMACO had no interest in Brazil whatsoever, Hugh reckoned he was safe. If Livvy was going to be involved in the whole thing then Hugh needed to throw in a name that would mean something, that would add credibility to what he'd just said. She'd never go to Brazil if she knew the truth about Manuello.

Putting a finger to his lips to indicate secrecy, Hugh leaned forward and said, 'What? IMACO?'

'Is that who it was?'

'Strictly between us, yes.' Hugh saw the excitement in Livvy's eyes flare. He was right to have chosen a well-known name. He lowered his voice. 'But I *mean* strictly between us, Livvy. Only two other people know it was IMACO. Duce had no idea who he was dealing with.'

Livvy was surprised.

'Duce went along with the whole thing because they had something he wanted,' Hugh explained. 'Simple as that.' He shrugged. 'Trouble is, I really don't know if we'd ever be able to repeat it. There's no reason on earth why he should speak to a film crew and a British reporter when he has nothing but invasion of privacy to gain.'

But all the time he spoke, Hugh's mind was working in its brilliant strategic and meticulous way. He was sure that Livvy in Brazil could really work for him, in more ways than one. She would be a good cover for James – a film crew, high profile and beyond suspicion – but more importantly, she would be there if James chickened out. Glancing across at James, Hugh realised that was something worth any amount of effort to track down Duce again. Knowing

James as he did, Hugh was under no illusions as to who or what would be sacrificed for James to save himself. Ah, to catch the spider in her own web, he thought again as he stubbed out his cigarette and smiled up at Livvy.

'But you know something, Livvy?' he said finally, watching her face for reaction. 'With a hell of a lot of effort, I think I just might be able to do it.'

Chapter Six

The following morning, James woke at nine and stretched out an arm across the bed expecting to touch Livvy. He opened his eyes, rolled over and looked at the unslept-in side of the bed.

'Livvy?' He sat up, rubbed his eyes and pushed the hair off his face. 'Livvy?'

'Hmmm?'

He could hear the faint tap of fingers on a keyboard in the next room. There was a pause, a sigh and then the tapping continued, this time at a faster pace. James climbed out of bed, pulled on his robe and wandered through to the sitting room.

'Livvy? What are you doing?'

Livvy, dressed in a pair of old silk pyjamas, sat cross-legged on the sofa with her laptop computer on her knees and a pile of scribbled notes spread out over the surrounding area. She didn't even look up as James walked over to her, picked up one of the glossy books she had pulled from the shelves and looked at the cover.

'*Lenny Duce and the freedom of Abstract Expressionism.* My

God! What on earth are you doing with this at . . .' He glanced down at his watch. 'Ten past nine on a Saturday morning?' He waited, and getting no reply, put the book back on the floor with the others and went into the kitchen.

'Coffee?' he shouted.

'Hmmm, yes, please.'

He put his head round the door. 'A response at last!' Livvy had looked up from her work. 'What are you doing, Liv? It's the bloody weekend, for God's sake!'

'I'm rewriting my proposals for the arts series on City.'

'What, now?'

'Yes, now! The proposal for the opening programme can't wait. I've rung Alan and Judy said he'd ring me back when he gets in from walking the dogs. I want to go down to Kent this morning and talk to him about it.'

James walked back in from the kitchen and stood looking down at her. 'Are you serious?'

'Of course I'm serious! Hugh said . . .'

James experienced a peculiar prickling sensation at the back of his neck. 'Hugh said what? What has Hugh got to do with City Television?'

'Quite a lot, as it happens.' Livvy suddenly smiled. 'Oh, James, I can't believe it! Hugh apparently met Lenny Duce in the late part of last year and he reckons he might just be able to get me an interview with him. He's huge, James! The most famous living artist of the twentieth century and the whole world has been unable to find him for ten years! It's just too incredible for words!'

James stood still and the prickling sensation continued down his spine; he recognised it as fear. Why he should fear Hugh he had no idea, but he did. It spread down along his spine and his whole body shivered momentarily.

'Are you all right, James?'

'Yes, I'm fine.' He turned as the kettle boiled and walked out of the room. The fear changed instantly to anger and he ignored Livvy's call to him. Why should Hugh do something for Livvy? And why did Livvy have to go down to Kent today, on a Saturday when the sun was shining and he'd have to spend the day on his own? He hadn't heard any of the conversation last night. What else did they say? He had been excluded, very obviously, and although he didn't realise it, the anger changed again, to jealousy.

'James?'

He looked round. Livvy stood in the doorway.

'You can come to Alan and Judy's if you want.'

'No. Thanks, Livvy, but I always find TV people a bit much.' He poured the scalding water on to the ground coffee and plunged the filter down into the jug. The telephone rang.

'I'll get it, it's probably Alan.' Livvy had walked back to the sitting room to answer it. 'Could you bring my coffee through?'

James nodded and she smiled her thanks.

'Hello? Alan! Hi, how are you?'

James listened to the first part of the conversation and then closed the connecting door. He switched on the radio, tuned it into Capital and, humming aggressively, he poured out two cups of coffee, took a sip of his own and left Livvy's on the side to get cold.

Livvy was dressed and stuffing her papers into her case when James came out of the shower. She smelled fresh and lemony and her hair was newly washed. James was cross that she was leaving him and he found it difficult to conceal.

'What time will you be back?'

Livvy clicked the case shut and stood straight. 'I won't, not tonight. I'm staying with Alan and Judy. I haven't seen them for ages and . . .'

'Yes, all right, I know! It's important to keep in touch with friends of your father's, blah, blah, blah.'

'Thank you, James.'

He ignored her sarcasm. 'Not to mention that Alan has an awful lot of clout at City,' he went on, 'and if you have to convince anyone that you're right for the job, you might as well start there.'

Livvy watched him, waiting until he'd finished and then said, 'Is there anything on your mind, James? A hangover perhaps?'

James shrugged. He knew he was being churlish but he didn't want to be left alone, it unnerved him. He knew damn well the temptation to call Hugh would be enormous and that made him decidedly uneasy. He was no longer at all sure that he had the advantage. 'No, nothing,' he answered finally. He smiled and Livvy forgave him his peevish outburst. 'I'm sorry, Livvy.' He crossed to kiss her. 'Have a good time. I know how much this job means to you.'

Livvy rested her head on his shoulder for a few moments and he stroked her hair. She worried very briefly why the job did mean so much to her but she dismissed the doubt almost immediately. She had been striving for too long to question it.

'I'll see you tomorrow then.'

She lifted her head and nodded. The embrace was comforting but she was relieved when James gently moved away. She bent, picked up her case, computer and weekend bag and turned towards the door.

'Good luck,' he said.

She smiled. 'Thanks.' And blowing him a kiss, she walked out of the room. Moments later he heard the front door slam and the noisy mechanics of the lift. He went back to the bedroom and began to dress.

It was after eleven when James picked up the telephone to ring Hugh. He had thought about it for over an hour, letting the idea nestle in his mind, letting it settle there so that when he came to dial there was no real doubt left, only the notion that it was a simple, friendly call. James never really questioned anything he did very deeply. He knew by now that Hugh was dangerous but somehow managed to ignore that. He only ever took into account the things that gave him pleasure or gain; the rest were easily forgotten along the way.

Hugh was sitting, propped up against a bank of pillows in bed, reading the *Telegraph* and listening to Herbie Mann live at the Village Gate. He was relaxed, pleased with himself in a way that he rarely felt, and he tapped his bare toe to the bass as he read. The telephone sounded on the bedside table and reaching over after several rings, he picked it up.

'Hello?'

'Hugh? Good morning, it's James.'

Hugh leaned back, pushed the paper away and, letting his head rest against the feather pillows, he smiled, a slow, triumphant smile. 'Hello, James.'

After weeks and weeks of his careful and meticulous pursuit, Hugh had finally got what he wanted. James couldn't stay away. 'Thanks for a super evening last night,' he said casually. 'How's Livvy this morning?'

'She's gone down to Kent,' James answered, unable to keep the irritation from his voice. 'She's all fired up about the idea you mentioned to her and she's taken off to discuss it with an old family friend.'

'Oh, really?'

'Yes, really.' James smiled. 'You didn't do it on purpose by any chance, did you?'

Hugh laughed. Don't flatter yourself, Jamie my boy, he thought, but he said, 'Well . . .' and after a pause, 'I don't suppose you'd like to come over and join me on the balcony for breakfast, would you?'

James looked out at the brilliant January sky, ice-cold blue, and said, 'Is that with our overcoats on?'

'It's with or without, whatever you want.'

'Yes, all right then, I'll be over in about half an hour.'

Hugh smiled again. 'See you in half an hour.' He leaned over and replaced the receiver without another word.

'Nat?' he called. He swung his legs over the side of the bed and stood up. 'Nat?'

The bathroom door opened and a young dark-haired man, not unlike James, turned his beautiful face away from the mirror towards Hugh; it was covered in shaving foam.

'Nat, I've got someone coming for breakfast, in about twenty minutes.' Hugh shrugged. 'Sorry.'

'OK.' Nat picked up the razor and began to trace the outline of his jaw with it. 'I'll finish dressing,' he said, rinsing the razor under the tap for a moment and then continuing. 'I'll be gone in ten.'

Hugh pulled on his bathrobe and picked up the two coffee cups from the floor. 'Thanks, Nat.' He walked out of the bedroom and across to the kitchen. The arrangement he had with Nat was very convenient for both of them, at least for the moment. No lies, no fuss, just sex; rare and satisfying. What he had with Nat was something he knew damn well he could never have with James.

Hugh was still in his bathrobe when James arrived forty minutes later; he had just stepped out of the shower. He released the lock on the main door and left his own front door open while he made the coffee in the kitchen. He heard James come in and called out to him. He was in a buoyant mood this morning; after all the waiting, he reckoned he just about had James in the palm of his hand and that meant he was ready to set things up. The thought of that exhilarated him, filled him with aggressive confidence. He turned as James came into the room.

'Good morning.'

James was immaculate in navy chinos, a pale blue Oxford cotton shirt, a light grey cashmere sweater and brown suede Gucci loafers. Hugh smiled at his appearance, always so perfect. 'Hello,' he answered. 'How are you? Was there much mess after last night?'

'A bit. Livvy rang Mrs Thing this morning and she's coming in this afternoon to clear up.'

Hugh knew as well as James the affectation of that expression but he let it go. James seemed to have conveniently forgotten how his mother worked to put him through college.

'Sit down,' he said. 'D'you want coffee?'

'Hmmm. Please.' James picked up the *Telegraph* and turned to the sports section. Hugh watched him for a few moments, the square, smooth shape of his jaw, the exact cut of his hair and the soft down on the back of his neck, but he looked away as James glanced up.

'What's all this about Livvy going to Brazil on some wild goose chase?' James said, leaning back on his stool against the wall. He sounded petulant and his voice whined very, very slightly. He was still irritated by Livvy's departure to Kent and jealous of Hugh's sudden interest in her. He knew it was childish but he couldn't help it. 'Since when did you have any interest in helping someone?' he asked sarcastically.

Hugh felt a sudden sharp jolt of anger at the easy insult and retorted without thinking, 'I don't, but Livvy may be useful there!' But as soon as he said it he knew he shouldn't have. He saw a truculent wariness come into James's eyes.

'What do you mean, useful?'

Hugh didn't answer, he was too unsure of what to say next. Something about James had begun to irritate him recently – his edge of possessiveness, his stupid paranoia that the whole world was watching him, waiting to catch him out; the covert gay. Truth was, Hugh thought meanly, the whole world couldn't give a shit, but James was far too arrogant ever to realise that. And besides, pretty soon he really would have something to be paranoid about. He'd know all about fear then.

'I asked you a question, Hugh,' James said angrily. 'I want an answer!'

'I want, I want,' Hugh retorted. 'You sound like a spoilt middle-class brat, James!'

'I wouldn't have thought you know much about middle-class brats, Hugh! Were there many middle class on that filthy housing estate in Manchester?' James saw Hugh's face change, his eyes harden and his mouth narrow into a tight thin line. 'You should be careful, Hugh my love,' James continued, unable to curb his spite. 'If you say things like that you'll give the tightly kept secret of that massive working-class chip of yours away!' He smiled nastily and looked away. 'You still haven't answered my question, Hugh.'

Hugh watched the sharp, perfect profile for several minutes, a profile he had loved all those years ago and saw quite clearly how beautiful James was and how well that masked all the ugliness inside. He had been waiting for the right moment to take control, for a subtle introduction of his strength. But now he couldn't care less. James would have to know and the sooner the power was asserted, the better.

Slowly Hugh said, 'I have a plan, James. It involves you mainly but Livvy may be useful to some degree, that's why I mentioned Brazil to her.' He saw that James sat very still, suddenly shocked.

'And what plan is that?' James asked coolly. He stayed outwardly calm but a peculiar sensation of fear had started in the pit of his stomach. He had a terrifying premonition that his life was about to fall apart.

Hugh leaned back against the side, casual and calm. 'I've been trying to set up a drug deal in Brazil for about a year now and I reckon that I'm almost there. I've got the distribution network set up, but up until about five months ago, until I received Eliza's wedding invitation, I was stuck for a courier. That was the last thing I needed, to put the deal into place. I needed someone with a very low risk, someone practically above suspicion, and when I got that invite it suddenly occurred to me that Eliza might be able to help.' Hugh stopped. James was staring at him now, open-mouthed. Hugh knew he had already guessed the next part of the story.

'Eliza was more than helpful,' Hugh continued. 'She gave me all the gossip, your complete history in fact. The Foreign Office, the posting to Lisbon, the position now on the Brazilian desk, loads of stuff on your rather half-hearted relationship with Livvy. The whole lot!' Hugh smiled. 'A stroke of luck, you might say, so I settled on you. It's really been a case, in the past month or so, of putting myself in a position to make you an offer you can't refuse.'

James shook his head, too stunned to answer. He just sat and stared at Hugh and all the time a dull icy fear crept through his whole body. 'You don't mean it,' he whispered. 'You can't be serious, Hugh?' He was whining, he could hear it himself. 'You don't mean it, Hugh, I know you don't.'

Hugh shrugged. 'Don't I?'

Suddenly the anger hit James. He jumped up and lunged towards Hugh, his right fist flying. 'You're fucking mad, Hugh! Mad!' he shouted. 'There's no way you're involving me in any of this, no fucking way!' But Hugh caught his hand before it hit him. He was shorter than James but physically much more powerful. He held James's wrist and twisted it painfully.

'Oh no? Too late, James!' he said icily. 'You're already involved, from your neck down to your tight little ass!'

'You're out of your mind, Hugh,' James spat. 'You're crazy!'

'Really?' Hugh still held his wrist. 'I don't think so. Who would suspect you, James? A senior secretary in the Foreign Office, in Brazil on business? You're above suspicion, it's one of the perks of the job. To stop you coming through would be laughable.' He loosened his grip slightly. 'Come on, James, think it through.' He dropped James's hand.

'There's no way!' James said, holding the skin-burn on his wrist. 'No fucking way!'

But Hugh simply shrugged and moved away. 'I said, think it through, James.' His face was completely emotionless. 'What would Livvy say if she knew that you had slept with me?'

'Oh for Christ's sake, Hugh!'

'That you'd put her health, even her life at risk by having an affair with another man? You have no idea how promiscuous I am, do you, James?' Hugh snorted with derision and then said sarcastically, 'I don't suppose that safe sex ever occurred to you, did it? You were far too eager to get your hands on me to think about that kind of thing.'

Suddenly Hugh saw James slump as if all the strength and aggression had deserted him. He went on, the feeling of power quite exquisite.

'The flat in Cadogan Square belongs to Livvy's grandmother, doesn't it? How much does Livvy earn? Hmmm? Enough to pay all the bills while you pay for your expensive suits from Gieves and Hawkes and the odd holiday to Mauritius?' Hugh raised an eyebrow. 'It's a nice lifestyle, James, costly, but nice.'

James looked at him with fear and disgust. 'You really think Livvy would believe you?'

'Of course I do. I wouldn't mention it if I didn't.'

The next moment Hugh realised that he was close to ultimate control. He saw all James's weaknesses come to the surface and knew that he had got him. He moved closer and put his hand on James's shoulder, swiftly changing tack.

'It's OK,' he whispered, 'I understand. You feel like I do, James. You don't want all the fuss and aggro of being gay, you want the safety, the wonderful things that Livvy can give you, the flat, the lifestyle. You always have done, ever since that first time in college when you realised just how much she was worth to you. You dumped me for Livvy, remember? You wanted it easy. You still do.' He leaned in even closer. 'I don't blame you, I'd have probably done the same. But you *can* have it easy, James. So can I. No one need ever know about us, about any of it.' James could feel the heat of Hugh's breath.

'We can carry on for as long as you like,' he said. 'You need it, so do I.' He saw James shiver, a slight involuntary shudder that went through his whole body. 'James, trust me,' he whispered. 'I'm not asking much, just that you trust me, do as I say.' He moved his hand down to James's groin and heard him moan. 'You see, I know what's best for you.' Unfastening the buttons of James's chinos, he slipped his short, thick fingers inside and felt the excitement there, regardless of fear and anger. He knew there was nothing to stop him now. 'Trust me, James,' he said, kissing his neck. 'Just trust me, baby.'

Livvy sat back from the table and ran her fingers through her hair. She swept it back off her face and Alan, looking across at her, thought how like her mother she was. It puzzled him why she was so determined to live up to an image of her father, an image that only she had, but he never mentioned that to her. He admired her for what she'd achieved and left it at that. And he had to admit, with the pile of proposal papers spread out in front of him, that this time Livvy was on to a story that would break round the world. It was a BAFTA winner, no doubt about it, if she could pull it off.

He picked up her treatment of the interview again and

looked at it for the third time that afternoon. The angle that she'd taken was new and innovative, not the same old 'What had Lenny Duce done for twentieth-century Art?' but 'What had twentieth-century Art done for Lenny Duce?' It was a look at the modern world through the eyes of one of the most brilliant and creative people of modern times, before and after his success. What changed him and why? If Livvy really could get to Duce, Alan thought, then the outcome would stun the world.

He glanced up from the paper and saw Livvy's intense gaze across the table.

'You've got one hell of an idea, Livvy,' he said.

'I know.'

He smiled. 'Ever modest. Do you really think this Hugh person will come up with the goods? You don't even know who his contact was.'

Livvy closed her bright blue eyes for a minute. She had been less than truthful with Alan – the one thing Hugh had insisted on was that no one should know it was IMACO. She realised how risky it must look and for the first time since Hugh had mentioned the name Lenny Duce, she felt a moment of hesitation. Why should Hugh do something of such huge importance for her? She hardly knew him, had spoken to him properly last night for the first time in eight years and he had made a rash and incredible promise. A promise that would make her career. She opened her eyes again. 'Yes,' she said, 'I do but I'm not at liberty to say.' And the second she said it she knew that whatever happened she would pursue it to the bitter end. She knew that nothing would come between her and the glory.

'Do you think Jake Parsons will agree?' she asked.

Alan chucked the piece of paper he was holding on to the

pile already on the table and grinned. 'My dear girl,' he said, 'do you think I would spend four and a half hours talking about a proposal without ringing the programme controller first to check if he thought it was a good idea?'

Livvy narrowed her eyes. 'And?'

'I don't really have to spell it out for you, do I?' Alan stood, placed his hands over his large, rounded abdomen and patted it affectionately. 'Come on, let's go and eat before my stomach has a revolt and we'll talk about who's available to direct over lunch.' He held out his hand. 'Better late than never, I suppose. Judy's been making signs at me behind your head for the past forty minutes. I only hope my spicy lamb isn't burned!' He pulled Livvy up and, placing his arm around her shoulder, led her out of his studio and into the main part of the house where the delicious aroma of food made her feel suddenly quite weak with hunger.

That same Saturday afternoon, Jack Wilcox took Nel's arm as they tumbled out of Bently's wine bar just off the Strand and pulled her lithe, shapely body close to his. She giggled as he lunged for her ear with a wet, rolling tongue, and pushed him away.

'Jack! People are watching.' She teetered on her high-heeled black suede ankle boots as Jack reached a hand out and ran it along the exposed length of stockinged thigh beneath her tight Lycra skirt.

'Got you!' He laughed loudly, his face ruddy from the vast quantity of champagne they had drunk and his eyes glazed. He squeezed her buttock and belched. 'Oops! 'Scuse me!' Then pulling her to the edge of the pavement, he shouted across the street at a black cab that was letting out its fare. 'TAXI!' He let go of Nel and darted across the traffic, whooping as he narrowly missed the bonnet of a passing sports car and stumbling on the kerb.

'Prince's Gate please, mate!' he called to the cabbie as he regained his balance. 'Come on, Nel!'

'Jack!' Nel materialised by his side in what seemed like the blink of an eye and Jack suddenly realised he was far more pissed than he had thought. He climbed unsteadily into the back of the taxi and slumped against the seat.

'Make that Mayfair, would you?' Nel climbed in beside him and he looked up at her through a haze of alcohol.

'Why are we going to Mayfair?'

She leaned over and kissed him on the lips, slipping her tongue expertly inside his mouth and over his teeth. Then she broke off and smiled. 'We're going back to my place this afternoon,' she whispered. 'I've got a surprise for you.'

Jack shook his head, grinning. 'Jesus, Nel . . .' She had eased one of her long legs over his and the top of her pale brown thigh was exposed above her stocking. He could see the black lace covering her crotch and his breathing quickened. She put her fingers up to his face and held it for a moment before kissing him again, this time deeper, letting her tongue go right down into his mouth, exploring, enticing. He strained towards her and pinched the skin on her thigh.

'Ouch!' She pulled away and laughed. 'You are wicked, Jack Wilcox!' She caught the eye of the driver and acknowledged his look; the more witnesses the better.

Jack strained again but she pushed him playfully away. 'You'll have to wait,' she teased, unzipping her leather jacket and letting him glimpse the sheer black see-through body she wore underneath and the hard, dark brown shape of her nipples. 'You'll get what you want in the end,' she said,

crossing her arms and forcing her large breasts up provoca-
tively. 'You did last night, didn't you?'

Jack closed his eyes as images of the previous night at his
flat came flooding back into his mind. She had been insa-
tiable, willing to do anything to please him with her
incredible, flexible body. She was literally the best fuck he
had ever had. He nodded weakly. 'How come you live in
Mayfair?' he asked, slurring his words slightly. He opened
his eyes as the cab swung round a corner and Nel fell
towards him. 'That's a pretty smart address.'

Nel giggled and stayed where she was, the heavy weight
of her body against his. 'Isn't it?' she said and purred as once
more Jack's fingers crept up to the top of her thigh and
towards her crotch. She eased her legs open and made sure
the driver had a full eye view.

Standing on the pavement in Clarges Street, Nel pressed the
buzzer for number three on the panel outside a tall, white
Regency house and waited for the door release. She pushed
the main door open and pulled Jack gently inside the big
central hallway, kicking the door shut behind them. She put
her arms up around Jack's neck and they fell against the wall
in a passionate embrace.

Minutes later, as Jack went to kiss her throat, she moved
her hands to his chest and eased him away a few inches.
'Wait,' she murmured. 'Let's go inside, it's much warmer.' He
nodded and she led him down the corridor to the open
door of her flat. He looked momentarily puzzled but she
turned to him and smiled as she guided him into the sitting
room. 'Close your eyes,' she said, 'for my surprise.'

He laughed, did as she said and felt her tie something
soft and silky around his head, covering his sight. He heard

her giggle and the rustle of clothes, then what sounded like whispering.

'Jack?' She was in front of him now, he could smell her perfume. She pushed him gently backwards and down, sinking him on to a sofa and he stumbled slightly, the drink and the lack of vision making him momentarily disorientated. Then he felt a hand on the zip of his fly, the fingers slipping down to stroke him, and he moaned loudly. The fingers were withdrawn and he heard muffled footsteps walking away from him.

'You can take off the blindfold now,' Nel said and Jack moved his hand quickly up to his face. Pulling the scarf away, he blinked in the darkness of the room and then saw Nel sprawled out on a red velvet chaise across the room. She was on her back, reclining like a Victorian lady, wearing only a pair of white silk stockings held up with garters and a pink feather boa. In front of her, lying back against the chaise, was a plump, big-breasted blonde, completely naked except for a pair of old-fashioned ankle boots and her stockings rolled halfway down her legs. She had her eyes half closed and an erotic smile on her lips as Nel draped her arm down over her body and gently stroked the pale pink nipple on the tip of her round, creamy white breast.

Jack stared, the blood rushing to his groin instantly, and his lips parted as his breathing grew faster.

'This is Alice, and we both want you, darling Jack. I think you will have to decide who you have first,' Nel said. She bent her head and tilted the blonde's head back to kiss her full on the lips. Jack moaned. Behind the couch he could see part of his own reflection in a huge gilt mirror and he began to undress, pleased at the size of his erection. Naked, he held it in his hands, looking at it and moving across to the girls.

'Get on top of Nel,' he said to Alice. She eased her body up and Nel opened out her arms. Alice came into the embrace and Jack moved to the end of the chaise. He watched the girls for several minutes, the plump rounded buttocks of the blonde moving gently, Nel's strong brown legs open and wrapped around the blonde's back. Then he edged forward, placed his hands on the white globes to part them and glanced down at his manhood. Nel moaned loudly, he found the right place and, lunging forward, he joined in the moving knot of flesh.

Much, much later, lying on his back, Jack lifted his arm from across his eyes and looked again at the two girls on the chaise. Even now, the sight of them was magnificent.

He tried to focus on his watch but he couldn't be bothered, it felt as if what had happened had occurred in a few seconds but he knew that must be wrong. He was exhausted and could see the mess on the glass coffee table: the debris of their cocaine, empty champagne bottles and cigarette packets, a full ashtray. He put his arm back over his eyes and just listened to the sighs and murmuring from across the room. He had never done cocaine before, never dared risk it, but with Nel nothing went untried. And hearing her groan in ecstasy, he let out a deep, heavy, spent sigh, rolled on to his side and curled up into the foetal position to sleep.

In a small, cramped space behind the large gilt two-way mirror, the video operator finally switched off his camera, unplugged the microphone and lit up the last cigarette in his packet. It was nearly nine a.m., Sunday morning, and he was shattered. A good night's work though, he thought, packing his equipment away; that Nel was one hell of a pro, God bless her. He glanced at the poor bastard asleep on the carpet and then shook his head. Deserves everything he gets, upper-class git, he thought savagely. Although quite what he would end up with was anybody's guess, especially with Hugh Howard behind the whole set-up.

Chapter Seven

James sat on the floor in the wide, open cream and white sitting room of Livvy's flat and looked through the final album in the pile he had by his side. It was Sunday night and he had been there for hours.

He opened it at the page of photographs they had taken on his return from Lisbon, the end of his three-year posting there and the beginning of their relationship proper. There were snaps of him moving into the flat, snaps of them together, unpacking, laughing helplessly in the panic to position themselves for the automatic timer on the camera, snaps of happy, uncomplicated days. He closed the album and leaned back against the sofa.

'Oh Christ,' he murmured, looking round him at the wonderful, rich luxury of the room. He picked up the first album in the pile again and turned to the page with his family photographs on. He stared at the small, bad quality print of his parents outside their council house in Norwich on the day he went up to Oxford, the day he had left home, promising to ring and knowing he never would. He could see them in his mind's eye: the thin frame of his father, the outline of his vest under the white nylon shirt, sleeves rolled up to the elbow and the false smile of his mother, her heavy red lipstick and the two front curlers hastily removed from her hair for the camera. He remembered the poky little house with its Reader's Digest collection of condensed novels and the enormous twenty-inch television screen that dominated the front room. He looked away from the photograph, hating himself for feeling the way he did, but unable to stop, nervous and ashamed of his parents.

It was so apparent, the gulf that stretched between them now, the gulf of experience that he knew he really owed to Livvy, to her lifestyle and her money. He couldn't give it up; he knew he couldn't even try.

Finally making it through the front door of the flat, Livvy dropped her overnight bag heavily down on to the carpet and let out a loud groan of relief. It had been a horrible journey up from Kent. She switched on the lights, kicked off her shoes and wandered through to the sitting room, turning the lamp on as she went.

'Oh!' She jumped, startled as James's form came into vision with the light, sprawled out on the floor. 'James!' She crossed to him and bent to kiss his cheek. 'I thought the flat was empty. What are you doing sitting here in the dark?'

As she bent, James caught her face with his hand and held her close for a few moments. He suddenly wanted to touch her more than he had thought possible. She kneeled and looked at him, surprised at the gesture. 'Is anything wrong?' she asked gently.

'No. I've missed you, that's all.' He smiled, a smile that he had mastered so long ago, that looked so real even when it was miles away from that.

Livvy smiled back, her momentary concern evaporated. 'Good.' She stood. 'Have you eaten?'

'No, I thought . . .' James broke off. He gazed up at the tall, graceful shape of Olivia Davis, beautiful and elegant in a pair of black jeans and a lambswool sweater, her pale blonde hair loose around her shoulders. He couldn't let Hugh win; he wouldn't let him take her away. 'Livvy, I thought we might get married,' he said.

Livvy stopped. She was on her way to the kitchen and she stood perfectly still then turned slowly. 'Are you serious?'

'Of course I'm serious!' He was cross.

'I'm sorry, it's just that I never expected . . .'

'What? That I might love you enough to want to get married and have a family?' he lied.

'No! That it would be now, that's all.'

James stood up and crossed to her. He placed his hands gently on her shoulders. 'This wasn't quite the reaction I had in mind.'

Livvy tried to smile and glanced down at the floor. 'I'm sorry, I . . .' She wanted to say, You can't just announce something like this, completely out of the blue, not when I've just made one of the biggest breaks of my whole career. How do you expect me to react? But she didn't, she continued to stare down at the ground and waited for him to speak.

James said nothing. He took her hand and led her back to the sofa, seating her next to him. 'Livvy, look.' He held her hand in both of his. 'I know it's a surprise but I've been doing some thinking lately and I've come to the conclusion that we both need a break, some time together, away from everything, jobs, London, England.' He paused and waited for that to sink in. He hadn't planned what he was going to say, he hadn't even thought it through. He just knew he couldn't let Hugh win, he wouldn't take the risks he was asking. A minute or so later he continued. 'Livvy, I'm sick of the merry-go-round and I want to get off. I don't want to go to Brazil next month. I don't like this Hugh thing, with you chasing after a rainbow. I just want some time off, to get married and be with you.' He let go of her hand and turned her face towards him. 'It's a sabbatical, Livvy, a fresh start for a while, maybe even a baby?' Whatever would tie them together, whatever it took, he didn't care, as long as Hugh couldn't destroy it.

Finally Livvy lifted her dark blue eyes to his and met his stare. Yesterday, with Alan, she had realised just how much success meant to her, and just how far she would go to achieve it. Pursue it to the bitter end, she had thought, let nothing come between her and the glory. She felt that now, it burned in her heart and made all else seem unimportant. She had to lay her father's ghost to rest with this, she had to. It would be her one major achievement to match his.

'James . . .' Livvy swallowed. 'I can't marry you now, not right now. I'm sorry but I can't.'

James dropped her hand. 'What does that mean? Why can't you marry me? What's stopping you, Livvy?' A note of panic had entered his voice; he hadn't expected this.

'I want to go to Brazil, James. I want this job and I've got more than a chance of getting it with this programme on Lenny Duce. If it works, this programme could . . .'

'This programme, this programme! Some wild goose chase across South America for an hour of tape? That's all it is, Livvy! There's no guarantee that Hugh will find him again, none whatsoever!' James's voice had become tight and strained. Livvy put her hand out to touch his arm but he pulled away. 'What makes you trust Hugh so much, Livvy?'

'Because I rang him this morning after a long meeting yesterday with Alan and a call from the programme controller. He told me he'd been working on the Lenny Duce thing since last night and was certain he could trace him.'

James's breath caught in the back of his throat, the chill of fear turning to icy panic. He jumped up, angry, disappointed and suddenly very afraid. He strode across to the window and stood, his back to Livvy, looking out at his beloved view across the square. Minutes later, he started as Livvy touched him on the shoulder.

'James, please.' She moved closer to him. 'There's no need for this . . .'

'Isn't there?' He longed, for one agonising moment, to tell her the truth, to blow Hugh's plan sky-high, to beg her forgiveness. But it passed; his strength had failed him again.

'We'll go to Brazil together, take some time off after the shooting schedule, after your conference, to be alone. Maybe even a few weeks?' Livvy pulled his shoulder gently round and James looked at her. 'Please, James?'

He was lost. There was no way out of it all, no choice. For once in his life he could not muster a smile; he could do nothing but look away, sick to the heart. He shrugged.

'James?'

'Yes, Livvy,' he said, 'whatever you want.' If success really meant that much to her, he thought, then Livvy would have to suffer the consequences. And although James wasn't aware of it, the germ of Hugh's idea had already taken root; Livvy had chosen her own destiny in more ways than one.

It was midweek, Wednesday night around nine o'clock, and the last person out of the office was Hugh's personal assistant, Mary. She called out to Hugh, still working, double-checked she'd left nothing of any importance on her desk and switched out the main bank of lights. She pulled her foldaway umbrella out of her bag as she walked along to the lifts and within minutes she was gone. Hugh looked out through the glass screen of his office at the semi-dark emptiness beyond, waited for three or so minutes and then picked up the telephone. He took a slip of paper out of his breast pocket, dialled the number on it and waited several seconds for the international line to connect and for the ringing tone of the Colombian exchange. The line was answered almost immediately.

'Hello?' Hugh waited for the sound echo to disappear. 'Manuello, please.'

The voice at the other end was Spanish and he couldn't make out what was being asked. It was a terrible line.

'*Manuello, por favor? Señor Manuello?*'

The line just crackled and the Spanish voice faded. Hugh felt his patience ebb. 'Manuello?' He shouted. 'Señor Manuello?' But the line went dead.

'Shit!' Hugh slammed down the receiver and glanced at his watch. The only time that he knew he could reach his contact was mid-afternoon local time and it was now just after nine in London. If he hadn't had to wait so long for Mary to clear out then he could have called an hour or so earlier. He glanced at his watch again and wiped a small film of sweat from his forehead. Time was running out. Manuello wanted a clear promise of the money by the end of the week and Hugh needed to reassure him it was on its way. He picked up the receiver again and dialled the number for the second time.

Moments later, he connected and the line was answered. It was clear.

'Hello? Señor Manuello, please.' Hugh breathed a sigh of relief and drummed his fingertips on the desk while he waited for someone to fetch his contact. He hated leaving things until the last minute. The deal had taken far too long to organise and he was working with the big boys now. They didn't take any prisoners and he didn't want to blow it.

He glanced up, still waiting for Manuello to come to the phone, and suddenly caught sight of Robson coming out of the lifts.

'Oh great!' he murmured under his breath. 'All I bloody well need!' Holding on for a moment longer, he saw Robson begin to approach his office and without thinking further, he replaced the receiver. Standing, he walked round the desk to the door and yanked it open, shouting across to Robson.

'What the hell are you doing here at this time of night?'

Paul Robson stopped in his tracks, taken aback by the attack. He swallowed down an angry retort.

'I . . . er . . .' He looked at Hugh's glowering face. 'I met a mate in the pub tonight, he's a journalist at the *Independent* and he's researching a story on IMACO.'

'So?'

'Well, he reckons that the reason they wanted to up their level of insurance a while back is because the MAFF are investigating Benzotytrin, their chief fertiliser and someone in the company is worried about that.'

'And this is what you trudged all the way back to the City for? To relay some overexaggerated news story to me?'

Robson flushed, angry at Hugh's tone. 'No, I thought it would be prudent, Hugh, to go over the files. We gave them such a big level that I want to be sure that we did the right thing.'

Hugh took a breath. He was out of order and he realised it. 'Look, sorry, Paul, it's been a long day. Why don't we talk about it some other time?' The last thing he needed was Robson sniffing around; he couldn't afford any awkward questions right now. The stress of his deal with Manuello was really getting to him and he still had tonight to deal with. 'Listen, I appreciate your concern, but I'd far rather you didn't bother with such petty problems . . . I . . .'

'With all due respect, Hugh,' Robson interrupted, 'I don't think this is going to be petty.'

Hugh suddenly lost patience; he didn't have time to mess about. 'Well, *with all due respect*, Paul, I'm the senior partner in this company and it's still my decision that counts! You do understand that, don't you?'

Robson glared at Hugh. 'Perfectly,' he answered coldly.

'Good.'

The two men stood their ground for a few moments, then Robson turned and left the office, slamming the door behind him. Hugh listened to his footsteps as they faded away, then he glanced at the clock and went back to the telephone. He would make it up to Robson tomorrow, take him out for lunch or something. He didn't like being a bastard, but sometimes it was the only way to deal with people.

Minutes later, he finally got through to Manuello.

'I've got the money organised,' he said. 'It'll be ready by the end of the week. The rest of the details I will let you know in due course.'

Manuello gave him the bank account number in Grand Cayman, which he noted on a scrap of paper. Seconds later the line went dead and he breathed a sigh of relief.

*

Jack stopped the cabbie and looked at the building in front of them. He checked the Soho address that Hugh had given him again and caught the knowing look from the driver. He leaned forward, paid the fare and climbed out of the taxi, unsure of what to do. Hugh had to be joking, surely? He looked up at the lurid multi-coloured photographs advertising the live sex show inside the bar and grimaced. He stood on the pavement for several minutes wondering what to do, then he glanced at his watch. He was already half an hour late; the least he could do was go in and have a look for Hugh. He descended the dark, grubby, staircase, paid his entrance fee to a fat man on the door and went inside.

Keeping his head down, Jack walked across to the bar and shouted over the noise of the music to order a drink. He told the girl he was meeting a friend and she shrugged as if to say, what the hell are you telling me for, asshole. He paid the four pounds fifty for his gin and stood with his back to the show, embarrassed and slightly sickened by the whole scene. One drink, he thought, and then I'll go. Just then someone tapped him on the shoulder.

'You waiting for Mr Howard?'

Jack turned round to face the fat man from the door. 'Yes, that's right.'

'Follow me, then.' He turned without any courtesy and Jack saw the shiny back of his suit. He finished his drink and hurried after the man, across the bar and through a door behind a red curtain. He glanced briefly along the darkened corridor, continued behind the man and followed him into a small dark room. The door was closed and he stood, uneasy and alone, unsure of what to do.

Minutes later, the door opened and Hugh appeared. Jack

moved across to him, his face flooded with relief, and took Hugh's hand.

'Hugh old chap, bloody good to see you! I was getting a bit worried, I must say. What kind of place is this?' He laughed nervously. 'Your idea of a joke, eh? You always were a bit on the wacky side at college.' He laughed again, this time more relaxed, and Hugh smiled.

'Come and sit down, Jack,' he said. 'Make yourself comfortable. I've got something I want to show you.' He led Jack to one of the chairs facing a large blank screen and they sat, Jack's sense of unease escalating again.

Hugh nodded behind him and the beginning of a tape came up on to the screen with the crackling of a soundtrack. Seconds later, Jack saw himself, blindfolded in the centre of a room he recognised as Nel's and a close-up of the naked blonde girl on the chaise. He jumped up, shocked and confused, and moved across to the screen to cover the image. The sound of Nel's voice came out of the two speakers on either side of the screen and then his own.

'What the fuck is going on?' he shouted. 'Turn that thing off! Turn it off!' He looked at Hugh, shocked and sickened, then back to the screen. 'Turn it off!' he shouted again, this time his face convulsed with anger. He lunged at Hugh, grabbed him and began shaking him, the rush of blood to his head making him almost completely blind. Seconds later, the room went dark. The flickering images on the screen vanished and Jack could hear the sound of his own heart hammering in his chest. He dropped Hugh and put his hands up to his face.

'You bastard!' he spat. 'You fucking bastard!'

Hugh watched him coldly. He waited until Jack regained some control, then he stood up, smoothed his suit where

Jack had grabbed him and walked across to a small metal filing cabinet. He opened it, took out a bottle of Scotch and two glasses and poured a large measure into each.

'Here.' He held out a glass for Jack and saw the man's hand tremble as he took it. He sat down again in silence while Jack wiped his face on his handkerchief.

Finally Jack had composed himself sufficiently to speak but he didn't look at Hugh, staring instead just above his head.

'You taped the whole thing?'

Hugh nodded and Jack seemed to crumble with the answer. 'So what do you want?' he asked. 'How much?' He took a gulp of his drink to steady his nerves. There was no point in pleas; he knew what Hugh had would ruin him. He knew that the trouble Hugh had taken to set him up meant serious blackmail. Hugh wasn't playing games.

'Did you know that Alice was under age, Jack?' The faintest flicker of a smile passed across Hugh's eyes. 'Wasn't your father recently on the bench for a juvenile sex trial?'

Jack swallowed hard, beads of sweat breaking out on his upper lip. 'How much?' he repeated.

'I want one hundred thousand pounds, to be transferred to a bank account on Grand Cayman, by Friday,' Hugh answered. Jack looked him in the face: what Hugh had was worth more than that. A tape of a barrister snorting cocaine while having sex with two women, one of them under age, would cause a scandal that could rock the legal world.

'That's not all, is it?' he said.

'No, but for the moment it will do.' Hugh took out his cigarettes and lit one up. He knew exactly how much Jack was worth but he didn't want it all at once, that would only cause suspicion, dissolving a portfolio that big in one go.

'Jesus . . .' Jack looked away and downed the rest of the whisky. A while later he said, 'So when will you want more?'

'Probably in about three months' time. Another fifty, in cash.'

Jack started. 'What the hell's it all for, Hugh?' He wanted to shout, Why me? I'm your friend, aren't I? But he knew it would be pointless.

Hugh narrowed his eyes. There was no reason to tell Jack but he had the sudden urge to show off, to exult in his power. He wanted Jack to know just how clever he was. 'I've set up a deal,' he said. 'With a Colombian gentleman. It's untraceable, funded by yourself, risk-free and should, by the end of the year, make me a very rich man.' He dropped the cigarette on the floor and crushed it under the heel of his shoe. 'It's taken a long time to organise, Jack, but I think I'm almost there.'

Jack felt an overpowering urge to hit him – it was almost as if Hugh wanted congratulations – but he didn't have the courage. He just stood and moved away from Hugh towards the door. He had to get out of there, he could taste the bile in the back of his throat. He would raise the money by selling a portion of his portfolio despite the rotten market conditions. He opened the door and looked out into the corridor.

'You're a fucking bastard, you know that, Hugh,' he said over his shoulder.

Hugh shrugged. 'Better than being an asshole, Jack. At least I always know what I'm doing.' He raised an eyebrow and Jack escaped, slamming the door behind him.

Hugh started to laugh. He didn't know whether it was the relief that that part of the deal was over, the exhilaration of finally achieving what he had planned for so long or the macabre enjoyment of persecuting someone he had always thought of as more powerful than himself. Whatever, he laughed long and hard and the echo of it followed Jack along the dark, dank interior and out of the emergency exit into the seedy, grimy alley behind the bar where his shock and fear overwhelmed him and he sank down against the black, oily brick wall of the building.

Chapter Eight

Paul Robson closed the Best's Insurance report for the second time that morning and let it slip from his fingers on to his desk. He put his head in his hands and closed his eyes for a moment, wondering what the hell to do next.

He had checked every other report he could lay his hands on after looking at Best's first thing that morning and the Brasilia Insurance Company weren't anywhere at all. Nowhere, not one single mention or listing, nothing. He opened his eyes again and let out a sigh. Where in God's name was Hugh? This was the last thing he needed on top of the worry about IMACO. Brasilia Insurance was Hugh's jurisdiction – he handled all the work for them, everything.

Paul stood up and wandered across to the window, looking out for a while at the winter sky. For a moment he wished he was away from all of this: away from Howard Underwriting, away from London, back in Manchester where he had grown up. But he was involved, he knew that, and as he tried to think it through, why Brasilia wouldn't be listed, despite the huge sums of money their business generated, and couldn't find any reasonable conclusion, he realised just what that involvement could mean.

He was worried sick. A South American insurance company, putting a considerable amount of money into the UK via Howard Underwriting and who couldn't be traced in any of the insurance reports – it stank of money laundering; of drug money. It stank to high heaven!

Maybe the fact that Hugh had made it pretty big, pretty fast had something to do with it? Sure, he had a talent for sniffing out the best deals and what seemed like a gift for making large profits, but was there more to it? Paul Robson had always had his suspicions, but that was all they were, vague suspicions, often prompted by envy.

Suddenly the phone on his desk rang and he started. The office was empty except for two of the secretaries chatting at a desk in the far corner. Everyone else was at lunch or in the market. Paul called out to the girls and went back to answer the call. He picked up the receiver, and heard the voice of Dave Webb over the din of a restaurant.

He knew instantly that he'd forgotten his lunch appointment. 'Oh God! Sorry, Dave,' he said. 'Yeah, I know, I know. As soon as I heard your voice I remembered. Listen, I'll be there in five minutes, the Leaden Hall wine bar, isn't it?' Robson opened his drawer and stuffed the file on Brasilia into it, locking it once it was closed. He didn't want anyone else to know what he was doing.

It was the strain of the past few weeks, the IMACO risk, and now all this Brasilia Insurance thing – it was getting to him. He never forgot appointments, especially not lunches. Calling across the room, he asked Sharon to transfer his phone and told her where he was going. Jesus, he wished Hugh was around a bit more. Bugger the money – the responsibility was killing.

Arriving at the wine bar, Robson hurried up the stairs

and into the light but crowded room, and made his way through the throng towards his broker at the bar. They shook hands and Robson took a large gulp of the wine he was proffered with relief. He looked at the board, ordered tapas, five different dishes, and then Dave Webb led him over to a table he had reserved in the corner by a window.

'How'd you manage this?'

'I'm rogering one of the bar staff.'

Robson laughed and looked across at the bar. 'Which one? The blond guy with the earring is rather nice.'

Webb choked on his wine. 'Actually it's the redhead, in the mini skirt with legs up to her armpits!'

'Oh yes, nice!' Paul Robson sat back in his chair, marginally relaxed for the first time in hours. Dave Webb was an excellent broker, he knew everyone on the market and always had one ear to the ground. Anything you wanted to know, you asked Dave Webb, from the price of a gram to the latest disaster rumour. He was very good company.

'So, how's business at the remarkable Howard Underwriting?'

'All right.'

'Just all right? Come on, Paul, you underwrite so much bloody business I'm surprised Howard hasn't bought himself a house in Cap Ferrat yet!'

Robson smiled tightly. Any reference to Hugh at the moment left a sour taste in his mouth. 'Listen, Dave,' he said on the spur of the moment, 'you ever heard of Brasilia Insurance?'

Webb thought for a minute or so and then shook his head. 'No, I don't think so. Where're they based?'

'Brazil.'

'Hence the name.' He narrowed his eyes. 'Hey, wait a

minute! Maybe I have heard of them . . . er . . . Brasilia Insurance, I'm trying to think . . . yeah, that's it!' Webb swallowed down the rest of his wine and poured himself another glass, topping up Robson's first. 'I think one of our younger brokers had something to do with them several months back, autumn last year sometime. Why, is it important?'

Robson shrugged, half relieved by the information. 'Fairly.'

'OK, hang on a minute, I'll ring the office and see if our young Geoffrey can remember what it was all about.' Webb took his mobile out of his pocket and dialled his office.

'Hi, Mags, is Geoffrey in the office?' He waited a few seconds. 'Ah, Geoff, I need a bit of help with something. Do you remember a company called Brasilia Insurance, by any chance? I think you had dealings with . . .' There was a pause and then Webb said, 'Really? Yeah, that's right, I do, now you come to mention it.' He took his notebook from his inside pocket and a pen and jotted a few lines down. Robson looked across but he couldn't read Webb's writing. He waited, uneasy as Webb continued to listen on the phone.

'Good lad! Yes, if I need to I'll do that. Thanks, Geoff. Bye.' Webb clicked off the phone and looked across at Robson. 'Sorry, Paul, I should have remembered. Geoff's just reminded me that he was approached by Brasilia last year for reinsurance but the intermediary we were using at the time advised us against any dealings with them. Said, Don't touch them with a barge pole, if I remember correctly. Apparently they're a pretty dodgy operation. Rumour has it they're run by some kind of drug baron as a laundering gaff. Manuello, or Conswello, or something like that.' Webb smiled. 'But you know what rumour is like in this place. Take an aspirin in the bloody bogs and you're down as a junkie!' He laughed. 'I hope that's of some use to you anyway.'

Paul Robson nodded and forced a smile. 'Yeah, it's great! Thanks, Dave.' He drank some wine and wondered how quickly he could get away back to the office. The name Manuello was so familiar he felt sick, he couldn't for the life of him think why, but he was damn well going to find out.

'Don't thank me, Paul,' Webb said, laughing. 'Give me some frigging business!' And with that, the food arrived and Robson got out of saying very much more about Brasilia Insurance and why what he'd just heard set a hundred alarm bells ringing in his head.

Back at his desk after lunch, Paul sat down and immediately dialled Joyce in the managing agent's office. He didn't want to waste any time.

'Joyce? Hello, it's Paul Robson.'

'Hello, Paul!' Robson heard the warmth in her voice. 'This is a nice surprise, what can I do for you?'

He could see her in his mind, pushing back her hair and sitting a little straighter in her chair, pulling in her tummy. He tapped a pencil silently on his desk.

'Joyce, I'm ringing for two things really. Firstly, to see if you're free for lunch on Friday?'

'Oh,' she sounded pleasantly surprised and then she added, more suspiciously, 'and?'

'And to see if you'd do me a little favour.'

'Ah!' she laughed. 'Thought there was a catch in it!'

'Not much of one. I'd like an update on our list of names, for some research I'm doing. Could you do that for me, sweetheart?'

'Er . . . let me see . . .' She paused, 'OK, I don't see why not, as long as you don't call me sweetheart!'

Robson smiled.

'But you'd better take me somewhere nice, because you know as well as I do that Hugh doesn't like me giving out the list without his authorisation!'

'Of course I'll take you somewhere nice, Joyce! Where would you like to go?'

'The Pavilion, downstairs.'

'Well . . .' Robson always enjoyed his banter with the delicious Joyce. 'You drive a hard bargain, Joyce . . . but . . . all right! Can you send the list over right away?'

'Yes, no problem.'

'Thanks. I'll come round to your office on Friday around twelve-thirty. OK?'

'Yes, lovely, Paul. See you then.'

Robson hung up. He sat back in his chair and wondered what the hell he was going to do if the name Manuello was on the list of names. He knew he'd heard that name somewhere but he didn't know how. It irritated him, like a bad itch, and he felt his blood pressure rise. Suddenly he sat forward and took a grip on his paranoia.

Listen, he told himself, the odds of it being there are pretty damn small! Dealing with South America he was bound to have heard the name before, it was a common name, like Smith or Jones. And even if there was a Manuello on the list, Jesus, the names were interviewed by a panel at Lloyd's – the chances of it being the one that Webb was talking about were so remote as to be almost laughable.

Robson stopped tapping his pencil and began to feel a little better. He knew the stress was getting to him; this was just another facet of it, worrying about nothing. He put the pencil down. Wait until the list arrives, he thought, then think what to do. And happy with this, he stood up and walked across to the coffee machine to get himself a drink.

An hour later, his frame of mind had completely changed. Manuello was on the list, one of the biggest names, based in South America. Robson had begun to sweat. He realised he had to know more.

Leaving the office, he made his way along St Mary Axe to Lloyd's and went in the main entrance. He stopped at the pay phones on the right and dug in his pocket for some change; he wanted no record of this conversation.

Dialling the number of his brother-in-law's nick, he asked to be put through to him and waited to be connected. He nodded at someone he knew walking past and seconds later his brother-in-law came on the line.

'Detective Sergeant Eastman.'

'Hi, Joe, it's Paul.'

'Paul, how are you?'

'Fine. Listen, Joe, I need some help. I want to hire a PI for a while. Know anybody good?'

'What's up? You in any trouble, Paul?'

'No, nothing like that, it's work. Some rather delicate insurance investigations, you know the sort of thing.'

'Oh, right.'

Robson heard a short silence and the background noise of the incident room. His brother-in-law came back on the line.

'I've got a couple of names here you could try. They're ex-met. One of them used to work with me.'

'Great, fire away.' Robson wrote down the numbers he was given. 'Thanks, Joe, I appreciate this.' He paused. 'Don't mention this to Sally, will you? She'll think the worst.'

'We never spoke, Paul.'

'Thanks, Joe. I'll see you soon, all right?'

'Yeah, take care, mate.'

Robson tucked the numbers away and replaced the receiver. He turned to go into the market.

'Oi, Hugh!' He spotted his boss just coming out of the café and waved across at him but Hugh was talking on his mobile. He ignored Robson and hurried out of the building before Robson had time to approach.

'Great!' he muttered under his breath. Whatever Hugh Howard was working on, he thought, it didn't look even remotely like insurance business; he'd never known him as edgy and aggressive as he'd been the past few months. Robson flashed his pass at the scout and went on up the escalator to the company box. And if it wasn't insurance business, he thought, then what the hell was it?

Hugh stood in the glass porch of a large Victorian terraced house in Hampton that belonged to Peter Mace. He could see and hear Mace inside the hallway on the telephone, the rough edge of his South London accent smoothed for the client on the other end, and thought how well organised the whole drug business had become. He looked at the black and white tiled floor, beautifully polished to a deep sheen, the George IV hall table with its high square vase of white arum lilies, and he knew that this was where the real money was today. Mace was a distributor, the man who organised the dealers, did all the groundwork and took a fair chunk of the profits for his pains. He covered his tracks with some sort of antiques business but Hugh recognised hard cash when he saw it. The house was stuffed with valuables, good art, ornate furniture, a collection of rare books and hundreds of pieces of fine porcelain. Mace was bloody sharp, but that was what he was paying for.

Hugh looked round as Mace finished on the telephone and waited for him to come out to the porch. Mace took a large bright red silk handkerchief out of his pocket and wiped over the mouthpiece before replacing the receiver, then he glanced in the mirror above the table, smoothed back a strand of hair in a gesture that reminded Hugh of James and turned to join him.

'Sorry about that, Hugh. Someone wants a William and Mary chair the same as one I sold last week,' Mace said charmingly. He rolled his eyes and Hugh nodded stiffly. He wanted the business done so that he could get out of there; the whole place made him edgy and he was acutely aware of showing his inexperience.

But Mace immediately picked up on the vibes. He had a sensitive nose that could sniff out fear a mile off. It had made his reputation, that and the fact that he was a nasty piece of work. The well-developed air of culture he wore covered a ruthless temperament and a complete lack of conscience. Cutting any conversation, Mace held out his hand. 'I'll expect to hear from you next week then, Hugh,' he said curtly. 'When everything is in place. Presumably you'll let me know the exact date you expect delivery?'

Hugh nodded.

'Good! I look forward to doing business with you then, Hugh.'

They shook hands and Hugh, much relieved, opened the glass door to leave. He glanced behind him.

'I'll ring,' he said, and Mace nodded. Then without another word, he walked down the small front garden to the curled iron gate and through it to his car parked right outside. He released the alarm, climbed inside and started the engine, all the time feeling the eyes of the other man on him. He glanced quickly over his shoulder but Mace had gone inside.

'Arrogant bastard,' he muttered and put his foot down on the accelerator. He was only too aware that Mace had him taped. Mace was Manuello's man – all the distribution went through him and all the profit came back through him. A third of estimated profit up front, Mace had wanted, for 'operational costs' and contingency. A whole third, Hugh thought tensely as he pulled out into the traffic of the main road. What with that and the money for Manuello, Hugh was in it right up to his neck. He sure as hell hoped that James was going to pull it off, one way or another, he didn't care how. If anything went wrong, then Hugh had real trouble. He was not so worried about using Jack to pay Manuello, but embezzling funds to pay Mace was a very serious offence.

Suddenly, stopping at a pedestrian crossing, Hugh began to laugh. What the hell was he thinking? If he was going to worry about embezzlement then he had no chance at all! After all, what was a bit of fraud in comparison to smuggling half a million quid's worth of high-grade cocaine into the country?

He arrived back in central London halfway through rush hour and queued at the lights approaching the Chiswick roundabout. He was meeting James at six-thirty in a bar off the Piazza in Covent Garden. He was running late and that made him really uptight. Getting the balance right with James was essential, he had to be in control. Swearing at another driver as she pulled in front of him when the lights changed, he stuck one finger up and accelerated off, nosing the back bumper of her car with his and flashing his lights.

'Stupid frigging cow!' he mouthed out of the side window. 'Learn to drive!' And swerving into the inside lane, he overtook her, beeped his horn and raced off up the A4 towards the city centre.

Hugh was seated in the back of the Crusting Pipe and had ordered a bottle of Laurent Perrier champagne when James arrived at the bar, irritated and tired from public transport in the rush hour. The wine sat in an ice bucket beside Hugh's table while he sipped an iced water and read a copy of the *Evening Standard*. He glanced up, saw James and stood to call him over. Hugh needed to dominate the situation, it was an intrinsic part of the game.

'Hello, James.'

'Hugh.'

They shook hands politely and James stood where he was. It was the first time they had met in weeks and he was unsure of the ground.

'Have a seat,' Hugh said, 'I've ordered some champagne.'

'So I see,' James answered curtly. He unfastened his coat and sat down, placing his briefcase on the floor under his chair.

'How have you been?'

James looked at Hugh and raised an eyebrow. 'I take that to mean, have I got everything organised for my trip to Brazil?'

Hugh shrugged.

'Well, the answer is yes. I've done what you suggested and I'm booked in for the conference in Rio in three weeks' time. Was there anything else you wanted, Hugh? Or can I go now?'

James stood and Hugh, glancing discreetly round the bar

first, put a hand out to restrain him. 'Sit down, James,' he said quietly, 'please.'

James looked in disgust at Hugh's hand for a moment, then he closed his eyes and turned his face away. All the time he felt it, all the bloody time. Whatever he did with Livvy, however much he tried, he felt it, the longing, the terrible, terrible ache of excitement that just the sight of Hugh provoked. It was as if it had been locked away for years inside him, coiled like a serpent, and was now stronger, more powerful and more deeply destructive for all its dormancy. He moved his arm, pulling it back aggressively, and bent to pick up his briefcase.

'James, don't go. Stay and have a drink, at least one drink,' Hugh said.

James turned back to face him. He hated Hugh now, he hated him and yet the very thought of him was an obsession. The sound of his voice, so low and intense, made James shiver. Silently, he nodded. More than he hated Hugh, he loved him, and the domination of that emotion filled him with a dreadful loathing.

Sitting again, he accepted a glass of champagne and took out his cigarettes, lighting one quickly before offering them to Hugh. He stared silently around the bar.

'So you leave on the fourteenth of next month?' Hugh asked, taking up the lighter. 'Is that right?'

James turned back. 'Yes, I'll give you my flight details and exact itinerary nearer the date,' he answered coldly.

'Good.' Hugh ignored the anger. He knew James too well; he was too much in control now to let it get to him. 'Whenever you're ready,' he said. He finished his wine and reached to pour another glass. 'I've got my car here,' he remarked as he refilled James's glass. 'Can I offer you a lift home?'

James didn't answer.

'I gather Livvy's away again tonight?'

James looked over and narrowed his eyes. 'So?' He didn't bother to question how Hugh knew that, he just took it as read now that Hugh somehow knew everything there was to know about him and Livvy.

'So, can I get you dinner?'

James shook his head and snorted. 'You never give up, do you, Hugh?' he said nastily. 'Isn't it enough that you already have what you wanted from me? Do you have to keep on? Do you?'

Hugh moved his leg under the table so that it touched James's and very slightly applied pressure to his thigh. Yes, he thought, I have to keep on, on and on until I hold that precious five kilo parcel in my own hands. Until I've done it again and again, used you, in the same way you used me, to get what you wanted until something better came along. But he said nothing. He dropped his hand down under the table and touched James's leg, feeling him flinch at the contact.

'Do you want dinner, then?' he repeated.

James drank down his second glass of champagne in two gulps and wiped the corner of his mouth with his hand. He knew what his answer would be and he hated himself for it. 'Yes,' he said, 'I want.'

Chapter Nine

Livvy hurried out of the bathroom wrapped in a towel, her hair piled up on her head and a rosy pink glow from the hot water on her skin. She dropped the towel in front of the huge pine mirror and looked briefly at her reflection as she squirted a handful of moisturiser into her palm and began to rub it in quick circular movements over her thighs and abdomen.

James watched her from the bed.

He couldn't deny that she was beautiful. The whole length of her was perfectly proportioned, lean and brown, her features even and balanced and her smile as warm as the golden hue of her skin. And yet he didn't feel anything for her. No physical response, no emotional stirring. Nothing. He tried to think back to when he had first realised it, when he had known that something between them wasn't right but he couldn't honestly remember. Perhaps it had always been like that? He really didn't know. He didn't seem to know anything any more.

Suddenly Livvy turned towards the bed and attempted to smile. 'It doesn't matter, James,' she said. 'Really. We can sort it all out in Brazil.' But it did, it mattered so much that she felt like crying. The romantic afternoon she had imagined had been a disaster. She watched James as he swung his legs coolly over the side of the bed and stood up, then she turned sadly back to the mirror and continued dressing.

'What time is the cab coming, Liv?'

Livvy looked at her watch. 'Oh God! In about fifteen minutes!' She began to panic as James pulled on his bathrobe and strode across to the bathroom.

'Calm down,' he remonstrated. 'The case is packed so all you have to do is get dressed and check your handbag.' He stopped at the door. 'OK?'

Livvy nodded, relieved. James always packed for both of them. She was far too disorganised to do it properly and had a nasty habit of forgetting something essential, like the passports.

Turning back to the mirror, she abandoned the lotion and hurriedly pulled on a black cotton thong and bra. She threw a tee-shirt on, then a long shirt and finally her LA Strikers sweatshirt over the top, with a pair of black Lycra leggings. Bending to tie the laces of her trainers, she picked her baseball cap up off the floor and crammed it on her head. Ready, she grabbed the large old leather handbag she used for travelling and walked into the sitting room, starting as the main door buzzer sounded.

'James! James!' She rushed across to the door. 'Oh my God, the taxi's early!' She shouted into the intercom that she'd be right down and darted about the flat frantically in a last-minute panic to check she had everything she needed. She was never usually this uptight. It must be the combination of the terrible hour in bed with James and the feeling that this time, she was really on the edge of making her whole career. She couldn't bear it if anything went wrong.

James appeared moments later with her plain black suitcase, and dropped it down by the front door, taking hold of her shoulders and forcing her to be still.

'Now, have you got everything?' he asked.

Livvy nodded. 'I think so.'

'Good. I'll come down with you to the car then.'

'No, you don't have to. I mean . . . unless you want to.'

James smiled. 'Of course I want to.'

Livvy reached up to kiss his lips lightly. 'Thanks,' she said. It was one of the few moments of tenderness they had shared for months and Livvy looked away sadly.

'Oh, by the way,' James said as he picked up the case. 'Fraser Stewart rang earlier this evening to wish you luck. I said you'd ring him back but I forgot to tell you.' He carried on to the lifts and glanced over his shoulder. 'Sorry,' he finished without much regret.

The moment of tenderness was lost.

'Oh, thanks a lot, James. I wonder if you do it on purpose sometimes!' Livvy's irritation was almost irrational. She hated missing a call from Fraser – he hardly ever rang and she loved talking to him. She'd never thought of their phone conversations as more than the chance for a really good chat, but she was suddenly quite unreasonably cross. She stood with James by the lift and looked the other way while the elevator cranked its way noisily to the top floor. Finally it arrived and she glanced at James, not wanting to part with bad feeling.

She smiled. 'Never mind,' she said, although she far from meant it.

James shrugged. 'Come on,' he said, 'or there'll be ten quid on the meter before you start.' He heaved open the ironwork doors and Livvy stepped into the lift. He followed her, pressed the button and they began to descend, both miserable and disappointed about the parting but neither of them prepared to admit it.

Livvy opened her eyes and moved her right arm stiffly, feeling the hot, uncomfortable sensation of pins and needles as the blood rushed back to her hand. She shook it and clenched her fist but the fizziness in her blood continued. She sat up and rubbed her hands over her face, lifting the tiny blind on the window and looking out at the brilliant sun high up over the clouds. She was instantly elated.

'Morning.' Roger Hardman looked across at Livvy from his seat across the aisle and smiled. He was remarkably fresh for a twelve-hour flight, clean shaven and smelling of cologne.

'Hi!' Livvy rolled the blanket down and stretched her arms above her head, aware but unselfconscious of her slept-in state. 'Isn't the sight of all that tropical sun out there just wonderful?'

'Wait till you see Rio, my darling!' Roger laughed. As one of the top independent producers in television, he was extremely well travelled. 'I guarantee you'll never have experienced anything like it.'

'I can't wait!' Livvy meant it. This whole thing – Lenny Duce, Brazil, the programme – no matter what it cost, was worth more than anything else she had ever done. She unfastened her seat belt and eased herself awkwardly out of her seat. Standing stiffly, she reached up to the overhead locker and took down her big leather bag.

'How long before we land?' she asked.

Roger glanced at his watch. 'About twenty minutes. We should be starting our descent now.' Suddenly they both smiled as the plane dipped and Livvy's stomach lurched for a moment. 'I think the pilot heard me!'

Livvy laughed and, pulling out her washbag, she tucked it under her arm and started towards the toilets at the back. 'I'll see you in Rio then, Roger!' she called over her shoulder, her voice ringing with excitement.

'Now this is the sort of service I could get used to!' Phil said as the porter loaded his camera equipment into the boot of the Mercedes parked right outside the arrivals door of the airport. He turned his face up to the mid-morning sun, just breaking through the light scattering of cloud, and sighed. 'Rio de Janeiro. Paradise!'

Suddenly he heard a loud knock and darted forward, ever vigilant about his precious equipment. 'Oops! Easy does it!' He took the expensive camera from the porter and reverently laid it on top of his soft bag, cushioning it against any blows. Then he turned to Livvy and rolled his eyes. 'Perhaps not paradise.'

She smiled and nodded to the porter as he started on her own case and laptop computer. She had a pair of black Raybans on, her baseball cap pulled down and with the accompanying fuss that the film crew caused, she was creating quite a stir. Several of the crowd on the pavement stared openly and a babble of Portuguese started up, an obvious argument as to who she was. The hotel driver came round to the side of the car and opened the door just as she heard the name Madonna and she quickly slipped inside the air-conditioned car with great relief and a suppressed giggle.

Phil climbed in beside her, and Roger Hardman, Hank the sound man and Debs the production assistant waved at them as the driver pulled off. Their car was in the process of being loaded. Minutes later, as the car sped up the highway towards the city, Livvy sat back against the leather of the seat and thought with a broad grin, This is it, I've arrived! Watch out, Lenny Duce! Watch out world!

The drive into central Rio took just over thirty minutes, the midday sun bouncing blindingly off the hot, black tarmac as it rose higher in the sky. The air-conditioning in the car gave no indication of the heat and dust outside and the whole scene, the land, the teeming mass of *favelas* and the dazzling view of the glittering sea seemed to pass by in a blur of dark tinted windows and cool comfortable air. In what seemed like no time at all, the hotel car drew up in front of the Rio Palace and a uniformed doorman stepped out of the shade to open the back doors to let the passengers out. He helped Livvy on to the pavement where she stood for a moment, excitedly breathing in the humid tropical air, and then coughed and spluttered uncontrollably on the heady mix of warm carbon monoxide fumes and sea air. Phil followed her out, patted her roughly on the back and turned towards the sea. He stopped, his eyes fixed on the spectacular chaos of people and noise on the Copacabana Beach and let out a long, low whistle.

'I've never seen anything like it!' he said. He was watching a group of young girls strutting about on the beach near the pavement, all wearing tiny bits of string and cloth that barely covered their nipples and pubic hair. Every other part of their beautifully curved bodies was a deep, rich, nutty brown. 'Jesus!'

Livvy swung round to follow his gaze. 'Wow!' She shook her head in amazement. 'So this is Rio,' she murmured.

But Livvy's excitement and good humour didn't last long.

Standing at the reception desk in the long, opulent lobby of the hotel, she checked for messages while Phil watched the parade of fashion-conscious Brazilians coming into the restaurant for their Saturday lunch out: a myriad of coloured silks and cottons, gold and diamonds, all sparkling under the bright electric light of the hotel's interior design, all hung on deeply tanned bodies with expertly coiffured hair.

Livvy took her baseball cap off and ran a hand nervously through her hair as she spoke again in pidgin English to the desk clerk. She was beginning to panic.

'You . . . are . . . sure . . . there is no message . . .? For Olivia Davis?' She had been expecting word from Hugh's contact, communication that everything was all right, and now she found she hadn't even got rooms in the hotel!

'*Non.* No message, Senhora. I 'ave nozing 'ere in the name of Senhora Davis. I don't hava Senhora Davis on my leest.'

'Oh God!' Livvy took a deep breath. That was all she needed, no message and no booking! What the hell was going on? She felt the prickle of nervous perspiration on her forehead. 'How about something for Senhor Hardman? Roger Hardman?'

'*Non.* Ai don'ta thinka so.' The clerk went through his small pile of messages one more time. 'Ah! Si! One momento, Senhora!' He pulled out a piece of paper and Livvy's spirits soared. 'Ai 'ave somesing for Senhor Hardman. A telefone message.'

'Yes?'

'It ees froma Primo Television.' The clerk smiled at this, obviously impressed.

Her heart sank again. 'Nothing else?'

'*Non. Desculpe.*' The clerk shrugged.

'Oh no!' Livvy turned away from the desk and attempted to stay calm. Here she was, three thousand miles across the globe with a prestigious film crew in tow and Hugh's contact hadn't shown up! They hadn't even heard of her at the hotel! What on earth would Roger say? What if the contact didn't show up at all? Livvy began to panic. She ran the back of her hand over her damp brow and tried to think it through.

Hugh had told her that someone would be waiting for her. He'd told her not to mention the IMACO connection to anyone, not even Duce, and that everything would be organised for them from the moment they arrived. He had recommended the hotel, booked for her and the film crew, informed the hotel of James's arrival at the end of the week. Suddenly Livvy had an idea. 'Do you have a booking in the name of Ward? James Ward?' She drummed her fingers on the reception desk and bit her lip.

The clerk sighed heavily and then flicked through his papers once more. He looked up and smiled. 'Ah yes! Senhor James Ward!' He pulled out the booking form and counted the number of rooms on it.

'Oh thank God for that,' Livvy murmured under her breath. 'How about any messages for him?'

The clerk shook his head.

'You all right, Livvy?' Phil had taken out his camera and was about to snap at random as people filed past him.

Livvy nodded, smiled brightly and kept her fears to herself. They had rooms, it was a start. All she could do was sit tight and wait. That and get on the phone to Hugh.

'Fine,' she murmured, 'just fine.' But her heart sank even further when she saw the expectant face of Roger as he strode across the lobby towards her.

'Any news, Livvy?' he called and she shrugged, unable to look him in the eye. A very real fear that she might be in right over her head had begun to take hold. 'Not at the moment, Roger,' she answered and bent to pick up her bag. 'I was expecting this though,' she lied. 'Hugh said it may take a while to get things organised.'

Roger glared at her. 'Well, let's just hope that his while and my while are the same thing,' he growled, 'or someone has made a very costly mistake!'

Livvy felt her stomach lurch. 'Yes, Roger,' she said and moved away to let him hassle the desk clerk.

An hour or so later, after they had finally checked in, Roger Hardman faced the whole film crew, his patience sorely strained by the wonderfully laid-back manner of the Brazilians and the lack of news from Livvy's so-called contact, and handed them their room keys, with the exception of Livvy. It had been found, after much heated discussion, that her name wasn't even on the list and that she was booked in under the name of James Ward.

'By courtesy of Primo Television,' he said, 'we've all been moved to super de luxe rooms.' A ripple of approval ran through the small group.

'Just like the BBC,' Phil commented and everyone laughed. Primo was the giant Brazilian television station co-producing the programme with City and covering much of the cost in South America.

'What I suggest,' he continued, only half smiling at Phil's remark, 'is that you get some rest, and then we'll meet up for drinks early evening to go over the script. Tonight we're having dinner with the team from Primo at the Copacabana Palace, a former haunt of fifties Hollywood, so smart dress is required.' Roger paused, then continued with more than a note of irritation in his voice. 'Apart from that, guys, there's little else I can tell you, I'm afraid. The brief from Livvy's man was to wait here for someone to contact us, which they'll do once they've secured the final arrangements with Duce – if they know we're here, of course.' He looked pointedly at Livvy. 'Is that right, Livvy?'

She nodded, embarrassed.

'So don't get too comfortable and don't get too eager.' He smiled. 'Right. See you all later.' And looking towards Livvy he said, 'Can I have a word?'

'Yes, sure.' She waited for everyone to pick up their hand baggage and wander off towards the lifts before moving over to Roger.

'Drink?'

'OK.' Livvy turned and bent to pick up her huge leather bag. As she did so, she noticed a man seated by the doors, someone she thought she'd seen at the airport. She glanced at him for a moment to see if she was right but he lifted his paper and covered his face. She shrugged and stood straight, slinging the bag over her shoulder and putting it down to paranoia. Following Roger towards the bar, she tried to think nothing more about it.

'So, Livvy,' Roger took a long gulp of his beer. 'What's the hold-up then?'

She shook her head and attempted to smile. 'I don't know but I'm sure it's nothing.'

Roger shrugged. 'It makes me very nervous, Livvy, waiting around. I hope it's not a bad omen.'

Livvy glanced away. He hoped it wasn't a bad omen! 'I have a contact number,' she said. 'I'll ring from the room, see if I can get hold of anyone.'

'You do that.' Roger finished his beer and stood up. 'Livvy, an awful lot is riding on this programme. We're on a tight schedule and a tight budget and we can't afford to sit in Rio for weeks on end.'

Livvy nodded. The easy-going Roger had vanished and there was absolutely no certainty that things would go according to plan. None. 'I'll make sure that won't happen,' she said sharply. 'It won't be more than a couple of days, at the most.' She had to maintain her confidence. She'd got this far and she sure as hell wasn't going to let it slip away now.

'All right, Livvy. I've gone with you all the way on this as a favour to Alan. I bloody well hope I've done the right thing.'

Livvy swallowed back her irritation. A bit late now! she felt like saying. But she had to maintain her confident façade. 'Of course you have. I guarantee it.'

Finally Roger smiled. 'There's more than a bit of Bryan Davis in there, Livvy!'

She smiled back. 'I hope so,' she answered, and Roger patted her shoulder. He moved past her and strode out of the bar.

Two days later, sitting in her room at the Rio Palace, Livvy wondered miserably just what her father would have done in the same situation. She prayed for a bit of his inspiration.

For three days now, ever since their arrival in Brazil, she had had no word from IMACO and it was really beginning to scare her. Added to that, she'd been unable to get hold of Hugh, James seemed to be either out or permanently in a meeting at the Foreign Office, and Roger Hardman was practically foaming at the mouth with impatience and charging City Television God knew how much for every minute of it. She groaned miserably and picked up the receiver to dial home for the second time that day. She didn't know how long Hardman was prepared to sit it out. Presumably until they had the lead but judging from his attitude the past three days she wasn't even sure of that. The line connected to London and she asked to speak to Hugh Howard.

'Oh? Is he? Do you know when he'll be back?' She waited for the echo to fade on the answer. 'Oh, I see.' Picking up her diary, she made a note of when to try again. 'Yes, yes I did. Yesterday and the day before. Yes, it's very urgent, I really must speak to him! If you could, yes I'd appreciate that.' She waited again, this time for several minutes, thinking all the time how much the call was costing and then the secretary came back on the line. 'Oh, no reply to the pager, I see. OK. Thank you. Yes, it's Livvy Davis and I'm calling from the Rio Palace Hotel in Brazil. Just to ask him if he'd call me back, please, urgently!' She sighed. 'Yes, thank you, goodbye.'

She kicked the side of the bed with frustration and stood up. Where the hell was Hugh? Why wasn't he returning her calls? If he wasn't going to deliver Duce to her then why had he bothered to send her all the way out to Brazil? All these questions kept buzzing round and round her brain as she picked up her bag and room key and crossed to the door. And where was James?

Stepping out into the corridor, Livvy closed the door behind her, slamming it shut and walked quickly up towards the lifts. She stopped, pressed the button and for a split second she could have sworn she saw a figure behind her, following her. She spun round but there was nothing there, only the empty silent space of the corridor. She shook her head and stepped inside the elevator.

First I see the man from the airport, she thought, not once but three times in the hotel, always behind me, and then I think he's following me. She looked at her reflection in the smoked glass mirror of the lift. 'This is really getting to me!' she said aloud to her own image.

She needed some time away from her room, from the terrible silence of the telephone. She pressed the button for the ground floor and for the first time decided to take a look round Rio.

Chapter Ten

Hugh sat in his office. It was eight-thirty at night, the place was finally deserted and he was waiting for the lines to Brazil to clear. He picked up the telephone again and dialled the number, only half holding the receiver to his ear, expecting the lines to be busy. He heard the familiar wait for the numbers to register and then the ringing tone.

'Jesus! About friggin' time too!' His call was answered ten seconds later.

'John?' The long-distance echo reverberated the name back into his ear and then his man in Brazil replied. Hugh wasted no time. 'John, it's Hugh Howard. What the hell's going on?'

Drumming his fingers angrily on the desk top, Hugh listened to the reply without taking any of it in; he wasn't interested in excuses. Livvy had been on the phone twice a day for the past three days because his man in Rio hadn't shown up and he'd had word from the Colombians that they were following her, waiting to make contact. But they were following the wrong person! If they approached Livvy then the whole deal would be blown out of the water. It was imperative that she knew nothing about it. Hugh swallowed hard and tried to keep the sheer frustration and fear out of his voice. He knew that in the last twenty-four hours he'd come inches away from discovery.

At last John stopped babbling and Hugh said, 'Quite frankly, John, I don't give a shit what excuses you have! I paid good money for that contact and I've sent someone all the way out to Brazil on the strength of it. Livvy Davis thinks she's meeting someone from IMACO who'll take her to Duce and that's exactly what she's going to get! Do you understand me?' He paused, trying to keep control of his anger. 'I don't care how you do it, or what it takes but I want her to meet up with Duce! You said you could deliver, so deliver!' If Livvy didn't meet up with Duce then she'd be out of Rio before James even got there. Hugh couldn't afford that kind of slip-up; he just didn't trust James enough. Livvy was the perfect scapegoat.

'Listen, John,' he said, smoothing his voice, 'I paid a lot of money for your promises. Manuello trusts you.' He stopped and let that comment sink in. 'And so do I. Now, why don't you get on the phone to the Rio Palace Hotel, speak to Livvy Davis, tell her you're from IMACO and arrange to get her and the film crew to Duce. All right?' There was a few moments' pause. 'Today!' Hugh said. 'I want her out of Rio and on a plane to meet Duce by tomorrow night!' And with that, he replaced the receiver, then leaned forward and smacked his fist down hard on to the desk.

Several minutes later, he picked up the phone again and redialled South America.

'Hello. *Manuello, por favor.*' He waited for what seemed like ages but was barely a minute and felt the heavy dampness of sweat on the back of his neck.

'Manuello, it's Hugh Howard. No, no everything is fine!

Just to let you know that my contact is *not* already in Brazil, no, no that's not her. That was a mistake, yes, I realise that, no, a mistake with the hotel booking. James Ward won't be arriving until the middle of next week, Wednesday the fourteenth. Yes, if you could. Thank you, I . . .' Hugh suddenly stopped and looked down at the phone. The line had gone dead. He put it down and took out his handkerchief, wiping his forehead and the back of his neck, and then returned the receiver to its cradle. He stood up and took a deep breath. That had been close, he thought, walking across to the window, that had been too damn close!

Livvy stepped out of the shower and reached for a thick white bath towel from the rail. She hurriedly wrapped it round her and ran through to the bedroom, lunging for the phone.

'Hello, Livvy Davis.' She slumped down on to the bed when she heard Roger Hardman's voice and sighed heavily away from the receiver. 'Yup, that's no problem, Roger, I can be down in twenty minutes. Oh, I see . . .' She stopped and cursed under her breath; a contingency meeting was the last thing she needed. 'Oh, do you? All right, if that's what you think. I personally think we should wait a little . . .' Roger cut her short. 'Yes, OK, see you then.' She sat forward and replaced the receiver. 'Damn!' she said aloud and stood up.

Roger wanted a meeting to discuss what to do next. He didn't want to make any decisions without full team approval. 'Very nice of you, Rog, I'm sure!' Livvy continued to herself as she went back into the bathroom, 'Very consider . . .' She stopped as the phone rang again. 'Yes, yes, I know,' she said, walking across the room, 'you forgot to tell me to meet in the bar!' She reached for the receiver a second time.

'Yes?' But instead of Roger's drawl, she heard a voice she didn't recognise. She stood perfectly still and held her breath. Then she suddenly smiled, a broad Cheshire cat grin. 'Yes, yes it is! Oh, thank goodness for that! Yes, great! I can't tell you how good that sounds,' she laughed lightly down the line. 'You know, I was almost beginning to think you wouldn't call.'

Fifteen minutes later, dressed and with all the details in her hand, Livvy rang reception and asked for Roger Hardman's room. She caught him just as he was on his way out to the bar.

'Roger? It's me!' She could hardly keep the excitement out of her voice. 'You'd better tell everyone at the meeting to get themselves some dinner and then go back upstairs to pack. Yes, yes they did! Just now. We're booked on the Varig flight out of Rio tonight, to Belem. Apparently Duce is somewhere up the Amazon, and we're off to find him!' She sat down on the bed and listened to Roger's reply. Then she looked down at the piece of paper in her hand and began to read out their instructions. Livvy Davis was on her way and nothing was going to stop her now.

Chapter Eleven

'OK. Let's call that a wrap!'

Livvy closed her eyes for a second to blot out the glare of the lamps and put her hand up to her neck. She loosened the cotton handkerchief at her throat and took a deep breath. It was over, thank God!

'Phil! You got everything you need?' Roger's voice was sharp, irritated and exhausted.

'Yup! It's all here!'

Livvy leaned back in the small canvas chair and lifted the hem of her tee-shirt to her face, wiping it across her skin and leaving a wet mess of make-up and sweat on it. The voices seemed miles away. Then she opened her eyes and looked across at Duce. He had stood up and walked away.

'Great,' she muttered. But there was no love lost between them, he couldn't wait to get out of her sight.

The heat of the jungle was stifling and the lights were making her feel sick. She shouted across to the small huddle of producer, cameraman and sound man: 'Can someone turn these lights off, please!' but no one took any notice. So she stood herself and pulled the plug on the two free-standing thousand-watt lights that were used for filming.

'That's better!' The natural light of the jungle seemed suddenly quite unnerving with its heavy pattern of light and dark but the heat had been reduced by half and at least she could breathe again. Livvy sank back into her chair and wiped her face for the second time. The bites on her neck began to itch.

The past week had been a living nightmare for all of them. The making of the programme had been riddled with problems: the heat, the damp, the humidity, the rain, Duce's tantrums, diarrhoea – the list was horrendous. Livvy snorted when she thought about what she had imagined halfway up the Amazon: some colonial outpost with cane chairs and huge overhead fans. The reality had been a bunk room for all five of them, an old shack of a place by the water where she'd lain awake every night listening to the sound of Phil's asthma, brought on by the damp air, and the horrible loud grunts of Roger banging away at a whimpering Debs astride him. That against the constant hum of giant mosquitoes as they bit their way through the nets and deep into the flesh of any half centimetre of her they could get to was almost too much to bear.

It was only the success of what they were putting on film that kept her going, she thought, as she put her hand up and scratched at the angry red welts on the side of her neck. That and the fact that she'd done one of the best pieces of interviewing she had ever done, got things out of Duce he'd had no intention of divulging. Livvy stopped scratching, realising she was drawing blood, and glanced across at Roger, who was instructing one of the boat crew on packing up the equipment. He was worth his weight in gold, she thought, knowing that he'd pushed her to probe for things she would never have had the nerve to try for on her own, even if he did sound like Guy the Gorilla when he came.

'Livvy!'

She stood up and stretched as Roger walked across to her.

'I get the feeling that the sooner we get out of here the better,' he said, nodding towards Duce. Duce was gesticulating at one of the Indian boatmen, indicating the pile of equipment to be packed. He had finally taken his little round black glasses off and his eyes were bloodshot and swollen. 'So if it's all right with you,' Roger continued, 'we're packing up right now and making tracks this morning.'

'It's more than all right with me!' Livvy answered.

'Good. It's a hell of a ride but I reckon we're better off doing it today, on the back of a high, than sitting around here for another twenty-four hours. Yup?'

'Yes, agreed.'

Roger strode off back to Hank and Phil as they sorted out their stuff and Livvy bent to pick up her bag. As she did so a small lizard ran across her hand and she screamed, more out of surprise than fear. Duce looked across at her and smiled. Bastard, she thought, regaining composure, but she knew he had a point. She had been more than a little unpleasant to get the answers she wanted in the past week, and she didn't blame Duce for resenting her. Turning towards the crew, she slung her bag over her shoulder. She was fatigued and sick from the heat and food and she felt guilty about exploiting someone for her own gain. It didn't feel nice. Ah well, everybody does it, she thought, shaking off any remorse, it's dog eat dog in this world. But it wasn't really right and even though she put her sensitivity down to the state of her health, in her heart of hearts she was slightly ashamed.

Standing on the jetty, waiting for the rest of the crew to settle into the long boat, Livvy turned, surprised, as Duce approached her. He had put his glasses on again and she couldn't see his eyes but she knew he was staring straight at her. He held out his hand.

'I can't say it's been a pleasure, Livvy Davis,' he said, in his North American drawl. 'It wasn't what I had been led to expect at all.' He had been persuaded to do the interview by the fact that the film crew knew where he was and in order to say something about the land he had reclaimed for the forest, but that subject had hardly been touched upon.

Livvy took his hand and noticed how rough and chapped it felt. It was the first time she had touched him. She looked at him and blushed scarlet.

'At least you have the grace to be embarrassed.'

'I was only doing my job, Lenny,' she answered.

He shrugged and dropped her hand. 'Sometimes we're so damn busy getting to the top that we don't see what's behind us or even what's really in front of us.'

Livvy stared at him for a few moments and then stuttered an apology but he cut her short.

'Your boat is ready, Livvy,' he said. She looked down at the boat and then quickly back at him.

'Yes, I, er . . .' Duce had walked away. Scrambling down into the boat next to Roger, she breathed a sigh of relief and with the heavy throb of engines, the boat moved off.

James Ward sat on the edge of the bed in the room at the Rio Palace with his head in his hands. He was sweating and

felt sick. He had been in Rio for four days now, the conference was in its last afternoon and for the first time the
realisation of exactly what he had to do had hit him, the
shock making him shiver, like a bad dose of malaria.

He knew he was being followed, he'd known since the
airport, but somehow he'd managed to put it out of his
mind. Somehow, he'd managed to convince himself for the
past few days, in the round of parties, drinks and dinners,
that this was a normal Foreign Office trip, that there was
nothing sinister about it, nothing more than a conference
on the environment and James Ward, the brightest of the
bright young men in the Foreign Office, charming his way
through the ranks of the crusty old ex-pats and their crinkly
old wives. Only now, the pretence was over.

Hugh had just called from London. Livvy was on her
way back from Belem and contact had to be made.

'Don't fuck up on this!' Hugh had warned. 'You know
what's at stake, don't you, James?' And James had said yes,
he knew, he wouldn't fuck up.

Lifting his head from his hands, he looked down at the
telephone and the small scrap of paper he had left beside it.
His contact number, to be used once and then thrown away,
burned, eaten. He managed to smile. Christ, he was scared.
He had to make contact before Livvy arrived back in Rio, he
had to get things sorted, so he knew what he was doing.
Reaching for the receiver, he picked it up and held it to his
ear. Still shaking, he dialled the number. This is all I have to
do, he thought, waiting for the line to connect, just get this
over and . . . Suddenly he dropped the receiver and
slammed his hand down on the button.

Jesus Christ! What the hell was he thinking? How had he
got it into his head that his responsibility ended with

collection? He looked down at his hands and clasped them tightly together to stop them trembling. In the back of his mind a terrible thought kept going round and round, the thought that he really could save his own skin, just as Hugh had said he could. Round and round it went, telling him he had nothing to fear, that it was all so simple and uncomplicated. He picked up the receiver a second time.

Dialling the number, he tried to put the thought down, ignore it, squash it, but as he waited for someone to answer and his fear escalated, it came to the fore and dominated all others. It suddenly seemed all so possible, so easy, so tempting. He heard someone answer and, swallowing hard, he asked for Manuello. He didn't really know it yet but he had already made up his mind. Livvy's trip to Brazil had turned out to be exactly as Hugh had planned it.

Chapter Twelve

Livvy woke early, in the warmth and comfort of her hotel bed, the sun streaming through the window and the sound of James breathing softly by her side. She stretched, glanced at her wristwatch and then, moving gently so as not to wake him, she eased her body out of bed. Walking naked to the bathroom, she switched on the light and ran the cold water to splash her face. The telephone rang.

Darting back into the bedroom, she picked it up and whispered down the line, glancing quickly at James, to see if he'd been woken by it.

'Yes, hi, Roger!' She kept her voice to a low murmur. 'No, no, it's just that James is asleep. Oh, right. Yes, I don't see why not. Give me five minutes, OK?' As silently as she could, Livvy hung up, went back through to the bathroom and hurriedly dressed.

Exactly eight minutes later, she was down in the hotel lobby. She spied Roger over in the corner, sitting on his own and reading an out-of-date copy of *The Times*. She walked across to him and sat down.

'Good morning.'

He looked up.

'Morning, Livvy.' Folding the paper away, he signalled to the woman at reception and pointed to the tray of coffee on the low table in front of him. 'I'm sorry to get you out of bed so early, Livvy, but I'll get straight to the point and let you get back to James.'

She smiled; she rather liked his bluntness now. 'Please do,' she said.

'OK. I've decided to go back to the UK early and get on with editing the programme. I hate sitting around and I've had enough of Brazil.'

'How early is early?'

'Tonight. I called the agent last night and there are still some seats left on the flight out this evening.'

'I see.' Livvy looked down at her hands, waiting for the next bit.

Roger smiled. 'I think you know what's coming.'

'Perhaps.'

'It's up to you, Livvy, entirely your decision. I know this is a bit of a holiday for you, I don't want to get in the way.'

'No.' A waiter arrived with coffee and Livvy watched him put the tray down, arrange the cups and pour. There wasn't really any decision, she thought, not if she wanted some control over the editing. This was her programme, she'd come this far and she wasn't going to give it all up for a few extra days in Rio with James. 'What time's the flight?'

Roger shook his head, still smiling. 'You're an ambitious woman, Livvy.' He meant it as a compliment.

'Can you leave all the details at reception for me? I'll collect them when we come down for breakfast.'

'Yup, no problem. Do you want some of this coffee?'

Livvy shook her head as she stood. 'I think I'll go back to bed for a while,' she said. 'Catch you later.'

'OK.' Roger picked up *The Times* again and turned to where he had left off. He began reading as Livvy walked away and he couldn't help thinking how glad he was that his wife Mary wasn't driven by ambition. Maybe he was sexist, but there was nothing worse for a man than always coming second.

Back in her room, Livvy undressed quickly and slipped silently into bed beside James. She pulled the sheet up and closed her eyes, settling down to sleep.

'What was all that about?'

She opened her eyes again and sighed. Then, rolling on to her side, she faced James. 'Nothing. I'll tell you later.' She reached her hand out and touched the lean length of his thigh.

He narrowed his eyes. 'Nothing at eight in the morning?'

Livvy smiled. 'Shut up and go back to sleep.'

He smiled back. 'OK. But come here first.'

She inched towards him and he encircled her with his arms. He was warm and smelled of sleep. Tilting her chin up, Livvy waited for his mouth, her eyes slightly closed, the wonderful luxury of being close to someone, warm and comfortable, overwhelming her. Seconds later, she felt the brush of his lips against her forehead and then the settling of his body as he closed his eyes to go back to sleep. She opened her mouth to say something but stopped herself. There was little point in protesting, it wasn't as if the situation was anything new.

Later that morning, rubbing a liberal amount of Hawaiian Tropic into the smooth brown of James's back on the beach,

Livvy realised that she had forgotten how lovely it was to run her hands the length of his body and how beautiful the line of his muscle was, with its sleek covering of dark brown skin. She trailed her fingers over his spine and he relaxed against her touch.

'Hmmm, that feels really nice,' he mumbled.

'Well, make the most of it,' Livvy replied without consciously thinking, 'It's your last chance.' And then suddenly she stopped, realising what she'd said, and sat back on her heels. James rolled over and looked up at her.

'What do you mean by that?' His voice was sharper than he'd meant it to be but he couldn't help the feeling of panic that rose in his chest.

'I mean . . .' Livvy answered with hesitation, 'that I . . . er . . . I have to leave Rio early.' She looked away from him, which was just as well, because he had gone white with shock.

'How early?' The sudden thought of being left alone in Rio to do what Hugh wanted him to was terrifying. He was overwhelmed with dread. He couldn't do it alone, he knew he couldn't do it alone. 'How early?' he demanded, his voice harsh.

'This evening,' she answered, unnerved by his reaction.

'Jesus Christ, Livvy!' James sat up, his heart pounding. The only thing that had kept him going all this time was that he'd planned for Livvy to carry the drugs, that they'd travel together, back from official Foreign Office business, and she would be carrying the packages, confidently and casually, and in complete ignorance of the whole thing. 'Jesus Christ!' he shouted again.

Livvy put her hand out and touched his arm. 'James . . . I . . .'

'You what, Livvy? You really feel it's necessary to leave so soon? I thought this was supposed to be our break away together, some time on our own?' He was using emotional blackmail but he couldn't care less. 'You promised, Livvy! You promised that we'd have this trip away. It was the only reason I came out here on business, the only goddamn reason!'

'Look, James . . . I . . .' Livvy was dismayed at his anger. She'd had no idea he'd take it like this. 'But why don't you come back with me? What's the problem?'

'Oh, it's no problem to you, is it, Livvy? Of course I can't come back with you, I booked my flight Apex, remember? I can't just change my ticket like that!' He clicked his fingers to illustrate the point and stared angrily at her.

'James, I'm sorry . . . I . . .'

He stood up, pulled on his tee-shirt. 'I'm sorry! Ha! I take that to mean that you've already made up your mind?'

'Yes, no! I mean . . .'

'I know exactly what you mean, Livvy!' He snatched up his towel and violently shook the sand out, much of it blowing in her face. 'You've just made one hell of a bad decision, Liv!' he shouted. 'That much is certain.' And regardless of the open stares from the crowd around them on the beach, James grabbed the rest of his things, slung the towel around his neck and stormed off, kicking a cloud of white sand up behind him as he went.

He crossed the road from the beach and stormed into the lobby of the hotel, went straight into the bar, ignoring the stares at his attire, and ordered himself a large Scotch on the rocks. He gulped it down in one go and ordered another, the heat of the liquid hitting the pit of his stomach and spreading a warmth through his body. He sat on a bar stool to wait for the second drink and began to think things through, his emotions heightened by the rush of alcohol to his brain.

There was no way he should be left to carry the whole burden, no way at all. A single man was far more suspicious than a couple travelling together, even if he was a Foreign Office official. If it had gone the way he'd planned Livvy wouldn't have known anything about it; she'd have carried the whole thing without the slightest unease, ignorant of the risk, self-assured and confident, in her usual upper-middle-class way. The second drink was placed in front of him and he drank it down again, in one gulp, the heat hitting his stomach a second time with a jolt. He began to feel better.

'Another one of these please,' he said to the barman, sliding his empty glass across the bar. 'Right away.'

He looked round the unoccupied bar as the thoughts started to take shape in his head.

There was no reason why Livvy would be stopped, was there? She was a well-known television reporter and presenter, she would be travelling with City's film crew and her reputation was completely without stain. She would have no reason to look suspicious – after all, she wouldn't know anything about the packages, would she? James picked up the third glass of whisky and held it in both hands, looking at the warm amber liquid. He was about to drink it down when he stopped. God, what was he thinking of? He loved Livvy, didn't he? None of this was her fault. He looked at the drink for a moment longer and then drank it down and stood up. He left the money on the bar and walked towards the door.

'James!'

He stopped in the entrance as Roger came towards him.

'Ah, James, glad I caught you! You couldn't tell Livvy we're booked on the flight out tonight, could you, mate? They just confirmed it.'

He nodded. James didn't like Roger, he was a cocky son of a bitch.

'Thanks,' Roger edged past him into the bar and James was dismissed, not worth any more conversation.

'Bye, Roger,' James said.

'Oh! Yeah, catch you later, James.' He had walked off without even turning round. James stood where he was for a moment, angry at his lack of status within Livvy's circle, and then in an instant he changed his direction and crossed the lobby to the telephones. Digging in the pocket of his shorts for his change, he dialled the number he had memorised and waited for the line to connect. He was angry and upset and he blocked out all thoughts save those of self-preservation. Suddenly, it was all perfectly clear in his mind.

Livvy shivered in the cool of the corridor as she made her way back to the room. She had given James half an hour to calm down and now she really should speak to him, smooth things over before she left. Opening the door to the room, she saw the light on in the bathroom and flung her bag down on the bed. She crossed to the bathroom door.

'James?' She stood where she was and waited for him to answer. 'James, listen, I want to try and explain . . .I . . .' She stepped closer, not able to hear anything but the whirr of the extractor fan. 'James . . . Look, I'm sorry, I . . .' Pushing the door open, she went inside. 'James?' The bathroom was empty. 'James?'

Walking straight out into the bedroom, she called his name again, knowing it was pointless, and then went back to the bathroom. She saw a damp towel on the rail and his swimming shorts flung down on the floor; he had obviously been in, showered and then gone out again. She picked up the swimming shorts and sighed heavily.

'Bloody hell, James,' she muttered. Nothing between them ever seemed to go right. Placing the shorts on the rail next to the towel, she reached into the shower and turned on the taps for herself. She pulled her tee-shirt over her head, stripped off her bikini and stepped under the hot torrent of water, taking up a sponge and gently soaping her entire body. She was sad and frustrated by the past few days and in the luxurious warmth of the water, she leaned back against the tiled wall and ran her hands over her body in the way that James should have done, the pleasure of it long needed and the release making her cry out in the empty, silent room.

James stood next to the tall, hefty Brazilian in the lift and tried not to breathe in the strong smell of rich, heavy cologne. He was nervous; he could feel the perspiration on the back of his neck and his hands were clenched tight behind his back. He watched the floors of the Copacabana Palace flash by on the panel and knew there was no going back. This was it, he hoped to God he didn't cock it up.

Stepping out of the lift, he followed the bodyguard along a corridor to the suite at the end and then through the door into a wide, modern room with a bank of windows over-looking the sweep of the bay and the Copacabana Beach. The bodyguard disappeared through a connecting door, leaving James waiting tensely just inside the room, the per-spiration now running freely down the side of his face. He wiped it away with his silk handkerchief and took a deep breath, glancing round the room, his eye drawn automatically to the panoramic view.

A minute or so later, a tall, distinguished Spaniard came through the connecting door and stood looking at him. James stepped forward and then suddenly stopped. He knew when to keep his distance.

'James Ward,' the Spaniard said.

James nodded. He felt his voice constrict in his throat and then thought briefly, No, not now, I've too much to lose.

'So what can I do for you, James Ward?' the Spaniard asked coolly. And taking hold of his fear, slowly James began to explain.

Livvy was lying on the bed reading when the phone rang at her side. It was mid-afternoon and she had begun to worry about James – he had been gone for over two hours. She picked up the receiver.

'Hello? Livvy Davis.'

'Livvy, hi, it's me.'

'James! Where are you, I've been worried . . .'

'I know, I know. I'm sorry, Liv, I shouldn't have stormed off. Look, I'm quite near the Sal & Pimenta and I thought maybe you could wander down here and we'll have some lunch and ogle the Brazilian celebs. How does that sound?'

Livvy hesitated. 'I don't know . . . I should pack and . . .'

'And nothing,' James interrupted. 'I'll pack for you later. Come on, Livvy, I feel bad, I don't want to part bad friends. It'll be fun too!'

Livvy smiled; James was a master in the art of persuasion. 'All right then. Where is this place?'

'It's Rua Paul Redfern 63. Just grab a taxi. And glitz it up a bit, I've heard it's pretty competitive in there!'

She laughed. 'Right! I'll see you in what? Twenty minutes?'

'OK. Don't be late!'

'Oh, I won't.' And with that, she hung up. Climbing off the bed, she walked across to the wardrobe and took out the only smart outfit she'd brought with her, an oyster-coloured silk suit, and laid it across the back of the chair. She glanced at her reflection in the mirror, took up a hair-brush and began to brush her hair, smiling as she did so, her spirits high and all her doubts about James suddenly lifted.

Ten minutes later, she crossed the lobby to the reception desk and asked the clerk for directions. She had plenty of time so she thought she'd walk to the restaurant. Tucking the map he outlined for her in her bag, she put on her Raybans and headed out into the sunlight. It was three blocks away and shouldn't take her long. She strode confidently and elegantly off in the direction that had been pointed out for her, looking forward to her lunch with James.

Approximately thirty seconds after she disappeared out of sight, James slipped out of the phone booth across the lobby and took the lift up to the fourth floor. He knew the distance she had to walk and he had seven or eight minutes at the most.

Unlocking the door to their room, he was greeted by the faint aroma of her perfume still lingering in the air and he held his breath to avoid it. He crossed to the bathroom, car-rying the bag with the four two-litre bottles of whisky in their presentation boxes and locked the door behind him. He placed the carrier bag on the toilet seat, unbuttoned his shirt and began to unstrap the body belt from his chest.

Then finally, his hands trembling slightly, he started for real what he had practised so many times at home. He had about five minutes left.

'Where the hell have you been? You told me not to be late and you weren't even here!'

Walking into the Sal & Pimento twenty minutes later, James bent and hugged Livvy, a humble and apologetic look on his face.

'I am so sorry, Livvy, really!' He pulled out a chair, sat and then took both of her hands in his own. 'I bumped into someone from the conference as I came out of the phone booth and they insisted I had a drink with them.' He kissed her palms and smiled helplessly. 'No, I said, *amigos, no*!'

'That's Spanish!'

'Oh yes, then no, my good man, in my best Portuguese, I am meeting my girlfriend, the love of my life, I cannot go. No! Please no!'

Livvy started to laugh. 'For God's sake, James! It's all right, I forgive you.' She pulled her hands away and picked up the menu. 'It was a bad tactical error though,' she said from behind the tall white card.

'Oh? Why's that?'

'Because you've given me twenty minutes to sort out the most exotic and expensive thing on the menu and it's going to cost you a fortune!' She lowered the card and looked at him over the top of it. He was relaxed and smiling at her, and she felt suddenly quite sad. It seemed like the first time in months he had been anything near happy.

'So what are you going to have?' he asked, avoiding her gaze. 'Apart from a huge champagne cocktail?'

'A what . . .?' She looked up, puzzled, just as the waiter

came over with two Kir Royals and a bowl of salted almonds. 'Oh, I see.' She waited for him to place the drinks down and then reached over and kissed James's cheek. Kir Royal was her favourite drink. 'Are we celebrating something?'

'No.' James shrugged off the smallest feeling of guilt that rose in his chest. 'Nothing at all.' He picked up his glass. 'Come on, now, drink up! We've got about five hours left together in Brazil.' He took a sip of the sparkling pink champagne. 'So we might as well make the most of it!'

Later that evening, having slept off the dizzy effect of five champagne cocktails and a huge lunch, Livvy woke, remembering those words, and opened her eyes to see James, seated by the side of the bed watching her. She rolled on to her side, pushed the hair out of her eyes and smiled at him.

'Why are you watching me?'

He shrugged. He had been watching her since he had hidden the bottles in her case, not sure why, but feeling strangely calm as he did so, strangely resolute for the first time in months, almost without doubt.

Livvy sat up and glanced down at her case, locked and ready to go. James pre-empted her words.

'I've left your wash things and some travel clothes out for you,' he said. 'I thought I'd lock your case up, it's getting late. The porter's coming for your bag in about half an hour.'

Livvy sat up and stretched. 'I'd better get up then.' She swung her legs over the side of the bed and stood, letting the sheet drop to the floor. Naked, she turned. 'James . . . I . . .'

He stood himself and started to move across to the window. 'Livvy, you'll be late.'

She nodded and moments later, he heard the rush of water from the shower in the bathroom. He looked down at the swimming pool, a bright glimmering blue in the early evening sun, and took a deep breath. Not long to go now, he thought with relief, another hour and it would all be over. Just one more hour to wait.

James and Livvy stood in the hotel lobby with the rest of the film crew while Roger attempted to keep an eye on their baggage as it was loaded on to the bus. They smiled at each other as he darted from porter to porter, shouting in his pidgin Portuguese to mind the frigging cameras and watch out for the bloody bags. He came back to the group, sweating and red in the face, and swore loudly about Primo and their insistence that they send a special bus for the City Television team.

'Why in God's name they couldn't have left the sodding lot to the hotel I don't know! They think they're doing us a favour sending some tinpot bloody driver who doesn't know one end of an expensive item of luggage from another! Jesus!' He hurried off again as Livvy's case was lifted and thrown on to the bus and started shouting anew. Livvy leaned against the reception desk and wished they'd just get on with it. She hated leaving places; once packed, she couldn't wait to get away.

Finally, several minutes later, Roger came back to the little group and wiped his face on a large spotted cotton handkerchief. 'OK, guys, we're ready for the off. I hope you've all got everything you need in your hand baggage because apparently this is the last time you'll see your cases.

Primo have arranged some kind of special treatment with the airline for the equipment's safety and the cases go, too.' He started towards the hotel entrance. 'Christ, it's like a frigging school trip, this!'

Slowly, the rest of the crew picked up their belongings and began to follow him.

'Listen, Livvy,' James said as Livvy turned to go. 'I'll call Hugh and get him to pick you up at Heathrow. All right?'

'Oh, James, I wouldn't bother. I can share a cab with Phil or something.'

'No, I'll ring him. He was going to pick us both up anyway.' He smiled. 'You know how he likes to feel important.'

Livvy smiled back. 'Yes, all right.' She stood where she was for a moment and James took her handbag, dropping it on the floor. He put his arms round her.

'Bye, Livvy,' he whispered, hugging her in close. He felt nothing, no fear, no doubt, nothing.

'Goodbye, James.' She kissed his cheek and he let her go.

'Have a safe flight,' he said. Of course she'd have a safe flight. What could possibly go wrong?

She smiled and put her hand up to her lips to blow him a kiss. Then she picked up her bag, turned towards the open doors and walked off. She didn't look back, it wasn't in her nature to do that.

PART 2

Chapter Thirteen

Twenty-five thousand feet in the air, somewhere above the coast of Spain, Livvy flicked aimlessly through an in-flight magazine, briefly glancing at the duty frees and dismissing the idea of buying anything. She kept one eye on the air hostess as she came up the aisle with a trolley stacked full of steaming plastic breakfasts and one eye on the man in the third row in front. She'd seen him before, she couldn't remember where, but she had definitely seen him.

Watching the back-up hostess pour the coffee, she tried to catch a glimpse of his face as he held his cup up but it was too difficult; he was at the wrong angle and the hostess bent in towards him, half covering him. Livvy sighed and closed the magazine, shoving it back into the pouch behind the seat in front. She looked round for Phil, hoping he'd hurry up before the breakfast arrived. She hated airline food, but after ten hours on a plane she'd eat anything to relieve the boredom. She saw Phil coming back from the toilets and smiled as he approached.

'Hello. You were a long time.'

'Well, I had to practically drag one of the hostesses in there with me to join the mile-high club and then once we'd locked ourselves in I got wedged on that ridiculously small seat with my trousers round my ankles and my erec . . .'

'Oh, please!' Livvy laughed and moved along to let him back into his seat. 'Spare me the details, Phil! I can't think of anything worse!'

'Thank you!' He sat down, placed his washbag back in the holdall under his seat and fastened his seat belt. He was a nervous flier and spent the whole twelve hours safely strapped into his seat with a large St Christopher medal pinned to his sweater.

'Listen, Phil, don't look now but there's a bloke over there that I think I've seen before. I think it was at the hotel in Rio.'

'Where?'

Livvy indicated with her little finger the row several yards in front. Phil immediately craned his head forward and took a good long look.

'Phil!' she hissed. 'Please!'

Phil laughed. 'For goodness sake, Livvy! I think you're paranoid!' He looked again and said, 'It could be a journalist from the *Sunday Times*, of course, who's been following you ever since you uncovered the whereabouts of the reclusive Lenny Duce and now he's hotfooting it back to Docklands to do a piece, a huge "World Exclusive" for this Sunday's edition of the paper.'

Livvy jabbed Phil in the ribs and he laughed. He leaned forward a third time. 'Hey, wait a minute! I think it's Andrew Neil!'

Now Livvy started to laugh. 'All right, all right!' She shook her head. 'Look, seriously, Phil. Do you think you've seen him before?'

Phil rolled his eyes and this time did take a proper look at the man, as discreetly as he could. 'Actually, I might have done.'

Livvy frowned.

'Come on, Livvy! It's just a coincidence if we have.' He smiled. 'You're surely not worried about it?'

'I don't know.' Something about him *did* worry her. She remembered now seeing him at the hotel on three or four occasions. Phil took her hand and tucked her arm through his. 'We'll be landing at safe old Heathrow in an hour or so, in safe old England, where nothing unusual ever, ever happens!' He looked up at the hostess as she handed him a breakfast. 'Does it?'

'I'm sorry?' She smiled, a perfectly made-up smile but a little worn at the edges from too long in the air and too long with the passengers.

'Never mind,' Phil said. He took his breakfast and peeled the hot tinfoil off the top. 'We'll be home soon, Livvy. Imagine! Steak and chips, HP Sauce and a bottle of Newcastle Brown.' He ripped open the plastic around his knife and fork and began to tuck into the rubbery omelette and the pale, rather tired-looking piece of bacon.

'Hmmmm, delicious!' he exclaimed and Livvy couldn't help but smile.

God, Phil is right, Livvy thought, stepping out on to the wet black tarmac at London's Heathrow Airport, even the weather in England is predictable. She put her collar up to stop the grey drizzle of rain seeping down the back of her neck and followed the stream of jetlagged passengers towards the terminal. She could see Roger and Hank at the far end of the plane and Phil was behind her, but she had lost sight of the man she had recognised earlier. He just seemed to disappear into the crowd.

Inside the terminal, the never-ending walk through to passport control began, along the miles of brightly lit walkways with their rolling pedestrian conveyor belt. Livvy trudged on after the people in front, relieved to be home and thinking about several hours of sleep in her wonderfully big, comfortable bed, and maybe supper later that night with Lucy at Orso's. She didn't say much to Phil behind her. She knew he was thinking about seeing his wife and baby and she felt a slight pang of envy that he had someone he loved there to meet him.

Finally entering the passport control area, she queued up at the desk for UK passport holders and went quickly through to the screens announcing the baggage reclaim. She dumped her bag down on the ground and waited silently next to Phil for their flight number to come up.

'BA flight 726 from Rio coming through now, Pete!'

One of the two customs officers at the entrance to the hangar shouted over to the dog handler as they watched the truck and trailer approach.

'OK, I'll be there in a minute,' he shouted back.

The truck stopped, reversed into position and two baggage handlers jumped down to begin throwing the suitcases on to the reclaim belt.

The officer with Gyp, a five-year-old golden Labrador bitch, crossed to the pile of baggage and waited for the handlers to finish their job. He chatted with the other two officers and then bent to let the dog off the lead. He held on to her collar until the suitcases were ready and then he let her off. 'There you go, Gyp,' he said, 'have a good old sniff round!' He stood back with the other two officers and watched the dog scrabble over the mound of bags. All three were silent for several minutes, concentrating hard. 'Whoa! Looks like Gyp's got one!'

All three officers watched the dog as it scratched and sniffed at a black suitcase, nuzzling it hard with her nose. She began to paw it as one of the officers switched on his radio. 'All Victor callsigns,' he said over the air. 'We've got a live one.'

Gyp's handler climbed up on to the belt and pulled the dog off the case. 'Black Samsonite,' he called over his shoulder. Pulling Gyp by her collar, he led her back to the ground and fastened her lead. 'Good girl, Gyp! Good girl!' He patted her head and stroked her ears as she sat obediently by his side. The officer with the radio got on the air again, knowing that several officers would already be positioned in the reclaim hall ready to watch for the case as it came through.

'Victor two one, Victor two three, the bag is a black Samsonite suitcase with metal trim, one handle. No other markings on it. It's going on after a brown case with leather trim, before a blue checked holdall . . . It's on now.' He nodded to the dog handler as he switched his radio off. 'Has John gone ahead?'

Gyp's handler nodded and, knowing everything was in position, they stood and watched the remainder of the bags on the belt go through.

Livvy stood alone by the baggage reclaim waiting for her bag. Debs had been the first one to make a hasty exit, realising that Mary, Roger's wife, was probably outside in arrivals, Hank had claimed his case and darted off to meet his girlfriend; and Phil and Roger had gone at her insistence. She knew that they both had wives waiting for them.

She saw her luggage coming through, in between a checked holdall and a brown case, and moved forward to pull it off the belt. Giving a good yank, she pulled it free and dumped it on the trolley. It was bloody heavy and she wondered what the hell she'd packed.

'Phew!' She positioned herself behind the trolley and pushed it forward towards the green customs channel. She glanced behind her to check that she had everything and then looked straight ahead. God, it was good to be home!

Wheeling the heavy trolley round the corner into the green channel, Livvy was craning her neck to see ahead through the glass doors into arrivals when a customs officer stepped forward and beckoned her over. She stopped, surprised, and smiled politely.

'Excuse me, madam. Can I ask you where you've just come from?'

'Yes, of course! Rio de Janeiro, Brazil.' She looked down at her bag. 'I have my ticket here somewhere.'

'Could I see it, please, with your passport, madam?'

Livvy looked at him, puzzled; she'd never been stopped before and she didn't know if this was usual procedure. 'Yes, of course,' she said, rummaging in her bag. She pulled out her travel documents and handed them over.

'Are you resident in the United Kingdom?' The officer held on to her passport.

'Yes.'

'How long have you been out of this country?'

'Oh, gosh, I'm not sure.' Livvy started to feel uneasy. 'I left on the twelfth of February, which was . . . er . . . eleven days ago. Why?'

The officer ignored her question.

'Is this all your baggage?'

'Yes . . . I . . .' She stopped and kept quiet. There was something in his manner that had really begun to unnerve her.

'Did you pack it yourself?'

'Yes.' It didn't occur to her to mention that she never packed herself, that James always packed for her.

'Are you carrying anything on behalf of anyone else?'

'No.'

'Do you know you are in the customs green channel?'

'Yes, of course I do, I . . .'

The officer interrupted her. 'Do you understand the customs allowances?'

'Yes.'

'Have you anything in excess of these allowances?'

'No.'

'Have you obtained anything or been given anything abroad that you are bringing back to the United Kingdom?'

The questioning seemed to be going on forever. 'No,' Livvy answered a little impatiently.

'I'd like to examine your baggage please.'

She looked at him, surprised again. 'Oh, well yes, certainly.'

The officer walked around to the trolley and lifted the case up on to the examination bench. Livvy's stomach instantly churned. She knew she had nothing to fear but she couldn't help it. She hated officials, they always made her feel guilty.

'Could you open the case, please?'

Livvy reached into her bag again and took out her purse. She unzipped it and found the key to the Samsonite in amongst some Brazilian change. Fitting it into the lock, she turned it and clicked open the case, then lifted the lid and stood back to let the customs officer look inside. She watched him as he removed the top layer of clothes, her oyster-coloured silk suit, and then suddenly her whole body froze. Nestling in amongst her shirts were four two-litre bottles of whisky in presentation boxes.

The customs officer reached over and removed one of the boxes. He opened it and took out the bottle inside.

'Oh my God, I . . .!' Livvy put her hand up to her throat, unable to breathe. There was no liquid in the bottle. It was packed full with what looked like talcum powder. Silently he did the same with the other two bottles and Livvy stumbled forward, holding on to the edge of the bench as her knees buckled under her. They were identical.

The customs officer grabbed her arm and held her up. She gasped for breath, her head swimming. 'Oh Jesus . . . I . . .' She slumped down on to the edge of the bench and put her head in her hands.

'Have you ever seen these bottles before?'

She shook her head, unable to look up.

'Please answer the question, madam.'

She raised her head. 'No! Never!'

The officer lifted the bottles out of the case and placed them on the examination bench. Livvy started to shake.

'I am arresting you on suspicion of importing a controlled drug,' he said. 'You do not have to say anything unless you wish to, but what you say may be given in evidence.' The officer then looked down at his watch. 'It is now exactly nine-fifteen a.m.,' he stated and closed the lid of the case.

Livvy blacked out.

Chapter Fourteen

Hugh stood behind a small crowd in arrivals and looked for the BA label on the bags of the people coming through. The flight had landed twenty minutes ago and he tensely scanned the stream of passengers for Livvy's face. He was nervous, his scalp itched and he could feel a knot in the pit of his stomach. This was not the plan. James had cocked up, bottled out, fucking idiot! If anything went wrong, Jesus! He'd . . .

Hugh looked across the heads of the people in front. He saw a man with a trolley-load of camera equipment come through, wave to his wife and child and move towards them. Just at the end of the crowd he was stopped by a customs officer and his face instantly registered alarm. Hugh peered closely at the equipment; it was stamped all over with City Television. The knot in his stomach twisted painfully.

Watching closely, he saw the woman with the child approach her husband and the customs officer. Something was explained to her and her face too registered shock and alarm. She nodded, looking up at her husband, and together they followed the customs officer across the floor to a door marked Private.

Hugh swallowed hard and edged along the back of the crowd towards the glass doors of the green channel. He pushed his way through to the front and leaned forward to see what was going on in there. The glass was tinted and it was difficult to get any clear picture. He strained a little further, pushing on a woman in front and it was then that he saw Livvy. He froze.

Seconds later, without looking again, he turned on his heel and shoved his way back out of the throng, striding, almost running across the terminal towards the car park. His gut hurt and the blood pulsed in his ears. Once out of the terminal, he started to run. He had to get away from there before Livvy told them she was being met, he had to get out of the airport. Fast.

Calming himself as he approached the pay kiosk, Hugh dug in his pocket for the ticket and some change. He paid at the counter, turning his face away so the man couldn't see him properly and collected his exit ticket. He took the stairs up to the right floor and ran across to his car.

Climbing in, he started the engine and gripped the steering wheel with both hands. He was shaking uncontrollably. Shifting the car into gear, he swung out of his space and headed towards the exit. The soft purr of the Porsche engine calmed him slightly. Once out on the road, he picked up his telephone and pressed the redial. He got straight through to his solicitor.

'Marcus, it's Hugh Howard.'

'Morning, Hugh. How are . . .?'

'Marcus, I am at a meeting with you right now, d'you understand? Put it in your diary.'

'Hugh, I'm afraid I . . .'

'Put it in your diary now, Marcus! And leave the office for

an hour or so. Go to a coffee place, and keep the receipt.'

'Hugh . . .'

'That's what I pay you for, Marcus, in case I ever need anything. Do it!' Hugh switched the phone off. He wasn't going to argue; he paid a hefty backhander for exactly this kind of insurance. Putting his foot down, he pulled into the outside lane and overtook the car in front. If the shit hit the fan, he was going to make damn sure he was way out of its range.

Livvy sat with her head in her hands. She had been like that for the past hour. Nothing that had been said to her had registered; the whole terrifying scene had gone on and she'd felt as if she wasn't there, as if it wasn't happening to her. She didn't know what had happened, she really didn't know. One minute she was collecting her suitcase, saying goodbye to the film crew and the next she was in an interview room with two officers and questions, words, rights, more questions, all going round and round in her head. She looked up as two women in uniform came into the room.

'Livvy Davis?'

She stared blankly at the woman who spoke.

'We are going to carry out a strip search. I'd like to draw your attention to the notice about appeals against the search.' The woman nodded at the wall. Livvy didn't look up. 'Could you stand up, please?'

The arresting officer who had been with her for most of the morning walked towards the door and quietly disappeared. The women moved forward and Livvy stood as she'd been asked to do. She saw the blank gaze of one of them and realised then what she had to do. She began to shake.

'Could you remove each item of clothing separately and hand it across to me. I will tell you when to remove the next item.'

Livvy looked down at the ground for a few moments, then she pulled her sweatshirt over her head and handed it to the officer. She stood awkwardly and waited while it was carefully examined, folded and placed on the table. She unfastened her shirt and took that off next.

Several minutes later, standing naked, she put her arms up across her chest and tried to control her shivering. She couldn't look at the women. She stared down at the ground, the tears thick and painful in her throat. After what seemed like ages one of the officers said, 'OK, you can get dressed now.' And she nodded, reached for her bra, then finally began to cry.

Fraser walked into his office just as the phone rang and leaned across the desk to answer it, his strong muscular body more flexible than it looked. He half held the receiver to his ear while he glanced down at some copy to go in that evening's edition and said, 'Yup. Fraser Stewart, the *Angus Press*,' in his usual curt and casual manner. He heard a silence and then said, even more abruptly, 'Yes? Can I help you?'

He dropped the copy he had just picked up and sat up straight.

'Jesus, Livvy! What is it? . . . Livvy?' He waited for several seconds, his heart hammering in his chest. 'Livvy, slow down, try and stay calm if you can. No, it's all right, sweetheart, I'm still here.' He grabbed a pen from the tray and ripped the end off the copy. 'Try and tell me slowly . . . yes, yes I've got that.' He tried to keep his voice even but his head was reeling from shock. 'How long have you been there? OK. I understand. Yes, I'll be on the next flight . . . Look, Livvy, where's James?' He gripped the receiver as he heard her sobbing again. 'Listen, never mind, sweetheart. Don't worry now, please. I'll be right there.' He wrote down what she'd told him. 'Yes, I understand, OK. Listen, try not to worry, Livvy. It'll be all right, I promise . . .' The line went dead.

He cursed and slammed the phone down, jumping off the desk. He walked through to the outer office.

'Carol?' He looked at the empty space and hollered, 'CAROL!'

Seconds later his assistant appeared, running into the office. 'What? What's the matter?'

'Carol, get on the phone now and book me on to the next flight down to London Heathrow! Then go out and buy me some overnight things, I haven't got time to go home.'

'OK.' Carol picked up the phone. 'You all right, Fraser?' She was concerned, she hadn't seen him this shaken up before.

'Yes. Well no, actually, but I haven't got time to explain.' He walked back into his office and a moment later poked his head round the door. 'Thanks, Carol.'

She shrugged and continued to dial.

Sitting on his desk again, Fraser waited tensely for directory enquiries to answer his call and felt as if he were back twelve years, in Oxford, with all the mixed emotions of shock and worry and incredible longing all coursing round and round his body, painful and exquisite. God, he remembered it well, he remembered it like it was yesterday!

Seventeen she was, far too young for Oxford but far too bright for anywhere else and so eager to get away from home, so desperate to escape the pain of her parents' divorce. He never knew why it was him, what had made her turn to him on that terrible night and afterwards, but he did know that he'd somehow managed to save her from her pain. He'd made love to her, all the time, night after night, with a force and energy he had never known before or since and she'd clung to him, crying out, writhing under him, making him ache for years afterwards at just the thought of it. Her father's suicide, halfway through the first term at Oxford, had marked the beginning of a painfully short affair, but he had never forgotten it. Never.

He started as his call was answered.

'Oh yes, er, Marshall. Gray's Inn, London. Thank you.' He waited. The computerised voice came over the line and he wrote the number down. He pressed the button and re-dialled. Seconds later he was through to the Clerk of the Chambers.

'Can I speak to Peter Marshall, please?' He was given the standard reply, that Mr Marshall was in court. 'I see,' he said. 'Can you get a message to him then, please? It's very urgent, regarding his stepdaughter, Livvy Davis. Yes, she's being held at Heathrow Airport Customs under some very serious charges. She rang me, my name is Fraser Stewart.' He waited impatiently for the clerk to write all this down. 'He can call me on the following number . . .' There was another silence and Fraser said, 'Have you got that? . . . Good! That number is only for the next hour, though, after that I'll be on a flight to London. Thank you.' Abruptly, he rang off.

Standing up, he crossed to the glass wall of his scruffy little office and looked out at Carol still on the phone to the airline. Why the hell had Livvy called him? But he didn't have time to think about that; the next moment the phone rang. He darted across and grabbed it.

'Fraser Stewart. Hello, Mr Marshall. Yes, I did. I'm sorry to . . . No, I'm an old friend from Oxford. No, I don't know why she called me . . . Yes, I realise that but she seems to be very upset, confused. We were quite close at one time and . . .' Suddenly Fraser lost patience. 'Look, Mr Marshall, I understand that you're worried but I know very little except that Livvy phoned me ten minutes ago in a terrible state and asked me to come down to London. I don't know exactly what happened and I'm as puzzled as you are why she rang me but I did help her quite a bit when her father died so maybe that's the reason.' He stopped, breathing hard, and then continued. 'Whatever, I'm flying out of Aberdeen this afternoon and should be in London by this evening. There's not much I can do except be there, that's why I rang you.' He listened to Peter Marshall's reply, calmer now and then nodded. 'OK, thank you, I appreciate that. I'll see you at Heathrow, then. I'll ring and leave a message with my flight details.' He noted down the home number that Peter gave him. 'Right, thanks again. Goodbye then.' He stood up and replaced the receiver.

'Carol?' he shouted from his desk, looking out at her. She put her thumb up in the air as she finished her call and then hung up.

'The next flight is two-thirty,' she called. 'You're on it.'

'Thanks a lot.'

She smiled. 'Right, I'm off to the shops, then.' She stood, grabbed her coat from the back of the chair and took up her handbag. 'I'll collect some petty cash on my way out.'

But Fraser didn't answer, he was already thinking two steps ahead. If he was going to be away for a few days, he had to brief Gordon on what he had been planning to run. He picked up the phone once more, dialled down to the print room and asked for the editor.

Peter swung his Jaguar into a space between two squad cars and slammed on the handbrake. He switched off the engine and glanced up at the cold grey building before climbing out of the car and reaching for his case. By anybody's standards the police station on the north side of Heathrow Airport was a bloody grim-looking place and he wondered how the hell Livvy was coping. He strode up the steps and into the waiting area.

'Hello. Peter Marshall, QC. I've come about Olivia Davis,' he said curtly. 'She's being held here in police custody.' The sergeant on the desk asked him to take a seat.

Minutes later, a slightly balding young man approached Peter. 'Mr Marshall? I'm Sergeant Reid, the custody officer for this case. If you'd like to follow me . . .'

'I'd like to know what's going on here first!' Peter interrupted.

'Yes, of course. I'll take you to one of our interview rooms where we can talk, then I'll have the prisoner brought up to see you.'

Peter winced at the word prisoner. 'I don't even know the charges yet, Sergeant.'

The sergeant glanced down at the clipboard he was holding. 'Miss Olivia Davis has been charged with being "knowingly concerned in the importation of a controlled substance", in this case, cocaine hydrochloride,' he said.

Peter's face registered nothing. 'What amount?'

'Please, follow me,' the sergeant answered. 'The interview room is just up here on the right.' He walked off and

Peter went after him. Entering the small and impersonal interview room, he placed his case on the table and turned to the sergeant.

'What's the full story?' he demanded.

'At nine-fifteen this morning Miss Olivia Davis was stopped coming through the customs green channel and asked a series of the usual questions. Her luggage was then searched and inside her suitcase four two-litre glass bottles were found, each containing what was thought to be a substantial amount of a controlled drug.'

'How much?'

'It's been sent to the lab for testing and weighing.'

Peter looked at the officer.

'Probably somewhere in the region of about three to five kilos,' he finally answered.

Again Peter's face registered no emotion but the shock hit him hard.

The sergeant continued, 'Miss Davis was then arrested, searched and the substance tested by customs. It proved positive for a test for cocaine hydrochloride.'

'What was Olivia's reaction?'

The police sergeant shrugged. 'The customs doctor was called, apparently she passed out on being arrested. Disbelief, shock, says she had no idea of the bottles, had never seen them before.' He shrugged a second time. 'It's a familiar story.'

'Your opinion? Off the record?'

He sighed. 'Off the record, I've no idea. Genuinely pretty distressed, I'd say, shocked, in a bit of a state.' He paused and then said, 'But aren't they all?' He was cynical, he'd seen enough drug smugglers, all types, to know the score.

Peter drew his case towards him and clicked it open. 'Can I see her now, please?'

The sergeant nodded. 'I'll have her brought up.' He stopped at the door. 'Off the record again. She hasn't asked for a solicitor, not once. That's odd, for someone that bright. It's as if she hasn't quite understood what's happened to her.'

Peter made a note of that on his pad. 'Classic sign of shock,' he said. The sergeant nodded and left the room.

Peter rubbed his hands over his face and let out a tense sigh. Livvy was in deep trouble here and at this point he wasn't at all sure how she was going to get out of it.

Looking up as the door was opened, Peter nodded to the custody officer and then glanced behind him at Livvy. She came silently into the room. Her face was ashen, her eyes blank and she seemed smaller than the last time he'd seen her, just before she went away, when she'd seemed larger than life with all the excitement of her 'world exclusive'. She seemed shrunken, weighted down by the shock.

'Visit commencing at thirteen-fifteen exactly,' a young PC said. 'Present are the prisoner's stepfather, Peter Marshall, the prisoner and the custody officer, Sergeant Reid.' He noted all this information down on his record sheet and then closed the door, leaving the custody officer in there. Sergeant Reid stood back a pace to give Peter and Livvy some degree of privacy.

'Livvy?'

She came across to the table and sat down. 'Hello, Peter.' Her voice was flat, confused. 'How come . . .'

'Fraser Stewart rang me,' Peter interrupted. The sergeant was right, she wasn't really with it. 'Livvy, I've rung a solicitor, David Jacobs. He's coming straight over. He'll probably be able to get Seb Petrie to represent you.'

Livvy blinked several times nervously. 'David Jacobs? Seb . . .?'

'Seb Petrie, he's a criminal barrister, a very good one. I . . .' Peter saw that Livvy had started to blink again, almost uncontrollably. He put his hand out and touched her arm. 'Livvy, it's all right, I know what I'm doing. You need some advice, some expert advice.' He moved his hand down to hers and held it; her fingers were ice-cold. He suddenly couldn't remember ever having held her hand before and the thought that he was doing so for the first time in such ghastly circumstances made him terribly sad. He glanced up at her and saw tears streaming down her face.

'Fraser, is he . . .?'

'Fraser's coming down this afternoon. They won't let him see you but he'll be here. He's going to stay with us at home.'

She nodded and moved her hand away, using her palm to wipe the tears. She sniffed loudly and Peter handed her a handkerchief across the table. He wanted to ask her why she had called Fraser Stewart rather than calling her mother, but he knew it wasn't appropriate. The fact that she had, hurt him, it hurt Moira, too, it was something they just didn't understand. Livvy kept the handkerchief and twisted it in her hand. Without looking up, she said, 'Peter, I don't know why I called him. All I remembered was the last time and being with him . . .' She broke off and swallowed painfully. 'I'm sorry,' she said, 'I should've called you and Mum.'

Peter nodded, it was the only thing he could do. Livvy had never made any reference to him like that before and the acknowledgement filled him with both pride and sorrow. He cleared his throat.

'Livvy, what about James?'

'James? I don't know, he's still in Rio, I . . .' She shook her head. James had nothing to do with it, how could he? 'Should he be told?'

'Yes, he should. I thought you were travelling back together?'

'We were but then Roger wanted to leave early to start the editing and so I had to come as well. It was a last-minute thing, he only decided the morning we left, booked flights for that night . . .' She stopped, remembering the lunch, how much she had drunk and James, sparkling, charming . . . on edge? She dismissed the thought. 'He's at the Rio Palace Hotel. You can call him there.'

'He didn't want to come back with you?'

'No, he couldn't! His ticket was booked and . . .' He hadn't even thought of it, but then that was nothing new. They had hardly been close for the past few months. 'No,' she said again, 'he didn't want to come back with me.'

Peter nodded. Of course he didn't, he thought, then he stopped himself. He would be the first to suspect James, he had never liked him, thinking him vain and selfish. He mentally crossed out the word 'suspicious' by James Ward's name and tried to smile reassuringly.

'OK, that's fine,' he answered.

Moments later, the door was opened and the young PC who had brought Livvy up from the cell looked into the room again.

'David Jacobs, legal representative is here,' he said. Peter nodded. 'Livvy, the solicitor is here. I'm going to have to leave while he comes in to speak to you. You can say what

you like to him, all right? His interview is completely confidential.' He stood up to leave. 'Are you OK?'

The colour had drained from her face again. She managed to nod.

'Visit ended at thirteen-thirty,' the PC said aloud as he
noted it down. 'No incident took place.'

Peter collected up his briefcase and went to leave the
room, squeezing Livvy's shoulder as he walked past. He
stopped as she held on to his hand, gripping it fiercely with
her icy fingers. 'It's all right, Livvy darling,' he said quietly.
'Come on, it's all right.' She let go and he touched her hair
briefly before carrying on to the door. He left the room,
striding down the corridor towards David Jacobs with a
sinking feeling of dread and fear.

James walked into his room at the Rio Palace and bent to
pick up the message from reception that had been slipped
under his door. He dumped his bag on the bed and unfolded
the slip of paper. Hugh Howard called from London, he
read, he will telephone back. He peeled off his swimming
shorts and walked naked to the bathroom, grabbing a towel
from the rail and tying it round his waist. His body was
bronzed and covered in a light film of suntan oil after his
morning on the beach and he felt good, relaxed, for the first
time in months. He glanced at his watch and decided to call
Hugh back. Livvy should be home by now and the bottles
safely delivered. He went back to the bedroom and dialled
reception for an outside line. He punched in the number of
Hugh's office, a number he knew off by heart, and waited for
the line to connect. Seconds later he was through to Hugh.

'Hello, Hugh? It's James! I rang to check everything went
ahead smoothly.'

There was a brief silence on the other end and then Hugh said coldly, 'Get off the line, James, this call can be traced.' And with that the phone went dead.

James sat looking at the receiver as the first chill of icy fear ran through his body. Then he clicked the button and rang again for an outside line. He dialled the flat and minutes later, sitting on the bed, he stared blankly at the wall as the line rang on unanswered, bleep after bleep, the echoing, empty noise ringing shrill and terrifying in his ear.

Chapter Fifteen

Livvy sat in the small, grey cell on a hard plastic-covered foam mattress and looked at the plate of fresh fruit on the floor. Her mother had been down to the station early that morning with a change of clothes and something to eat. She was wearing the suit, one of Moira's, Jaeger, navy blue wool, but she couldn't face any food; her stomach churned and the acid kept coming up into her mouth as an aftertaste. So she sat perfectly still, just looking at the shiny green apple and the perfect plump skin of the orange, thinking how odd they looked on the small white plate against the cold, drab concrete floor. She heard the sound of footsteps and glanced up.

'Olivia Davis.' The custody officer Sergeant Reid was back on duty that morning. He smiled at her through the iron grille in the door and slotted the key into the lock. 'Time for your appearance at Uxbridge magistrates,' he said, pulling open the heavy metal door. 'Follow me.'

Livvy stood and smoothed her skirt down over her knees. Silently, she followed the sergeant along the corridor into the main part of the station and then to a back door leading out to the car park. Sergeant Reid turned to her as they reached the door and held up his handcuffs. He saw her wince and avoided her eye.

'Both hands out in front, please,' he said. She did as he asked and he clamped the metal cuffs round her wrists. For one terrible moment she thought she might scream but she bit the inside of her lip hard, until she tasted blood, and the moment passed.

Still silent, she walked out of the door and climbed unsteadily, her hands in front of her, into the back of the police van. The door was slammed and locked behind her. She glanced at the WPC already in the van then turned to stare blankly out of the grilled window as the vehicle drove off.

'I'm standing outside Uxbridge Magistrates' Court now, waiting for the arrival of Livvy Davis, the well-known television presenter and reporter due to appear in front of the magistrates this morning on a drug-smuggling charge. Miss Davis was allegedly caught yesterday coming into the UK from Rio de Janeiro with over three kilos of cocaine in her luggage . . .'

The reporter clicked off the microphone. 'Mike? Shall we do the rest when the van shows up?'

The cameraman nodded. 'Let's get in at the front, over by the steps. You can do it from there and I should get a good angle on the crowd and Livvy's face as she gets out of the van.'

The reporter started moving across to the throng of people and caught the excited buzz of the photographers. This was a good story, they were all on to it.

'Here all right, Mike?'

The cameraman held up his thumb. 'It's OK but move to

centre a bit if you can,' he shouted. The reporter did as he asked. 'Great!' He gave her the thumbs up again and she smiled. They were ready.

Livvy saw the crowd before she saw anything else. They were three deep outside the court, reporters, photographers, ITV news. She swallowed and looked down at the floor.

'If you stick in tight to me we'll get you through,' the WPC said as she looked out of the window. 'Bastards!' Livvy kept her head down and nodded.

The van drew up in front of the entrance to the court and Livvy's heart pounded in her chest. She waited while a policeman came round to the back to open up, all the time feeling the pressure from outside, as if the van were being physically pushed and shoved. Then she stood, her legs weak, and, protected by the WPC, moved forward. She heard her name, several times, shouted above the noise of the crowd and looked up instinctively. She saw faces, hostile, greedy, sneering; cameras flashed and a roar went up, a triumphant, bloodthirsty yell. Livvy held on to the WPC as they pushed forward through the bodies and her lip bled again, from the sheer effort of holding back the screams.

Fraser stood inside the entrance to the magistrates' court with Peter and Moira, his heart wrenching at the sound of the crowd outside. He saw Moira's mouth twitch as she held back her tears and noticed that Peter was gripping her hand so tightly that it was white and bloodless. They started as the doors were flung open and Livvy was shoved brutally inside, a policeman on either side of her, her tall slim body literally battered between the two of them. Fraser glanced down at the handcuffs and turned away before Livvy could see him staring.

'Livvy!' Moira went to rush forward but Peter held her back; he could see that she was too distressed to do any good. He looked at Fraser and Fraser nodded. He stepped towards Livvy, trying to keep his face impassive just as the custody sergeant began to move her on.

'You all right, Livvy?'

She stared at him for a moment and a painful ache shot through his body. He desperately wanted to touch her.

'Yes,' she murmured. She put her head down, unable to look at him, and he felt completely helpless. Seconds later, the custody sergeant moved her forward and she was gone.

Livvy was led into the court, a miserable, characterless room, and took a seat next to David Jacobs. Her handcuffs had been removed and she rubbed her wrists painfully. Jacobs smiled at her reassuringly but she hadn't the heart to smile back. They stood as the magistrate came in and remained standing while the charge was read out by the clerk.

They sat and the Crown Prosecution spoke next. 'This is a matter for trial only on indictment,' he said, 'therefore we need to set a date for the committal hearing.'

The magistrate, a woman of sixty odd, peered at him over the rim of her half-moon spectacles and nodded.

'May I suggest six weeks from now, the fourteenth of April?'

'Yes, that's fine.' The magistrate made a note on her pad.

'That just leaves the question of bail in the interim,' he went on. 'The crown object to bail in this case for the following reasons . . .'

Livvy clenched her fists by her side.

'The possibility of abscondsion. The accused has a family house in Spain with adequate financial resources there. And secondly, owing to the scale of the case, if the accused is at large it may well jeopardise the enquiry.'

David Jacobs put a reassuring hand on Livvy's arm.

'Would the defence like to reply?'

Jacobs stood and nodded to the magistrate.

'My client would be willing to hand over her passport and adhere to any restrictions imposed on the bail and she and her family would be able to raise surety to the amount of twenty-five thousand pounds,' he said.

The magistrate made another note on her pad, then looked at the prosecutor and Jacobs. After several minutes, she said, 'I am afraid that I don't feel it's appropriate in this case to grant bail.'

Livvy dropped her head down.

'The defendant will remain in custody until committed to trial on April the fourteenth.'

Livvy swallowed back the tears and felt Jacobs pull her to her feet as the magistrate left the court, then she slumped down and covered her face with her hands just as the dock officer appeared to take her down to the cells.

Peter grabbed Jacobs as he came out of court. 'I want you to put an application into court right now to appeal!'

Jacobs gently removed Peter's hand from his arm. 'It's virtually done, Peter. I was expecting this. I'm going down to see Livvy now, to reassure her, and then I'm seeing the CPS to get them to send someone over to the court this afternoon. After that I'm driving straight back to my office. I instructed them last night, it's a question of finalising the papers and faxing them to the court office.' He patted Peter on the arm. 'Don't worry,' he said, 'I'll have her out by tonight.' Then he hurried off towards the cells and left Peter wondering what the hell he was going to tell Moira about Holloway.

Chapter Sixteen

'Stand by to record the opening . . . Roll the clock . . . 3 to go . . . Eng. 1 roll . . . 3 . . . 2 . . . 1 . . . And we're on air!'

'Cue, Pam!'

'Magistrates coming from Eng. 2 . . . 30 seconds on this . . . Eng. 2 on standby . . . 10 seconds . . . 5 . . . 4 . . . 3 . . . 2 . . . 1 . . . Roll Eng. 2 . . . caption . . .!'

'I'm standing on the steps of Uxbridge Magistrates' Court waiting for top television presenter Livvy Davis to be taken from here to Holloway prison. She was remanded in custody this morning on a drug-smuggling charge after bail was refused by magistrates. Her solicitor is appealing against the decision, but until then she will be transported to Holloway women's prison where she will await the committal hearing set for six weeks from now . . .'

Hugh Howard sat in a bar on London Wall and looked up nervously at a large screen opposite as he drank a bottle of Becks. He lit up a cigarette and watched the silent pictures against a background of noisy conversation and loud music. His stomach hurt and he felt sick but he was maintaining some semblance of normality. He had to, he couldn't afford to look suspicious. He didn't know what to do next, except wait. So he sat and watched the screen, in a grimy dump on the London Wall, checking his watch every few minutes and waiting for the lunch-time news bulletin. Suddenly he shouted across to the barman.

'Can you turn it up, mate?' The barman looked round. 'Turn the bloody volume up, I need to hear this!' The sound came over the Nicam speakers of the television and Hugh watched the headlines flash up on the screen.

'Shit!' Jumping down from the bar he looked at his watch and tried to think straight. All the time he watched the screen as Livvy was shoved and pushed, handcuffed, a policeman on either side, through the crowd towards a white police van. He began to sweat, the acid rising from his gut.

He had to get to a phone, a public phone, he had to call James, make sure he didn't cock it up again. He pulled a fiver out of his wallet and left it by his glass. Seconds later he had left the bar.

It took only a few minutes to get to Moorgate tube and buy a five-pound phone card. Hugh found an unoccupied phone and slotted the card in, dialling an international line. He punched in the numbers and after a short pause was through to Rio direct. The phone was answered by the hotel reception and he asked to be put through to James Ward. It was picked up by James almost immediately.

'James?'

The voice on the other end was nervy. 'Hugh, is that you? What the hell's happ . . .'

'Shut up, James! Just listen! I want you to ring Livvy's parents and say you haven't heard from her and you're worried. They'll explain the situation and you'll tell them you're getting on the next plane home.'

James began to panic on the other end. He didn't know what was going on, he was scared, he thought he was being watched. 'But, Hugh, I . . .' He was whimpering.

'Shut up, James! There's no time to explain. There's one hell of a mess here . . .' Hugh stopped and swallowed hard. 'Just get yourself back. Don't argue, and don't speak to anyone except Livvy's parents. Just do as I say. Now!'

Hugh hung up. He took out a handkerchief and wiped the back of his neck on it, then he removed the phone card and glanced around him at the other callers. He had been ignored. Tucking the card in his pocket, he moved off across the station and stopped to buy an *Evening Standard* by the entrance. Livvy Davis was front-page news and that was all he needed!

At the same time Hugh left the station, Paul Robson took a big bite out of his curried chicken sandwich and stopped in front of the window of Curry's on Cheapside to look at the CD players. His attention was caught by the news story on one of the portable TV's.

Livvy Davis. He'd seen her loads of times on the telly, rather liked her actually, she was more than just a cute ass. Holloway! Jesus! Poor girl, he didn't envy her now. He finished the sandwich and dug in the bag for his drink, popping the ring and taking a long gulp. Drugs. He wiped his mouth on a paper napkin and felt the familiar knot of tension in his chest at the thought of the drug industry. That was what it was, an industry, expertly run and highly profitable. Drugs.

He turned away from the window and wondered if he should call Loman again for more news. He was beginning to get scared, beginning to wonder just where the hell this was all going to leave him. Loman had uncovered a handful of companies, all over South America, companies that weren't listed in Best's, companies that he knew damn well had a hefty amount of premium incomes that were more than likely nothing to do with premiums. Drug money, that was his guess. They were laundering the money through bogus insurance companies, shipping it to the UK into a legitimate syndicate and using it to underwrite legitimate business. That was his guess, but he had to be sure. Before he went any further, he had to be sure. That was where Loman came in. Private investigators cost, but Robson had the money and Loman was good; as far as he knew, he was the best.

Robson crumpled his sandwich bag into a ball and chucked it at the rubbish bin on the lamppost. It hit the top and bounced in. He squashed his can and did the same, glancing back at the screen before he walked off. He saw Livvy Davis climb up unsteadily into the police van, assisted by a WPC, and the doors slam shut behind her. God only knows what happens to her now, he thought, striding off in the direction of Bank with his hands in his pockets. It was a bloody dangerous business to be involved in, that was for sure, and he damn well hoped he was doing the right thing.

David Jacobs picked up the telephone almost the instant it rang. He turned down the volume on his portable five-inch television screen and grabbed a pen.

'Jacobs . . .'

'What the hell's going on, David? You seen the news, for God's sake? Jesus! It's all over the place!'

'Yes, Peter, I've seen the news. Calm down, OK? It's all under control.' Jacobs put his hand up to his temple to ease the tension.

'I bloody well hope it is, Jacobs! What time's the hearing?'

'No word as yet but we're hard on it. Look, Peter, I'll ring you as soon as a time's set. We're seeing Judge Haltman and I'm hoping for around four-thirty this afternoon. The CPS are briefed.' Jacobs heard Peter Marshall sigh anxiously on the other end of the line. He felt for him, but they were doing everything they could. Appeals took time, it'd be a bloody miracle if they got this one through by the end of the day. 'Peter, I'll ring you as soon as I hear anything.'

'Yes, OK, David.' Peter knew the procedure only too well. He knew it took time, but with Livvy involved, and Moira, he understood for the first time the agony of waiting. 'I'll be in Chambers this afternoon,' he said. 'Ring me there.' He felt better being in London, near at hand if he was needed. Besides, he couldn't bear to see Moira so distressed.

'Peter . . .' Jacobs paused. 'Look, try not to worry . . .'

'Yes, I know, David. It's a fair system and all that.' He couldn't keep the irony out of his voice. 'I'll speak to you in an hour or so.' And with that he hung up.

Jacobs replaced the receiver and looked up at the small television screen on his desk. He leaned over and turned up the volume again to catch the last few seconds of the news bulletin on Livvy Davis. He saw the scuffle outside the magistrates' court, the white police van – the type with the locked cubicle compartments – and he closed his eyes for a moment, wondering how the hell Livvy was going to cope with it all. That was the trouble with an early hearing, he thought; they left you waiting until lunch time to take you down and in this case it was just enough time for the whole bloody circus to gather to watch. He switched off the television before he had a chance to see her face properly and spoke quickly into the intercom.

'Janice? Anything from the court office yet?'

It took several seconds for his secretary to get to the phone. He heard the noise of the fax in the background. 'I've something coming in now,' she said.

Jacobs felt his spirits lift for the first time that day. 'Bring it in as soon as it's off the machine, will you?' He released the speak button and said, 'Thank God for that,' quietly and to himself, then he went over the copy documents that had already been sent into the list office one last time.

Chapter Seventeen

The door of the cubicle slammed behind her.

It was a tight space, three by three foot at the most, a tiny cell, with no room to move, only to stand or sit. Livvy slumped down on to the ledge seat and put her head in her hands. She could hear the noise outside, ugly, wild voices, and she put her hands up to her ears to try and blank out the sound. The engine started, she could feel the vibration of it, and finally the van moved off. The voices began to fade, until only the roar of the engine could be heard, bouncing off the metal sides of the van, that and the dull, aching silence inside her head.

'Olivia Davis?'

Livvy stood silent as the prison officer came forward and nodded at the WPC. She was a large woman, nearly six foot, and heavy, the sort of weight that didn't look like fat, solid and compact. The sort of weight that intimidated. She took in Livvy's navy Jaeger suit, the shoes and bag, and a faint, sneering flicker of dislike came into her eyes. She hated middle-class offenders, they were the worst. They didn't have background or underprivilege to blame; in her book they were simply evil.

'You are now being handed over to the prison authorities,' the WPC said. She glanced at the prison officer and then very briefly at Livvy. 'This is procedure.'

Livvy looked down at the ground. She had ceased to exist, she was spoken to without any personal contact, almost as if she wasn't even there. She saw the big, black shoes of the prison officer, the heavy, thick ankles in dark nylon tights, the calf-length black skirt, the uniform, and suddenly she wanted to cry. She bit her lip, now swollen and bruised inside from all the pressure, and managed somehow to glance up again. She swallowed hard, held her head up, and followed the prison officer into the main reception area.

'Olivia Davis, Flat 19, East Mansion House, Cadogan Square, WC1.'

Livvy stared blankly at the officer who was filling in the form.

'Davis, number 1732,' the officer continued. 'Personal belongings?' She looked up and right through Livvy. Livvy took off her earrings, a pair of large eighteen-carat gold Chanel knots, and her Cartier Russian wedding ring and bracelet. She handed them over. Then she unfastened her watch, a brightly coloured fluorescent Swatch watch and handed that over too.

'You're allowed to keep the watch.'

Livvy shook her head. She didn't want it, she didn't want to be reminded of time or home or anything normal.

The two officers exchanged glances. They didn't like concessions to be refused – this one had high opinions of herself, obviously. The jewellery was dropped into a plastic bag, sealed and numbered.

'Take each item of clothing off and place it next to you on

the chair ready for inspection,' the officer said. She handed over a white cotton robe, starched and pressed into a small neat square. Livvy took it and held it, she hadn't quite understood what was about to happen. She felt a sharp prod in the back.

'Over there. Remove each item of clothing and fold it on the chair ready for inspection.' She looked behind her at the large, overbearing woman. There were two other officers in reception and one other prisoner behind her.

'I don't think . . .' Livvy stopped. Slowly she moved across the room to the row of chairs along the wall. She hung her head, aware that every pair of eyes in reception was on her and began to unbutton the jacket of her suit.

Sometime later, dressed in the starched white robe and shivering in the draught of the cold, grey reception area, Livvy sat with the other prisoner, waiting to be taken down to her cell. She hugged her arms about her, frightened and confused. She had been like that for nearly two hours.

'1732.'

Livvy heard the number but it didn't register.

'Davis! 1732!'

Suddenly she looked round and the other prisoner indicated with a slight flick of her eyes that she should stand. She did so as two guards came towards her.

'The governor has put you in a cell on your own,' the smaller of the two said derisively. She addressed the comment to a space just above Livvy's head, not wanting to speak to her directly. 'Here.' She held out a small pile of clothes. 'Put these on.'

The two guards stood while Livvy placed the pile next to her and unbelted the robe. She braced herself and took it off, turning her eyes away from the stare of one of the guards. She pulled on the underwear, her fingers slipping on the catch of the bra because her hands shook so much, and then the blue serge dress, buttoning it through. She sat to put on the tights and knot the laces of the shoes but again her fingers fumbled painfully over the thin ties. She heard the smaller guard sigh irritably and that made her even more nervous and clumsy. It took several minutes finally to manage the laces and stand.

'Fold the dressing gown up.'

Bending, she took it up and folded it.

'Follow me.'

The smaller of the two guards had a sharp, piercing voice, with no trace of softness. She turned on her heel without looking again at Livvy and walked off. Livvy followed, through the door out of reception, down along a grey glossed corridor and into the main part of the prison, one guard in front, one behind her. She focused on the black uniformed back of the guard in front, too frightened to look around, too humiliated and ashamed to take any of it in. They reached a cell several minutes later. The door was open and it smelled of disinfectant. Livvy hesitated for a moment and the jab in the back came immediately, only this time more painful. She started, inched forward and was inside the cell. Seconds later, the heavy iron door swung shut, the key turned in the lock and the footsteps of the guards echoed on the stone floor as they walked away. Livvy sank down against the cold, hard wall and slumped to the floor. She had reached the bottom, there was no way up.

Fraser sat in the kitchen at The Old Rectory with Moira and looked through a pile of old photographs that she had found tucked away in a drawer in the study. She sat beside him, smiling over the faded snaps, talking about Livvy continuously, in a way that he knew gave her comfort. They drank tea, the warmth of the Aga making little impact on Moira's icy fingers as she passed him photo after photo, the shock and distress having drained all the blood from her face and hands. And they listened with dread, every time the phone rang, to the answering machine as it recorded each message from yet another pushy journalist who'd somehow managed to get hold of the number.

Fraser felt helpless. He knew that Peter needed him there with Moira but he felt out of it, frustrated that he couldn't do something, anything, to help Livvy. He gazed mindlessly at the snapshots, noticing how few of the early pictures showed any sign of Livvy's father. He kept thinking back to Livvy's face at the magistrates' court that morning, so pale and defeated, so shocked and afraid, years away from the laughing, happy girl in the pictures. He dropped the last one Moira passed him on to the pile and noticed her staring at him. He glanced away quickly.

'I wonder why you let her get away,' she said quietly. Fraser looked back at her. Her eyes were the same as Livvy's, sharp, blue, intelligent eyes that looked harder than most. He shrugged and glanced down at the table for a moment.

'Did she ever tell you about . . .'

'No.' Moira touched his hand and again he felt the iciness of her fingers. 'She has hardly ever talked to me since her father died, not properly anyway.' Moira began to stack the photographs into a neat pile to keep her hands busy. 'I don't think she's really talked to anyone.'

'Not to James?'

She smiled, a small ironic smile. 'No, certainly not to

James,' she said and they both jumped as the phone rang again, piercing the intimate quiet with its intrusive bleep. Three rings and the machine clicked on. They sat silently and listened for the voice.

'Hello, Moira? Peter? This is James . . . I'm ringing from Rio, I'm worried bec . . .'

Moira looked across, surprised, and then indicated quickly that Fraser should answer it. He ran to the phone, grabbing it before James could finish his sentence.

'James. Hello? It's Fraser Stewart, I'm staying here with Moira and Peter . . . I . . .'

'Fraser!' James lost his train of thought for a moment. He had been practising the words to say to Moira and Peter in his head and this threw him totally off course for a few seconds. 'Fraser?'

'Yes, James, I . . .'

'What the hell's going on? I rang to speak to Moira or Peter! What are you doing there?'

Fraser bit back an angry retort; James's reaction was way over the top, it didn't make sense. 'Look, James,' he said, 'something's happened here . . .'

'I know that . . . what's it got to do with . . .' James broke off suddenly. He realised his mistake the moment he'd said it; he wasn't supposed to know what had happened, that was why he was phoning Livvy's parents. He thought quickly and then said, 'I was sure something was wrong, I've been trying to call Livvy for the past twenty-four hours and there's no reply. What's happened?'

Fraser hesitated. James didn't sound right; he was edgy, his voice was guarded, wary. He decided to put it down to distance – he could easily misinterpret across six thousand miles.

'James, Livvy's in a lot of trouble. She's been remanded in

custody for allegedly attempting to smuggle nearly five kilos of cocaine into the country. It's a bloody set-up, of course, but . . .'

'What do you mean, a set-up? Do they think that?'

'No but . . .' Fraser's face darkened with anger. 'James, it's obvious, for Christ's sake! Why would Livvy try to smuggle drugs?' For a moment he couldn't believe that he had had to say that. James was silent.

'You still there, James?'

'Yes . . . I'm shocked, that's all. I can hardly believe it!'

Fraser softened slightly. 'We all feel the same. When are you coming home?'

'I'll come straight away.'

Fraser breathed easier. This was the sort of reaction he'd expected. As much as he disliked James, he knew that Livvy would need him there. He glanced across at Moira and pointed to the receiver. She shook her head.

'Listen, James, we're hoping to get Livvy out on bail by the end of the day. What's the earliest you can get home?'

'I don't know . . . Perhaps the day after tomorrow? I'll ring when I've booked my flight.'

'All right. Ring here, I think Livvy's going to come home for a while.'

'How long are you staying?'

Fraser snapped, 'Does it matter, for God's sake?'

'No, I . . .' James stopped. He had never liked Fraser; he didn't need him prying, looking too closely at the way he behaved. 'I'll ring when I have the details,' he said. 'Give Livvy my love.' And quickly he replaced the receiver.

'Jesus!' Fraser looked at the dead telephone in his hand and then slammed it down. He stood silent for a few moments, glowering.

'I take it there's no love lost between you and James?' Moira said.

'Ha!' Fraser walked back to the table. 'That bloke doesn't sound right to me! It was as if he already knew, had been warned off, you know? He didn't once ask me how Livvy was. Doesn't that strike you as strange?'

Moira shrugged. 'Nothing James Ward does strikes me as strange. He doesn't really care for anyone, I don't think, Fraser, apart from himself.' She stood and rested her hand affectionately on Fraser's shoulder for a moment before crossing the room. 'He's probably worrying about the damage this could do to his diplomatic career.' Filling the kettle at the sink, she plugged it in and turned. 'My guess is that if you rang him back right now the line would be busy; he'll be ringing someone in order to cover his back.' She smiled to show the joke in what she said but her eyes were cold.

Fraser looked down at a recent picture of Livvy with her half-brother Giles and his stomach wrenched. Moira saw it so plainly in his face and thought, If only it were him instead of James. She had seen more emotion inside Fraser in the past twelve hours than she had ever seen in James Ward. Turning back to the tea things, she let Fraser alone with his thoughts and wondered what the hell was going to happen next.

Halfway across the globe, pacing his hotel bedroom, that was exactly what James Ward was thinking as well. The telephone call to the Marshall house had thrown him; he had begun to panic.

Fraser Stewart, that was all he bloody needed! He should never have listened to Hugh, should never have rung! Stewart saw through him, he just knew he did. Christ, the

bloke was an inquisitive bastard; his voice had dripped suspicion. James paced, his hands clasped together tightly, and
tried to think it through.

Bugger Hugh, that was for certain! There was no way
James was going to rush home to the sceptical glare of
Fraser Stewart. He didn't trust himself, he was too nervous
not to give something away. No, he'd have to stay in Rio for
a few days more. He'd ring and say he couldn't get a flight
out, he'd been delayed by business. Christ, he should never
have listened to Hugh. Well, he wasn't going to any more.
Hugh was freaking out, he'd lost control. He'd lost it completely and from now on James was going to play it *his* way.
He was in the Foreign Office, for fuck's sake! He should
know how to play the game by now.

Picking up the telephone again, he dialled an outside
line and then the number of Hugh's office. He waited several
rings for the line to be answered.

'Hugh? It's James.'

'Where are you?' Hugh was instantly wary.

'I'm in a pay phone,' James lied, 'stop panicking!' He
heard Hugh snort derisively down the line and his anger
flared. 'I'll be home in a couple of days,' he said sharply. 'I've
got some business to finish.'

Hugh's voice was suddenly icy. 'I don't think that's very
wise.'

'I don't care what you think, Hugh! I'm not coming back
until I'm ready.' He was oblivious to the whining petulance
in his voice.

There was a silence, then Hugh said: 'Grow up, James,
for . . .'

But he never finished the sentence; James had hung up.
He wasn't listening to anyone any more; this time he knew

what he was doing. This time he was taking control.

Ten floors below, in a basement room the hotel had given over to its hardware, the computer logged on the second call that morning from room 1101. It listed the number dialled, the date, time and length of the call and it added it automatically to the others already on the bill. Every call that James Ward made was traceable.

Judge Haltman swept into his chambers at twenty past four that afternoon. He sat, still in his wig and gown, and lit up a cigar. David Jacobs and the representative from the Crown Prosecution Service followed him in and stood while he went through the papers on his desk. He motioned with his hand, his attention taken by the application, and both parties sat opposite him. Jacobs lit up a cigarette.

Judge Haltman looked up. 'The date for the committal hearing is April the fourteenth?'

The CPS representative spoke first. 'Yes, that's six weeks away.'

'I am aware of the timing, thank you,' Haltman said stiffly.

'Of course.'

Jacobs glanced at the young woman from the CPS and attempted a brief conspiratorial smile. It was ignored.

She was thirty-four, new in the job and intensely earnest. She leaned forward very slightly in her chair to see where the judge had got up to in his reading and Haltman looked up at her, scowling.

'When I'm ready, Counsel,' he said quellingly.

She nodded and leaned back again.

Jacobs finished his cigarette and curbed the urge to light up another almost immediately. He knew Judge Haltman of old and he knew when to sit tight and keep his mouth shut. Haltman was a stickler for authority in his chambers, no verbal, one cigarette, speak when invited to. Jacobs folded his hands on his lap and kept still. After some time the judge looked up.

'What is the main opposition to bail please, Counsel?'

The young woman rustled her papers importantly.

'Absconsion, primarily,' she said. 'The defendant may have contacts in South America, there is a family property in Spain . . .' She glanced down again at her notes. 'And secondly, the defendant being at large may jeopardise the enquiry. Miss Davis has a very high profile with the media.'

Haltman puffed on his cigar and looked at her, blowing great clouds of grey smoke out of the side of his mouth. Her nostrils flared in distaste.

'Your reply?' Haltman turned to Jacobs and he knew then that the decision had been made.

'The defendant is prepared to offer up her passport as security and would adhere to any restrictions imposed on the bail. Also, she and her family would be able to raise surety to the amount of the bail.'

'It's Peter Marshall's stepdaughter, isn't it?'

Before Jacobs had a chance to answer, the young woman snorted contemptuously, a very low, muffled sound, but unmistakable. Judge Haltman raised one bushy grey eyebrow for a moment but ignored the indignation.

Jacobs coughed. 'Yes, that's right.'

Haltman turned to the CPS representative. 'I think it's highly unlikely, given the family background and the nature of the defence, that the defendant will make any attempt to abscond . . .'

'But . . .'

Haltman glared at the young woman to silence her. 'And,

as I am of the opinion that this is the only reason of any value for objecting to bail, I must overrule the magistrate's decision.'

Jacobs let his hands relax.

'However . . .' Haltman was determined to keep the young woman quiet, 'I will impose certain restrictions on the bail, and owing to the opposition from the CPS and the recommendation from Customs and Excise, I feel duty bound to set bail at one hundred and five thousand pounds.'

Jacobs breathed in sharply: that was an impossible amount of money for this kind of case! He could see the flicker of a smile on the young woman's lips but restrained himself.

'That's an extraordinarily high sum, Your Honour,' he said.

Haltman stubbed out his cigar. 'Considering the information, Mr Jacobs, it is the only path left open to me.' He took another almighty puff on his cigar. 'Will there be a problem with it?' Again the smoke came out in the direction of the young woman.

'No, not at all.' Jacobs spoke quickly and assertively, although he was far less confident than he sounded.

'Good. This hearing is dismissed.' Haltman sat back in his chair and looked at both parties.

Jacobs stood, picked up his case and nodded politely to the young woman.

'Thank you,' he said, 'I'll make arrangements at the list office. I'd like to have my client out by the close of day.' Judge Haltman nodded, and, not quite sure how he was going to tell Peter, Jacobs turned and left the chambers.

*

Peter waited on the end of the line for the manager of Coutts to come back on. He had known Adrian Kirk for years and felt sure that he would do everything he could to raise the money, but it was now four forty-five, officially after bank hours and he was beginning to worry about what could be achieved this late.

'Hello, Peter?'

'Yes, Adrian.'

'Peter, the arrangements have been made. There wasn't any problem, I'm glad to say. I'll have a banker's draft biked round to the Crown Court Office immediately.'

'Thank you.' Peter covered the mouthpiece with his hand for a moment and took a deep, relieved breath.

'I'll need the signatures tomorrow morning, if that's all right?'

'Yes, that's fine, Adrian. I'll drop them into the bank myself on my way to Chambers.'

'Good. Look, Peter . . . I . . . er . . . I hope everything turns out all right.'

'Thank you, Adrian. I appreciate all that you've done.'

'Right.' Typically British, Adrian Kirk was embarrassed by sentiment and kept it to the minimum. 'I'll speak to you tomorrow, then,' he said curtly.

'Fine. Goodbye, Adrian, and thank you again.' Peter smiled at Adrian's manner and replaced the receiver. He redialled immediately, got straight through to Jacobs, who was waiting for his call, and finalised the arrangements. Minutes later he was on the line for the third and last time to Moira, to tell her that he was bringing Livvy home.

Chapter Eighteen

Peter sat at the long pine table in the kitchen at The Old Rectory and watched Moira helplessly as she stood and crossed the room to the window, her arms hugged tightly around her. They had reached a stalemate and he was unable to comfort her. She looked out at the garden, its darkness broken through the trees by the flicker of candles in the summer house where Livvy and Fraser sat.

'Moira?' She kept her back to him so he too got to his feet and crossed the room. He stood behind her and placed his hands on her shoulders.

'Moira, there's nothing we can do,' he said quietly. 'It's Eadie's choice.'

But Moira jerked away. 'Eadie's choice! The pernicious bitch!'

'Moira, please!'

She spun round, her face distraught. 'Please what, Peter? I earned this house, the hard way! All the years of infidelity, boozing, cruelty, and the bastard left half of it to his mother! Jesus! . . . I put up with it, for peace, for Livvy and you, but now this!' She stopped and took a breath to calm herself. 'It was Bryan's ultimate revenge, eh?' she said bitterly. 'For my affair with you, my only bit of happiness!'

'Moira . . .' Peter tried to comfort her but she pushed his hand back.

'Why, Peter? Why? Olivia is her only grandchild, why wouldn't she sign the papers? What does she have to lose? It's Livvy's freedom we're asking her for!' She shook her head. 'Why wouldn't she let us buy her out years ago? God, we were fools to let her hang on in there, gripping on with those evil claws of hers!'

'Moira, it doesn't matter. I can ask the bank to accept my portfolio at Capel's as security on the bail. Really, Moira, it doesn't matter.'

'Well, to me it does! You shouldn't have to do that, Peter! Livvy isn't your daughter.'

'But you're my wife,' he said patiently, 'and I do it for you as much as for her.'

'Then she should know. She should know everything! That her father left nothing but chaos and grief, that you paid for everything, for Oxford and . . .' The strain and the terrible disappointment of Eadie's malevolent refusal to sign her half of the house for surety had finally worn her down. She put her hands up to her face and quietly sobbed.

Peter took her in his arms and held her close. 'Blood is not always thicker than water, my love,' he whispered, stroking her hair. 'Livvy will find out, when she's ready.'

'Oh, Peter . . .'

'Ssssh . . . please . . .'

Moira pulled back for a moment and looked up at him. 'What will happen? What are we going to do?'

'We're going to see Livvy through this and we're going to get her off. She didn't do anything wrong and I'm going to make sure we can prove it.'

'Do you really believe that, Peter?' She searched his face with her piercing blue eyes.

'Yes, I do.'

Then she put her hands up to his hair and touched the grey at his temples. 'Thank you,' she whispered. She reached forward and kissed his lips. 'Thank you.'

Livvy and Fraser sat side by side on the Victorian wrought-iron seat in the summer house, the soft flicker of the candles in their terracotta pots lighting the pitch black of the winter night. They had their coats on, sat on two blankets folded double and their breath made small clouds of white steam in the freezing night air.

They were silent.

Fraser watched Livvy as she traced a pattern with her fingertip in the dust of the window pane. She didn't want to talk, she needed the silence, she said, and the peace. She had hardly spoken since Peter brought her home from the prison. She had withdrawn from them all, sat in front of the fire for hours, just staring at the flames. Then she had asked Fraser to walk with her and they'd gone for miles across the fields in the damp, cold night, the open countryside stretching way beyond them and the wide empty sky above them.

'This is freedom,' she had said quietly as they gazed up at the dark clouds overhead. 'I wonder if I am going to lose it.' And Fraser had put his arm around her then and tried to comfort her, holding her body, so rigid with fear and shock.

They had ended up back at the summer house in the garden, a Victorian glass structure, icy in the dead of night, and he sat beside her, frustrated and helpless, not knowing what to do, what to say, just holding her hand and watching her face as she drew her patterns in the dust.

'Livvy, we ought to go in, you know,' he said, noticing as he gazed at her how her brow wrinkled in concentration. 'You'll get cold sitting here in the damp.'

She didn't look at him. 'Not yet,' she answered. 'Let me do as I please for a bit longer.'

'All right.' He tucked their clasped hands down inside his coat and saw the flicker of a smile on her lips.

'That's nice,' she murmured. They stayed like that for a while longer and then Livvy scrubbed out the mindless patterns on the window and finally turned towards him.

'Fraser, thank you for coming here.'

He shrugged. 'It's OK.' He paused for a few moments, then said, 'But I'm not really sure what I'm supposed to do.'

She looked at his face. She had forgotten how strong and kind it was, how warm the brown of his eyes was. 'Nor am I,' she replied, and smiled a little self-consciously. 'Do you remember, when my father died?' she went on. 'All that happened?'

Fraser nodded. He had a desperate urge to pull her to him and tell her over and over that he remembered every last detail, every single moment of that intense love. But he didn't, he sat still and impassive and waited for her to continue.

'When they stopped me . . . when they found the drugs . . .' She broke off and tried to swallow back the tears that had come suddenly and painfully into her throat. Fraser dug in his pocket for a large checked handkerchief and passed it across to her. 'I just wanted to speak to you,' she went on, wiping her eyes, 'to hear your voice . . .' She laughed, to cover a sob that had escaped her tight control. 'Oh God, it was so stupid . . .' She was crying now, she couldn't stop it. 'All I could think about was you, not James, or Mummy or Peter . . .' She put her hand up over her face and Fraser moved towards her, encircling her with both arms. He pulled her in close.

'It was like a deep need . . . to be comforted . . . to be loved . . .'

'Ssshh, please.' He cradled her head to his chest and gently stroked her hair.

Suddenly she jerked away from him. 'But it all happened years ago! It doesn't make any sense. I'm in love with James!' And in the next instant, she smiled, a small, half-smile through her tears, exasperated, as if she had just realised how ridiculous it all sounded. Fraser put his hand up to her face and wiped the wet from her cheek. She touched his hand and held it there for a moment. Then she looked at him and met his gaze. He moved his fingers to the back of her neck and eased her forward so that her face was inches away from his. Moments later, he kissed her.

He touched her lips with his own, softly, lightly, his tongue darting across the line of them, wetting them, and she started with the intensity of the ache that ran through her. He pulled away from her. 'Are you all right . . .?'

She put her hands up to his hair. 'Yes, don't . . . don't stop.' And she parted her lips, lifting them to his, drawing their mouths together and finding his tongue with her own. It was what she wanted, what she needed, to be loved, to feel the deep physical comfort of that, and her response to him was involuntary: it was a basic human need.

Suddenly their embrace was almost violent in its intensity. He pulled her on to his lap and his mouth moved down over her face to her neck as he wrenched at her clothes, pushing them away so that he could find her skin.

She moaned and her hands ran the length of his back under his clothes, the hard, taut line of his body. She tipped her head back as he pulled open her shirt and kissed her breast, licking and teasing her nipple with his tongue. His hands held her hips as she drew her skirt up over them and eased her underwear down. She unfastened his trousers, her fingers trembling, and lifted her body, moving her hands to grip the flesh of his back. He pulled her down on to his lap and she cried out, the exquisite joy of it echoing in the stillness of the night, and slowly, their moving shadows merged as one against the flickering light of the candles.

When it was over he held her and she laid her head on his shoulder, her breathing heavy and her heart pounding in her chest. The skin on the back of her neck was damp and he stroked it with his fingertips. They stayed like that for some time.

Finally he moved, and looked up.

'We've steamed the windows up,' he said. He sensed her smile. 'And I think we'd better go in, before I freeze my bollocks off.'

Tilting her head up, Livvy laughed and kissed his cheek; it was the first time he'd heard her laugh since she had come home. She lifted her hips and moved off him, standing to sort herself out. Straightening her clothes, she faced him.

'Fraser, I don't know . . .'

He cut her short by putting his fingers up to her lips.

'Don't say anything,' he said, afraid of what it was she wanted to tell him. 'Not yet.'

She nodded. How could she explain? She was confused, hardly knew what she was feeling, except that she needed to be loved, needed the warmth of it, the security of being wanted. She went out first and waited while he blew the candles out and followed her, closing the door behind them.

'You don't mind?'

He couldn't see her face now in the darkness and he didn't really know what it was he was supposed to mind.

'No,' he answered, 'I guess not.' He didn't want to ask, he was afraid to. He had waited too long for this moment; he had wanted her almost without respite ever since that day she had left him at Oxford. It was his own fault. He hadn't had the courage to go after her and he'd had no idea of what he'd lost until she'd gone. He reached for her hand and held it tight, tucking it down into his pocket with his own. Gone to James, he thought angrily, and wasted all those years. He glanced up towards the lights from the house, forced the past from his mind and together they made their way silently back home.

Peter called out from the hallway, keeping his voice low so as not to wake Livvy. Moira was putting the last few items into the basket she had prepared, and she went through, still holding a carton of milk. Fraser could hear the low murmur of their voices. Minutes later she was back.

'Peter wants to get away,' she said. 'He wants to give one or two of them the run around.' She was wearing a pair of Livvy's leggings and a long sweater, and with her hair tied up she could easily pass for her daughter through the tinted windows of the Daimler. She smiled. 'I'm not sure they're going to fall for it.'

Fraser smiled back. 'It's worth a try.'

'Yes, I suppose it is.' She glanced at the window, at the ominous presence of the press at the end of the drive. The

Old Rectory was set back off the road, protected by a long gated drive and several acres of tree-lined gardens. At least the house was safe from prying eyes, she thought, until they started scaling the coach house, that was, with zoom lenses on their cameras. Moira placed the milk with the other things in the picnic hamper. 'I think that's everything,' she said. 'You'll ring us, will you?'

Peter came into the kitchen. 'Yes, let us know that everything's all right, won't you?'

'Of course, as soon as we get there.'

Peter looked briefly at Fraser with something near doubt and then picked up his briefcase. Moira walked into the hall to put on Livvy's velvet floppy hat, one of her trademarks, and a pair of Raybans. She came back, kissed Fraser on the cheek and Peter said, 'You know the back route and which . . .?'

'You've been through it twice already,' Moira interrupted. 'Come on, Peter, let's go!' She picked up the black Armani rucksack, slung it over her shoulder and made for the front door. Peter and Fraser followed.

'I'd stay out of sight, so they think that only Moira's left here.'

Fraser nodded and stepped back as Peter opened the front door. 'Bye,' he said. 'And good luck!'

Peter nodded and went out after Moira. Fraser heard the car doors slam and walked back into the kitchen. He picked up the telephone and began to dial his office. Now that he had everything in place for the next few days, he had to tell the paper that he wouldn't be in.

Moira fastened her seat belt and waited for Peter to start the engine. She was digging in the rucksack for a tissue.

'Moira, I'm really not sure about this, you know. I can't help feeling that we should be staying and thinking about Livvy's defence. We need to get organised . . .'

Moira touched his arm. 'Peter, Livvy needs some space, a little time to get over the shock of the past few days. She needs some rest, to get her thoughts together.'

'But what about Fraser? I worry about him getting involved.'

'He's already involved,' Moira said. 'My guess is he's been involved for a very long time.'

Peter looked at her for a moment. 'Maybe they should stay here,' he offered, 'where we can be in touch if anything goes wrong.'

Moira nodded towards the end of the drive where a small crowd of press waited. 'I don't think so. Come on, let's get going. To the flat to put them off the trail and then to the bank.'

Peter finally started the engine. 'OK, but I only hope we're doing the right thing.' He gently eased the car into gear.

'So do I,' Moira replied and briefly they both smiled.

Livvy woke up to silence and the familiar safety of her own room; she opened her eyes and felt the relief flood through her. Climbing out of bed, she pulled on her dressing gown and then quickly glanced in the mirror before going down. She brushed the hair off her face with her hand, pinched her cheeks to put some colour in them and unfastened the top button of her nightdress. Foolish, she knew, but Fraser would already be up and about.

Padding down the stairs barefoot, she crossed the stone floor of the hall and entered the kitchen, the wonderful aroma of fresh coffee hitting her as she opened the door. Fraser had his back to her and was on the phone.

'OK, Gordon, if that's what you think. Can we have a header on the main page for tomorrow's follow-up, then? Something eye-catching, maybe a small colour print? If it's that good, let's sell it hard . . .' He looked up as he heard the door open and saw Livvy. Just her presence in the room excited him. He stopped, watched her walk across to the coffee and then cleared his throat. 'Listen, Gordon, can I call you back, in about five minutes? . . . Great. Speak to you then.' He hung up and waited for Livvy to turn. There was something about her, in her half-awake, slept-in state that made him hard. She looked round at the silence.

'You didn't have to hang up on my account.' She smiled. 'I won't give away the trade secrets of the *Aberdeen Angus Press*!' But she was pleased that he had. 'D'you want some coffee?'

'Hmmm, please.' Fraser stood and went to the cupboard for two cups. He watched Livvy as she walked to the window, still holding the coffee pot, and looked out at the front garden. She saw several figures in the distance, gathered by the front gate.

'Oh no . . .!' She started and some of the scalding liquid spilled on to her hand. 'Ouch!' Hurriedly backing away from the window, she dropped the pot down on to the table, holding her burned hand. Fraser was by her side in seconds. 'Ouch! Fraser? What the hell's going on?' He took her arm and led her to the sink, turning on the cold tap and holding her hand under the running water.

'I meant to tell you,' he said, looking at the red inflamed skin. 'Stay away from the windows, the press are everywhere.'

'Oh no!' Livvy yanked her hand away and slumped back against the unit, hugging her arms about her. 'Oh God, that's all I need!'

Fraser gently took her arm again and inspected the minor scald on her hand. 'I've got it under control, don't worry.' He held her hand and resisted the temptation to put it to his lips and kiss the palm. 'Does Moira have any Burneeze in the kitchen?'

Livvy shrugged, amazed at how gentle Fraser was, for someone so large and powerful. 'It's all right, honestly.' She glanced up at his face, half smiling. 'Just kiss it better.'

He flushed suddenly, thinking that she must have read his mind, his face turning a dark red, and Livvy burst out laughing.

'Well, thank goodness you can still laugh,' he said gruffly, dropping her hand. He was embarrassed and moved away.

'So what do you have under control?' Livvy asked, realising that she'd been insensitive. She had moved further into the kitchen, away from the window, and she hovered nervously, keeping one eye on the scene outside.

Fraser picked up the pot and poured the coffee, adding milk and sugar. He handed one to Livvy and told her to sit down at the table while he went to fetch his map. 'They can't see you if you sit round the side,' he said. 'Moira and I tested it early this morning.'

Livvy did as he said and waited for him to return. She heard the phone ring, moved to answer it and then realised that she couldn't. She waited for the answerphone, listening as the smooth voice of one of the tabloid editors came on to the tape. He wanted to do an exclusive, fee negotiable, he said. Livvy scoffed derisively and stuck her fingers in her ears.

'It's all right, you can take your hands away now.' Fraser had come back in, smiling. 'The nasty man's gone.'

Livvy pulled a face at him but she was suddenly near to tears and he saw that instantly. 'Where've Mum and Peter gone, anyway?' she said, trying to keep her voice even. Fraser came round to her side of the table and sat down next to her. He opened the road atlas at the page for Sussex and Livvy saw that he'd marked their village.

'Moira and Peter are all part of the plan,' he said. 'That's if you agree to it.' And quickly he went on to explain what he had spent the early hours of the morning thinking up.

Livvy had showered, dressed and thrown some things into a rucksack; all in fifteen minutes, all behind the drawn curtains of her bedroom. Fraser had told her it was essential that she wasn't seen from any of the windows.

She went downstairs to find Fraser ready to leave. He had the small leather holdall that Carol from the office had packed for him and the hamper that Moira had prepared. He looked up and smiled.

'Ready?'

Livvy nodded.

The Range Rover was already at the back of the house; Peter had driven it round, over the lawn, several hours earlier and it was hidden from view by a screen of trees. Fraser looked out, saw that the coast was clear and Livvy darted from the back door into the car, sinking down low into the seat, the top of her head barely visible. Fraser locked up the house, dumped the two bags and the hamper into the boot and hurriedly climbed into the car, started the engine and shifted the gears. He drove down Peter's perfectly manicured sloping lawn, through the gate at the end between the trees and into the field, the suspension of the car bouncing easily over the uneven, muddy land surface. They travelled as fast as they could across the field, mud flying, avoiding the sheep, and finally hit down on to the muddy track that led off The Old Rectory's land and on to the farm road. The suspension of the Range Rover righted itself and Fraser accelerated off. He glanced in his mirror, hoped that Peter wouldn't come home to find a lawn demolished by sheep and swung round the bend of the winding lane and out on to the main road. There was nothing in front of them and nothing behind. Livvy sat up, smiled tentatively and they were on their way.

From the trees at the bottom of the lawn emerged a wet, tired, young, trainee journalist with a mobile phone. He dialled his boss round the front of the house and told him that a Range Rover had just left The Old Rectory in a bit of a hurry. The reporter out front dashed back to his car, looked at the map and jumped in, starting the engine. He roared off. It wouldn't take him long to meet up with the road that led round the back of Heston Wye Village, not if he really put his foot down and hacked it all the way.

Fraser had just leaned forward to adjust the radio on to a station with no news when, sitting straight again, he glanced in his mirror and saw a red Cavalier behind him, some distance but keeping pace, with only one driver in it.

'Uh oh,' he muttered under his breath and Livvy looked round.

'Is that . . .?'

'Could be . . . Livvy, have a look at the map, will you? You know the area better than me, you navigate, I'll drive.' He kept one eye on the car behind. 'Better to be safe than sorry.'

'OK . . .' Livvy found the road they were on and followed it with her finger. 'Er . . . turn left . . . here!' She pointed to a small lane and Fraser yanked the steering wheel, hardly slowing, and turned into the lane, his tyres screeching on the wet tarmac.

'Bloody hell!' Livvy gripped her seat and the map went flying. 'Was that really . . .'

'He's still with us!'

'Oh no!' She bent, retrieved the map and focused her attention on the area. Fraser had picked up speed.

'Right . . . In about half a mile there's another left turn, take that and then first right . . .' She held the map firmly, ready this time. Fraser crashed down through the gears and swung round the corner, then again, the car very nearly skidding across into a hedge. He straightened and accelerated.

'Now . . . Great! Sharp right, then stop, reverse and turn down a mud track. There's a barn there, I remember it from our cycle trips.'

'OK.' Fraser was watching his mirror. 'Shit!' He saw a flash of red in the distance. 'Here goes . . .'

Speeding along, he swerved into the turning, screeched to a stop, slammed the Range Rover into reverse and spun round. Then accelerating off, the mud and water spray flying, he drove along the track towards a barn at the top of the slope. The great structure was open and empty. He drove straight in and pulled on the handbrake. Jumping down from the car, he ran to the doors of the barn and looked down at the main road. 'There's the bastard!' he shouted to Livvy. The red Cavalier carried on along the road they had turned off, for miles into the distance, round a bend and then disappeared from sight. He ran back to the car.

'OK. Back the way we came, yes?'

Livvy smiled. 'Yes.'

Fraser climbed in, started the engine and meshed the gears, accelerating off, still in rally mode.

Livvy, gripping the seat once again, looked across at him and said, 'Why do I get the feeling you're enjoying this?'

Fraser suddenly grinned. 'I have no idea,' he answered, and handled the car round the bend in true Nigel Mansell style.

It was a long drive. They stayed on the A roads, avoiding the motorways for fear of being spotted, and wound their way along through the counties towards Devon. They didn't talk much, there didn't seem any need, but it was a comfortable silence, companionable and easy. Livvy slept for an hour or so, her coat pulled around her and her legs tucked up on the seat, but she woke suddenly, tense and afraid, knowing that she was on the run and scared by that fact.

They stopped for lunch, parked in a picnic area, and ate the food in the car. Livvy didn't want to go to a pub – she didn't want to be recognised and stared at – so they opened the hatchback, put a rug across the boot and sat there, looking out at the cold sky and drinking hot coffee from a thermos.

By three o'clock, they reached Lustleigh on the edge of Dartmoor and followed the winding lane through the centre of the village and up a steep hill where the hedgerows were nine feet tall and the road narrowed to the width of a single car. Finally Fraser pulled into a drive, a single track that wound up through some woodland to a long, low house, only just visible in the distance. Livvy climbed out to close the gate after them. She stood for a moment, looking down over the valley that spread out into Dartmoor, miles and miles of perfect green pockets of land, gently sloping and cut by immaculate hedges and stone walls. It was so fabulously lush that it looked like a picture, not real at all.

'This place is beautiful,' she said, clambering back into the car.

'I know.' Fraser looked at her face. She was smiling for the first time since they'd left Sussex. 'Come on, I can't wait for you to see the house.' She slammed the door shut and they drove on, under the green covering of the trees and out into a clearing where the rhododendron bushes began the gardens that led up to the house.

Fraser parked in the cobbled courtyard in front of the old, white cob building and switched off the engine; Widcombe House was exactly as he remembered it. He glanced again at Livvy's face and knew that she instantly loved it as much as he did.

'It belongs to my uncle; my mother's brother,' he said. 'He lives in France for part of the year and comes back here for the summer.' Fraser opened the car door and climbed down from the Range Rover, stretching his back. 'I came here for a while after my father died, in the summer before Oxford. Sim wasn't here then, he'd gone off to Peru and I had the place to myself.' He walked forward, still looking up at the house. 'It's a good place to think,' he said over his shoulder. It was the place where he had finally come to terms with his inheritance, the *Angus Aberdeen Press*, and the fact that he would never be a barrister, that when he finished his degree he would have to return to Scotland to run the paper. He turned and smiled, to rid himself of the memory of his father's death. 'There's not much else to do here!'

Livvy came to stand beside him. 'Thanks,' she said. 'For bringing me here.'

Fraser shrugged and took her hand. 'Mrs Westly should've been in this morning. I rang her and told her we were coming down.' He led Livvy up to the front door and bent to a huge old terracotta pot filled with winter flowering jasmine. He felt round the back of it and pulled out a key. 'Ah-ha!'

Livvy smiled and waited for him to open the door. Then she walked into the house and straight away felt the comfort and warmth of it, the sense of safety. She stood in the centre of the hallway, saw the tall vase of winter flowering jasmine placed on the table for their arrival and suddenly put her hands up to her face to cover the fact that she was crying. It was all so beautiful, so normal and it made her so acutely aware of what she might have to lose.

'Hey, Livvy!'

Fraser moved towards her and put his arms around her. He hugged her close. The sheer bulk of him was comforting, a weight to lean against, and she thought briefly how physical he was, how easy it was to touch him. A fleeting sensation of the previous night came back to her and she blushed, moving away from him towards the kitchen, suddenly embarrassed.

'Shall I make some tea?' she asked, wiping her face on the hem of her sweatshirt. It was a childish gesture and it made Fraser smile.

'Yes, tea,' he said, 'that would be nice, and I'll bring in the set of Vuitton luggage!'

Livvy carried on to the kitchen and Fraser stood where he was for a moment just watching her. Then he went out to the car to fetch the rucksack, his holdall and the hamper with Moira's food in.

Later that day, when they were settled and the night had begun to descend over the valley, Fraser and Livvy walked out of the house and down through the gardens at the back towards the open land of the valley. The light was disappearing, everything seemed to be tinted by a deepening purple sky and the greens across the landscape had become intense, vivid in colour, with odd patches of swirling, rising mist from the river.

Fraser and Livvy tramped for miles. As they walked, the night came down completely and engulfed them in darkness, the smell of wood smoke filled the air and the lights from the village across the valley could be seen above the branches of the trees, reflected in the now cloudless sky. They made it to the other side of the river and stopped in the Black Cow for a drink, sitting by the fire in an almost empty pub, sipping thick, dark cider and talking about the gulf of time that had stretched between them, filling in on the years apart, as lovers do.

Livvy hardly spoke about James. She talked about her career, admitting to Fraser and herself for the first time that maybe she had pushed too hard, had thought too little about the other aspects of her life, and Fraser told Livvy about his paper, the *Aberdeen Angus Press*, how it had dominated his life from the moment he had inherited it, all through his time at Oxford, even though someone else ran it for three years. He told her how he had built it from the ailing local rag that his father left him into one of the biggest local circulations in the UK. She asked him about his women and he laughingly shrugged the question off. He had had his fair share – he was an attractive man, powerful and dynamic – but he couldn't tell her that no one had ever been the same for him after he had loved Livvy Davis, nearly ten years earlier. That would have sounded unbelievable, almost as unbelievable as it felt. He didn't ask her about James though; he didn't want to know.

When they left the pub it was late and they took the road way back to Lustleigh, not touching but bumping every now and then as people do when they walk too close. Approaching the house, they saw the front porch light shining out in the darkness and hurried towards it, under the rustling branches of the trees; the shape of the moon, a fraction bigger than the night before, just visible between the gaps in the trees.

Fraser opened the front door on reaching the house and Livvy went ahead of him, her cheeks flushing at the sudden warmth of the hallway. She pulled off her coat, threw her scarf down on the chair and released her hair from its woolly hat. She shook it free and turned, to find Fraser staring at her again. She looked away and moved towards the stairs.

'I think I'll go up,' she said. She had not acknowledged the way she felt; she had tried to stop it, worried by it, confused by the overwhelming desire she had for him on top of all the other crowding emotions. 'I'm tired,' she added lamely. She just couldn't cope with any more, she told herself.

'OK.' Fraser unfastened his Barbour as she turned and ascended the stairs. He didn't watch her go, but took his coat off, hung it up and went through to the kitchen to make himself a cup of tea. He had brought Livvy to Widcombe House to help her, to protect her; the last thing he wanted to do was confuse her, or himself for that matter.

Twenty minutes later, he finished his tea and left the cup in the sink. Switching off all the lights downstairs, he made his way up to the bathroom, his footsteps hardly making a sound, and undressed by the large, white old-fashioned sink, filling the bowl with hot water. He stood naked to wash, too tired to be bothered to take a bath. He splashed his upper body with hot water, lathered on some soap and then sluiced himself clean. He reached, eyes closed, for the towel on the hot rail, put it up to his face and rubbed hard at his skin. The next moment the door opened.

Livvy had drifted off to sleep the moment she laid her head down, leaving the light on and then woke twenty minutes later with a start. She was thirsty, so she climbed out of bed to get a glass of water. She fumbled her way wearily to the door, across the landing and, only half-awake, opened the bathroom door and walked straight in, her eyes suddenly blinded by the light. She blinked several times, adjusted her vision and saw Fraser as he dropped the towel and stared at her in surprise.

'Oh, I'm sorry . . . I . . . ' She gaped at him, unable to stop herself, her eyes travelling the length of his lean, strong body, powerful and athletic, the hard line of muscle running up from his thigh to a ridge at his abdomen and then his chest. She took a pace back and crashed painfully into the door handle, still staring at him. 'Ouch, damn . . .!'

He moved towards her. 'Are you . . .?'

'Yes!' she yelped. 'Fine.' Her own body had responded, it was pulsing and she knew her cheeks blazed. She put her hand behind her, unable to move her gaze, and struggled with the handle. She couldn't get it open and she began to panic. The urge to run was overwhelming.

'Livvy.' Fraser stepped forward and put both his hands either side of her shoulders, resting them on the door. She pressed herself back but she could see the movement of her chest as her breath tightened. He was inches away and she stared over his shoulder at the painted yellow wall above the sink. Very slowly he removed one hand and undid the three buttons on her nightshirt with his fingers. He moved the cotton apart and looked down at her breasts, then placed his hand back on the wall. He moved half an inch closer so that the hard pink tips of her nipples just brushed the skin on his chest. She bit her lip.

'Fraser, I don't know why I'm doing this . . .' Her voice broke as the words came out. She looked down and saw how hard he was. 'I . . . I . . . don't know where it's all going to end.'

'Do you need to?'

As he spoke, the rise and fall of his chest touched her nipples and her legs had started to feel weak. She was aching, desperate to pull him against her, but she wouldn't let herself.

'Do you need to know that?' he asked again.

'I . . .' She moved her hand up to his chest and traced the outline of the muscle with her finger. 'No, I don't,' she said at last and he bent his head, kissed her mouth and slipped his hands under her bottom, lifting her up and over his arms. He kept his mouth over hers, kissing her as he carried her out of the bathroom across to his bedroom, to the huge old carved pine bed where he laid her down, pushing the shirt off her shoulders and looking down at her body for several moments before opening her legs, pulling her thighs up high around his back and moving over her. She closed her eyes and pressed her hips towards him, crying out when she felt him and opening her eyes again to look at his face, to watch the pleasure in it and to search for the love that she knew instinctively was there.

Chapter Nineteen

It was seven a.m. and Fraser carefully pulled the sheets back, eased his legs over the side of the bed and stood up. He padded quietly to the door, opened it and stepped outside on to the landing, glancing behind him at Livvy, still sleeping. Once there, he took the clothes he had left hanging over the banister the night before and hurriedly dressed. He descended the stairs, jumping over the ones he knew creaked, unlocked the front door and eased it open. He stepped out into the dull early morning and headed up the drive towards the village. He had to phone Peter.

As he walked, Fraser looked up through the trees at the sky and thought about the past two days with Livvy, two days that, whatever happened, would be etched forever in his memory. He hadn't thought about the risks, about the fact that he might lose Livvy, that great tragedy might await her. He had simply loved her, in much the same way as he had done years earlier, surrounding her in that love, leaving no room for any other thought; and he'd watched the lines of sadness disappear from her face, he'd watched a peace settle over her and he'd known, right from the first time, that James didn't love her, not the way he did.

Of course being at Widcombe helped. There was no telephone, no television; his uncle Simcox had an aversion to modern technology. There was an old Roberts radio, its tuning broken and locked into Radio Three, and they'd not been near the village to buy a newspaper. She'll have enough of that when we go back, Fraser had argued to himself, knowing how hard he was trying to protect her, she doesn't need it now. But he'd often found Livvy sitting at the window, looking out at the wide open landscape and the unending expanse of sky overhead and he realised that even though he had insulated her from what was happening for a while, he couldn't make it go away. She was scared. He eased her fear but he knew it was there. She was really scared.

Reaching the phone box, Fraser dug in his pocket for the bag of change he kept for these calls and swung open the heavy door. He left it open, holding it with his foot, and dialled The Old Rectory, a number he now knew by heart, and waited for someone to answer. He didn't know why, but this morning he was dreading speaking to Peter.

'Hello, Peter?'

'Ah, Fraser! How are you? How's Livvy?'

'Fine. I'm fine and Livvy's looking a lot better. I reckon it'll be a few more . . .'

Peter cut him short. 'We had a call from James last night, Fraser,' he said. 'He's on his way home. He'll be arriving at Heathrow this morning and he's coming straight down to The Old Rectory. He wants to see Livvy and Moira and I really think that she should come back today. He's an important figure in the case, Fraser and . . .'

'Yes, I know.' Fraser didn't need any explanations. 'Look, don't worry, I'll go back and wake Livvy now and we'll make a start in about an hour or so.'

'Good, thank you, Fraser.' Fraser could hear the relief in Peter's voice. 'James should be with us by midday.'

'Right. We'll see you later, then.' The money was running out on the call. 'It'll probably take about three, three and a half hours. We'll be home around the same time as James.' There was only ten pence left. 'See you.' Fraser hung up as the panel flashed and slammed the receiver back in its cradle. 'Shit!' he said loudly to the empty phone box. He walked out, let the door bang shut behind him and took a long kick at a large stone lying in the road. There was nothing he could do about it. He'd been waiting for James to come back and he'd always known they only had a few days. That didn't make it any easier, though. The thought that what they had just shared might be over was too painful to think about. So he didn't; he kicked the stone up the road as he made his way back through the village towards the house and made up a whole sequence of possible events that he knew in his heart would never happen. He just needed something to hang on to, something to get him through the next few hours.

When he got back to the house he made some tea, laid a tray with the pot, two cups and some orange juice and carried it upstairs to the bedroom. He entered, saw that Livvy was asleep and placed it on the floor, crossing silently to the bed. He sat down, brushed a strand of hair off her face and looked at her for some time before gently touching her shoulder to wake her.

'Livvy.' He saw her eyelids flutter. 'Livvy, wake up.' She opened her eyes and stared blankly at the wall for a moment. Then she turned and looked up at Fraser, a smile hovering on her lips. She reached one arm out from under the covers and hooked it round his neck, pulling him gently forward.

'Hmmm. That's not a very nice good morning,' she whispered, her warm breath caressing his neck. 'Why don't you get in?'

But Fraser gently eased away from her, taking her arm and placing it back on the bed. He looked away.

'Livvy, we have to go back to Sussex today,' he said quietly. 'James is on his way home.'

Silence.

Not daring to look back at her, he waited for a few moments and then stood, unsure of what to do with himself. 'I've made some tea,' he said hopelessly.

Livvy sat up. She hugged her knees and rested her chin on them, staring blankly out of the window. Of course they had to go back to Sussex, she had been expecting it, waiting for it. So why did it come as such a shock? She stayed as she was for some time, feeling numb, and a heavy silence hung between them. After some time, Fraser spoke and she looked across at him, having almost forgotten he was in the room.

'I'll leave you to get dressed then,' he said.

She nodded. The stupidity of this observance of propriety, after such intense and abandoned love, crossed her mind for a second, but she let it go. He moved towards the door and she felt his misery but was unable to say anything to comfort him. Just the mention of James's name had shattered everything. It had brought the real world back into their lives and Livvy knew that what had happened between them would struggle to survive outside the idyllic setting of Widcombe House.

They were up and packed within an hour. They ate the last of the food in the hamper, made a thermos of tea and, just before eight, Fraser took the bags out to the car and stowed them in the boot. He stood, looking at the view and wondering if he would ever be as happy there again. Livvy came out of the house as he turned and slammed the door behind her, taking the key and placing it under the terracotta pot by the door. She stood straight and smiled sadly at the ritual.

'You could always come back to Scotland with me,' Fraser said.

She looked at him. She wanted to agree, to lessen the pain of leaving. 'Yes,' she answered, 'I could.' Then she joined him by the car and took his hand, kissing the palm of it briefly as she too looked out at the amazing Dartmoor view for the last time. 'Come on,' she said, a moment later, 'we should go.' And dropping his hand, she opened the car door and climbed up into the Range Rover.

Moira listened to the smooth tone of James's carefully cultivated voice as she made the coffee and he sat at the table, talking about himself, about the trip to Brazil and how frantic it all was for him. He seemed to be distancing himself from Livvy and if she hadn't already known it, Moira would never have guessed that they were actually there together.

Moira didn't like James, she never had. He was charming, impeccably handsome, witty, and clever but somehow it didn't click with her, she just didn't buy it. There was something undeniably cool about him, something insincere that she wasn't able to pin down. Livvy said it was Moira, that she was an involuntary snob, but Moira knew it wasn't that. She never told Livvy that she worried because she didn't think James loved her daughter enough, or even at all. Moira didn't say much really; she believed that Livvy had to get on with her own life. Only now she thought that maybe she *should* have said something.

'Moira?'

She turned, realising that she had missed most of the last few minutes of James's conversation.

'I'm sorry, what was that?' She pushed the plunger down in the cafetière and brought it over to the table.

'Where did you say that Livvy had gone?'

'I didn't.' She reached for the milk jug. 'Milk? Sugar?'

'But she went with Fraser Stewart?'

Moira shrugged, looking vague; she had been a good actress in her day. 'I think so, I'm not really sure. I left it all to Peter, I was too upset.'

'Oh, yes, of course.'

There was something in James's voice, something wary. He didn't like Fraser, she guessed – perhaps it was jealousy? She poured two mugs of coffee, passed one to James and walked out into the hall to call Peter. As she stood there, she heard the scrunch of tyres on the gravel drive and hurried to the front door.

'Peter? I think they're back!' she shouted in the direction of his study. She pulled open the door and stood in the porch as Fraser parked the Range Rover and switched off the engine. She watched as the two of them sat together silently in the car for a minute and then Livvy climbed out.

'Hello.'

'Livvy.' Moira moved forward and hugged her daughter. 'How are you?' Moira stood back and surveyed her. Livvy looked better, her face was less strained and her eyes were clearer, less troubled. Livvy glanced over her shoulder at Fraser and he opened the car door to climb out. He smiled at her and Moira saw quite clearly the brightness in her daughter's eyes as she smiled back. Then all of a sudden it died, just vanished, as she looked towards the house and saw that James had come out to greet her.

'Hello, James.' She edged awkwardly into his embrace and he held her, but not warmly or closely. He kissed her forehead and stroked her hair, then he stepped back and his attention was diverted to Fraser. Well, it's definitely not jealousy, Moira thought, watching the scene; it was more a distinct uneasiness. He moved aside and put his arm about Livvy's shoulder, walking her across to Fraser. He held out his hand.

'Thank you for looking after Livvy. I don't know what we would have done without you.'

Fraser shook his hand briefly and nodded. He said nothing. He wasn't the type of man to be pleasant to someone he didn't like, just for the sake of it.

Peter came out at that point and the uncomfortable tension was broken. He hugged Livvy but as usual she stood passively and didn't return the affection.

'Come on inside,' he said. 'Let's have a drink.' He smiled at Fraser. 'I should think you could do with one, couldn't you?'

'Yes, I could,' Fraser answered, visibly relaxing, and Moira took his arm and led him into the house.

In the kitchen, Peter sat at the table with Moira and Fraser while James stared out of the window, oblivious to the conversation around him. He was desperately trying to work out what to do next. He needed to get Livvy back to London, he thought, away from the eagle eye of Stewart and into a position where he could watch her every move. James had to protect himself and the best way to do that, he had decided, was to stay as close to what was happening as possible. He needed Livvy under control so that he could stay one step ahead. If she went down, he was going to make damn sure there was no way she could take him with her.

Livvy was curled up on the window seat, her knees tucked under her, her head resting against the glass and her face blank. James stood and walked across to her.

'Listen, Livvy, I've been thinking,' he said, stopping directly in front of her. 'You really must come back with me. I accept that you needed a rest, but now you've got to get yourself together and start your defence. It's about time we started to get things sorted.' He glanced briefly at Fraser and Livvy felt a stab of guilt. He went on. 'You have to speak to Jacobs, Livvy, get things moving. I'm sure Peter will agree with me.'

Peter nodded.

'We need to head back to London today. It's hard, but that's the truth of it. You can't just sit around hoping that this is going to go away.' Again there was the briefest of glances at Fraser which made Livvy feel foolish for ever having agreed to go to Lustleigh. 'It isn't. It needs action.' He sat down next to her and took her hand. 'Livvy, you've got to face up to things, go back to work and try to carry on as normal. Hiding like a fugitive is only going to fuel specula-tion.' He dropped her hand and stood up again, preferring this position of advantage. 'Look, there's a crowd of press out there waiting for you to make a statement. They've writ-ten what they want to up until now but if you give an interview, say what really happened, you could gain a good deal of public sympathy and that's essential in a case like this.' He turned to Peter. 'Isn't that right?'

'Yes and no. It's not supposed to be, but juries do read newspapers.'

'Right!' Turning back, James caught a look between Livvy and Fraser and instantly changed tack. He squatted down in front of Livvy and, taking both her hands in his own, he began to speak softly, persuasively. 'Livvy, let's go home, eh? Let's just try and forget this and get on with our lives, at least for the time being, until the magistrate's hearing. I want to take you home, babe.' He kissed her hand and smiled at her and eventually she smiled back. James was right; she had never really entertained the idea of going to Scotland, it wouldn't have worked. He pulled her forward and hugged her. 'Why don't you go and change and we'll make tracks.'

Livvy nodded. She uncurled her long legs and stood stiffly. On the way past her mother she touched Moira's shoulder and Moira patted her hand. She heard her mother ask James if they wouldn't stay for lunch and James mumble an excuse as she made her way up the stairs but the rest of the conversation was inaudible. In her bedroom, she looked through the small collection of clothes she kept at home and then down at her jeans and baggy old cardigan. Funny how Fraser never commented on her clothes, she thought, taking out a jacket and a cashmere sweater on its padded hanger – things like that just didn't seem to bother him.

Showered and changed, Livvy pulled the strings on her toiletries bag. Someone knocked on the door and she turned and called out, then began to brush her hair.

Fraser walked into the room.

'Oh, hi.' She dropped the brush on to the bed.

He stood awkwardly by the door. 'Hi. I came to say good-bye. Peter just rang the airport and there's a plane leaving in an hour. He's going to drive me to Gatwick.'

'I see.' Livvy didn't know what to say. She was too confused to recognise the sinking feeling in her heart and Fraser wasn't going to push her. She had always said she was in love with James, he was under no illusions there. He might not trust James but he knew there was nothing more that he could do for Livvy, not until she asked him. And, despite hurting, he had already decided to try and make light of it all.

'I wondered if I might have my handkerchief back?' he asked, smiling. 'The one I lent you in the summer house.'

Livvy blushed but she couldn't help smiling back. 'Yes, it's . . .' She bent to rummage in her rucksack. 'Oh!' Standing straight, she went to her drawer and looked in there. 'I don't seem to be able to find it.' She turned towards him. 'I'm sorry, I must have lost it . . . in the er . . . heat of the moment.' And suddenly they both burst out laughing.

A minute or so later, they suddenly became serious and Livvy looked across at him. 'I'm sorry.' Unable to meet his penetrating gaze, she hung her head.

Crossing to her, he tilted her chin up and kissed her gently on the lips. 'Hey!' He shrugged and attempted to smile. 'For what?' Then he moved away and winked at her before turning and walking back to the door.

He stopped there, as if wanting to say something else, but thought better of it and stepped out on to the landing without another word. Livvy stood and listened to his footsteps down the stairs and then sat down on the bed and put her head in her hands.

Minutes later, the front door slammed, the Range Rover started and he was gone. James called up the stairs to her that they really ought to leave.

*

Fraser checked in fifteen minutes before the flight and, carrying his holdall as hand baggage, went straight through security to the boarding gate. He showed his card to the ground crew and took a seat with the other passengers waiting to go on to the plane. He opened out his paper and, without taking in a word of it, began to read.

Beth Broden sat across the small lounge from Fraser and took out her glasses to have a closer look at him. She slipped them on and peered at him, recognising him instantly and then smiling at her good fortune. Putting the glasses back in their case, she fluffed up her short, neat brown bob, wet her lips with a flick of her tongue and stood up, smoothing her skirt down over her high, plump hips. She walked across to Fraser.

'Hello, Fraser Stewart?'

Fraser lowered his paper and looked up at the owner of the soft Scottish accent. He saw a round, attractive face, lightly touched with make-up, shiny brown hair and a warm smile. He automatically smiled back.

'Hello. I'm sorry, I must have forgotten your name . . .'

'No, you haven't, we've never met.' She laughed lightly. 'You'll know me, though, I think. My name's Beth Broden.'

Fraser sat up straight. 'Yes, I do know you! Doctor Broden. I remember your evidence on the two IMACO cases.'

She nodded. 'Still speaking to me, then?'

He laughed. 'I didn't agree with it but . . . I do find plane journeys pretty boring!' He moved his holdall. 'Here, sit down.'

Beth Broden put her case on the floor and took the seat offered. She inched her skirt up to show her nice legs but Fraser didn't notice. When Dorsey had mentioned that it might be a good idea to get to know Fraser Stewart she had tactfully ignored the suggestion, banked her cheque and forgotten all about it. Now she realised she might have made a mistake. Stewart was far more attractive than his picture and Beth Broden had never missed a good opportunity to mix business with pleasure. She turned to him and said, 'The plane doesn't look terribly full, does it?'

Fraser glanced round the lounge. 'No, not at all.' And right on cue he asked, 'Where are you sitting, by the way?'

Beth smiled. 'I'm not sure, but I'm certain I could change seats if I wanted to.'

Chapter Twenty

Livvy and James had been back in London for three days but Livvy had not returned to work and carried on with her life as normal as James said she should; she just couldn't face it. She was plagued by calls from the press, and from all sorts of cranks who'd somehow managed to get her number and rang leaving odd and abusive messages on the answerphone. She had to dodge the photographers when she ventured outside and ignore angry stares from the other residents in the block, fed up with the constant parade of people outside the main door. And she had phoned the office every day to speak to Bill about the new series of programmes, each time to be told by the switchboard that he was out and could she call back. She had no idea what was happening on the Duce interview. Roger Hardman was unavailable, off on location, so his assistant said, and she just didn't have the heart to call round the rest of the film crew to find out what was going on.

So, apart from meeting with David Jacobs and Seb Petrie, her barrister, she did nothing but sit inside the flat and stare out of the huge bank of windows at the health club across the square and envy the people whose lives were simple enough to be able to go out in the evening to the gym.

By the fourth day, Livvy had had enough. She called the office early that morning, knowing damn well that Bill would be at his desk, and was told again that he was out. She slammed the phone down, stormed into the bedroom and started yanking clothes from the wardrobe and flinging them on the bed.

'He can bloody well tell me if something's wrong,' she muttered under her breath, 'instead of hiding behind the bloody receptionist!'

She pulled several things from the pile, tried them against herself in the mirror, discarded them and tried some others. Ten minutes later she had decided what to wear, unconsciously dressing for battle in a very fitted, long black skirt, a hip-length tailored red waistcoat, cream silk shirt and her black swirl coat with the huge fake fur collar. She strode into the bathroom, turned the shower on full pelt and stripped off her dressing gown, stepping under the steaming jet of water. She was filled with confidence that she was about to restart her life.

An hour and twenty minutes later, her confidence began to slip as she entered the reception of City Television, its black and chrome interior polished to a reflective gleam, and saw the security man Ron look up, surprised, then look down at his paper again until she had crossed to the desk.

'Morning, Ron,' she said brightly. 'How are you?'

'Fine.' He picked up the telephone, flicked down a switch on the panel and finally looked at her. 'I'll tell them up at *Take Five* that you're here,' he said.

'Oh.' Livvy hadn't expected this; it was like she didn't

work here any more. She began to feel very uneasy.

'I'll go on up,' she said as Ron hung on the line waiting for someone to answer, 'I think I know my way.' She smiled and Ron reluctantly smiled back.

Innocent until proved guilty, he reminded himself sharply as he watched her climb the stairs, but he couldn't help feeling terribly disappointed in their Livvy nevertheless.

Livvy reached the second floor and stood for a moment to get her breath. She was suddenly nervous and it made her chest feel tight. She took out her compact and glanced at her reflection in the small magnifying mirror, patting a loose strand of hair back into place. She had it swept off her face and twisted up into a chignon at the back, chic and sophisticated with her high cheekbones and the slash of scarlet at her lips. If you have to go, you should go with style, she thought briefly as she folded the mirror and tucked it back inside her bag. Then she scolded herself for her lack of confidence, realising that the sudden spurt of drive that morning had simply vanished. But there was no going back now, so she took a deep breath and swung open the doors of the *Take Five* office suite.

'Ah, Livvy.' Bill stood the moment she walked in, as if he'd been waiting nervously for her, and crossed to the doors. He kissed her lightly on each cheek and led her over to his space. She noticed a sudden quietness in the room and stared ahead, trying to ignore the air of embarrassment that hung over it. They reached his work station.

'Here, sit.' He pulled out a chair. 'Coffee? Tea?'

Livvy slipped off her coat and watched Bill as he fiddled with some papers on his desk, not really clearing any space, simply covering his embarrassment. Her heart sank and the very last of that morning's determination disappeared. She wanted to cry.

'Nothing, thanks,' she said, 'just an explanation.'

Bill slumped down in the chair opposite her and looked depressed. He shook his head and Livvy braced herself for what was coming.

'We're putting together a new series,' he said, 'with Amanda Dunn.'

'Amanda Dunn!' She sat back and stared at him. 'But she's . . .'

'She's got the F-Factor . . .' he interrupted quickly, then he paused. 'And we needed someone quickly. I'm sorry.'

'So this means that I'm officially off the programme?'

He nodded.

'And?'

'And Jake Parsons wants to see you upstairs. He rang down when he heard you were in.'

'Oh.' Livvy stared down at her lap and resisted the temptation to cry. She had had a phenomenally successful career and had never had to face a moment like this one. She dug her nails into the palm of her hand until the tears receded, then she looked up again at Bill and reached for her coat.

'You could have told me earlier,' she said, 'when I rang.'

'No, I couldn't.' Bill avoided her eye. 'I've been arguing myself stupid for you to stay. I didn't want to tell you anything until I was beaten.'

The tears that Livvy had successfully put down rose again in her throat and she swallowed painfully, her eyes filling. 'Thanks,' she mumbled. She stood, pulled her coat on and turned away towards the door. Bill accompanied her across the room and she managed to smile at several of the team on her way out. In the corridor he kissed her.

'Sam will be sorry she missed you.'

Livvy shrugged and Bill put his hands on her shoulders. 'She will, really!' He still held her. 'Look, if you need anything . . .'

Livvy cut him short, 'Yes, I know. Thanks.' She stepped away and pressed the button for the lift. 'Go on! Go back to your desk, there's work to be done.' She smiled and Bill smiled back.

'Bye, Livvy. Good luck.'

She nodded. 'Goodbye, Bill.' She looked up at the panel as he left and put the tip of her finger up to her eye to wipe away the beginnings of a tear. The lift arrived. She stepped inside it and travelled up to the top floor.

'Come!'

Livvy removed her hand and dropped it by her side; she had barely knocked. Turning the handle, she walked into the corner office on the top floor of City Television and strode over to the huge black ash desk in front of the window. She shook hands with Parsons, let her coat fall off her shoulders and sat down, a good expanse of long, sheer black-stockinged thigh exposed by the split in her skirt. She crossed her legs.

'Livvy, I'm very sorry for what's happened,' Parsons said blandly, 'it must be very difficult.'

'Yes, it is,' she answered directly. 'Very.'

He nodded and smoothed the expensive hand-painted silk of his tie. 'Quite.' He leaned forward. 'However, I'm afraid that the wider ramifications of it are already starting to be felt by the company.'

'Really?' Livvy was straining to retain her composure. All

she kept thinking was: For God's sake get on with it! If you're going to sack me, do it quickly.

'Yes. I'm afraid that we've had to replace you on *Take Five*.'

'Yes, I understand that.'

'Then I'm sure you'll understand the decision, albeit a very difficult one, to end your contract with City as from today.'

Livvy was silent. Although she'd been waiting for it, the words still came as a shock. She took a few moments to calm herself and then said, 'What about the Duce programme?'

Parsons shrugged. 'Jeff Ridges is working with Roger Hardman now, editing it. He's changing the slant of the report but we're still using your interview.'

'I see.'

Parsons smoothed his tie again and Livvy took it that the interview was over.

'My contract . . .?'

'Our lawyers have taken care of all the details. There'll be a final payment and a copy of the release clause sent to you within the next day or so.'

'Right.' Livvy stood. She didn't know how she did it, but she shook hands with Parsons, smiled and turned to leave the room. She crossed to the door, her high-heeled black suede shoes leaving a mark in the deep pile of the carpet as she walked, her stride elegant and self-assured. She left without looking back, smiled at the secretary in the outer office and made her way along to the lifts.

Five minutes later she was outside on the street. She hugged her coat in tight around her, whistled loudly for a taxi and climbed inside. She gave her address, sat back in the seat and stared blankly out of the cab window. Within seconds she was crying, the tears streaming down her face, making a mess of her make-up and mingling horribly with the jet black of her mascara.

By the time the cab had wound its way through the traffic to Tottenham Court Road Livvy had dried her eyes, wiped her face and composed herself. She began to think over what had been said. The Duce interview was the thing that had really got to her. It was her baby; she had put the idea together, trailed the Amazon to get to him, dragged the most incredible things out of him in interview and ruined her whole damn fucking life for it! All that, and City had simply given it to someone else to rehash and pass off as their own. To someone else to reap all the glory for.

'How dare they?'

The cabbie slid the glass partition back. 'What was that, love?'

'Oh! Nothing,' Livvy answered quickly, flushing. She continued to stare out of the window and the cabbie slid the glass panel back again. But as they drove on towards Chelsea, Livvy's self-pity and distress began to turn, with each click of the meter, to anger. The more she thought about it, the more it incensed her. The programme wouldn't have existed without her – they would *never* have got to Lenny Duce without her input! She twisted her handkerchief round and round in her fingers, the anger building up inside her until suddenly the cab screeched to a halt as someone stepped out into the road and Livvy lurched forward, grabbing on to the seat for safety.

'My God!'

'Sorry about that, love.' The cabbie shook his head at the couple of art students who had just risked their lives to get across Long Acre. He glanced at her in the mirror and rolled his eyes. 'Bloody students,' he said.

Livvy nodded in agreement, and still on the edge of the seat, leaned forward. 'Would it take long to get back towards Chancery Lane from here?' she asked quickly.

The driver narrowed his eyes. 'You want to go to Chancery Lane?'

Livvy made her decision on the spur of the moment. She would go to Peter's chambers and see if there wasn't any way she could keep some control on her programme. 'Yes, please.'

'All right.' The cabbie checked his meter. He'd drive the lady round all day so long as she paid him. 'Chancery Lane it is, then, love.' He looked in his mirror, then glanced over his shoulder and swung the heavy black cab round. Minutes later they were heading up Kingsway towards the City and Livvy sat back to think about what she was going to say.

Peter looked up as the clerk came into his office and stood by the door. He spoke into the phone: 'Moira, can you hang on a moment?' then put his hand over the mouthpiece and motioned for the clerk to come in.

'Olivia Davis is here to see you, Mr Marshall. She doesn't have an appointment.'

'Oh.' Peter sighed heavily. 'Can you ask her to wait, Wilson?'

The clerk nodded, disappeared and Peter went back to his wife on the phone.

'That's all I need at this minute,' he said. 'Livvy's here, now I'll have to tell her about the flat. I had hoped to be able to leave it for a few days, see if we couldn't sort something out for her.'

'D'you suppose Eadie's already told her?' Moira's voice was weak, she'd been crying earlier on the phone.

'I doubt it.'

'Is there any kind of redress legally, do you think?'

'No, I'm sorry, love, that was my first thought, after all the goddamn money she's spent on doing the place up! She doesn't even have a tenancy agreement – legally she's living there as a favour.'

'I don't know what to do.'

He could hear the tears in Moira's voice again and he was filled with fury.

'There's nothing we can do. Livvy needs this like a hole in the head.' Peter sighed again. 'Listen, Moira, I'll have to go. I'll call you later, try not to worry.'

'Good luck.'

'Thanks.' He went to hang up.

'Oh, and, Peter?'

'Yes?'

'Thank you.'

Despite his tension, Peter smiled. Whatever he did for Moira was always acknowledged, even the smallest thing, as if she were just so relieved to have someone to care for her after the desperate, pointless years with Bryan.

'It's OK. Look, I'll call you later.'

He went out into the clerk's office and saw Livvy, beautifully dressed, her face ashen except for two feverish spots of colour high on her cheeks and scarlet lips.

'Hello,' he said. 'Come on through.'

Livvy stood up and smiled. 'Peter, I'm so glad you're in. I'm sorry for just turning up like this but I need some advice.' She spoke in a rush, the words tumbling out, and Peter thought for a moment that she'd been drinking. As he ushered her, still talking, into his office, he realised she was in a state of extreme tension.

'Livvy, sit down.' He went over to his desk. 'Would you like some tea?'

'No thanks, Peter. I don't want to take up too much of your time but I felt I had to come and see you.' She paused, sucked in her breath and went straight on. 'I lost my job this morning, at City, they've apparently terminated my contract!'

'Oh, Livvy. I'm so sorry.'

'Hmph!' She snorted and waved her hand in the air. 'I was expecting it. But the thing that I really need advice on is this programme with Lenny Duce I was making for them. They've booted me off it and put Jeff Ridges on – he's working with the producer right now. I'm absolutely furious, Peter! It was my programme, my concept, my research and it was going to win me a BAFTA award, I know it was! There must be something legally that I can do. They can't just do that, there must be copyright or something.' She was pacing as she spoke and suddenly she stopped and announced, 'I need a barrister. I'm going to sue them. How much do you think it'll cost me? Not that money's important at all, it's the principle I'm fighting for, that's beyond co . . .'

'Livvy!' Peter had to raise his voice to stop her mid-flow. 'Livvy, calm down.'

She looked across at him with a mixture of surprise and indignation. 'What? What is it?'

He let out a long, low whistle and shook his head. 'Come and sit down. Please!'

Reluctantly she walked over to the desk and perched tensely on the edge of a chair.

'Now let's get a few things straight. Did you have a copyright agreement with them? Any kind of agreement stating your artistic rights to the programme?'

She eyed him for a moment. 'No,' she said. 'Not anything specific.'

'What do you mean, not anything specific? Was there anything at all?'

She was silent. Then she said, 'No. Nothing.'

Peter kept his voice as calm as he could. 'Then what are you going to sue them for? There's a clause in your contract that gives them an option to let you go, there always is.'

'Really?' Her voice was edged with sarcasm.

'Yes, really! I looked the contract over, I remember it.' He stopped, not wanting to upset her, and softened his voice. 'Livvy, you've very little to go on. Nothing actually, unless you have some sort of legal agreement about the programme that City are in breach of.' He shrugged. 'I'm sorry, I can't offer you any help and I don't think anyone else can either.'

Livvy stared at a space above his head. The finality of his words hit her hard and she struggled to control her emotions. All the bitter disappointment and humiliation of the morning at City suddenly exploded inside her and it seemed as if Peter were out to spite her, to make her suffer even more.

'Are you sure it's that?' she said coldly. 'Or is it that if I no longer have a job in television then the last reminder of my father will have died away and you can step out of his shadow?' She kept her face impassive but the pulse in her neck beat visibly, pounding, as the blood rushed to her brain.

'I hardly think that's fair,' Peter protested. He had never

fought with Livvy; he had no idea of the complex emotions inside her. He looked away, hoping to defuse her anger.

'Not fair? His death was a relief for you and Moira. It gave you a clear future and you've been trying to wipe him out ever since! To tidy things up!' Livvy stood. She didn't know what she was saying now, except that they were things she should have said years ago or never at all. She had lost control. 'If I won an award then everyone would say I was my father's daughter and you couldn't stand that, could you?' She spat the words at him, holding on to the edge of the desk for support. She was way out of control now and Peter didn't know what to do.

'Livvy, I . . .'

She cut him short. 'You couldn't stand it, could you?' she said again, her voice high and tight. She turned towards the door. 'He was ten times the man you are,' she shouted, her face suddenly crumpled with pain. 'He would have helped me! He would have known what it meant!' She yanked the door open and whacked her leg with it, stumbling slightly as she ran from the room. Peter hurried after her but he heard the main door of the building slam and he knew it was pointless. She had gone. He stood where he was for a moment and smiled weakly at Wilson who'd come to see if he was all right. Then he closed the door, walked wearily back to his desk and slumped down in his chair.

He knew it was the hurt and anger of her situation that had spoken but as he sat and remembered all the times he'd been unable to get through to Livvy, all the times he'd felt she had never forgiven him, he also knew that some of the things she had just said she really felt, deep down inside, and that he should have had the courage to deal with them years ago, to tell her the truth, no matter how painful. It was too late now, he thought sadly, and he wasn't even sure if she would believe it when she heard it.

Livvy sat on the long cream sofa in her flat and stared blankly at the television screen. She had her feet up on a stool, her shoes were discarded, along with her coat, on the floor near where she sat and by her side was a second bottle of red wine, only half full. She held the wine glass drunkenly, close to her mouth, so she could sip continuously, and a packet of cigarettes was open on the sofa beside her, an ashtray slowly filling up with butts on the floor. She sighed heavily and flipped the switch to change channels.

It was half past eight in the evening and Livvy had been sitting there since she arrived home from Peter's office. She hadn't eaten that day and the wine had taken effect even after the first glass. She knew she shouldn't have spoken the way she did to Peter but somehow at that moment, she just didn't care. She was beginning to get maudlin, seeing everything through a wine-sodden fog, and feeling too despondent even to get up off the sofa. She reached forward, tipping a little of the wine on to the sofa, and rubbed at it with her grubby finger, making the dark red stain even worse.

'Oh dear,' she muttered, picking up her ashtray. 'Thilly me . . .' She lit up, blew the match out, scattering ash over the sofa as well and flipped the channel over with the remote control again. She hit City and watched an advert for cat food, thinking that what she needed was a cat. She settled back, took a long drag, holding the smoke in her mouth, and then blew tiny, perfectly formed rings up into the air. She squinted at the screen, her vision now beginning to really blur and saw the first two seconds of a trailer for *Take Five*.

'What?' She instantly sat up, dropped the cigarette, swore again and scrambled on the carpet for it with one eye on the TV. She saw a tall, leggy blonde, horribly similar to herself, standing in a short black dress in the middle of a huge white art gallery talking to the camera. The music was Dave Brubeck in the background and she screamed, picking up her shoe and hurling it at the screen.

'Amanda Dunn!' she cried, finding the cigarette and grinding it into the ashtray, but not before it had burnt a small brown hole in the cream Wilton. 'Amanda bloody Dunn!' she shouted again and then slumped back against the sofa as the trailer came to an end and the music of City's current affairs programme rolled around the room. Livvy put her hands up to her face and started to cry, loud, drunken sobs hiccupping almost in time to the beat of the music. Seconds later, she dropped her hands away, pressed the remote and the screen went blank.

She sat forward, unsteadily manoeuvred herself to her knees, held on to the edge of the table and stood, swaying for a few moments and trying to clear the terrible spinning inside the room. She staggered into the bedroom, smacking her hip on the door frame, and then realised she'd forgotten the wine. She staggered back, hitting herself in exactly the same spot, found the bottle and managed once more to get back to the bedroom.

She slumped on to the bed, settled the bottle on the bedside table and after some effort, struggled under the covers, pulling them up to her chin and laying her head back against the heap of pillows. She thought about having another glass of wine but it remained a thought. Within seconds, the room had stopped spinning, Livvy's head rolled slightly to the side and she fell heavily and drunkenly asleep.

James stood in front of the mirror and knotted his tie. It was after nine and he had begun to worry about getting back to Livvy. Hugh watched television from the bed, ignoring James, eager for him to go.

'You know I won't come again,' James said suddenly, turning from his reflection.

Hugh dragged his eyes slowly from the screen and shrugged. 'Please yourself,' he answered. He leaned over to pick up the remote control and James saw the angry red marks on his shoulder. He smiled. They both knew that James would be back, and they both wanted it. They were locked in now. They had dangerous information on each other and James knew that Hugh needed him as much as he needed Hugh. He reached for the jacket of his suit and eased it on, smoothing the front and pulling the sleeves down over his shirt cuffs.

'Yes, I will please myself,' he taunted and Hugh looked away from the screen once again.

Their sex had become almost violent in the past few days and it excited Hugh like nothing else. It was the danger, he realised, that excited him. He stared at James and the flicker of a smile hovered on James's lips.

'You'll come again,' Hugh said finally. 'At the weekend, when Livvy's gone home.'

James raised an eyebrow and picked up his briefcase but he knew Hugh was right. He turned towards the door, not bothering to say goodbye; there was little warmth between them now. He walked out of the bedroom, across the sitting room and out into the hallway, collecting his overcoat on the way.

He arrived home at the flat a little before ten and smelled the cigarette smoke as soon as he opened the door. He thought that Livvy must have had Lucy Deacon round for supper and was pleased; it meant that hopefully she wouldn't ask too many questions. He took his overcoat off and hung it up, switched off the hall lamp and went through to the sitting room, expecting to hear voices. He saw the discarded black coat, the shoe that had rebounded off the television screen and the half-full ashtray on the sofa, just by the red wine stain. He walked silently into the bedroom.

Over by the bed, he looked down at Livvy, still fully dressed and crashed out under the counterpane. He removed the red wine bottle and the half-full glass, drew the blinds and left her, quietly closing the door behind him. He took a blanket down from the linen cupboard, threw it on the sofa and cleared the sitting room of her debris before he went to clean his teeth. He was relieved that he didn't have to sleep with her, relieved to have some space. The thought of spending another night in the same bed as Livvy was beginning to seem unbearable. He just wasn't sure how much longer he could keep up the pretence.

Chapter Twenty-One

Livvy woke with a stinking hangover. She felt it before she even opened her eyes, the terrible throb in her head, a gruesome, furry taste in her mouth and the overwhelming sensation that if she moved she would be sick. She lay in the darkness of the room, wondered how the hell she was going to get up and then realised with a sinking feeling that she didn't have to. She heard the buzz of voices in her head and thought: Christ, I must have drunk a lot! But as she rolled over to try and get back to sleep, she recognised several words and sat up sharply to listen, yelping at the pain in her head. The voices were real, they were coming from the hall.

Stumbling out of bed, Livvy reached for her dressing gown and noticed she was still fully dressed. She pulled her waistcoat down and attempted to straighten her skirt. Her hair was a fright but she didn't think about brushing it. She rushed from the bedroom into the sitting room to find out what on earth was going on. She stopped short just by the sofa and stared at two men, one in a sharp grey pinstripe suit and loud tie, the other in jeans and a leather jacket, brandishing a camera.

'Who the . . .?'

The suit and Livvy both spoke at the same time, both with the same amount of shock and indignation. They stopped, looked at each other, then Livvy jumped in first.

'What the hell are you doing in my flat?' she demanded, 'Who the hell are you?'

The suit looked momentarily confused. 'Your flat?'

'Yes!' Livvy cried. 'My bloody flat!'

He shuffled from one foot to the other while the photographer rolled his eyes and glanced down at the floor. Then he took out his enormous filofax and looked at several notes. 'Is this number fifteen?'

Livvy narrowed her eyes. 'Yes . . . So?'

The suit breathed a sigh of relief. 'I'm sorry,' he said. 'We weren't told that there were any tenants in the flat.'

'I'm not a tenant!'

'You're not?'

This was becoming farcical and Livvy suddenly felt sick. She eased herself down on to the edge of the sofa and looked up at the young man in the suit. 'Please explain what is going on,' she said weakly, putting her hand up to her temples.

He took a step forward and glanced at his notes again. 'We were contacted by a Mrs Eadith Davis yesterday morning who said she was the owner of this property.'

Livvy nodded. 'Eadie,' she said. 'That's right, she's my grandmother.'

'Ah.' The suit closed his filofax and cleared his throat. 'Well, Mrs Davis asked us to come round this morning and value the flat for rental. She said she wanted to put it on the market right away.'

Livvy dropped her hand down and gripped the edge of

the sofa. 'She what?' It came out as a shocked croak. 'Could you explain that again?'

'Oh dear,' the suit said. 'You don't know?'

'Of course I don't know!' Livvy cried. 'I had no idea.' She closed her eyes and tried to calm herself. 'Are you telling me that my grandmother has put the flat up for rent?'

The photographer glanced at Livvy as if she were incredibly stupid but the suit kept his face impassive and nodded.

'But I don't think she can do that!' Livvy exclaimed. 'Not without my permission.'

The suit was silent for a few moments taking stock of the situation and Livvy suddenly felt very, very sick.

'Look, Miss er . . .'

'Davis.'

'Miss Davis. Why don't you telephone your grandmother and find out what's going on while we pop back to the office for half an hour? Here's my card – you can ring this number and let us know what the outcome is and, if necessary, we'll make an appointment then to come and photograph the flat at your convenience.'

Livvy nodded, she didn't even have the strength to look up. She knew that if she moved right then she would vomit all over the carpet.

'Right, we'll let ourselves out then.'

'Yes,' she managed feebly. She heard them move towards the door but she couldn't lift her head. There was some intense muttering out in the hall and she thought she saw a flashbulb go off but a few minutes later the door slammed and she knew that they'd gone. She stood, clapped her hand over her mouth and ran to the bathroom to be sick.

Ten minutes later, Livvy had washed her face, downed some Resolve, two Nurofen and nearly half a litre of orange juice. She found her address book, sat down by the phone and dialled Eadie's number in Sussex, not feeling much better but knowing that she had to have some answers. She waited what seemed like ages for Eadie to answer then heard the customary snap of her grandmother's voice and said, as brightly as she could muster, 'Hello, Granny. It's me, Olivia.'

Silence at the other end.

'Granny? You still there?'

'Yes?' Her grandmother growled. 'What do you want?'

'Oh, I . . .' Livvy reminded herself that Eadie always sounded like that. She took a breath and went on. 'Granny, some men came round to the flat this morning to tell me that you've put it on the market. That's not right, is it? Is there some mistake? Could you explain?'

'There's no mistake, Olivia,' Eadie said coldly. 'And no, I won't explain!' She snorted derisively. 'I told your mother's husband as much. If you want to talk, talk to him, I hold him responsible anyway!'

'Responsible for what?' Livvy's voice was thick with tears. '*What*?'

'Oh, stop whingeing! If it hadn't been for him, none of this would have happened in the first place. I've always said it and I'll say it again!'

'But, Granny! What is . . .'

Eadie interrupted her sharply. 'And you can forget the "Granny" as well, young lady! If you think I'm going to have drug dealers in my family then you've got a big shock coming!'

'Drug deal . . .'

'You move your things out by the end of the month at the latest, Olivia, or I'll have to take legal action.'

'Legal . . .' Livvy's voice broke. She listened to Eadie

ranting in her familiar abusive manner until finally she had the courage to replace the receiver. She sat for a few minutes in silence, then she looked around at her beautiful flat, put her hands up to her face and burst into tears.

She was still crying when the phone rang. She started, remembered that the answerphone was on and waited for the voice of the caller to come on to the machine. It was James. She rushed to the phone. 'Oh, James! Thank God you've rung!'

'Livvy? What's happened?' He was immediately wary. 'What is it?'

'James, Granny's put the flat on the market to rent!' She started to cry again and James tried to calm her, all the time wanting to tell her sharply to pull herself together. He waited for the sobbing to subside and then said, 'Livvy we need advice, legal advice. You must call Peter now and ask him what to do. If he can't help then he'll recommend someone who can.'

'I can't . . .' she said weakly. 'I'm sorry, James, but I can't call Peter.'

'Why not?' This time he couldn't keep the impatience out of his voice. 'Don't be stupid, Livvy! Of course you can call him, he's your bloody stepfather!'

Livvy thought back to Eadie's words and the anger of the previous afternoon rekindled itself. She was silent.

'Livvy? I insist you call Peter!' James said again. 'I don't care what's gone on . . .'

'Look, Granny said that Peter is responsible,' Livvy interrupted angrily. 'That's why she's chucking us out.'

'What the hell does that mean?' James exploded.

'I don't know! How should I know?' Livvy shouted back.

There were several seconds of icy silence and then James said, 'Well, I suggest you ring and find out, Livvy.' His voice was cold. 'And by the way, after you've done that, you should tidy the flat a bit. After an awful lot of hassle, I've managed to get Mark Green from the *Independent* to come round this morning to interview you; they've had a feature fall through for tomorrow and it's a bloody good opportunity for you to speak out.'

Livvy immediately softened, knowing how hard James was working for her. 'All right, I'll ring Peter now.'

'Good.'

She heard the relief in his voice. 'And thanks for the interview,' she added as a peace offering. The last thing she felt like was the press, but at least it would give her a chance to put her side across, to sway some of the public opinion James was always talking about.

'OK,' James said. He wasn't thinking about the *Independent* or the row with Livvy; his mind was on losing the flat. It filled him with despair. 'Ring me when you know what's happening.'

'I will.'

And without another word, he hung up. Livvy shook her head and clicked the button to redial. Then, not wanting to lose her nerve, she punched in the number of Peter's chambers and got through to the clerk.

'Peter Marshall, please,' she said. 'It's Olivia Davis.'

She waited nervously for the line to connect to Peter and realised that she had absolutely no idea of what she was going to say.

Peter closed the meeting with his clients and stood as the two men prepared to leave. He walked round his desk, shook hands with each of them and showed them to the door. Wilson was hovering, waiting to catch him. The two men left, and Wilson followed Peter back into his office.

'Mr Marshall, Olivia Davis is on the phone for you,' he said in an intense whisper. 'She's been holding on the line for about ten minutes.' He remembered the previous afternoon's scene and shook his head disapprovingly. 'I told her you were in a meeting but she insisted on waiting.'

'That's fine, Wilson.' Peter brushed Wilson's air of controlled panic aside. 'Could you put her straight through?' He smiled and Wilson scurried away to his office. Peter walked back to his desk and waited for the line to ring.

'Peter?'

'Hello, Livvy,' he said. He had no idea what to expect after yesterday's scene, a scene he hadn't had the heart to mention to Moira.

'Peter, I've just rung Granny.'

'Oh.' He should have known Eadie wouldn't waste any time.

'She's put the flat on the market, to rent.' Livvy tried to keep her voice even but failed. 'She can't do that, Peter!' she cried suddenly. 'Not after all the time and money I've spent on it!'

'Livvy, I'm sorry, really I am, but I'm afraid that she can. I've already looked into it. You've no legal tenancy agreement, nothing in writing at all.' He sighed and went on, 'The flat belongs to Eadie and she's every right to put it up for rent. She will have already checked this out with her solicitor, Livvy, you know what she's like.'

There was a long pause and Peter thought he could hear Livvy struggling not to cry. Then she said accusingly, 'Eadie told me that she held you responsible. What does that mean, Peter?'

Peter was taken aback. He knew that Eadie had always disliked him but the extent of her maliciousness now shocked him, even after all that he'd had to put up with over the years. He was silent for a while then he said quietly, 'Livvy, it's a long and complicated story and I don't want to explain it now, over the phone. Suffice it to say that it has nothing to do with anything real or concrete. I don't know exactly what she means but I can guess and it's pretty pathetic.' Peter knew that Eadie had held him responsible for any failing in Moira or Livvy's lives for the past ten years. She had maintained throughout that if Bryan were alive, which he wasn't because of Peter, then everything would have been perfect.

'It may appear pathetic to you,' Livvy said coldly, 'but it seems to have lost me my flat.'

Peter sighed. 'Livvy, it's not that, it's . . .'

'It's what, Peter?' Livvy's anger was quick and sharp; every way she turned Peter blocked her. 'It's not your fault? Nothing is ever your fault, is it? The only thing I know is that ten days ago Eadie paid my bail money quite happily, and now she wants to chuck me out of my home for reasons she holds you responsible for. You!'

'Wait a minute!' Peter found himself raising his voice and immediately stopped; he hated to shout. 'Who told you that about the bail?' he asked coolly, his professionalism getting the edge. He had no intention of rowing.

'No one,' Livvy answered sharply. 'I thought it was obvious! Who else has that kind of money?'

Peter held back an angry retort. He heard a knock on the door and saw Wilson enter quietly to let him know it was time for him to get over to court. 'Livvy, I have to go. We'll discuss this later.'

But Livvy was really angry now. Peter will help, James had said, it was exactly what she'd thought the day before, only Peter wasn't about to help anyone but himself!

'No we won't, Peter!' Livvy said bitterly. 'There's nothing more to discuss. I get the message. Get out of your life and leave Mum to you. Ha!' She laughed, a high-pitched, harsh sound and then just as Peter was about to speak, she hung up. He looked across at Wilson, embarrassed, and replaced the receiver. He just didn't know what to do.

Livvy clenched her fists by her side and fought the urge to smash the telephone on to the floor. In the past few days she had felt a frustration and anger like nothing she had ever experienced before and she struggled to control it. She stood where she was for quite some time, motionless, just staring at the phone, torn between tears and violence, and then she jumped visibly as the main door buzzer sounded. She hurried to the intercom and spoke into the panel.

'Who is it?'

'Mark Green, from the *Independent*.'

'Oh no!'

'Sorry?'

'Nothing, hang on, I'll press the buzzer.' She did so and ran into the bathroom to brush her hair. She hadn't even bothered to shower and change that morning and her clothes were stained and crumpled from the night before. She looked terrible, deep shadows around her eyes and a puffiness on her face from too much red wine. She grabbed the mouthwash and gargled, swishing it rapidly round her mouth, then attempted to untangle her hair with a comb before brushing it.

The doorbell sounded and she ran from the bathroom into the hall, panicking and in a foul temper, still with the comb stuck in the side of her head. Yanking the door open, she faced Mark Green, a journalist she had come across several times before in the course of her career and someone she had never really had much time for. She smiled, a little too enthusiastically, opened the door wider and ushered him in.

'How are you, Livvy?' Green held out his hand.

'Oh, all right.' They shook hands and he turned to the young man behind him. 'This is my photographer, Leo.'

'Hello, Leo.' Livvy suddenly laughed. 'It rhymes,' she said but both men pointedly ignored her flippancy.

'Come in.' She pointed to the sitting room and watched them both go on ahead, Leo taking in every detail for the right kind of shot. Livvy rolled her eyes and followed them after closing the door. She walked across the sitting room towards the kitchen and noticed that they were both staring at her clothes. She pulled at the waistcoat but knew that fussing was useless; she felt immediately on edge.

'Would you like some tea, coffee?'

Green shook his head and Livvy stopped.

'I haven't got long,' he said. 'If it's OK with you I'd rather just get on with it.' He exuded an air of pompous professionalism as he spoke and Livvy couldn't keep the look of derision off her face. Jumped-up little jerk, she thought briefly, as she came to sit down on the sofa.

'Where would you like to start?' she asked, as politely as she could manage, but Green didn't miss the irritation in her voice.

'How about the picture?' he answered, catching sight of the comb still in Livvy's hair. 'Standing over by the Dufy drawing. It is Raoul Dufy, isn't it?' The slant for the article was beginning to form in his mind.

'Yes, but . . .' Livvy didn't know what was worse, to be seen and written up as fiercely vain by requesting to go and change, or to be photographed looking as awful as she did.

Green sensed her unease but he wanted it just the way it was, it fitted perfectly. He'd never really liked Livvy Davis, thought she was a trifle too big for her Maud Frizzons. 'You look fine, Livvy,' he said easily. 'Don't worry, we'll probably only use a head-and-shoulders shot anyway.'

'Oh, all right.'

'I tell you what,' he went on, 'why don't we talk while Leo snaps?' He had learned that trick years ago; it always caught them off guard, made them say things without really concentrating.

'Well . . .'

'Time's short, Livvy. It'd be a great help.'

'OK.' Livvy stood, tired, still feeling sick, dishevelled, upset and in an extremely bad mood. 'Where shall I stand?' she asked wearily.

'To the right of the picture, I think,' Green answered. That way he got a good slant of the very chic, very expensive room. 'There, that's great!' He took out his pad and a pen and sat down at the dining table to make notes as Livvy talked. 'Why don't you tell me what's happened over the past two weeks or so,' he said. 'Who's been involved, who's tried to help et cetera.' He glanced at her face. 'We could start with your stepfather, he's a barrister, isn't he? He must be doing everything he can to help?'

'I don't want to talk about him!' Livvy snapped angrily, as the shutter on the camera clicked away.

'Oh?'

'Pick another opener, Mark,' she said icily, her face flushed and Green covered a smile as he looked down and began to write. 'No problem, Livvy,' he answered lightly.

No problem at all, he thought. The lie of his article had been well and truly set.

James came home early, let himself into the flat and called out to Livvy as he walked into the sitting room. There was no sign of her. He went through to the bedroom and sighed heavily as he saw the curtains drawn, a wine glass by the side of the bed and a small brown chemist's bottle on the bedside table. He picked it up, read the label for valium, unscrewed the lid and checked the number inside; Livvy had taken two. For the second night running, he removed the wine glass, took the pills and quietly left the room, closing the door behind him. He stood in the sitting room and surveyed it.

With the drinking and the pills, he reckoned that Livvy's news on the flat was pretty bad. He had called a friend himself that afternoon and found out that legally there wasn't much hope. He hated himself for doing it, of course, but he knew that it was time he took some action. He had no intention of losing if things went badly wrong. Crossing to the phone, he rang Hugh. They had a brief conversation, then James dialled a local taxi firm and ordered a taxi for an hour's time. He put the phone down, walked round the sitting room and made a mental note of what was really valuable and what he ethically had a right to. He started with the Dufy landscape sketch.

Within the hour he was ready. He had wrapped the valuables he wanted in brown paper, padded them and packed them into a cardboard box, which he left standing by the front door. He had neatly packed a holdall with enough things for a few days, his beautifully laundered shirts immaculately folded with tissue, his suit on a padded hanger inside a suit bag and his brown suede Gucci shoes in their soft felt bag. He sat on the chair in the hall and waited for the driver to buzz for him. Right on time, the door went. He answered, keeping his voice low, opened the front door and picked up his holdall and his box. Without a single thought for Livvy, he stepped out into the hall, pulled the door gently shut behind him, and called the lift, listening to it slowly clanking up towards the top floor and wishing it would hurry up. Minutes later he was gone.

Chapter Twenty-Two

Paul Robson sat at his desk with the *Independent* open in front of him and stared down at the article on Livvy Davis, his chin resting in his hands. He had read it earlier, on the tube, and now he just gazed blankly at the picture, his mind on something else, something different but indirectly connected, and began to feel afraid.

SET-UP OR UPSET? the article headline read and it archly questioned whether Livvy Davis really was an innocent pawn in a gruesome game as she protested or whether she had been lured, like so many other young professionals, into a world where profits were high, and, providing they were smart, the rewards still outweighed the risks. It outlined her history, her connection with the law, with the media, her boyfriend in the Foreign Office, and argued that she might have been brilliantly duped, as an extremely low-risk courier, or she might just have thought she was beyond suspicion, like so many upper-middle-class people did. It was that final line that had filled Robson with unease.

Young upper-middle-class professionals dealing in drugs, where the profits far outstripped the risks and especially when the operation was highly sophisticated and expertly run . . . He thought about Loman's last message, a slip of paper in an envelope pushed under his door at home two weeks ago. Since then Robson had heard nothing, not even a phone call. Loman wanted to meet, the message said. He would ring in the next few days or get a message to Robson; he thought he was on to something but made no mention of what. So Robson had waited, heard nothing and then telephoned Loman at home; the line was unobtainable.

But like most things unpleasant, Robson had put it to the back of his mind until it came up again. He was in it up to his neck with claims against IMACO, and Annie his wife was beginning to think he was having an affair he spent so much time in the office. He didn't need the complication of Loman; he didn't even want to think about it, at least he hadn't until now. Now he couldn't *help* but think about it. Everything he'd found out on his own, before he hired Loman, had pointed to some pretty odd dealings with South America, some kind of involvement with Howard Underwriting that didn't exactly add up, and the article had stirred the whole thing up in his mind.

Looking up suddenly, he glanced at the clock on the far wall and made a spur-of-the-moment decision. He had been cautious about ringing his brother-in-law. He'd wanted Loman kept a secret, out of harm's way. But now he reckoned he had to find out what was going on, go round and see Loman and just check things were all right. He picked up the receiver and dialled his sister's house in Peckham, hoping that Sally would be busy getting the children's breakfasts and Joe would answer the phone. Seconds later, he heard his brother-in-law's voice and breathed a little easier.

'Joe? Morning, it's Paul.'

'Hello, I've been waiting for you to call.'

'Really?' Robson tried to cover the edge of panic in his voice.

There was a short pause and then Joe said, 'Did you ever contact that private investigator? Loman?'

Robson held his breath. He decided to be honest, or half-honest, at least. 'Yes, to ask him about a routine insurance investigation. Why?'

'He's dead. Found in a back alley down in Brixton, two bullets in the chest, fired at point-blank range. Nice job, professional.'

Robson's chest tightened painfully but he kept his voice as even as he could. 'Jesus! Poor bloke. Any idea why?'

'Drugs. We reckon that maybe he was involved in some kind of drugs investigation and got in the way. It's not that rare an occurrence in that part of the world. Snooping round asking awkward questions was probably enough.'

'You reckon?'

'Yeah. We've been through his stuff but there's nothing in the files, we haven't got any kind of lead. So . . .' Robson heard Joe take a slurp of tea. 'Anyway, it's not your problem, is it? Presumably you didn't have much to do with him or you'd have rung earlier?'

Robson paused for a moment. 'No, not that much. He started something for me but we didn't get very far. I don't even have his address.'

Joe was silent and Robson heard the muffled sound of a door closing; the background noise of the house disappeared. 'D'you need it?' Joe asked.

Robson knew an explanation was required. 'I need a copy of what he'd found out for us.' The *us* implied Howard Underwriting – Joe knew that investigators were used for some of the bigger claims.

'All right. I've got it in the office, strictly off the record. I'll ring you later this morning with it. Where are you?'

'I'm at work.'

'Christ! At this time? No wonder you're so bloody well paid!' Robson smiled; it was a bone of contention between him and his brother-in-law, his salary.

Joe lowered his voice. 'Listen, Paul, be careful, all right? Loman's death is still under investigation.' He didn't need to say any more; he trusted his brother-in-law.

'Yeah. Thanks, Joe.' Robson replaced the receiver.

He looked down at the photograph of Livvy Davis and took a couple of deep breaths to try and ease the tension in his chest. He knew he had to go round to Loman's, see what there was, see if he could find any clues to the note. But Jesus! The bloke was dead! He put his hand up and rubbed the sore spot in between his heart and lungs, taking another couple of deep breaths. Funnily enough, the initial fear he'd felt that morning had gone, replaced by a grim determination to get some answers. That and a painful ache of what felt like indigestion in his chest. I'd never make a hero, he thought sourly, reaching for the Rennie in his desk drawer, my stomach couldn't cope.

Livvy woke at eight. Her head was stuffed full of cotton wool and she couldn't work out where the piercing bleep was coming from. She sat up, bleary-eyed, and felt on the bedside table, trying to locate the noise. She put her hand over her small electronic alarm clock and the bleeping finally stopped. She relaxed back but then the telephone rang.

'Oh God!' Climbing out of bed, not able to remember where she'd put the phone, she walked round to James's side to look for it. It registered that James wasn't in his side of the bed, and that he hadn't been all night, but it didn't register why. The effect of the valium still had several hours to wear off.

Finding the phone under a pillow she had chucked on the floor, she retrieved it, sat on the edge of the bed and picked up the receiver. She tried her voice, got only a croak and cleared her throat. 'Hello?' she said again, this time a fraction louder.

'Livvy? You all right?'

'Yes. Lucy? Where are you? What time is it?'

'It's eight o'clock and I'm in the office.'

'Oh.' Livvy shook her head to try and clear it. Everything seemed a little unreal, even Lucy's voice. 'What's the matter? Why are you ringing at eight in the morning?'

'Livvy, have you seen the *Independent*?'

'No. Why?' Livvy was momentarily confused.

'So you haven't seen the article?'

Sudden realisation hit her. 'Oh my God! The article! No, I haven't. What's it like . . .?' She stopped. 'Oh God!' Panic entered her voice. 'It's bad, isn't it?'

Lucy didn't hesitate. 'Yes, it's bloody awful! You need to get a copy, then I think you should talk to Peter, find a solicitor.'

Livvy felt as if the wind had been knocked out of her. She put her head forward between her knees, still gripping the telephone, and tried to breathe. The dopey effect of the tranquilliser had evaporated and her head spun in panic.

'Livvy? You still there?'

'Yes . . . I . . .'

'D'you want me to come round?'

'No.' She struggled to take control of her anxiety. 'What

does it say, Lucy? Give me some idea.' She held the telephone in the crook of her shoulder and hugged her arms around her, rocking back and forth. 'Please?'

Lucy sighed heavily. 'All right.' She was loath to read it out, but she didn't know what else to do; Livvy sounded desperate. So she picked out a part that didn't sound too awful and quietly began to recite.

When Livvy finally hung up, she held the telephone, unable to put it down, and stared blankly at the wall. The words ran round and round in her head, cutting, sneering words. They mocked her and made her hate herself. Was that how she really looked? Of course it was. She stood and glanced over at the bedside table for her pills. She needed one, to get her through the next hour or so.

Not able to see them, she crossed to the bathroom and found the small brown bottle there, unscrewed the lid and took out a tiny white tranquilliser. She dropped it into the palm of her hand and walked to the kitchen for a glass of water. She ran the tap, turned to look at the station clock as she did so and saw that it was missing. She started. Her hand opened. She dropped the pill and the glass, which shattered on the quarry-tile floor.

Leaping back, Livvy cried out as a piece of broken glass hit her on the leg and she looked down at the cut, instantly oozing a slow stream of dark red blood which dribbled down the length of her shin. She bent, wiped it with her finger and stepped over the pile of splintered glass to the wall where the clock had been. She looked round; two of the eighteenth-century fruit prints were missing as well and a heavy aching sickness started in the pit of her stomach. She had been burgled! She put her hands up to her face and cried out loud. On top of everything else, she had been burgled!

Attempting to pull herself together, she walked into the sitting room, skirting the edge of the kitchen to avoid any fragments of glass, and stood by the door surveying the room. She knew at a glance what was missing. The Dufy drawing had gone, several pieces of modern silver and the two rare hand-coloured editions of *Alice in Wonderland* that she had bought in Brighton with James. She was motionless for a moment, not quite believing what she saw, then a sudden realisation hit her. Everything else was in its place, the television, the video, her handbag. She crossed the room and took out her wallet with its neat stack of credit cards in the back. It was all there, the cards, the cash. It was then that the anger hit her. She hadn't been burgled at all. At least, not by strangers!

Running back into the bedroom, Livvy threw open the cupboard to look for his clothes and then rushed into the bathroom to search for his wash things. She gripped the edge of the marble sink for support and closed her eyes. Her legs felt weak and her heart pounded. James had gone! He had left her, coldly and with calculation, he had gone. And with him, he had taken the most valuable of their possessions.

Livvy stayed like that for some time, the cold marble reassuring under the trembling dampness of her hands. She hung her head and concentrated on trying to dispel the panic, big breaths, in and out, listening to the rasping sound of her lungs. It took nearly twenty minutes but finally she managed to raise her head and let go of the sink. She walked unsteadily back into the bedroom, slumped down on to the edge of the bed and reached for the telephone. She dialled the Foreign Office.

James answered the line on the first ring. Livvy heard the smooth tone of his voice and was instantly so angry that she almost hung up. For a moment, she couldn't think straight as the blood rushed to her head.

'Hello, James Ward.'

'James . . . it's Livvy,' she stuttered.

'Oh.' There was a short silence and then he said, 'How are you?'

'How am I?' She swallowed back the initial impulse to cry, struggling for control. 'I think you owe me an explanation,' she said tersely.

Again a short silence. 'I can't talk now,' he said, 'I'll have to ring you later.'

'No!' She stopped; she didn't want to shout, she didn't need a slanging match. 'No, James,' she went on more quietly, 'you can speak to me now. I want an explanation *now*!' Her voice had a desperate edge to it and James hesitated before hanging up. She was at her lowest ebb, he knew it and he couldn't just cut her off. Besides, he didn't want to end it badly; he didn't want to alienate her, just in case he ever needed her. He could persuade her when she was like this, make her see it his way.

Trying to inject some sympathy into his voice, he spoke again. 'Livvy, I've done what I thought was best, for the time being anyway. You, we, need some space, both of us, some time apart. I'm trying to think of you.'

'Me?' she cried. 'You're trying to think of *me*? How can you . . .?'

'Livvy, calm down!' he interrupted. 'You won't achieve anything by getting yourself in a state.' He waited a few moments and then went on. 'One of us has to think straight, get things organised, you must see that? I thought that you needed some time alone, you're not well, you're not being rational at the moment and I . . .'

'You . . .! You took my picture!' she cried. 'How could you, James?'

'I thought that after what you had said about Eadie renting out the flat, I should look after our interests. You weren't capable of it. I've taken some of the most valuable things we own and put them in a safe place. For insurance purposes more than anything.' He stopped and took a breath. His reply had been sharper than he'd intended. 'Livvy, I thought you'd understand,' he pleaded. 'I thought you'd be glad of some freedom.'

Livvy was silent.

'I know how hard it's been for you, Liv, really I do. I am trying to do what's best for you, for both of us.' He could hear the faint sound of her quickened breathing as she struggled not to cry. He had persuaded her, he knew he could get her on his side. 'You do understand, don't you Livvy?' he finished softly.

Suddenly Livvy felt deflated. All her anger had simply evaporated and it left her weak and tearful. 'Yes . . . I think so,' she whispered, wiping her eyes on the corner of the sheet. Perhaps James had only been doing the best he could for her. She certainly knew that she wasn't coping at all well. And maybe he was right, maybe she did need some time on her own, some space. 'Yes, I understand,' she said quietly. What did a few pictures matter anyway? If she went to prison then . . . She stopped and bit her lip hard. What did any of it matter anyway? 'Look, I'd better go, James.'

'Yes, so had I.' She sounded dull and lifeless and James couldn't wait to get off the phone in case she started weeping.

'I'll ring you later,' he said, 'when I've got more time.'

She sighed; there wasn't any point. 'No, don't bother,' she

answered and placing her finger over the button, she cut him off. There was nothing more to say.

Dropping the phone down, she left it hanging over the side of the bed and curled up into the foetal position, cradling her head on her hands. She pulled the covers up, shut her eyes tight and let the tears slide out from under the lids, down over her face and into a damp stain on the white linen pillowcase. She couldn't even be bothered to cry properly and that in itself seemed a fitting end.

Moira parked the Range Rover in a residents-only parking space and ignored the signs. She was too worried to concern herself with bloody parking tickets! She clambered out and headed off in the direction of Cadogan Square, her Barbour zipped up against the cold, a floral silk headscarf over her hair. She kept hearing the engaged tone on Livvy's number in her mind as she strode on, her imagination running wild. After the scene with Peter the previous night, she had been trying to call her daughter since early that morning, nearly every twenty minutes, and in the end had despaired, put on her coat and shoes, climbed into the car and headed for London.

Peter had told her last night that Livvy was in a state. He described what she'd said to him and Moira had had to agree. Livvy had never been one for confrontations – she had always kept a tight rein on her feelings, had hardly ever talked about her father – and now she was ranting and raving at Peter, saying things they had never imagined she felt.

Moira turned the corner at Milner Street into Cadogan Square and stopped to cross the road at the Hyatt Carlton Towers, her mind in turmoil. She stepped off the pavement, narrowly missed a black cab whose driver blasted her with his horn and darted across to the other side, her heart pounding with the shock of the loud noise but her mind oblivious to how close she'd been to an accident. She walked along to Livvy's apartment block and stopped determinedly in front of the panel, locating Livvy's name and pressing hard and long on the buzzer. She looked up at the very top floor of the building and waited for a reply.

Livvy heard the buzzer. It penetrated her dream and she opened her eyes for a moment. It stopped. Still enveloped in the last, dull numbness of the valium, she let her eyes close again and her mind drift away. The buzzer sounded once more, only this time it didn't stop. It went on, an irritating, monotone drilling noise, and she lifted her head, shook herself out of her torpor and dropped her legs over the side of the bed.

'All right, all right!' she muttered, yanking on her dressing gown and moving through the flat. 'I'm coming!' She bent to the intercom and demanded rudely, 'Who is it?' Preparing the appropriate abuse.

Moira's voice came out of the small grille, loud and clear. 'Livvy, it's your mother!' she said sharply. 'Can you please let me in.' Relief made her sound harsher than she felt.

Livvy pressed the lock release, opened the front door and left it like that while she went to put the kettle on. She didn't feel anything, no surprise or pleasure at the thought of her mother, just a small irritation and the heavy remains of the drugged numbness.

Moira let herself in and gently closed the door behind her. She walked through the flat towards the kitchen, took stock of the mess, of the missing picture and the stale fusty smell and stood in the doorway to the kitchen, waiting for Livvy to turn to greet her. She saw that Livvy's hair was lank and dirty and that the dressing gown looked as if she'd lived in it for the past year but she said nothing. She just stood and waited for Livvy to stop fiddling with the top of a tea caddy. Finally, unable to stand the rudeness any longer, she coughed and Livvy glanced up.

'I suppose you've come to tell me how badly behaved I was towards Peter,' Livvy said. She spooned some tea into a pot and poured the boiling water on top. 'I won't apologise if that's what you've come for.'

Moira stared at her daughter. She was instantly insulted, but reminded herself of Livvy's situation and kept her cool. 'No, that's not what I've come for.'

Livvy raised an eyebrow. 'No?'

Again Moira held her anger in check. 'No,' she answered, 'I came to see if you were all right. I couldn't get through on the phone and it worried me. I . . .'

'You came up to see Peter, Mother, don't lie.' Livvy shook her head. 'In the past twelve years, when have you ever put me first? Come on, let's be honest! I've upset Peter and you thought you should come up to town, have lunch with him, cheer him up a bit and while you're here, kill a morning reminding me what a nice bloke he is.' Livvy rolled her eyes. 'Please, spare me!' She was leaning insolently against the sideboard and she could hear what she was saying but the nastiness of it didn't register, she was too numb. 'You've always been a slag where Peter is concerned, Mother, you'd do anything to please him. You . . .'

Moira had crossed the kitchen and slapped Livvy hard across the face before she even knew she was doing it. Livvy started violently with the shock and put her hand up to her cheek.

'Jesus! You bitch!'

Moira's chest was heaving and her face was flushed. She thought she was going to cry but she clenched her fists and stood firm. 'No,' she retaliated, 'not me!' She moved back a pace and looked at her daughter. 'You know absolutely nothing,' she said. 'We've always tried to protect you, we . . .'

'Protect me? Christ, that's a joke! Protect me from what? Certainly not your affair, in all its rampant glory.'

'That's enough, Livvy!' Moira warned.

'Enough! Did you protect me from your obscene pregnancy, the reason you left Dad, did you ever try to spare me the spectacle of a thirty-eight-year-old, my mother, with a newborn and a lover? Did you?'

'That's *enough*!' Moira shouted. 'Enough, I said!' Her voice was strong and she hardly ever shouted. It took Livvy by surprise and she stared at her mother. 'I will tell you why I left your father,' Moira yelled. 'I left him because I was sick. Yes, Livvy, sick! I had been physically and mentally abused for so many years that I was completely run down, numb, sick.' She stopped to catch her breath and saw the look of horror on her daughter's face. She had to say it, though, it was half out now and Livvy needed the truth. They all did.

'Livvy, Bryan Davis was a brilliant newsman,' she said, more calmly, 'but he was a lousy husband and not a very nice human being. From the moment I first fell pregnant with you he took off; he said he needed "sexual expression", that it was a part of him he couldn't deny and that I couldn't give it to him, at least not the way he wanted, not all night and heavily pregnant. So he started one of his "affairs", even asked if I'd like to meet her.' Moira paused and smiled bitterly. 'After that, after staying out all night and coming home sodden with drink he just assumed that he could do whatever he liked and . . .' she shrugged, 'I suppose, frantic with a new baby, young, lonely, inexperienced, I let him. More fool me!'

Moira relaxed her hands; now she had started to speak, she couldn't stop. It was the lifting of a huge burden. 'Bryan was a violent drinker, Livvy. He gave me a wallop on more than one occasion when I objected to him coming home in the state he did, and in the end, Eadie had to step in, not for me, I might add, but to protect her son – she didn't want the police involved, or the media. It might ruin his career.'

Moira couldn't look at Livvy. Every time she stopped, she had to gaze down at the floor, not wanting to see her daughter's pain. 'Eadie warned Bryan never to drink around you and when you were old enough, it was Eadie who insisted you went away to school, and paid for it, so that you wouldn't come into contact with any of this.' She smiled again, only this time more affectionately. 'You saw only the good side of your father, the great side. We made sure of that,' she said quietly. Then she went on.

'When I met Peter I was at a terrible low. The small bits of acting I had done to keep me sane over the years had dried up, you were away at school and my marriage was non-existent. No, more than that, it was painful.'

Suddenly her face changed. 'Peter fell in love with me the minute we met,' she said gently. 'And I can't tell you how wonderful that was, after all the years of abuse and lack of self-esteem. I don't need to explain my actions, Livvy; I fell in love with him as well, simple as that. I saw a man who would look after me, look after us, and that was a blessed relief.' Now Moira did look up at Livvy. 'You have never known what Peter has done for you, Livvy,' she went on quietly. 'He wanted it that way. When Bryan took his own life he said that he thought that was enough of a burden for a young person to have to face, that you should be allowed your memories and I agreed with him.' She swallowed and then continued. 'Peter paid for you to go to university; he set up a fund so that you could have a bit of financial independence and go into a badly paid job at the BBC, and it was Peter who persuaded Eadie to let you have this flat. He . . .'

But it was too much for Livvy; she couldn't make sense of it. 'He still killed my father though, you both did! Whatever he did, he still did that.' She started to cry. She had been fighting to control it all the time Moira spoke but was no longer able to. 'You both killed him!' she shouted.

Moira was taken aback. The violence of Livvy's emotion shocked her. 'No, Livvy,' she said, moving forward. 'Bryan took his own life. No one forced . . .'

But Livvy shook her head, tears streaming down her face. 'If you hadn't run off with Peter he wouldn't have . . .' She didn't finish her sentence. She ran from the room and out into the hall. Moira rushed after her and tried to seize her as she pulled her coat on over her dressing gown and stuffed her bare feet into some shoes.

'Livvy, stop it!' Moira pleaded. 'Stop being silly.'

Livvy shoved her away. 'No!' she screamed, openly sobbing now. 'Leave me alone!' She wrenched open the front door, grabbed her keys and ran out of the flat. Moira went after her but stopped by the lift and stood helplessly as Livvy fled down the stairs, her heavy shoes clattering on the stone, the terrible sound of her sobbing echoing around the huge Victorian staircase. Moira leaned her head against the cold iron of the lift cage and closed her eyes. And, quietly, she too began to weep.

It was dark by the time Livvy finally looked up and realised where she was. The wind was bitter and it was raining. She moved, her limbs painfully stiff, and stood up, her feet numb from the cold. Pulling her coat tight around her, she put a hand up to her face and touched the swollen lids of her eyes; her face felt tender and bruised from all the crying. She began to walk towards the Queen's Gate entrance to Hyde Park, thankful that the afternoon had closed in early and that it was too dark for her face to be seen.

She headed back to Knightsbridge, crossed the road by Harvey Nichols and made her way down along Sloane Avenue to Cadogan Square. The streets were fairly empty even though it was only four o'clock and she was grateful for that. She made it to her apartment block unseen and took the keys from her pocket, letting herself wearily into the building and slowly climbing the stairs to the top floor. She walked inside her flat, felt the warmth rush the blood to the surface of her skin and finally crumpled, collapsing against the wall in the hallway.

Moira stood in the doorway to the sitting room and looked at her daughter. She was silent for some time, until Livvy finally opened her eyes and saw her there.

'I waited to see if you were all right,' she said quietly.

Livvy nodded. Moving towards her, Moira bent to help her up but she backed away. 'Don't! . . . Please, I'm fine.' She raised herself up and rubbed her hands wearily over her face.

'Can I . . .?'

'No!' Livvy shrugged. 'Sorry . . .' She took a breath. 'Look, I'd just like to be alone, Mum, OK? I need some time to think.'

Moira hadn't moved; she didn't know what to do. She nodded, still standing in the same spot, and watched Livvy as she walked past her into the sitting room. The urge to reach out and hug her was almost unbearable. She turned round to face her daughter. 'Are you sure you're all right?' She felt completely helpless.

'Yes. I'm all right.' Livvy had slumped down on to the sofa. 'Really, I'd rather be . . .'

'OK!' Moira held up her hands to silence Livvy. 'I'll leave.' She took up her bag and coat from the hall table. 'Livvy, if there's anything that you want . . . anything . . . well . . . I am always there for you . . . OK?' She paused. 'Peter and I will always care,' she finished. And without waiting for an answer, she crossed the hall and left the flat.

Livvy stared out at the dark sky through the huge bank of windows along the far wall of the flat, then she closed her eyes and rested her head against the warm, soft leather of the sofa. She had always thought that she had everything. How dangerous that had been. Now she had nothing. And after what Moira had told her, she didn't even have the luxury of her memories.

Paul Robson watched his boss snake his way through the throng of people in Lloyd's towards his own box, and thought that whatever else Hugh Howard was, he was certainly a bloody smooth operator. He stopped on the way to chat, smiling effortlessly, exuding confidence, and Robson envied him that. At that moment he himself felt nothing like confident; he was scared out of his wits.

As Hugh reached the box Robson stood up and slung his overcoat across his arm, and then picked up his briefcase. 'I'm off then, Hugh, if you don't mind.'

'Not at all, Paul.' Hugh turned towards one of the underwriters to say something and dropped a file down on to the desk. Robson read the name on it and an alarm bell sounded in his head. Porto Insurance: another new South American company.

'What time's your appointment?' Hugh had turned back.

'Four forty-five,' Robson answered. 'They'll probably keep me waiting an hour, though, you know what doctors' surgeries are like.'

Hugh smiled and picked up the file. 'See you tomorrow then. Hope it's nothing contagious.'

Robson laughed lightly and nodded at his secretary. 'Bye then. Cheerio, Marian.'

He moved off towards the escalators, his heart hammering in his chest, and felt in his trouser pocket for his car key. It was there and just the shape of it gave him a feeling of relief. He was better off doing what he had to do by car: if anything went wrong he would be able to make a quick getaway. He stepped on the moving staircase and looked down at Lloyd's trading floor below, his stomach already starting to ache. In an hour it'll all be over, he kept telling himself, trying to calm the acid in his gut. He simply wasn't cut out for detective work, he thought glumly – whoever heard of Dick Tracy with irritable bowel syndrome?

He reached Loman's place at five-thirty. Trying to be inconspicuous, he parked his new Rover one street down from Loman's. He gathered up his briefcase, fastened his overcoat and straightened his tie, then set off smartly in the direction of the next road and Loman's house. He looked like a professional businessman making a house call; no one would consider him in the slightest bit suspicious.

Arriving at number fifty-seven, Loman's three-bedroomed semi-detached house, Robson went up to the front door, rang the bell and waited for a couple of minutes, just as he'd planned to do. There was no reply. He glanced round the back of the house, saw that it was clear and casually followed the path towards the back garden. He unlatched the gate, stepped on to the patio area by the kitchen door and took out the small chisel-shaped instrument that Annie used for taking out tacks in her upholstery class. He slipped it between the door and the frame, gave a good wrench and snapped the lock. He glanced nervously round as the noise shattered the suburban silence, thinking, Jesus, I hope Joe doesn't do me for this. He gently prised the door open and quickly entered the house.

Robson moved hurriedly through the rooms on the ground floor, looking for Loman's office, shining his torch around each one. Papers were scattered around the place but there was nothing that could be described as a work area. Swiftly he went upstairs.

Conscious that the light could be seen more easily in the upstairs, Robson kept his torch low as he moved about, all the time listening hard for any noise downstairs. He found Loman's office behind the second door he tried. He walked in, crossed to the window and drew the curtains, then put his torch on to full power and looked around at the two high metal filing cabinets and the Amstrad PC. Silently, his movements quick and controlled, he began to go through everything he could see.

Forty minutes later, he sat in front of the computer screen and held his breath as he switched on the machine, praying that Southern Electric hadn't cut off the supply. He heard the whirr of the power drive, a couple of sharp bleeps, and the screen came to life. He inserted a disk he had found in a file marked with the numbers 1275 – the last four digits of his telephone number – and bit his fingernail nervously as he tried to follow the software. It had to be the right disk, it was the only one that could be! Within minutes he was into the system.

Quickly he pressed A : and the enter key, then realised he needed a password. He began to sweat. He tapped in his name first, then Lloyd's, then Brasilia, then Hugh Howard . . . His stomach churned. Finally he tried the rest of his phone number as a trickle of sweat ran down the side of his face. The machine bleeped and he was into the file.

Seconds later a list of names came up. He moved the cursor down the list, his fingers hot and sweaty inside the leather gloves, and the information unfolded itself, like the pieces of a jigsaw. For the first time since he'd started the whole thing three months ago, he felt really and truly terrified. With no time to waste, he pressed the save key, flipped the disk out and clicked the machine off. His hands were trembling.

Shoving the disk into his pocket, Robson switched off the computer at the mains, replaced the chair and did a final check round the room with his torch. Satisfied that he had left no trace of his visit, he ran down the stairs and hurried through the house back to the kitchen, clutching his briefcase. He shut the kitchen door, securing it as best he could, slipped his torch away and walked casually round to the front of the house and down the path to the street. He strode away, watching out for any prying eyes, turned the corner into the next road and saw the safety of his car. He pressed the alarm pad, released the central locking system, and climbed inside, slumping back against the seat.

He had thought that searching Loman's house would bring the whole business to some sort of conclusion. But it had turned out to be just the beginning. What he had on that disk might well be what had got Loman killed! It was certainly enough to put Hugh Howard away for a number of years, and anyone else involved. Robson eased his gloves off and took out his handkerchief to wipe the sweat off his face. His heart was still pounding and the pain in his stomach stabbed relentlessly. He was involved. A junior partner in the company – he was more than involved, he was right in it! And if Loman had been killed, then who the hell would be next?

Chapter Twenty-Three

It was nine-thirty and Jack Wilcox had been drinking since lunch time. Sometime in the middle of the afternoon he'd moved on from a bar on Fleet Street to a pub off the Strand that was open all day. From there he went to Bently's, where the whole thing with Nel had started, and sat in a corner downstairs, the torn page from the *Independent* in front of him, now crumpled and damp from beer, the photograph of Livvy, tired, strained and shabby, staring up at him as he drank.

He was past the maudlin, self-pitying stage; he'd gone through that at about six. Now his thoughts were muddled, not incoherent but blurred, and he was angry, the dull, useless anger that comes from too much beer, the type of anger that would have made him hit someone if he'd been in the least bit violent. He was angry that he'd been set up, that they'd all been set up. He was angry at himself, for his own fucking stupidity, and at Livvy for ending up in a worse mess than him. He gazed down at the photograph and swore at Livvy's distraught face. Why hadn't someone warned her? Why hadn't he? He traced the outline of her head and shoulders, his finger way off the mark but too drunk to notice it, and thought: Now it's all going to happen again, another deal, more money from Jack the asshole, and maybe some other dupe getting caught, ruining their life. He shook his head, put his finger up to his lips and kissed it, placing it back on the photograph. 'Sorry, Livvy,' he murmured.

Drunkenly he looked up and shouted in a slurred voice at the barman. 'Hoi! You . . . gotta . . . phone?'

'Yeah, mate. It's over there, by the cigarette machine.'

Jack hoisted himself unsteadily to his feet, holding on to the table and swaying visibly. He grabbed the torn sheet of newspaper and staggered through the small crowd at the bar towards the phone. He dug in his pockets, pulled out his small leather address book along with a handful of change, dropping several coins on the floor in the process, and picked up the receiver. He found Livvy's number, propped himself up against the wall and began to dial. He had to tell her he was sorry, tell her he was a coward. He had to tell her that he knew she hadn't done anything wrong.

Livvy stepped out of the shower and wrapped herself in a huge, warm white towel. She stood by the radiator for a while, still feeling cold and shivery. Her head ached, she was exhausted and it seemed as if her flesh had been chilled to the bone. She couldn't think straight, she was too confused. Hugging the towel tight around her, she leaned against the hot metal and let the heat press deep into her muscles, relaxing them slightly. She thought about her father, trying to evoke a memory, something personal that they had shared, and she realised that she couldn't. All the memories were distant, intangible ones; there was nothing like – the day Dad and I went to the beach. All she had was a *sense* of him and she didn't clearly know how she had built that up. Maybe, just maybe, in all her grief and confusion, she had clung to something that didn't exist, had made him into the kind of man he wasn't. She honestly didn't know, but she had an intuitive feeling that that was exactly what she had done.

The phone rang and she started, then moved into the bedroom to hear who it was on the answerphone. She dropped her towel on to the bed and pulled on a clean XL-sized sweatshirt, bundling her dirty dressing gown into the laundry basket. She heard the end of her recorded message and then the background noise of a pub. Jack's voice boomed out suddenly, seeming to fill the whole flat.

'Livvy? It's Jack.'

She moved quickly towards the phone to pick it up but stopped as he went on. She realised he was drunk.

'Shorry you're not in, Livvy . . . but . . . er . . .' His voice trailed off drunkenly and then after a few moments he started again. 'Shorry you're not in, Livvy, but I wanted to shay someshing to you.' The words were so slurred she had to listen hard to make them out. 'I wanted to shay shorry, I should have shaid it, I should have told you . . . Oh God!' It sounded as if he'd dropped the phone but after a while he came back on. 'Livvy, don't trust anyone!' He shouted this suddenly and she jumped. 'Not James, not anyone! You shee . . . Fraser knew . . . well . . . I think he did. Livvy, watch your back, all right? I love you, I should never have let it happen . . . I love you really . . .' He broke off and Livvy thought for a moment she heard a muffled sob. She lunged across the bed for the phone, grabbing the receiver from its cradle.

'Hello, Jack? Jack?' There was no reply but she could still hear the background noise. 'Jack!' she shouted. 'Jack, speak to me. What do you mean? What did Fraser know? Tell me! Jack?' But a few seconds later the money ran out and the line cut off.

'Oh Christ!' She slammed the phone back down and dropped her head in her hands. She felt desperate. What the hell did he mean? *Why* shouldn't she trust James?

She stood up abruptly and strode into the sitting room. Picking up her filofax, she quickly scanned it for Fraser's home number, then reached for the phone. Fraser answered on the second ring.

'Hello?'

Livvy paused. She was momentarily shocked by her reaction to his voice but then her anger and fear took over.

'Fraser, it's Livvy.'

Fraser felt a tiny piercing stab of excitement but kept it tightly under control. 'Hello, Livvy,' he replied coolly. 'How are you?'

'Fraser, Jack Wilcox just rang me,' she said quickly. 'He was drunk, he said that I should watch my back, that I shouldn't trust James, or anyone, that you knew something . . .' She broke off and Fraser heard her try to catch her breath, to ease the tightness in her chest. 'What did he mean? What's going on?' Her voice faltered and despite all the times in the past week Fraser had told himself that he should have left well alone, that he had simply ended up in exactly the same position he had been in twelve years ago, he felt his heart constrict at the sound of her distress and knew that he wouldn't hesitate a second to go to her if she wanted him to.

'Fraser . . . Please . . .'

He closed his eyes for a moment, bracing himself to lie to her. 'Livvy, I don't know what Jack meant. I don't know anything.' He couldn't tell her now; she wouldn't be able to take it, he knew she wouldn't.

She was crying again. It seemed to her that for the past twenty-four hours she had done nothing but weep; it was uncontrollable, like the bursting of a dam. 'OK,' she managed to say, 'thanks . . .' and she replaced the receiver, without giving him the chance to say anything else. She sank down on to a chair and fumbled in her rucksack for a handkerchief.

She pulled out a clean, large, red-and-white check cotton square and wiped her face, then looked down at the handkerchief and wondered whose it was, because she couldn't remember ever seeing it before. She twisted it in her fingers, watched the checks change shape and suddenly it all came back to her. Putting the handkerchief up to her face, she started to laugh, then cry, and then laugh again, remembering the scene in the freezing summer house barely ten days ago, but which felt like a lifetime away. She ended up crying again, only this time she stood up, gently sobbing, and walked into the bedroom, throwing some clothes on to the bed – shirts, jumpers, leggings, jeans, underwear.

She pulled on a pair of jeans, some thick socks, a huge wool sweater on top of her sweatshirt, and then her Timberlands. She wiped her face on the handkerchief again, the tears streaming down it and splashing on to the neck of her sweatshirt. Fetching a holdall, she began stuffing the clothes into it. Several minutes later, without thinking again about what she was doing, she grabbed a coat from the cupboard and went to the front door.

Stopping suddenly, she turned and went back to the

phone. She picked it up and dialled a number she knew off by heart.

'Mum, it's me. I rang to tell you I'm going to Scotland. Can you take care of my things in the flat?' She paused and wiped her nose on her sleeve. 'I also rang to tell you I'm sorry and to ask you . . .' She stopped, swallowed, then said quietly, '. . . to ask you to say I'm sorry to Peter, for everything. And to tell him thank you.' She heard a silence on the other end and realised her mother was crying. 'I should have said it years ago,' she murmured. 'Thank you.' She hung up.

Turning the answerphone off, she walked back to the front door. She had an idea that the last train went from Euston; she remembered Fraser telling her that once. She didn't care what time it left, so long as she got there. She took a last glance round a flat that was no longer hers, closed the door on it and ignored the lift, making her way down the stairs to the main door.

Out on the street, she took a deep breath, the damp, cold March air filling her lungs, and whistled for a taxi. She was on her way, first to Euston, then to Aberdeen and, finally, to Fraser.

Paul Robson parked his car in the car park below Euston station and made his way up to the concourse, nervously checking behind him as he did so. He had picked Euston because it was the gateway to Manchester, to home. He walked past the row of platform entrances, the café and toilets, and on to the Left Luggage sign halfway down the length of the station. He stopped at the open hatch and buzzed for service. A middle-aged man appeared in uniform and Robson nodded.

'I'd like to leave this, please.' He handed over a small piece of hand luggage, empty except for the three-and-a-quarter-inch computer disk named Prima.

The official took it, surprised at how light it was, and made out a ticket. 'You pay on collection.'

Robson nodded. He tucked the ticket away and watched the man find a place for his bag on the shelf.

'Anything else?'

Robson shook his head. 'No, thanks.'

He turned and walked away, digging his hands deep into his pockets. He felt relieved to have got rid of the disk but he was still scared. He wondered, as he made his way back to the car, how long that feeling was going to last.

As he left the station, he noticed a tall, leggy blonde climbing out of a taxi. He watched her for a minute to take his mind off himself, thinking that she looked vaguely familiar. He tried to place her as she came towards him, but he couldn't think where he'd seen her before. Her eyes were blank and he obviously meant nothing to her. So he shrugged and gave up, wondering vaguely why she'd been crying, and continued on down to the car park.

He unlocked the Rover and climbed into it, feeling the gut ache he'd had all day finally begin to ease off. He started the engine, put the car into gear and drove off, leaving all the evidence and fear behind him in a left-luggage rack on Euston station.

PART 3

Chapter Twenty-Four

Fraser walked from the bathroom to his bedroom, drying his face on a towel. He dropped it on the bed, untied the towel from around his waist and reached for his shorts, pulling them on in one swift athletic movement. Crossing to the chest of drawers, he took out some clean socks, a freshly laundered navy-and-white striped shirt and his cufflinks box. He sat on the edge of the bed to finish dressing, staring out of the window at the slate-blue sky over Aberdeen and thinking about Livvy Davis.

He cursed himself for doing so. He had been cursing himself every day since arriving back from Sussex; he just couldn't get her out of his mind. He had no idea what the previous night's phone call meant. It worried him and yet he would not call her back, not this time. This time he had to give her some space; he had to give himself some space and try to let it go. Only the sound of her voice made him ache and he couldn't help wondering, as he'd been wondering all night long, what the hell was going on down in London.

He looked down at his lap as he finished buttoning his shirt and took the lid off his small leather stud box.

Selecting a pair of red-and-blue enamelled silver cufflinks, he held one in the palm of his hand and fiddled with the other, trying to ease it through the eyelet in his sleeve, swearing with the effort. He had just got it in one side of the cuff when the phone rang.

'Damn!' He reached back for the phone, dropped the other cufflink on to the floor, and swore loudly. The first cufflink popped out of its hole. He picked up the receiver and snapped, 'Hello!' irately searching the duvet for the little enamelled stud.

'Fraser? Good morning, it's Beth.' There was a slight pause and then she said in her soft Scottish voice, 'Fraser, are you all right?'

Fraser sighed. 'Sorry, Beth, I'm fine. I'm trying to put some cufflinks in and failing miserably.'

'You need a woman for that kind of job.' She laughed lightly.

'I think that's a sexist comment,' he answered, smiling.

'Aw, Fraser, don't be such a sissy now!'

He laughed. 'What can I do for you, Beth Broden? It must be something important, calling me at seven forty-five in the morning.'

'No, not really.' Her voice was flirtatious, light and easy to listen to. She paused. 'I thought I'd ring before I set off for the surgery and ask you for that lunch you promised me, in return for supper.'

'Lunch? When?' He had located the cufflink and was concentrating on putting it back in the eyelet, holding the telephone in the crook of his shoulder as he did so.

'How about today?'

He slipped it in and secured it the other side. 'Today? Er . . .' He stood and looked on the bedside table for his diary. 'Beth, my book's downstairs. Can you hold on while I go down to the study?'

'Yes, sure.' Beth would hold on for as long as it took to secure the date. She heard a click as the phone went down, then a minute or so later Fraser came back on the line.

'Lunch today, I don't see why not.' He didn't have much enthusiasm for it but he owed her for dinner the other night. 'Where would you like to go?'

'Oh, I don't know. How about the Skean Dhu Hotel at Ddyce?'

'OK. That's fine. Shall I pick you up?' He was glad she had suggested a weekday – that way he always had the excuse of the office to get back to. It wasn't that he didn't like Beth; more that he didn't really have the heart for her, or anyone else, at the moment.

'No, I'll make my own way there. I have a couple of house calls to make before lunch anyway. What time shall we meet?'

'One, one-thirty?'

'One o'clock is better for me, Fraser.'

'Right, one at the Skean Dhu. I'll see you then.' Fraser glanced at his watch, eager to get off the phone. He should have been at the office right now.

'Oh, Fraser?'

'Yup?'

'Good luck with the cufflinks!'

Fraser smiled, wrote their date in his book and walked back upstairs to finish dressing. If only Livvy hadn't got in the way, he thought irritably, his mind wandering helplessly back to the phone call last night, an affair with Beth Broden might have been rather good fun.

*

305

Gordon Fife sat on the edge of Fraser's desk and tapped his pen on his thigh as he spoke. He had a harsh Glaswegian accent that he hadn't lost at all in the twenty years he had been in Aberdeen and his vowels curdled the words, stringing them into what sounded like one long sentence. He was explaining an idea for a new layout that the chief sub had put forward. He was enthusiastic about the idea, but he wanted the boss's approval before he gave the go-ahead. He was like that, Gordon Fife, an exceptional editor with a lifetime's experience on the paper but with an old-fashioned courtesy that meant the boss had to have last say. Fraser Stewart owned the paper, and with ownership came the right to be consulted, even if he did usually end up agreeing with Gordon.

Fraser stared at a space somewhere in the middle of the room and nodded every now and then when a word punctured the bubble of private thought around him. He wasn't listening; he had no idea of what Gordon was on about because his mind had irrepressibly slipped back into thinking about Livvy. However much he tried to deny it, the phone call last night had really upset him. He couldn't help wondering if he should have told her his suspicions about Hugh and James at college, but it had all happened so many years ago that he wasn't sure he even believed them himself any more. And how would she have reacted to them? She had enough to cope with; he didn't want to add to her burden. Besides, would she really thank him for digging up the past like that? Telling her things that he either should have told her years ago or never at all?

He sighed heavily and shook his head, wondering why she kept messing up his mind like this. Jeeze, he had enough to think about without worrying about a woman four hundred miles away in the kind of trouble he had no way of getting her out of. He'd hardly begun going through the stuff on IMACO, for a start. Sometimes he really wished he'd never even gone down to Sussex. Glancing up at Gordon to try and catch the end of his monologue, he saw that the older man was suddenly silent, staring at him, his dark features glowering. He was so far away he hadn't even heard Fife stop talking!

He waited for Gordon to speak.

'What's tha matter wi' yae, Fraser? Yae haven't heerd a single worrrd I've bin sayin'!'

Fraser shrugged. 'Gordon, I'm sorry. I've got something on my mind.'

'Yae're noot wrrong there.' Gordon looked across Fraser's head and nodded towards the plate-glass wall of the office. Fraser looked round. 'Looks like shae has an' all!' His secretary Carol was gesticulating at him. 'Reckon someone wants yaer attention,' Gordon said dourly.

Fraser nodded. 'Listen, Gordon, go ahead and do what you think best on this layout. I'll have a look at the rough drafts and tell you what I think.' He stood. 'Is that OK?'

'It'll have ta be.'

'Thanks.' Fraser moved towards the door.

'They're rarely worth it, Fraser, yae know,' Gordon observed drily.

Fraser glanced over his shoulder. 'Tell me about it!' he answered, and smiling hopelessly, he went out to speak to Carol.

'Fraser, there's a young woman in reception who wants to see you. She said it's personal.'

He nodded. This wasn't a rare occurrence. With the

amount of cases he brought to the small claims court for various people across Aberdeenshire, he always had someone or other asking to see him on a private matter. 'I'll go right down. Could you give me a buzz in reception in time for the editorial? It'll give me an excuse to get away.'

'Yes, sure.'

He picked up a notepad from Carol's desk and took a pen out of her basket. 'Can I borrow these?'

She pulled a face at him. 'Oh, go on then.'

'Thanks.' He headed across the office to the lifts and she watched him go.

He's such a good-looking man, she thought wistfully, then she pulled herself up sharply and sat down at her desk. Out of your league, Carol, she reminded herself as she went back to her screen. Still, no harm in dreaming. And she smiled as she got on with her work.

Fraser swung open the double doors that led from the main part of the building into the smart grey reception area of the *Aberdeen Angus Press* and strode over to the desk. He smiled at Rhona the receptionist and asked who wanted to see him. She pointed to the far corner of the seating area where a tall blonde stood looking at some of the *Angus Press* back editions that had been framed for the wall, a huge holdall by her feet and the black rucksack slung over her shoulder. He knew who it was even before she turned round.

'Livvy?'

She glanced over her shoulder, saw him and then smiled. Turning towards him, she dropped the rucksack on to the floor and Fraser burst out, 'My God! What are you doing here?'

The instant he said it he felt stupid; he should have been

able to think of something a little more inspired as a first greeting. He crossed reception, trying to smile but not really managing it, feeling too confused and stunned to get his thoughts properly together. He stopped just in front of her and wondered if he should kiss her but decided not to, embarrassed by the interested stares of the girls on reception.

'I can't believe it!' he said. 'How come?'

Livvy shrugged. This wasn't the type of welcome she'd expected. 'I don't know,' she answered. 'I did it on the spur of the moment.' She wasn't going to tell him what had happened, not here and now, not with the response he'd just shown. She felt herself closing up and struggled to stay relaxed, smiling uneasily.

Suddenly Fraser took her hands – he couldn't stop himself – and pulled her forward to hug her. She felt good, just as he had known she would in all the times he'd imagined it over the past week. He stood back, still holding her hands, and laughed. 'Well, this is just so great!' The excitement welled up inside him and he started to say how much he had missed her and how much he wanted her, even now, standing right there in reception, when a vague nagging doubt suddenly sprang up in his mind and stopped him before he'd uttered a word.

What are you doing? he thought with instant panic. Look at where all this got you last time. And the time before that. He clamped his mouth shut and the doubt got a real grip. She doesn't even know why she's here, the tiny voice inside his head echoed, she just jumped on a train and expected you to be there, ready and waiting to smooth over the cracks. She wants you only for a limited time, don't you know that already? And when she's feeling better, more able to face the world again, she'll hurry back to James and get on with her life. Uh-oh, Fraser, get a hold of yourself, man! Stand well back, give the woman a wide berth!

Livvy was smiling, looking up at Fraser's face with relief when she saw it change. She watched a clear conflict of emotion in his eyes, witnessed the laughter die in them and a wariness replace it. Then she saw a coolness there that she had never seen before and it made her instinctively pull her hands away and hold them tensely by her side.

'Fraser?'

He glanced back at her and she realised that his face had closed up. 'Listen, Livvy, I'm sorry,' he said hurriedly, 'but I've got a lot on my mind. I have a meeting in a few minutes.'

'Oh.' She nodded, a biting anger rising in her chest. She had come five hundred miles for this! She wanted affection, she needed warmth and reassurance, and he was too busy – he had a meeting! 'Well, do you think you could recommend a hotel?' she said icily. 'I need a bath, I've been travelling all night.'

'Oh God, yes!' He shook his head. 'I mean, no! You can stay with me, you must, I won't let you go to a hotel.'

She stood awkwardly while he strode over to reception and asked them to ring up to Carol for his briefcase. Looking at his back she thought how well cut his suit was over the wide muscle of his shoulder and how the dark navy made him look more powerful, more distant. She felt her breath catch in her throat and was angry at it. There was no place for those feelings, she told herself furiously; he had made that quite clear.

After a few minutes a girl popped her head round the double doors and held out a briefcase. Fraser thanked her, took the case and opened it on the reception desk. He took out his house keys and clicked the case shut again.

'Rhona, could you ring for a taxi, to 54 Rubislaw Terrace?'

'Yes, sure.'

'Thanks.' He turned and walked back to Livvy. 'Here are my house keys.' He held out the small bunch and Livvy took them silently. 'The heating's on, there's loads of hot water, just do whatever you want.' He stopped for a moment and flushed slightly, then went on, 'You can sleep in my room for the time being; the spare room isn't made up.'

'Oh.'

He rushed on, 'Mrs Avery is coming in this afternoon to do the house; I'll ring her and ask her to do the other bed. It's just if you want to sleep now, that's all.'

Livvy forced a smile. She could see the girls on reception looking at her with open curiosity and she had an over-whelming urge to turn and shout, it's all right! There's nothing between us! But she merely mumbled her thanks and glanced away.

Fraser looked out of the window for any sign of the taxi, desperate to get back to the safety of his office. He wanted to touch her so much that if he didn't leave he would end up just marching her out of the building, into the privacy of a dark alley and practically jumping on her.

Livvy noticed his tension and misinterpreted it. 'I'm sure the taxi will be here any minute. Don't let me keep you.'

He hesitated. 'Are you sure you don't mind?'

'Of course not!' she snapped.

'OK. Fine!' he snapped back. Oh God, this was all going wrong. 'Look, I'll call you at lunch time, maybe drop home for an hour or so, just to check everything's all right.' He had completely forgotten his lunch with Beth.

Livvy softened slightly. 'All right,' she answered. 'Thanks.' She felt stupid all of a sudden. She should have known he had work to do; he couldn't just drop everything.

She glanced up at the wall. 'Your paper is much bigger than I thought.'

'Yes,' Fraser smiled. 'We're one of the biggest independent regional newspapers in the UK. We've got a distribution of nearly a hundred and fifty thousand daily, which isn't bad considering we started right down at the bottom of the heap ten years ago. Actually, it's bloody marvellous, but it's not been easy—' He stopped suddenly. 'I'm boring you.'

Livvy smiled. 'No, I'm very pleased for you.' She watched him as he stared up with pride at one of the front pages framed on the wall and realised that she really didn't know this man at all. He'd been working and building this paper for ten years and yet had hardly ever talked about it. Perhaps she'd never asked, she thought, and wondered how many other things there were about him that she'd been too self-obsessed to notice. She looked away from his face and said, 'You'd better go up to your meeting.' The thought had saddened her and she felt terribly tired all of a sudden.

'Yes, I guess so.' He shrugged and stepped back a pace. He didn't want to kiss her, or rather he did, but not politely, and he sure as hell wasn't going to make that mistake. 'I'll see you later, then.'

'OK.'

He turned and walked back towards the double doors, collecting his briefcase off reception as he went. He held up his hand in a salute and disappeared into the main part of the building. Livvy stared after him until the double doors had stopped swinging and were still. After a while, she tore her gaze away and saw that Rhona and her friend on reception were ogling her again. She picked up her holdall and rucksack, feeling decidedly uncomfortable, and headed towards the entrance. 'I think I'll wait outside for the taxi,' she said. She was sure they recognised her and it made her stomach churn. 'I could do with the fresh air.'

Without looking over at them again, she hurried out, down the steps of the building and on to the street where it was pelting it down with heavy, sleeting rain. 'That's all I need,' she muttered and dropped her holdall so as to cover her head with the rucksack and at least provide some cover until the taxi arrived.

'OK. Just to recap.' Fraser sat on the edge of his desk and glanced round the faces in the meeting. Gordon had already been through most of this but it was his job to sum up at their daily meetings; Gordon liked it that way. 'We'll run the stabbing story on page three; five and seven can take the two lead local stories; and on the right in the boxed column on three we'll have the feature headers.'

The chief sub made a note of this on her pad, knowing it was her responsibility to shuffle everything around on the screen in order to make sure it all fitted on to the page in the right format.

'That's it, everyone. Thanks a lot.' Fraser smiled and the team began to stand, stretch and head for the door. It was after eleven and they were all eager to get on. The copy had to be ready by one for the first edition to print at one-thirty. Fraser watched them go, Gordon leading the way, and noticed Andy, one of the special reporters on industry, waiting to see him. He motioned for him to come over and called for the last person to shut the door.

'Right, Andy,' Fraser said when the room was empty. 'What can I do for you?'

'I spoke to Gordon last night about a lead I've just had on a story down at IMACO,' Andy answered. 'He told me to discuss it with you before I went any further.'

'What's the lead?'

'Well, it's come from a confidential source and at the moment I don't have that many details, but it's to do with the fertiliser they produce, Benzotytrin. I think there's been a few problems with it.'

'Problems?'

'Yes, the MAFF are investigating it, routine tests apparently, but I think there could be more to it.' Andy spoke in a rushed, excited voice. He was young and fairly new to the paper and probably thought that this, if it went through, could be his biggest story.

'I see.' Fraser was well aware of the investigation by the Ministry of Food, Fisheries and Agriculture, but he had his own contact at IMACO working on it and so far there was no reason to suspect anything untoward. He didn't want any interference right now and he couldn't afford any risks or complications; the last thing he needed was a junior reporter blundering around.

He thought for a short while and then said, 'Look, Andy, what I'm going to say isn't going to be easy to take when you've just got an excellent lead on a story, but' – he looked directly at the young reporter – 'I'd rather that you didn't take this any further at the moment.' He saw the disappointment clearly on Andy's face but he wasn't going to give anything away. 'I'm not in a position right now to give my reasons, but I can tell you that I've got a personal interest in this whole thing. The information you've just given me is important, but I don't want to break a story on it, not now. I'm sorry.'

'So you don't want me to research it?' Andy was clearly upset.

'No, not on your own.'

'You don't think I've enough experience, is that it?'

Fraser hesitated for a moment, wondering how much to give away. Andy was a good reporter, one of the paper's rising stars, and he didn't want to risk losing him. He adopted a conciliatory tone: 'It's not that at all, Andy. What I'd like to do is put it on hold for a couple of weeks, no longer, until I find out exactly which direction it would be best to go in. Once I'm clear, I'd like you to carry on with it, work with me. Does that sound fair?'

'What if the story breaks in another paper, in the nationals before then? We've missed a bloody good opportunity!'

Fraser nodded. 'If I think it's going to break, we'll run it first, but' – he paused – 'there could be a lot more to it, if we wait and see.'

Andy shrugged. He was loath to let it go but Fraser was the boss and he knew from his short time there that the guy never missed a trick. He decided to give him the benefit of the doubt, even if it did mean a little snooping round on his own.

Fraser stood up. 'Andy, take a piece of advice, will you? Don't go snooping around on your own, not yet. All right?'

Andy looked up sharply and flushed. The boss could mind-read as well! He shrugged again. 'All right,' he said grudgingly.

Fraser smiled. 'Thanks. I appreciate this, Andy.'

'Yeah, sure.'

As Andy left the office, Fraser motioned to Carol to come

in. 'Carol, could you field my calls for an hour or so? I want to get through a pile of work this morning and I need the quiet.'

She nodded.

'Oh, and don't let anyone in unless they have a world exclusive for the *Aberdeen Angus Press*. OK?' He grinned and she smiled back. She held her two fingers up to her brow in a mock salute and left the office, closing the door behind her. Fraser watched her go back to her desk, jab a few buttons on her telephone to transfer his calls to her extension, and then settle behind her screen. He sat down, switched on his own PC and opened the middle drawer in his desk to take out his disk file.

This was something he should have done days ago, as soon as he heard from his contact in IMACO. Bloody Livvy – his mind just hadn't been his own! He pressed the enter key and flipped up the first case he'd taken to the small claims court against IMACO five years ago, his finger working the cursor down the list of contents in the file. Before he got the report back on the MAFF-banned chemicals, he had to be certain of his facts. It would save a hell of a lot of time in the long run if he knew right from the word go that there could be a connection. Peering closer at the screen, he worked down through the list, noting the pages he specifically needed to look at, and then pressed the key to flip up the first one. Within minutes he was totally absorbed.

It was just before one when Carol finally buzzed him. He started, picked up the phone and for the first time in nearly two hours, looked away from the screen.

'Yup, Fraser Stewart.'

'Fraser, it's Carol. Sorry to disturb you, but in your book you've got a lunch pencilled in, for one o'clock at the Skean Dhu Hotel. I didn't know if it was cancelled or you'd forgotten . . .'

'Oh damn!'

'You'd forgotten.'

'Yes. Can you look up the number of the Green Oak surgery for me, Carol? I'll have to ring and cancel.' He glanced at his watch and saw it was nearly one. 'Forget that. Ring the hotel for me, could you? And tell them I'm late but I'm on my way.'

'Sure.'

He hung up and turned again to his screen. He saved the file, switched the machine off and locked the disks in the drawer. Grabbing his jacket from the back of his chair, he stood, took his wallet out of his briefcase and headed out of the office.

'Thanks, Carol,' he called as he made his way across to the stairs, 'I owe you one.'

Beth was waiting at the table when Fraser arrived at the restaurant. She was reading the menu, one of only three women in the businessmen's eating place, and was attracting glances from all parts of the room. Fraser crossed quickly to her, thought how different physically she was to Livvy, and then stopped, closed his eyes for an instant and murmured, 'Oh damn,' under his breath as he realised he had promised to go home and check on Livvy. He had no hesitation as to where he'd rather be and he knew that was unfair. Just as he was about to turn and head for the phones, Beth put the menu down and glanced up. She saw him immediately halfway across the room and called out to him.

'Fraser, over here.' He smiled, continued over to the table and bent to kiss her cheek.

'Hello, Beth.'

'Is that all I get?'

He laughed. 'Beth Broden, I hardly know you!'

'Don't worry, we'll soon take care of that,' she said. 'Come on, sit down. I've been here for ages, I'm starving!'

'I know, I'm sorry, Beth.' Fraser hovered uncomfortably for a moment and then said, 'Look, I know I'm terribly late, but would you excuse me for five minutes? I have to make a phone call.'

She shrugged. 'Of course. Nothing serious, I hope?'

He shook his head. 'No, nothing serious. I won't be long. Could you order me a gin and tonic?'

'All right.' She watched him go and then ordered him a large measure of Gordon's and a small tonic. After the call from Dorsey last night, she knew she had to get things moving with Fraser, and a double gin was as good a place as any to start. Not that she wanted him drunk, of course. No, Beth liked her pound of flesh and knew full well that too much booze only ruined it. More pliable than drunk, she thought, as the waiter brought the G & T over to the table; relaxed and pliable, that would do for starters. And she sat back, sipped her Perrier water and looked down the wine list the waiter had just left on the table, pondering on what bottle they should have.

Livvy sat in Fraser's huge, messy kitchen, showered, changed and waiting for him to come home as he had promised. She was cross with herself for her earlier pique and although she put it down to tiredness, she desperately wanted to make it up to him, to pretend she had just arrived again and get everything off on the right foot. She felt miserable and alone in the big old house. It seemed very much like a family home – it had probably belonged to Fraser's mother – and reminded her of The Old Rectory with its faded, well-used elegance. This thought merely made her feel even more wretched, made her long for Fraser, for the warmth and comfort of him.

She glanced over at the clock on the cooker and saw that it was coming on for half past one. She began to worry. What if he didn't want to come home, had only said he would to please her? What if she'd made a ghastly mistake coming to Scotland? She stood up and paced the length of the kitchen. A faint ringing suddenly interrupted the thoughts going round and round in her mind. She ran out into the hall, wondering where the ring was coming from, and frantically opened several doors before she found Fraser's study. She lunged for the phone and gasped, 'Hello?' before collapsing into a chair.

'Hi Livvy, it's Fraser.'

'Oh.' A phone call meant no visit. She tried to push down the crushing disappointment that rose in her chest and said as brightly as she could, 'Is everything all right?'

'Yes, fine. Except that I forgot a business lunch today. I'd have forgotten to turn up if it hadn't been for Carol reminding me.' He paused. 'I'm sorry, really I am. Are you all right there? Did you find everything you need?'

Livvy felt slightly reassured by his tone; he did sound sorry and concerned. 'Yes, everything's fine,' she answered. 'Don't worry.'

Fraser breathed easier. He was about to say that maybe he'd be home early that night if he could when he felt a light tap on his shoulder. He turned, forgetting to put his hand

319

over the mouthpiece, and said, 'Oh! Beth?'

'Hi.' She leaned forward and much to his surprise brushed his lips with her own. 'I thought I'd bring you your drink,' she said softly, handing him the glass. 'On my way to the ladies.'

'Oh, er, thanks.' Fraser was cross and embarrassed by her tone. It was far too intimate for their level of friendship. He waited for her to wander off to reception and then said quickly, 'Livvy? You still there?'

But her voice was icy on the other end. She had heard everything, even what sounded like a kiss, and was filled with a raging fury. 'Yes,' she snapped, 'enjoy your business lunch.' And close to tears, she slammed the phone down.

He was left looking at the receiver and feeling more than a little angry himself. Why did she always expect the world to revolve around her, for God's sake? And when it didn't, she jumped right off the deep end. He hung up and stood for a moment wondering whether to call again, just to explain. But he sighed and decided against it as Beth came towards him; it was rude to keep her waiting any longer than he had done already.

'You OK?'

She nodded. 'Sorry to interrupt your phone call,' she said, smiling. 'You looked so serious, I just couldn't resist it.'

Fraser shrugged. 'Oh well, no harm done,' he lied and she slipped her arm through his. 'Come on, or they won't take our order.' And together they made their way back to the restaurant.

Livvy sat in the study and stared at the phone. Her anger had almost instantly changed to distress and was now slowly working itself into a hefty dose of bitter self-pity.

She put her head in her hands, closed her eyes and let it all wash over her.

Sometime later, when the afternoon had started to close in and the room was almost dark, she looked up and decided she needed a drink. She walked into the hall, found her rucksack and took out the bottle of vodka she had bought at Euston Station. She carried it through to the kitchen, found a glass, half a carton of juice and some ice in the freezer, and then decided that she might as well take a valium with the vodka and orange, to calm herself before she had to face Fraser that evening. She went back to the rucksack for the bottle of pills, took two for safe measure and popped them into her mouth, swallowing down a gulp of the Smirnoff and feeling instantly comforted by the warmth in her stomach.

Still holding the bottle, along with the carton of juice and her glass, she climbed the stairs to Fraser's room, closed the door behind her and sat down on the bed. Safe from the arrival of Mrs Avery, she tucked herself under the covers, topped up her glass and switched on the radio. She lay, alone in semi-darkness, swigging vodka and listening blankly to the noise of an afternoon play while the pills took effect and slowly her mind slipped into oblivion.

Fraser glanced down surreptitiously at his watch as he stood in the car park of the Skean Dhu with Beth and saw that it was way after three. Lunch had been a much longer affair than he had planned and he'd drunk far more than he'd wanted to, but it was such a relief to be able to talk to someone at last about Livvy and all the problems that came with her. And Beth understood; she had talked some sense into him, made him see that pandering to Livvy's every need would only make things worse. Livvy had to stand on her own two feet, Beth said; that way she would build up the strength to face whatever she might have to in the future. Fraser couldn't spend his life nursemaiding her, however much he wanted to. Livvy would never respect him if he did.

He looked up from his watch at Beth's face as they stood in the cold and saw how the wind had already whipped some colour into her cheeks. Her curly brown hair was blown out of its habitual neat style and she held one hand up to it to keep it from sweeping across her face. She looked both wild and vulnerable at the same time and Fraser smiled at her, reconciling the thought of the senior partner in the Green Oak surgery with the funny, sexy woman in front of him.

Beth noticed the look, and the smile, and she knew that she'd moved things up a level this lunch time. She was pleased with herself. 'What's funny?' she asked.

He shrugged. 'Nothing.'

'Well, it's good to see you smile, after the doom and gloom earlier on.'

Fraser pulled a face. 'I know, I'm sorry. Thanks for all the advice.'

She shook her head at him. 'As long as it doesn't go to waste. Remember what I said about leaving well alone, letting her get on with it and giving her some space.'

'Yes, doctor.'

She laughed, but underneath the laughter was a steely determination to get her message across. She needed Fraser's undivided attention over the next month or so if she was going to distract him, and it wouldn't be at all easy if he was constantly drooling over the love of his life. She moved an inch or so closer to him and put her hands on his shoulders, holding the velvet lapels of his overcoat.

'You know what doctors always prescribe for the worst kind of upset?'

He smiled. 'Tell me.'

Pulling him towards her, she held her mouth just by his, barely touching his lips and said, 'To kiss it better.' Then she opened her mouth and kissed him.

Fraser stood perfectly still and tried to locate his feelings. The kiss was nice – he could feel the warmth of her tongue and he kissed her back, an easy, relaxed kiss – but there wasn't any fire. There wasn't the intense ache in his groin that he had virtually every time he looked at Livvy.

Moments later, Beth stood back and gazed at him. She had no idea of the incredible passion he was capable of with Livvy and so was pleased with his response. She touched his face and said, 'I really should go, I have surgery.'

He nodded.

'To be continued?'

He leaned forward and brushed the tip of her nose with his lips. 'I think so,' he answered. Taking her arm, he walked her across to her car. Opening the driver's door, Beth threw her bag on the passenger seat and slid in, exposing a good expanse of thigh for him as she did so. She fastened her seat belt and looked up.

'If you want to talk at any time, just call me, OK?'

'Yeah, thanks, Beth, I really appreciate . . .'

She put her hand up to his mouth and silenced him. 'Any time,' she said again and then started the car.

He slammed the door shut and watched her manoeuvre out of the parking space and drive off towards the exit. He turned and, digging his hands in his pockets, struggled against the wind towards his own car, whistling, and feeling better than he had done for a week.

It was getting on for seven when Fraser finally made it home from the paper. The wind of the afternoon had brought with it another sleet storm and he was drenched walking from the car to the house on Rubislaw Terrace. He fumbled with the key, his hands frozen, and rang the bell a couple of times, hoping that Livvy would come and open the door for him. But there was no reply and after some time with an icy lock and numb fingers, he swung open the heavy front door and stepped into the warmth of the house.

He called out to Livvy.

Walking into the kitchen, he saw that Mrs Avery had been, turned on the lights for him and left something there for his supper. He blessed her silently, as he did most nights and went to the fridge for a beer. Drinking straight from the can, Fraser walked into the sitting room looking for Livvy, then back into the hall. He noticed her rucksack, open at the foot of the stairs, and picked it up to close it. As he did so, the bottle of valium fell out, its lid undone, and several of the little white pills spilt on to the carpet.

'Oh blast!' He bent to retrieve them, glanced at the label on the bottle and frowned, seeing they were tranquillisers. Taking the rucksack upstairs, he went first to the spare room, saw that it was empty and then to his own bedroom, reassured by the sound of the radio coming from it. He opened the door and peered in.

'Livvy? Hello? Are you awake?'

The room was dark and it looked as if Livvy was asleep. He crept in, switched the radio off and drew the curtains, the light from the landing making it easier to see. He turned, looked down at the bed and saw that Livvy was flat out, curled up under the covers and breathing deeply. He wanted to touch her, so he moved closer and squatted down, bringing his face even with hers and stroked a fine strand of hair off her cheek. She moved, opened her eyes for a moment and blearily said, 'Fraser, is that you?' The force of nearly half a litre of vodka hit him full in the face.

Recoiling instantly from the smell, he glanced up at the bedside table and saw the empty bottle. Livvy had closed her eyes and passed out again. Standing up, he took the bottle and the glass and strode from the room, closing the door behind him. He still had the valium in his hand.

Sitting on the top stair, he looked again at the label, saw the date of the prescription and the number of pills in the bottle. Carefully he emptied the remainder into the palm of his hand and counted them. There were four left. Calculating how many days she'd had them, he worked out that Livvy was taking three to four pills a day, which, along with half a litre of vodka, was a pretty stiff cocktail! He sat and stared down at the tiny little opiates, then, suddenly angry, he got up, walked into the bathroom and threw them down the toilet. He flushed, made sure they had all disappeared and breathed a sigh of relief.

If he really was going to help Livvy he had to make her face up to what had happened and attempt to get on with her life. It sounded hard, Beth said, but it was the only way. He still didn't know if Beth was right, but what he did know was that pills and booze weren't the answer; and that was something he knew from very bitter experience.

Chapter Twenty-Five

Fraser's alarm went off at the usual time: six-thirty. He reached out, put his hand over the button and stopped the sharp, piercing bleep. He was awake anyway; he'd been awake for ages, listening to Livvy downstairs.

He pulled back the heavy wool blankets on the spare bed and stood up, stretching slowly before finding his towelling robe, wrapping himself in it and tying it as he went out on to the landing. It was cold in the house – the heating had only just come on – and his bare feet were chilly. He descended the stairs and followed the noise of the radio into the kitchen, pushing his hair out of his eyes and rubbing his hand wearily over his face as he went. Opening the door quietly, he saw Livvy, curled up in an old Victorian armchair in front of the Aga, wrapped in a tartan rug and staring blankly out of the window. He walked into the room, closed the door behind him and waited for her to look round.

'Oh, Fraser?' She tucked a long strand of hair that had fallen over her face behind her ear and smiled, a jaded half-smile that had no warmth in it. She looked tired and ashen, and her face was slightly puffy from the vodka.

'It's cold,' she said. 'I couldn't sleep.'

He moved over to the sink and filled the kettle. If this had been two weeks ago, he thought miserably, I'd have gone to her, lifted her up and carried her back to bed, warmed her, made her sleep. But now he said nothing. He was silent as he brought the kettle over to the Aga, then he looked at her and asked her if she wanted some tea. She nodded.

'Fraser, I know this sounds odd,' she said, looking away, 'but I had some pills here yesterday and now I can't find them.' She held her hands in her lap and niggled at the raw edge of a fingernail for a few moments, then she faced him. 'They're on prescription from the doctor. Have you seen them?'

He put the two cups he was holding on the table. 'Yes,' he answered calmly. 'I flushed them down the toilet.'

Livvy was uncertain if she'd heard him correctly. 'I'm sorry?' she asked. 'What did you say?'

'I said I flushed them down the toilet, Livvy.' He watched the look of sheer disbelief on her face and then saw it swiftly change to anger. 'You don't need them,' he said. 'Believe me, you really don't.'

'Don't need them!' Her pale face had suddenly flushed a deep red and her eyes glittered dangerously. 'I have just had the worst experience of my life, I'm facing up to fifteen years in Holloway prison for a crime I didn't commit and you tell me "Lay off the valium, Livvy, all you need is some fresh air and a good bracing walk"!' She stood up. 'Shit! You make me sick, Fraser! What in God's name do you know about it anyway?'

Fraser swallowed hard. He had never seen her angry and he'd never heard her swear before. His mind was in turmoil.

'You don't need them,' he said again, keeping his voice calm. 'Pills and booze won't get you anywhere, Livvy.'

'Oh yeah? Since when did you become such an expert in emotional problems?' she yelled. 'How dare you!'

Fraser's equilibrium snapped. 'Oh, I dare, all right!' he shouted back. 'This is my house and I . . .' He stopped abruptly. He was going to say, I love you, I won't see you destroy yourself like my father did; but he just couldn't bring himself to admit it. The words died in his throat.

Livvy saw the emotion on his face and looked away. All of a sudden she just wanted to sit down and weep. She bit the inside of her lip and the old sore opened up. The taste of blood kept her from breaking down; it reminded her of her strength. 'You what?' she asked.

Fraser took a breath. 'I think you should face up to it,' he said. 'I know it sounds hard but it's the only way to get through it.'

She looked at him and shook her head. 'Hard? It sounds impossible.' Sitting down again she said, 'Where do you suggest I begin, Fraser?' He had no idea of what had happened to her and she couldn't keep the sarcasm out of her voice. 'Tell me, I'm curious.'

He moved closer to her. 'Well, for one thing you're out on bail and, even though you have to go back for the committal hearing, it'll be six months before your case is heard.' He was getting into his stride and his voice took on an edge of tension. 'You didn't commit this crime, Livvy, but someone did. You're a first-class reporter – investigate it, find a lead and go for it. You've done it in the past, with stories, with the most tenuous of leads. You could get a job, something low-key and . . .' Fraser stopped.

Livvy had put her hands up to her face and was laughing,

not nicely, but with malice, and almost hysterically.

'What's so damn funny?' he said icily.

'You!' she screeched. 'You're a complete bloody joke!'

He stepped back as if she'd slapped him. 'Thank you for that!' He was angry. 'I don't see what's so amusing about what I've just said.'

'You don't? Really?' Livvy's laughter died as suddenly as it had started. 'Well, how the hell do you think this ace hot reporter is going to get started? Eh? Who's going to give me a job, Fraser? Me, a former City Television presenter dropped like a hot brick owing to her impending imprisonment! I've nowhere to live, I have been hounded and humiliated by the press . . . I have nothing.' She suddenly shouted. 'Nothing! And you expect me to carry on like the *Cook Report*.' She stopped, knowing that if she went on she would just end up sobbing.

She turned away and crossed to the door. 'You asked me to come here,' she said, her voice breaking. 'Remember? And now I'm here you don't want me.' She said it with such startling pain that Fraser winced, his whole body feeling it. He moved towards her but she held up her hands. 'No! Don't!' she cried. 'Don't mess me up any more.' And pulling open the door, she fled from the room. Fraser heard her footsteps in the hall and then on the stairs. He was frozen to the spot for a minute, not knowing what to do. Then he started and looked up as the phone rang.

By the time he'd hung up, he knew she'd gone. He sat at his desk with a sick, sinking feeling in the pit of his stomach and put his head in his hands. He'd had to answer it; then he'd had to sort out the problem with the print room and find the number of the engineering company that had installed the machine so that they could fix it in the next few hours. Christ, why did it have to happen just then? And he knew he had to sit tight for at least half an hour, to make sure someone turned up and saw to the problem. He stood and walked out into the empty hall, feeling as if the house was suddenly far less homely than it had been last night.

That's ridiculous, he told himself, going upstairs to dress. How can twelve hours make any difference? You were perfectly happy here before.

But as he went into the bathroom, he saw Livvy's wash things on the side of the bath, forgotten in her hurry to leave, and knew it wasn't ridiculous. Having Livvy in his home, even for that short period of time, made him realise now how lonely he was, how much time he'd dedicated to the paper at the expense of his own life. He picked up the small collection of things and took them into his bedroom, leaving them on the bureau while he sat on the bed to make a call. He would go after her, he knew that, and dialling the station, he hoped to God that he hadn't already missed the first train out of Aberdeen.

Livvy sat on a hard wooden bench in Aberdeen station with her knees tucked under her and her arms hugged around them, huddled inside her thick jacket and still absolutely frozen. She thought miserably back to the row with Fraser and wished with all her heart that it hadn't happened. She was still angry at his blithe dismissal of her dilemma but here she was, running away again, only this time she really had no idea where she would end up. She stared across at the poster for the *Aberdeen Angus Press* and thought, What am I doing? I have nothing down in London, nothing to go back to.

She dropped her head down on to her knees and continued to gaze at the advert, a well laid-out front page of the paper, with colour photographs and snappy headlines; and she thought about Fraser, about the paper he'd built up from the scrappy, twenty-page local journal he'd once shown her at college, all those years ago. Maybe he does have some right to spout off about courage and facing up to things, she thought grudgingly. After all, he'd done exactly that, made something out of nothing. But what did he seriously expect her to do? It wasn't as if she were even particularly employable.

Perhaps I'll just sit here forever, she reflected, cold, hungover and confused, until they find me, frozen solid, the imprint of the wooden slats on my bum. She smiled at the last thought, imagining how they would have to bury her, once rigor mortis had set in, in an upright position, possibly with the bench still attached. She started to giggle, the picture in her head becoming more and more ridiculous until suddenly she was genuinely and openly laughing, for the first time in weeks, the pleasure of it warming her right through to the heart.

She sat up and wiped the tears from her eyes, still looking directly at the ad for Fraser's paper. She felt refreshed by her laughter, her energy felt regenerated and she thought that maybe, just maybe, Fraser did have a point. Certainly she knew she didn't want to go home – the further away from the mess she was the better. What was there to go home to anyway? She had no flat, no job; she didn't want to see James, at least not until they'd both had time to think. But what would she do if she stayed here? Get a job? How? She had no idea where to start. She'd never really had to look for a job – the BBC had taken her straight from

Oxford, probably off the back of her father's reputation, trained her up and then the rest had quite literally fallen into her lap. She couldn't even remember writing a CV!

Standing up, Livvy stamped her feet on the ground to warm them and thought hard about what to do next, ideas flashing through her mind. She took one final look at the *Angus Press* poster before turning towards the café to get another coffee and suddenly a brainwave hit her. 'You're a first-class reporter,' she heard loud and clear in her mind, Fraser's voice insistent. 'Investigate, follow leads, find stories!' The words went round and round as she stared at the ad and the first seeds of hope began to grow inside her.

Yes, she thought, I *was* good at my job. She'd done some cracking investigative journalism for the BBC; she knew how to present stories; she'd written scripts, reports – she could work on a paper, she was sure she could. She could work on the *Angus Press*! But, as soon as the bubble of optimism rose in the air, it burst. Don't be insane, she told herself angrily, it's Fraser's paper. You're in deep trouble, your life is a mess and you think you can just walk into a job like that. Oh, grow up, Livvy dear!

Miserable again, she walked across to the huge, six-by-six billboard, and studied the layout of the *Angus Press* and the tone of the paper. She'd seen it all before, of course. She'd seen it in television several years ago when marketing and consumerism had suddenly hit the air waves and everything was about viewing figures and a more consumer-friendly approach. That was what her own job had been all about: arts, leisure. She could see exactly where Fraser was taking the paper and she smiled at his good sense. She looked closely at the headers on the top of the page advertising what was inside and thought that he'd done it well, but that it could have done with more of a consumerist feel; he could have dressed it up more. Small colour pictures, jazzy one-liners, that sort of thing; more to get people looking inside, more than just news.

Consumerism, she mused, consumer affairs, that was what everyone was concentrating on now in the media. Maybe it hadn't hit Aberdeen in full force yet? But when it did . . . She stopped suddenly as something hit her. Maybe, just maybe that was where she might have something to offer. She mulled the idea over and over in her mind for a few minutes, thinking hard. The *Aberdeen Angus Press* had already gone halfway down that route – why not suggest to them a way to finish it off? Surely it was worth a try, she thought, with a dose of her old optimism returning. At the very least it was worth asking, wasn't it?

Turning away, she glanced up at the station clock and saw that it was nearly seven-thirty. If she was going to leave Scotland, she still had another twenty minutes to wait for the first train. She felt in her jacket pocket for her ticket, pulled it out, looked at it and then hastily put it back again. She made her decision without any more thought, knowing that if she gave herself even one more minute she'd lose her nerve and change her mind. No, she decided, she wasn't going to leave, not yet, not until she'd done what Fraser suggested, and had a go at facing up to things.

Heading over to the bench, she bent and grabbed her rucksack, slinging it over her shoulder, then took hold of her bag. The first thing she had to do was find a hotel, shower, change and ring the paper. She didn't even think about coming into contact with Fraser – that had completely gone out of her mind. She just thought about the job, concentrated on that. The surge in her confidence was so fragile that that was as much as she could cope with for the moment.

Locating a guard on the far side of the concourse, she made her way over to him to ask about where to stay and was directed to the Victoria Hotel on Market Street. Hurriedly she left the station. She called for a taxi on her way out, jumped straight into it and sat back, relieved that she'd finally done something positive, just as the big hand on the clock hit the half hour exactly.

Fraser pulled up at the station at seven-thirty on the dot. He knew the first train left Aberdeen at seven fifty-five for London King's Cross and he'd rushed like crazy to get there on time. He locked the car and ran into the station, glancing up at the departures board to see that the train left from platform three and was just in. He ran over the bridge to get to it and then slowed to a jog, peering through the windows of each carriage from one end of the train to the other to see which one she was in. He couldn't find her.

Doing the same thing again only the other way around, he rechecked every carriage and then stood back, wondering if perhaps she was in the café and hadn't boarded yet. He started to feel nervous; he was desperate not to miss her. He ran back to the café on the main concourse and went inside, quickly surveying the cluster of empty Formica tables and nodding to the girl behind the counter. Livvy wasn't there either. He left, stood under the clock and decided that the only thing to do was to wait on the platform until she showed up. If she hadn't arrived by the time the train left, then he reckoned she must have gone back to Rubislaw Terrace.

If she hasn't gone back there, he thought miserably, then God only knows where she's disappeared to.

Livvy stood in the hotel bedroom and took a good, hard look at herself in the full-length mirror. Dressed and almost ready to go, she peered at her face and thought how tired she looked, wondering if the grey pallor would ever go from her skin. Moving closer, she took her make-up bag out of her rucksack and searched for the relevant tools necessary to do a major repair job on her face. She had to make some attempt to turn herself back into the glamorous City Television presenter of a month ago, she realised, however much she hated the thought of it. She knew, after her brief conversation with Gordon Fife earlier, that that was exactly what the editor of the *Angus Press* was expecting.

Fifteen minutes later she was done. She grabbed her jacket from the back of a chair. It wasn't exactly Armani, her outfit, but it was put together from the meagre things she had brought with her and it would have to do. Gordon Fife had said that his boss was out of the office for the morning and she wanted to make sure she had arrived and left before he came back into it.

She reckoned Fife was only seeing her out of curiosity. Once she'd explained who she was he seemed amazed to have her on the end of the phone. But she had a good idea now of what she was going to sell him and how she was going to do it as well. He could be as curious as he liked, she thought, stuffing the old copies of the *Angus Press* she had filched from reception into her bag and closing the door of the hotel bedroom behind her, as long as he gave her a job. She made her way down to reception and to the taxi that was waiting for her outside.

Fraser arrived back at the station for the second time that morning having been home, then to the airport, back home again and finally to the place he had begun in, just in case she had missed the first train and was trying for the second. He had a good look round, asked if anyone in the ticket office remembered her and, by then feeling pretty despondent, decided for a last-ditch attempt in the guard's office.

The office was tucked away on platform two, marked only by a small sign and with no windows or immediate access. Another of British Rail's incentives to help the public, Fraser thought grimly, as he finally located the door and knocked loudly. Someone shouted and he turned the handle, pushing forcefully to unstick the door and making it inside the small room only after considerable effort.

'Excuse me,' he said, slightly out of breath, as three uniformed guards turned to look at him. 'I was wondering if anyone remembers seeing a woman here this morning, a Londoner; it might have been early, around seven?' He surveyed their faces. 'She's about five foot eight, pretty, blonde?'

'There was a gerl I spoke ta this mornin', laddie,' one of the men said. 'I gave haer directions to the Victoria Hotel. I dunnae know if it's tha same one, of course, but . . .'

He didn't finish his sentence. Fraser had thanked him and left the office before he got the chance. Hurrying back to his car, he felt the lifting of a huge weight. Of course it was Livvy; no one could mistake her once they'd spoken to her. It had to be Livvy! He reversed out of his space and set off in the direction of the hotel.

*

Gordon Fife looked at Livvy Davis and thought, she's got brains, this one, and a cute way of packaging them an' all. He listened to the way she spoke, not pushy or aggressive but confident all the same, as if it never entered her head that he might not like the idea, that she might not be successful. She had a kind of professional ease and he admired her for it. She'd done her homework too. Her idea for a LIFESTYLE section featuring arts, local interest, leisure and TV was just right for the paper, perfectly pitched. But the one thing that really bugged him was, why? This was the *Aberdeen Angus Press*; it wasn't the *Scotsman* or Grampian TV. It was big for a regional, admittedly, but it was still small fry for someone in her league. And what made her think that if the big boys wouldn't ignore her impending conviction, he would? He tuned back into the last of her outline and saw that she had been watching him closely as she spoke.

She finished, put away the page of rough notes and said, 'I think you probably want to ask me some questions, don't you? About my reasons for being here?'

He raised an eyebrow. The one thing Fife really respected was honesty and he was pleased that she'd saved him the bother of pussyfooting around. He liked things to be straight, so he answered her yes, he would like to ask some questions.

'How aboot yae tell me why I should employ yae when yae have an impendin' conviction hangin' over yaer heed?' he said. 'For starters anyways.'

Livvy faced him squarely. 'I've got a committal hearing down in London in about four weeks,' she said. 'My case will be committed to trial at the crown court, which will probably take about six months, maybe less, maybe more.

In that time, Gordon, I could have set this whole thing up, produced say three issues of a LIFESTYLE section, possibly four. I'm not looking for a lifetime's commitment, just a job for the next few months.' She paused and met Fife's steely, penetrating stare for a moment before carrying on.

'I can't guarantee that I won't have some of my time taken up by the court case, that's obvious, but it won't affect my work. One of my reasons for asking for this job is that I'm pretty sure I can manage it, do it bloody well actually and still have some time to . . .' she paused. 'To do my own thing.'

Fife said nothing but he did nod and it gave Livvy the small lift of courage she so badly needed. He was silent for a few minutes, thinking over what she'd said. She had pre-empted his next question, which was why the *Angus Press*, but he still didn't understand the Scottish link. He said, 'Why Scotland?' and saw the faint flicker of wariness in her eyes.

'Because it's far enough away,' she answered. She had no intention of telling him about Fraser. 'I've been hounded by the press,' she went on, 'and I need the distance. I'm not as well known up here, it's easier.' The penetrating stare continued. 'And there's a personal reason,' she finished, 'but I'd rather not say what it is if you don't mind.'

Fife nodded again and she breathed a sigh of relief. She waited for him to speak but again he was silent for a few minutes. Then he stood up and reached for her page of scribbled notes, something she'd put together in the taxi on the way over.

'Livvy,' he said, looking down the page. 'As far as I'm concerrned there's nae rason why we can't set this thing up for yae.' He was impressed – this was exactly the type of thing they'd been looking for and thinking about for months. OK, she had no experience in papers, but he had an excellent team for her to work with and she had the most important thing: the ideas. She was fresh to it as well, and that was a great bonus to bringing in something new. 'I'd have ta discuss it with tha boss, of course. I dunna like ta make any decision wi'oot his approval but I canna see nae problem.'

'Of course.' Fraser would go mad when he found out what she'd done! She put it to the back of her mind for the moment and thought, Well, if he has any sense, he'll keep whatever it was between us exactly that: between us!

Fife went on, 'Would yae be prepared to work a trial period? See if tha whole thing's going to work?'

'Yes, no problem.'

'And salary? I've no doubt it's going to be a bit of a shock for yae after the television.'

Livvy shrugged. There was no point in discussing it at this stage, particularly if Fraser threw a fit. 'Why don't you discuss it with Mr Stewart? And then we can talk about the money.'

'Right.' Fife stood up. His time was short and with the boss out of the office he had more than his usual share of work. The interview was over; he didn't believe in wasting time. 'We'll see yae in tha morning, then? We get going here around eight, eight-thirty.' He held out his hand and Livvy shook it.

'Thank you, Gordon,' she said. 'I look forward to working with you.'

He nodded a last time. 'Right,' he muttered and held the door open for her. 'Tomorrow then.'

She smiled. 'Yes, tomorrow.' And she made her way

across the open-plan office to the doors, conscious that she had just done something positive for the first time in weeks and feeling really very good about it.

Mitch McDonald looked up from where he stood, leaning over Carol's desk, and let out a low whistle as Livvy left the office. 'Christ, Carol! Who's that?'

Carol tutted and turned his head back to the photographs in front of her. 'I've no idea,' she said huffily, 'but if you want my opinion on which of these to show Gordon you'd better hurry up and go through them. I haven't got all day, you know.'

He coughed. 'Ah, sorry, Carol.' He leafed through the collection of black-and-whites for her to view them and surreptitiously glanced up at the door again whilst she was looking. The blonde had gone. Whoever it was, Mitch thought, turning his gaze to the plate-glass wall of the editor's office, he wasn't the only one she'd got going! And he smiled at Gordon Fife, the hardest newsman in the country, standing motionless by his desk and staring after a girl in tight black leggings who had long since disappeared.

Fraser sat in the reception area of the Victoria Hotel and wondered for the millionth time whether he should stay or go. He had been there the whole morning, taken a snack in the bar for lunch and sat there again for a good part of the afternoon. He was bored and frustrated, but he was also terrified of leaving in case she turned up, collected her things and departed Aberdeen without him having had the chance to see her.

He had called the office three times and Gordon had said

everything was under control. It was a quiet day, with not much news around, and the printer had been fixed by mid-morning ready for the lunch-time run. There was something he wanted the boss's decision on, Gordon had said, but it was nothing urgent, it could wait until the morning; Fraser told him to go ahead with whatever it was, as he usually did, and Gordon told him he had already done so, more or less.

Apart from the phone calls and the delivery to the hotel of the paper's first edition, Fraser had done nothing but sit and wait for Livvy. He looked down at his watch, saw it was after three and decided finally that he would give her five more minutes and then he'd have to go. Besides the boredom and the numbness in his legs, he was slightly concerned that he might get picked up for loitering with intent, as the young girl behind reception had given him more than a few choice looks. He turned his head towards the entrance of the hotel for the last time and just as he did so, Livvy strolled into reception, two big carrier bags in her hands and the colour high in her cheeks. She looked better than she had done for weeks.

'Livvy!' Fraser stood and hurried over to her. His legs were a bit stiff and she smiled at the way he was walking. 'It's good to see you smile,' he said. 'Are you all right?'

'Yes, Fraser, I'm all right.' She dropped the bags down on to the carpet. 'Have you been here long?'

'No, not at all,' he answered quickly. 'About half an hour or so.'

She nodded, eyeing him cautiously. 'Did you want something?' she asked, waiting for the outburst about her appointment with Gordon. But he just shrugged. 'No, not really,' he said, 'except . . .' He paused. 'Look, why don't you come back with me and we can at least talk about what I said this morning.'

Livvy stiffened. 'I think you made yourself quite clear this morning, Fraser.' The last thing she wanted to do was go over the same ground. He'd told her to face up to things and that was what she'd done; end of story. She felt a sharp stab of anger and bent to pick up her bags. She didn't need him, or his pity; she'd wanted love and affection and all she'd got was sanctimonious advice. She went to move past him but he stopped her with a hand on her arm.

'Livvy, I was thinking,' he said quickly. 'You could maybe get a job on the paper, to tide you over. It wouldn't be much but it'd be . . .'

Livvy removed his hand. 'I've already got a job, thanks, providing the boss agrees. I saw the manager today and he offered it to me on that proviso.'

'Really? Where?'

'I don't think that concerns you.' He followed close behind as she crossed to the desk and asked for her key. The girl on reception watched the scene with open fascination.

'Livvy, please.' Fraser raised his voice as she turned. He was cross at her attitude. 'Don't be so childish! This morning, I was only acting for the best . . . I . . .'

'You made your point, Fraser,' Livvy snapped. 'You told me to face up to things and that's exactly what I intend to do. So, please, let me get on with it.'

They looked at each other for a long moment and then Fraser turned on his heel and stormed out of reception. Livvy glanced up at the girl, whose mouth had dropped open, and gave her a withering look. The young girl blushed, clamped her jaw tightly shut and stared down at the reception desk as Livvy strode over to the lifts and went up to her room.

Fraser stopped at the traffic lights on Union Street and stared blankly across at the car beside him. He was still steaming, the anger pulsing through him, and he was finding it hard to concentrate on his driving. He saw what looked like a familiar profile and then the woman in the car turned to stare back at him. It was Beth Broden. They both exchanged surprised looks, then smiles and Beth reached over and wound down the window on the passenger side.

'Fraser, hello!'

'Aberdeen is a small city, Beth,' he said laughing. 'Where are you off to?'

'I'm going home, actually, it's my afternoon off. You?'

'Back to the office. Unfortunately.' He pulled a face.

'D'you fancy skiving off for the rest of the day?' She glanced at her watch. 'There's only about an hour of it left, anyway!'

'I'd love to, Beth, but I haven't been in today.'

'Ah, well.' The lights changed and she blew him a kiss, shifted her car into gear and accelerated off. She held up her hand to wave and Fraser suddenly thought, oh hell, why not? There wasn't anything urgent to do in the office and he could use a little company. He pulled off behind her and flashed his lights, beeping his horn and waving out of the window. At the first opportunity, Beth drew up and stopped her car.

Fraser pulled up behind her, climbed out and walked up to her open window. 'Can I change my mind?' he asked.

She laughed. 'Of course you can!'

'OK. What shall we do?'

'How about coming back to my place and having tea, then we can take it from there.'

'Sounds wonderful!'

'Good. Follow me.'

Beth pulled out into the line of traffic, waiting for Fraser to catch her up, and headed for home, feeling thoroughly delighted with herself and just a tiny bit smug.

Chapter Twenty-Six

By the time Livvy woke up the following morning, she had completely lost all her confidence from the previous day. She walked into the bathroom and stopped, did a double take and then stared hard at her hair, its short, boyish cut around her face emphasising the shape of it, her extraordinarily high cheekbones and the oval line of her jaw. She pulled at it nervously and sighed. It suited her, there was no doubt about that, but it made her look about seven years younger and waifish, and she wondered once again what on earth had possessed her to do it.

She had her reasons, the reasons she had given herself as she rushed from the hotel after seeing Fraser, down to the hairdresser's she'd noticed on Union Street where she had asked for several inches to be lopped off. She was angry; she wanted to show him that she was in charge of her own life, could make her own decisions; and she wanted change. If she had to face up to things, then she wanted to be a new person, with more courage and strength to do what she had to. Long hair belonged to the old Livvy, short hair to the new.

But now, in the cold light of day, it felt and looked so

different and so strange that it made her nervous just staring at herself. She wasn't sure who it was in the mirror in
front of her and she wasn't at all sure what that person was
capable of. Reaching for a comb, she flicked it through the
cut, sprayed some mousse into the palm of her hand and
fingered it in, arranging her hair the way the hairdresser had
shown her; then she turned away from her reflection, hoping that she wasn't going to appear as terrified as she really
was, and went into the bedroom to dress.

Fraser overslept.

The office was buzzing when he arrived just before nine.
Most of the staff were in – some had been in for hours working on pieces for that day's press – and the open-plan space
was full, noisy, and smelling strongly of freshly brewed coffee. He walked across to his office, a glass-walled corner of
the huge room and said hello as he went, stopping en route
to exchange comments with several of the reporters.

'Hmmm, you smell nice this morning!' Carol had followed him in and handed him a stack of post. 'New
woman?'

He stared at her, surprised. 'No!' he answered sharply. He
was tired and grouchy. He had stayed far too late at Beth's
and had hardly slept for thinking about Livvy. What was
Carol on about? He smelled no different from any other
morning – all he'd done was get in the shower, shave, dress
and come to work. Then he realised. Livvy had left her
shower gel; he'd used that. Hell! When he wasn't thinking
about the woman, he was smelling like her. He looked
down at the desk and scowled.

Carol immediately thought she'd upset him. 'Are you all
right, Fraser?' she asked nervously.

He glanced up and saw her face. 'Oh, yes, sorry, Carol, I'm fine.' He smiled to reassure her. 'Any messages?'

'Just from Gordon.'

'Oh yes?'

'He's down in the print room with the new girl he's just taken on. He said could you go straight down when you come in; he wants to introduce you.'

Fraser was puzzled. 'New girl?'

'Yes, she came in yesterday.'

'Ah yes!' He remembered Gordon wanting his approval on a decision yesterday; it must have been that. He stood up, eager to find out what had happened. 'I'll go now. Was there anything urgent from yesterday?'

'Nope.' Carol smiled. He'd get a shock when he saw the girl; she was an absolute stunner.

''What's so funny?' he asked as he came round her side of the desk.

She shrugged. 'Nothing.'

He eyed her warily. 'You sure?'

'Yes, sure.' She wasn't going to let on but she wished she could find an excuse to go down and watch his reaction. Turning, she led the way out of his office, sat down at her screen and switched it on as Fraser carried on across to the stairs. If it was anything like Mitch's or Gordon's, he'd be up with his head lolling sideways and his brain like scrambled eggs, she thought, glancing up at the letter she was typing; and she laughed, amused and entertained if only a tiny bit jealous.

Fraser saw Gordon across the print room, half hidden by the enormous bulk of machinery and talking to a tall, young woman who could only be seen from the back. He took in the shape of her, long, thin and elegant in black tights, a bright lime-green mini skirt, black polo-neck sweater and an orange wool jacket, fitted and short. His eyes travelled up to her head, to the cropped blonde hair and large silver earrings and he realised with a jolt that she reminded him of Livvy, if it hadn't been for the hair, although he had no idea of what her face was like. God, he thought, making his way over, is she ever going to get out of my head?

Gordon waved and looked over the young girl's shoulder. 'Ah, Fraser,' he called above the noise of the machinery, 'I'd like ta intraduce yae to our new employee, Livvy Davis.'

Fraser was feet away but he stopped dead in his tracks as Livvy turned round. His stomach somersaulted and he stared into her piercing blue eyes, made to look bigger and sharper than ever by the short, boyish hair. He swallowed hard and then a surge of fury rose up in his chest. His nostrils flared and his eyes hardened, but he remained silent. He just stared, an icy, angry gaze.

'Hello, Livvy,' he said.

She smiled but her eyes were anxious. At least she has the grace to be embarrassed, he thought; though it didn't soften his anger.

'Fraser,' she answered. 'How are you?'

Gordon watched the scene with open curiosity. A perceptive man, he could almost smell the tension in the air; it crackled, like electricity. 'You two know each other, then?' he asked. Livvy spoke first.

'We were at college together,' she answered, looking directly at Fraser and daring him with her eyes to question what she was about to say. 'At Oxford.' She stopped, waited for Fraser to say something, and then continued as he remained silent. 'It's been a long time. It's good to see you.'

She walked towards him, held out her hand and Fraser stared down at it for a moment, incensed. He very nearly just walked away; then she said, 'Fraser?' and her voice was soft, almost pleading.

He glanced up at her and saw that she was scared of him, that her confidence was brittle and close to snapping. He took her hand. 'Yes, it has,' he agreed coldly. 'So you have a job on my paper. What a surprise.'

Gordon moved quickly forward into their space. 'I took the responsibility on meself but I did say the boss's worrd was final, Livvy.' She nodded. 'Perhaps yae and I can have a private worrd aboot it, Fraser?'

Fraser suddenly saw that the two people in front of him were both painfully embarrassed by his reaction and he stopped himself before he went any further. 'That won't be necessary, Gordon,' he said. 'I'm quite happy with any decision you want to make.' He turned to Livvy. 'Livvy, welcome to the *Angus Press*, I hope you'll enjoy working here.'

The relief in her face was apparent. 'Thank you,' she murmured. 'I'm sure I will.'

At that moment, Carol's voice came loud and clear across the din of the machinery as she hollered at Gordon, only her head and shoulders visible round the door of the print room.

'Reg is on the line from the regional office, Gordon! He's got that story you wanted.' She paused to rest her voice for a second, then she screamed out again. 'He's sending it down the wire now but he wants to speak to you.'

Gordon waved to acknowledge her request and she disappeared. He excused himself quickly and asked Fraser to finish showing Livvy round; he would meet them back in his office when they were ready. He hurried after Carol, leaving the two of them together, glad to be out of the firing range and wondering just what the personal reasons Livvy Davis had for staying in Scotland were.

The moment Gordon had gone, Fraser took Livvy's elbow and guided her forcefully out of the print room and the view of the technicians into the relative privacy of the corridor. He stopped, glanced round to make sure they were alone and then hissed, 'What the bloody hell are you playing at, Livvy?' still gripping her elbow painfully.

She pulled away from him, rubbing her arm, and answered sharply, 'I got myself a job, just like you told me to! Remember?'

He shook his head, exasperated. 'But why my paper? And why the hell did you do it behind my back?' He just didn't understand it. 'I'd have given you a job. All you had to do was ask.'

Livvy looked at his face. It showed an uncomfortable mix of bewilderment, hurt pride and anger, but she couldn't see any sympathy or understanding. 'But that's exactly it,' she answered. 'Don't you see?'

He didn't, obviously.

'I had to do it on my own! I didn't come here to get back at you or anything like that; I came because I thought, in a highly rash moment admittedly, that I stood some kind of a chance of getting a job here.' She continued to look up at him, willing him to understand. 'I thought up a way of offering something the paper didn't already have, an idea for a consumer section, and I sold that idea to Gordon Fife.' She touched Fraser on the arm. 'He offered me a trial period because he thought I was good, not because he felt sorry for me. You must understand how important that was!' She stopped. She wanted to add that she needed it, that after his awful pity she wanted to show him that she could do it, but she had already said enough, she could see that. Fraser didn't understand, he probably never would.

'Look,' she began again, 'if it really upsets you I'll leave now, forget the whole thing. I really didn't think about you when I came here; all I thought about was the job.' She dropped her hand down and turned towards the stairs. 'I'll have to get my things from Gordon's office.'

Fraser nodded and she started up the stairs.

'Livvy! Wait!' He honestly didn't know what to do. He was struggling with his emotions and with the knowledge that Gordon's judgement was usually one hundred per cent right. 'What sort of consumer thing did you discuss with Gordon? Can you talk me through it?'

Livvy held on to the stair rail and felt the relief flood through her. It made her legs weak and she suddenly sat down, trying to conceal the fact that if she hadn't she'd have fallen down. It was stupid, she knew it was, pinning all her hopes on one thing, on a job at the *Angus Press*, but it had been a start, it had seemed to her some small way out of the mess of nothingness and depression.

For a moment she was silent, then the part of her that had kept her afloat in the past few weeks took hold again and she began to explain. 'It's a LIFESTYLE section, Fraser. A once-weekly pull-out section that covers all sorts of things that aren't necessarily news.' Her voice had gathered strength as she spoke. 'Things like fashion, TV, what's on, gossip on personalities, book reviews. A kind of colour supplement, only with a hugely local slant.'

He nodded.

'It's not a brand-new concept, admittedly. Other papers have done it – like the *Evening Chronicle* in Newcastle and the *Evening Standard* in London – but it's new for here, and I think it could be really successful.'

Fraser remained cautious but her idea was exciting, he had to admit that. 'What did Gordon offer you?' he asked.

'A trial run,' she said. 'Put together a dummy issue, see how it looks, how it works and then take it from there.'

'And you're happy with that?'

'It's a start,' she answered honestly. 'I can't ask for more in my position, can I?'

'I guess not.' Fraser was silent for a while and Livvy couldn't bear to look at him. She stared down at her lap and wished he'd say something. Anything! Finally she had the nerve to look up and saw that he had been watching her.

'I think,' he said, 'that the best thing I can do is let you and Gordon get on with it. We've talked for a long time about something like this and I guess if he's convinced then I'll trust his judgement.'

Livvy couldn't stop herself from smiling and Fraser smiled back. For the first time since she had arrived in Aberdeen she felt the familiar warmth between them and she relaxed.

Fraser moved towards the stairs. 'Come on.' He held out his hand to pull her up. 'There's an editorial meeting starting in a few minutes. I'll introduce you to the rest of the team.'

Livvy stood with his help and he kept hold of her hand for a moment longer than was needed. It seemed as if all the anger and misunderstanding between them had suddenly evaporated and he could feel the same deep physical reaction to her that he always had. She felt it too. Their eyes met for a brief second and then Livvy gently pulled her hand away and turned her head, blushing. Fraser hesitated and finally led the way up the stairs.

'I forgot to say,' he called over his shoulder, 'your hair's terrific! It makes you look completely different.'

'I *am* different,' she replied, smiling and following him up. 'And it's not just the hair!'

The editorial meeting lasted longer than usual as the story Gordon had had in from the regional office was a front-page headline and the rest of the news had to be shuffled to fit round it. The chief sub groaned loudly when Mitch McDonald came in late with the photos and wondered, what with those and with rearranging the other pages, if she was going to even have time to go to the bathroom in the next few hours!

Towards the end of the meeting, Fraser introduced Livvy and she stood to give a five-minute spiel on what she was planning for the paper. Gordon listed the three people he wanted to work on the LIFESTYLE section and Fraser watched Mitch try unsuccessfully to suppress a broad grin as his name was mentioned. He had been staring at Livvy from the moment he walked in, not subtly or discreetly but quite openly and lasciviously, and it was really beginning to piss Fraser off. As Livvy rounded off what she was saying and Gordon stood to end the meeting, he saw Mitch wink and Livvy smile at his cheek. I'll give him winking, Fraser thought, bloody know-it-all. He moved across to have a word with Livvy, asking her to stay back a minute, and glared at Mitch as he left the office. Livvy turned to smile at him and he said sourly, 'You'll have to watch Mitchell McDonald, he's a terrible womaniser.'

Livvy raised an eyebrow. 'Oh?'

'Yes, oh!' Fraser snapped and she held down a giggle. 'I can't say I approve of Gordon's choice but he is a bloody good photographer, I'll give him that. Just be careful, don't get taken . . .' He stopped and turned, interrupted by a light knocking on the glass, and then flushed a deep red as he saw Beth, watched by most of the office, waving at him from outside. He strode over to the door.

'Beth! Oh, er . . . Come in,' he stammered, aware of Livvy's steely gaze behind him. 'Livvy Davis, this is Beth Broden.' For the man who had had virtually no personal life since he started at the *Angus Press* ten years ago, the arrival of two attractive women on the scene at the same time was a bit too much. He was embarrassed and he could see Carol and what seemed like the rest of the office as well staring at the situation through the glass wall of his office.

Beth crossed to Livvy and held out her hand. She had the advantage – she knew all about Livvy Davis, whereas Livvy knew nothing about her. 'What luck that you're actually here,' she said, 'because I came to ask Fraser for the address of your hotel.'

'You did?' Both Livvy and Fraser asked the question at the same time, looked at each other and then looked away.

'Yes, I did! Fraser and I talked a great deal about you last night, Livvy, and you've been on my mind ever since.'

'I have?' Livvy shot a glance at Fraser but he ignored it. It wasn't at all like Beth made it sound but he could hardly say that now, could he?

'Yes. You see, the thing is, a patient of mine told me last week that she had a small attic flat at the top of her house which she wanted to rent. She was asking my advice, actually, because she didn't want to advertise it and she wondered if I knew anyone who might be interested.' Beth's voice was deceptive; it was soft, with a charming Scottish lilt, and it gave no hint of the tough and self-motivated character it spoke for. She went on. 'It was only after Fraser had left last night, in the small hours of the morning, that I thought about you. He'd said that you had found yourself a job and would probably need somewhere to live.'

'Well, not quite,' Fraser interrupted. He had actually said that he wanted to try to persuade Livvy to come back and live in the house with him, and he hadn't left in the small hours of the morning, he had been in at midnight! He started to explain but Beth talked over him.

'Anyway,' she said quickly, 'I thought I'd call you and see if you were interested in this little flat. It's terribly nice and a lot more cosy than a hotel.' She smiled encouragingly. 'I could take you over myself and show it to you if you like?'

Livvy had been silent all the time Beth spoke. The slow warming to Fraser that had begun ten minutes earlier was brought to an abrupt halt. She looked at him, at his embarrassment, and realised in an instant what an incredible fool she had made of herself. The blood rushed to her cheeks and a hot anger bubbled inside her, giving way almost immediately to a burning shame and humiliation. Why hadn't she seen it? Why hadn't she guessed? He'd given her enough clues, for God's sake! He had someone else and that explained everything. She slumped down on a chair, feeling as if someone had suddenly knocked her sideways and taken all the air out of her body.

'Livvy?' Fraser moved towards her but she warned him off with her eyes and Beth watched on, thinking, Well, that wasn't half as difficult as I thought it would be. She went on as if nothing had happened.

'I'm sure Fraser wouldn't mind if I took you away to look at this place now, would you, Fraser? It's just that I'm on my way over there to see my patient.'

Fraser shook his head. 'No, of course not, if Livvy's interested . . .'

'Yes, I'm interested!' Livvy snapped, cutting him off. Just the sound of his voice incensed her. 'But I'll have to check with Gordon that I can have an hour or so off.'

'With Gordon?' Beth smiled sweetly.

'Yes, Livvy has a job on the paper,' Fraser answered.

'Oh, how nice,' Beth said, realising that she had obviously arrived just in the nick of time. 'You're so kind, Fraser, you think of every . . .'

'It has nothing to do with Fraser,' Livvy said sharply. 'He had no idea until this morning. Gordon Fife, the editor, hired me.'

'Oh! Well, congratulations then.'

Livvy smiled sarcastically and for a moment the atmosphere was icy. Fraser said hurriedly, 'Look, Livvy, why don't you go off with Beth and see if you like this place?', more for something to say than because he really wanted her to do it. She glared up at him and he continued quickly, trying to make amends. 'If you decide you do like it, you could take the rest of the day off to get yourself settled there. Start here tomorrow instead of today.'

Livvy sighed heavily. He had made it almost impossible for her to refuse now without looking bloody-minded. So she stood, smiled again at Beth in her best theatrical manner and ignored Fraser. 'I'll just check it with Gordon,' she said to Beth. 'I'm sure it'll be fine. I'll get my coat and see you down in reception, if that's all right?'

Beth nodded. Perhaps this wasn't going to be as easy as she had first thought. 'Well, Fraser,' she said, as Livvy left, 'I guess I ought to be going. I hope you didn't mind me stepping in and trying to help?'

Her manner of phrasing things made it terribly hard not to sound ungrateful. Fraser nodded.

'Thank you, Beth. I'm sure Livvy will appreciate having somewhere of her own to live.'

Beth nodded.

'After all,' he went on, trying, as kindly as he could, to get his message across, 'she'll probably be in Aberdeen for quite some time to come.'

Beth pulled on her leather gloves and turned towards the door. 'How super for you!' she replied and, looking back over her shoulder, smiled her most dazzling smile.

But not if I can help it, she thought, as she made her way across to the stairs.

Chapter Twenty-Seven

Two weeks later, Beth Broden sat in her small consulting room in the surgery and gave herself a few minutes' breathing space before the next patient. She had been irritated by the woman who had just departed – a moaner, in Beth's opinion, and she'd told her as much, sending her away with a flea in her ear. Beth had a policy, a very personal one, that gave her clear guidelines within which to operate. She wouldn't tolerate moaners: people with problems other than medical ones were wasting her time. Depression, stress! Other names for moaning, as far as she was concerned; you either came to Doctor Broden with a serious complaint or not at all. And, after the last twenty minutes, not at all, she felt, was often more preferable.

She thought about Fraser in her few moments of peace as she frequently did when irritated by something. She thought about all the wasted phone calls, the amount of useless effort on her part, and nothing but a casual friendship, a chat, a drink, and the boundary line well and truly marked out to show for it all. She didn't like to be ignored: Beth Broden wasn't used to not getting things exactly her own way. Still, she mused, a little brighter, there was always tonight.

She reached for her bag and took out her small leather-bound notebook, opening it at the page of her shopping list. She ran her eyes down it to make sure she had remembered everything, added cream to the list of ingredients, and then, in tiny writing, added the final thing right down in the left-hand corner of the page: condoms. Tonight she was determined to put their relationship on to a more intimate level and for that she needed to be prepared.

Carefully zipping up her bag, with the notebook safely tucked away, Beth buzzed the intercom for the next patient. Her receptionist immediately rang through on the telephone.

'Hi, Beth. There's a Mr Derek Dorsey on the line for you. He's been waiting for about twenty minutes, or rather his secretary has.'

'Oh.' This was the third time Dorsey had rung in the past week but she'd managed to escape him so far. Little wonder she was edgy about Fraser, with Dorsey hassling her all the time. 'Is there any way you can put him off?' she asked.

'No, 'fraid not. He said he'll hold until you're free.'

'Oh God.' Beth sighed heavily. 'All right, Maggie, put him through. Thanks.' She waited for Dorsey to come on the line.

'Hello, Beth.' The voice was unmistakably charming, dark and smooth, the diction well rounded. Beth remembered what it used to do to her and still did if she let herself go.

'Hello, Derek. I'm sorry I haven't been able to get back to you.'

'Not at all, Beth, don't worry. I know how busy GPs on the NHS are nowadays!' She could hear the smile in his voice. She could hear everything in his voice, even when he got an erection. 'I was ringing to find out if you had anything for me on Fraser Stewart, our local newspaper magnate?'

Beth hesitated. Apart from Fraser's reluctance to get involved she also had the problem of Livvy Davis and that one hadn't proved at all easy to deal with. Fraser she reckoned she could cope with, but Livvy Davis was quite another matter. She wasn't quite sure whether to tell Derek all this, so she simply said, 'I'm working on it,' and hoped that would keep him satisfied for the time being.

There was a short silence. 'What is that supposed to mean, Beth?' he asked coolly. 'Don't piss me around, I'm not in the mood.'

She heard the warning in his voice. Despite his jocular opening remark, this wasn't a friendly call and Beth knew it. 'We're friends,' she said. 'We're having dinner together tonight in fact.'

'Are you fucking him?'

'I don't think that's . . .'

'Cut it out, Beth!' Dorsey's voice was suddenly sharp. 'Don't get coy with me. I told you I needed tabs on Stewart and you know full well what that means. We've found a leak in the system up there and I need to know how much information's gone missing. In the wrong hands it could cause a lot of damage, and you know what that means, don't you, Beth?'

'Do I?' Beth wasn't going to be drawn in on this. She was an innocent party; she wasn't involved.

'I hope so,' Dorsey said. 'If the fertiliser is banned, then a great deal of the medical evidence on it will be reassessed.'

'So? I only wrote what I believed.'

Dorsey laughed but there was no mistaking the malice in his laughter. 'You wrote what I paid you to write, Beth my darling, and there's very little point in saying otherwise. I have a very accurate set of accounts and Doctor Beth Broden is listed for freelance consultation.'

Beth felt her anger rise but she knew better than to vent it on Dorsey. She knew the extent of his power and it scared her. Indeed, that was how it had all begun in the first place – she found that fear incredibly erotic.

'So, what do you want from Fraser Stewart?'

'I want you to find out how much he already knows.'

'And how am I supposed to do that?'

'Oh, dear Beth,' Dorsey said sarcastically, 'do you really have to ask me that? I'd always had you down for a bit of an expert in these matters.'

Beth held down an angry retort. 'All right. I'll need a few days.'

'As long as it's only a few days. Ring me on Saturday, at home.'

'OK.' She went to hang up.

'Oh, and Beth?'

'Yes.'

'IMACO won't be the only thing to go down if all this gets out of hand; you do understand that, don't you?'

She drew in a breath to answer him but the line went dead.

'Bastard!' she muttered, replacing the receiver and buzzing for the next patient. And it was only when she uncrossed her legs that she noticed the wetness between them. The bastard still had that effect on her.

*

Livvy sat alongside Mitch McDonald on a table near the darkroom with a pile of photographs in front of them and a couple of rough sheet layouts for the first three pages of the LIFESTYLE section spread out over the entire length of the workspace. They were choosing the shots to fit the stories for the first issue.

The past two weeks for Livvy had been sheer hard work. They had been much harder than she had imagined and much more enjoyable. She liked Mitch; he was funny, slightly mad and wholly involved in the work. He tussled with her for every decision she made on the issue, challenging her, making her think; and, contrary to what she would have believed, she loved it, fighting for every inch, having to convince not only him but the rest of the team that what she was doing was right. For an awfully long time, Livvy Davis had had life very easy. She was famous in London and with that fame came a sort of reverence for her judgement, a lack of willingness to question her, and only now did she realise that perhaps she hadn't always been right. She also realised how much more gratifying things were after a struggle – they meant more.

At the *Angus Press* Livvy wasn't a TV personality, she wasn't the daughter of a TV personality; she was simply part of a team and that felt really good, much better than she had thought it would.

'Oh, I don't know why we bother with all these mindless model shots,' Mitch said wearily, leafing through some fashion pictures and dropping them despondently on to the desk. 'Put you in these and it'd be a whole lot more interesting.'

Livvy smiled. It was part of his manner. He liked to flirt constantly, it added excitement to his day. 'How about we put you in some of them instead?' Livvy said passing him a choice shot of a model in a black lace basque, stockings and suspenders. 'Now that really would be a whole lot more interesting!'

They both laughed and Mitch pinched her on the arm. 'Ouch!' She pinched him back and they went into a slapping routine, giggling like children and scattering the photos.

'Bloody hell, Mitch!' Livvy pulled out of the fray, still laughing, and scraped her chair back rapidly before he could get her again. 'Ha! Missed me!' she cried, standing up abruptly and squealing as he lunged for her again. She literally fell over the person behind her. 'Oh! Jeeze! Sorry!' She spun round, was about to apologise again, and stood face to face with Fraser.

'Oh! Fraser!' She blushed, put her hand up to her burning cheeks and tried to smile. 'Oh gosh, sorry. I hope, er . . .' She felt such an idiot. Mitch had stopped laughing and was busying himself picking up the photos off the floor, pretending to be invisible.

'Sorry,' she mumbled again and looked down at the ground. Fraser felt a moment of insane jealousy and then calmed himself, fighting back the urge to say something sarcastic to Mitch.

'I thought I'd have a look at what you'd done this week,' he said tightly. 'Gordon seems very pleased.'

Livvy nodded and looked up again. 'Yes, I think he is.' She reached for the layout sheets and her notes, making everything easy to see. Her manner was tense. She had been icy with Fraser since she started, glad that she'd seen so little of him but confused as to why, unlike anyone else she had ever known, he still preyed on her mind even when she hadn't set eyes on him for days. He looked down at the work and nodded as she talked him briefly through it.

'When will you have it ready to send out to our advertisers?' He could see the potential right away; each story had been set up to provide an opening for advertisers in that field and space left on the right-hand side for them to use. The fashion spread on underwear had already attracted interest from two major retailers, Gordon had told him, and at three and a half thousand for a quarter page, Fraser was well pleased with that.

'By the end of the week, hopefully,' Livvy answered. Fraser smiled. 'It'll be incomplete, of course,' she went on, encouraged by the smile. 'A good-looking dummy, but it'll give them some idea of what we're running, and we'll fill in the rest a few days before we print.'

'Good.' He looked up from the work and directly at her.

He looks tired, she thought, and she suddenly wanted to touch his face. It was an impulse, something powerfully physical, and she held her arms tightly by her sides, shocked by the force of it. They stared at each other for a moment and then Fraser looked away as Carol shouted to him across the office.

'There's a call for me,' he said, not moving. She gets on well with Mitch, he thought miserably, everyone's noticed it.

'Yes,' she answered. Don't give an inch, she told herself, just act casual. They continued to stare at each other.

'I'd better go.' Perhaps that's what she needs, no complications, a laugh.

'Yes.' I wish he wouldn't keep breaking off like this.

Mitch coughed loudly and they both turned round.

'Right, well . . .' Fraser glanced across at Mitch and then briefly back to Livvy. He could see the way Mitch felt; he'd be a fool if he couldn't. 'I look forward to seeing the finished thing,' he said tartly, then strode off to answer his call.

Livvy turned back towards Mitch and knelt down to pick up the remaining photographs; she needed a couple of minutes to regain her composure. It was the anger, she told herself; she was still furious with him and it had a very powerful effect. Handing the pile to Mitch, she said, 'So where has the boss been for the past ten days? I've hardly seen him.' She glanced up at his face, expecting to see him staring at her, but the incident had gone completely over his head.

'I don't know for sure,' Mitch answered. 'But Andy Roberts let slip last week that it was something to do with IMACO again.'

'IMACO?' That name was all too familiar to Livvy and it shocked her just hearing it. She concentrated hard on looking at the floor so that Mitch couldn't see her face. IMACO, Hugh, Brazil, the whole court case came flooding back into her mind and for a moment her fear was so strong that her hands trembled. She clenched them, forcing that image back to where she'd kept it for the past two weeks, locked away, desperate not to think about any of it, not now, not until she was ready. 'What's Fraser got to do with IMACO?' she asked quickly, her voice panicked. 'What do you mean, again? Is he involved with IMACO?'

'Whoa!' Mitch held up both hands. 'Stop! Not guilty.'

Livvy smiled. 'Sorry.'

Mitch hoisted her to her feet and they sat down at the table again. 'OK, for what it's worth,' Mitch said, 'ever since I've worked on the paper, Fraser's had this kind of hobby, I guess you could call it. He's got a reputation around the city for helping people with any minor claims against

IMACO, unfair dismissal, industrial injury claims, that kind of thing; on a very small scale, you understand. But apparently he does a whole load of legal work for people so that if they have to employ a solicitor, then it cuts their bill in half. Often it's a small claims court thing and he does it himself. He read law at Oxford, apparently. He's pretty bloody bright – wanted to be a barrister, Carol told me – but had to come back here to run the paper when his father died. Gordon Fife looked after it while he was at college on the understanding that he came back when he'd finished.'

'Oh.' Livvy took all of this in. She knew the part about Fraser having to give up law already; she'd known that since Oxford. But she knew nothing about his 'hobby', as Mitch called it, and she was quite shaken by it. It was beginning to seem that the man she thought she had known intimately twice in her life, she hardly knew at all. The idea was both fascinating and terrifying. She shuffled the pictures round the table for a while, not wanting to appear too interested, and then she said, 'So why IMACO?'

Mitch put his hand over hers and stopped her moving the prints. 'Why all the interest?' he asked back.

Livvy shrugged. 'Curiosity.'

'It killed the cat.'

Livvy leaned close to Mitch and whispered in his ear, 'But I'm not a cat.' Then she roared loudly and he jumped back in surprise, holding his eardrums.

'Christ, Livvy!'

'I'm a lion,' she said and burst out laughing.

'Very funny!' Mitch was particularly sensitive around his ears; they were high on his list of top ten erotic zones. He scowled at her and she stopped giggling.

'Sorry.'

'All right.' He'd had a serious sense-of-humour failure but after a while he did smile grudgingly. 'I don't know why it's IMACO and not Elf Oil or some other company, but I think it's something to do with the paper, years ago, and Fraser's father.' He shrugged. 'Satisfied?'

'Yes, thank you.' She leaned over and kissed his ear, the one that she'd shouted in. 'You?'

'Yes, thank you.' He smiled.

'Now, these photographs,' she said, not wanting to waste any more time. 'Let's get them down to the best five or so.'

'Right.' He picked up the top one. 'I still think you'd look better than . . .'

She cuffed him on the head and they finally got down to some work.

Mitch left the office around seven that night. After bullying Livvy for a good thirty minutes to have dinner with him, he finally gave up and went home alone. She insisted on staying to edit a piece that Jenna had given her late that afternoon and although she was tempted by Mitch's playful manner, she had begun to think that maybe there was more to his flirtation than just pure fun. He was an attractive man, Mitch, five years younger than her, tall, thin and with short blond hair that always looked as if it needed a comb, the sort of hair it was really easy to imagine tangling her fingers in. But she didn't need the complication of an affair and certainly not with her photographer.

Glancing up as Carol called goodbye, Livvy waved at her and saw that the office was finally empty. She had been so involved in what she was doing that she hadn't even noticed the noise of people leaving. She also saw that Fraser's lights were on and, on impulse, she stood up, stretched wearily and made her way across to his office, standing in the doorway and looking at his empty desk. She leaned against the doorframe and thought about what Mitch had said earlier, about the Fraser she had no idea existed, and she wondered what else she had just assumed about him. She thought back to her arrival in Aberdeen, to her meeting with Beth, and she remembered, with a sharp ache of desire, the few days in Devon. It was all so confusing. Maybe she had misjudged him? She just didn't know.

'Livvy?'

She spun round, startled out of her reverie.

'Oh, Fraser!'

He smiled at her. 'You look as if you've seen a ghost!' He was in his shirtsleeves, holding a plastic cup of coffee and waiting to go back into his office. 'May I?' He indicated that he wanted to get past and she moved hastily, embarrassed.

'D'you want a drink? Can I get you a coffee?'

'No. Er, thanks.'

He sat down at his desk and looked across at her. It never ceased to amaze him that every time he saw her it felt like the first time and he had to consciously drag his eyes away from her face. He glanced down at his papers.

'Actually, I was, er, wondering if you might, er . . .' Livvy broke off suddenly, thinking, Oh my God! What am I asking?

'If I might what?' He smiled again at her and the fine creases around his eyes deepened. He tapped a pen on the desk.

'If you might like to come for a drink,' Livvy blurted out. 'Now . . . ish.'

Fraser had to force himself to sit tight and restrain an

overwhelming urge to jump up, grab his coat and hurry her out of the door before she had the chance to change her mind. He pretended to think about it for a few minutes so as not to look too eager and as he was doing so the realisation that he was already busy suddenly hit him. Oh shit, he thought miserably, Beth! And he wanted to snap the pen he was tapping in half.

'Livvy, I'd love to, really,' he said, 'but I can't.' Beth was coming to the house to cook him supper. She had dreamed up the idea days ago and put him on the spot. He'd been unable to refuse and now he couldn't get out of it. He could hardly tell Livvy about it either – she already had the wrong idea about him and Beth and he just didn't have the nerve.

'I'm sorry,' he said, 'honestly. Maybe some other time?'

Livvy shrugged. He did look sorry but she was relieved in a way. 'Yes, some other time.' She moved backwards out of the office. 'I'll see you tomorrow, then. Don't work too hard.'

Fraser winced; he'd be following her out in a few minutes. 'I won't,' he answered. 'Goodnight, Livvy.'

She smiled. 'Goodnight.' And no longer wanting to continue with her work, she went back to her desk, packed up her things and silently left the office.

Livvy's attic flat was a haven of comfort after a long day's work and as she let herself in the front door of the house and made her way up the stairs to the four rooms she occupied at the top, she thought about a long bath, a glass of wine and Mrs P's lovely, comfy battered old sofa. The home that she rented was well worn, with big ancient armchairs stuffed with horsehair and covered in tartan rugs, blissfully snug, a high antique brass bed, plumbing that took an age but that finally filled the enormous Victorian bath with gallons of hot water and a tiny compact modern kitchen that Mrs P's son-in-law had fitted earlier that year. It had everything she needed. It wasn't elegant or coordinated but it was warm, it was cosy and it was hers.

She made it to the top stair, three flights up, and stopped to catch her breath, rummaging in her bag for her key. She found it, inserted it into the lock and heard the door down on the ground floor open and the shuffling footsteps of Mrs P. She sighed, thinking, that's all I need, but she didn't have the heart to ignore her. Leaning over the banisters, she called down, 'Evening, Mrs P! How are you?'

'Och, I'm fine, Livvy dear!' Mrs P's small tartan-shawled figure stood in the vast chilly hall and peered up through inch-thick spectacles at Livvy. 'I came oot to tell ya that the telephone people werrre heerre today. They put yaer phone in!'

'Oh, wonderful!' Livvy grinned down at Mrs P. 'That's great news! Thanks for letting them in.'

'Och, no problem, Livvy dear.' Mrs P bent and picked up Tilly the cat. 'I'll let yae get on then.' She stood and waited for Livvy to ask her up for a cup of tea.

'Would you like to come up?' Livvy called, knowing the routine by now but still puzzled by it.

'Och, no thanks, Livvy dear. I've got things ta do.'

And she shuffled back to her sitting room, firmly closing the door behind her. Livvy smiled, thought, as she did most evenings, what a queer old thing Mrs P was, and finally turned her key in the lock, letting herself into her flat.

The first thing she did when she got inside was to go over to her new telephone, pick it up and listen to the dialling tone. She smiled, put it down again and went to fetch her address book. She had to call someone, just to test it out. Sitting down on the sofa, she stretched the cord across and placed the phone on her lap, opening her book at Mitch's name. This is ridiculous, she thought gaily, to get so much pleasure out of one little telephone. She looked round the flat as she dialled and an image of her place in Cadogan Square suddenly sprang to mind. She realised, as she waited for Mitch to answer, that despite all the love and work she had put into it, she didn't miss it at all. 'Granny's welcome to it,' she said aloud, 'cantankerous old bag!'

'Hello. Who's this?'

Livvy cupped her hand over her mouth. 'Oops! Sorry, Mitch. It's me, Livvy. I was talking to myself.'

Mitch, furious at being dragged out of the bath, felt his anger instantly disperse. 'Hold on, Livvy,' he said. 'I'm going to take this on the portable.' He put the phone down in his bedroom, ran the length of his flat naked and dripping, grabbed the portable phone from the kitchen and darted back to the bathroom. Easing himself down into the hot water, he switched the phone on and said, 'Ooh, lovely! That's much better.'

'What is?'

'I'm in the bath.'

'Mitch! You decadent person!' Livvy teased. 'Not naked I hope.'

'Of course I'm not naked, Livvy. I'm sitting here in full evening dress!'

She laughed. 'I've got my telephone installed,' she said. 'You were the first person I rang.'

'No, really? Livvy, I'm touched.'

'Well, the first person I rang that was in, actually.'

'Cheers!' Mitch loved the quickness of her mind. Lying

naked in the bath with a semi hard-on talking to Livvy
Davis was almost his idea of heaven. Completely, his idea of
heaven was if she was in there with him. 'Livvy, new telephones can be awfully complicated, you know. Should I
come round and show you how to work it? Maybe go
through the instruction booklet with you?'

'Will you get dressed first?'

'If you like.'

She laughed again. 'That's very kind of you, Mitch,' she
said, 'and I really appreciate the offer, but I'm going to
phone my mother now, then I shall have a glass of wine, a
bath and go to bed.'

'Alone?'

'Yes, alone.'

He sighed heavily down the line. 'You're a tough one,
Livvy Davis.'

'Someone has to be.' She smiled as she heard the sound
of the taps in the bath. 'I'll leave you to your ablutions then,
Mitch. See you tomorrow.'

'Ah, Livvy, don't go!' But it was too late, she'd rung off
before he had a chance to ask her for her number. 'Damn!'
he muttered, turning the tap off with his big toe and settling
back into the water. Still, the thought of her alone had rejuvenated his flagging energy and he decided, soaping himself
luxuriously, to finish his bath, buy a bottle of champagne
and go straight round to her flat to celebrate the instalment
of her telephone. A freshly laundered, sweet-smelling Mitch
McDonald would be pretty hard to refuse, he reckoned,
particularly with a bottle of Veuve Clicquot in his hand.

Livvy put the phone down on Mitch and immediately
picked it up again to ring her mother. She had rung Moira

several times in the past couple of weeks, but always from the office and always in a rush. If she had been honest with herself she would have admitted that it was a relief not to have the time to talk, she hadn't felt ready to. But now, for some reason, she did. She wanted to hear the sound of her mother's voice and for the very first time in her life she also wanted to ask for some advice.

She didn't have long to wait before she heard the line connect and Moira's well-rounded 'Hello,' against the background noise of the dishwasher in the kitchen.

'Hi, Mum,' she said. 'It's me.'

'Livvy! Darling! How are you?' Moira was delighted, then her voice suddenly changed. 'You're not still in the office, are you? It's gone eight o'clock.' She worried constantly about her daughter's wellbeing.

Livvy laughed. 'No. I'm ringing from home, I've just had my telephone installed.'

'Oh good. At least we can get hold of you now. Give me your number right away or I'll hang up and forget to ask you for it.' Moira reached for a pen. 'Oh, by the way, Peter's gone to new chambers and he's had some more time to look at your case. He's . . .'

'Have you got a pen, Mum?' Livvy interrupted quickly.

Moira sighed silently on the other end. She wanted to tell Livvy about the court case, about everything that Peter was doing on her behalf, all the information he'd gathered. They desperately needed to talk about it, but every time she even mentioned Peter, Livvy clammed up. She decided to let it go again; Livvy obviously wasn't ready to face it and she didn't want to push, at least not yet.

'Yes, I've got one. Go on.'

Livvy read out the number the telephone company had

left for her on a small card by the phone and Moira jotted it down.

'Right,' she said. 'Now tell me how you are and what's been happening at the Fraser Stewart empire.'

Livvy laughed. 'Well, I'm fine,' she answered. 'I've been working so hard on this new LIFESTYLE section that I've hardly had time to think. And as for the Fraser Stewart empire, well . . .' Livvy paused, wondering quite what to say.

'Well, what?' Moira gently probed. She sensed that Livvy wanted to talk and was delighted. 'How's Fraser? Do you see much of him?'

'No,' Livvy replied. 'I don't see much of him at all.' Then she took a deep breath and launching in at the deep end, said, 'Actually, Mum, I really don't know what to think.' And she told Moira the full story, confiding in her mother in a way she hadn't done since she was a little girl.

Beth folded the oven cloth she had just used to open the Aga and check on her casserole, placed it in a neat square on the side and reached for the bottle of wine. She could hear Fraser coming down the stairs so she poured two large glasses and went out into the hall with them.

'Here.' She handed him one. 'Shall we sit down?'

'Yes, fine.' He followed her into his sitting room and they sat on the sofa. Beth looked at him as he moved several old newspapers off a footstool and put his feet up.

He had been up for a shower, a good sign, she thought, and she had prepared the type of meal that could be left for hours without ruining it. In her experience, stuffing a man full always meant that he hadn't the stomach for much else. Sex before dinner was always a much better affair. She sat back on the settee, sipped her wine and waited for him to look at her.

Beth had taken a lot of trouble with her appearance tonight. She was wearing a very tight black lace plunge bra that plumped her already well-rounded breasts up to almost page-three proportions, a matching pair of black lace French knickers and her killer black stockings with the lacy tops. Not that Fraser could see any of this, yet. On the top she wore a black cashmere cardigan, unbuttoned to show a good portion of cleavage, a classic knee-length black wool skirt and a pair of high-heeled black shoes.

'You look different tonight,' Fraser said, finally turning towards her. 'I can't work out what it is but it's definitely different!'

She laughed lightly. 'It's probably the first time you've seen me not dressed as "Doctor Broden",' she answered. 'I hope it's not too much of a shock!' She leaned forward to place her wine glass on the floor and Fraser caught a glimpse of the black lace bra under her cardigan.

'No, not at all,' he said, glancing quickly away and feeling the beginnings of a hard-on. Beth noticed it instantly and moved towards him.

'Fraser,' she purred in her soft voice. 'Do you find me attractive?'

He nodded, taking a gulp of wine. 'You're a very attractive woman, Beth.'

'Oh?'

She reached out for his wine glass, took it from him and placed it on the floor by her own. 'Well, you know, I'd never have guessed you thought that.'

Fraser was aware of an excitement at her closeness but it was a take-it-or-leave-it sort of feeling. There was no misjudging the messages she was sending out but he wasn't at all sure what to do about them.

Beth ran her finger along his arm and up to his face. She touched his lips.

'Fraser, I think we've known each other long enough,' she said. 'Don't you?'

'For what?' He was starting to feel distinctly edgy, trapped.

'For this,' she whispered, and, leaning towards his face, she kissed him on the mouth and slipped her hand down to his crotch, giving it a gentle but probing squeeze. Fraser's leg shot off the stool in surprise and he knocked both glasses of wine over, soaking Beth's foot.

'Oh Christ!' He jumped back, bent down to pick up the glasses and touched Beth's leg to see how wet it was.

'Hmmm.' She moved her leg under his hand. 'That's nice. Why don't you see if it's wet further up?'

Fraser's hand froze. 'Yes, um . . .' He stood up. 'I think I'll get us some more wine,' he said quickly.

Beth pulled a face and reclined back on the sofa. 'Do you have to?' she moaned in her baby-girl voice.

'I won't be a minute,' Fraser said. God, he needed some air! 'Promise,' he murmured, hurrying across the room.

'You'd better not be,' Beth pouted and she unfastened another button on her cardigan. 'We don't want to waste that.'

'What?'

She smiled at the bulge in his trousers and he glanced down. Oh Christ! It had nothing to do with the way he felt; it just happened, whether he wanted it to or not. And he certainly didn't want it to, not now, not tonight. He left the room, his hands hot and sweaty on the glasses, and escaped to the kitchen with a mixture of relief and an overwhelming desire to laugh hysterically.

Beth listened to the silence of the big, old house for a moment and then stood up, switched the standard lamp off and glanced at her reflection in the mirror over the fireplace. God, Fraser needed some encouragement, it was like getting blood out of a stone! She unfastened another button on her cardigan, eased a little more breast into view and then thought, Oh bugger it, I might as well make it obvious! and pulled the cardigan over her head. She unclipped the bra, knowing the sight of her thirty-eight D cups always did the trick, unzipped her skirt, squeezing it over her hips, and sucked in her tummy. Then she went back to her position on the sofa, lay down with her legs artfully placed, her large pink nipples erect, and waited for Fraser to come back. This, she thought confidently, he wouldn't be able to resist.

Livvy put down her umbrella as she went up the steps to Fraser's front door and stood in the porch light, running her fingers through her damp hair and hoping nervously that her mother was right. After she had put the phone down to Moira, she hadn't given it a moment's extra thought. She had simply grabbed her coat and umbrella, thrown her key into her bag and hurried out of the flat, buoyed up by Moira's words of encouragement and thinking that if at least they could become friends again then maybe there would be a chance to find out if there was anything more.

'I saw his face,' Moira had said to her on the phone, 'and I think you've misjudged him. Please, Livvy, put your friendship back on a level, don't carry your anger round, it's really not healthy.'

So, not bothering to phone, Livvy had rushed out into the night, calling out to Mrs P that she wouldn't be long, and hurried straight round to Fraser's house. At least he was in, she thought, finally plucking up the nerve to knock; she could see a light on in the kitchen.

Fraser came out of the kitchen carrying two more glasses of wine and thinking that he would have to make things quite clear to Beth, before they got out of hand and anybody got hurt. It wasn't that he didn't find her attractive or sexy; she'd certainly proved that; it was just that he wanted someone else and until he had given up hope there, he just wasn't interested. Feeling slightly more in control now he knew what he was going to say, he walked towards the sitting room and suddenly caught sight of a figure at the front door.

Placing the wine on the hall table, Fraser carried on to the door and peered through the stained-glass panel trying to make out who it was. He saw Livvy, damp but waving to him, and his stomach lurched. Forgetting everything else at the sight of her, he swung open the door and exclaimed, 'Livvy! My God! What are you doing here?' He grinned, genuinely delighted to see her, and pulled her inside the warmth of the hall. Then he remembered Beth.

Beth was feeling a little chilly, half naked and reclining alone on the sofa, and she decided to go and seek out Fraser. He was taking rather a long time in the kitchen but she didn't mind surprising him there. She wasn't averse to sex in unusual places; in fact she remembered one of the best screws she'd ever had was standing at the sink while Derek took her from behind only minutes before her dinner guests had arrived. She fluffed up her hair in the mirror, thinking how creepy old houses were, not being able to hear what was going on in the next room, and pulled open the heavy oak door to the hall.

'Fraser,' she called, 'where are . . .'

Both Livvy and Fraser turned at the same time but it was Fraser who uttered the loudest proclamation of shock.

'Oh my God!' He leaped back and stared helplessly at the thirty-eight D cups as Livvy cried out, slapped him hard around the face and turned in panic, fleeing down the steps and into the street. Fraser ran after her.

'Livvy! Please! Livvy, come back,' he shouted as her figure, tall and lithe, sprinted down the road in the pouring rain and he knew he had no hope of catching her.

'Oh, damn you, Livvy Davis!' he shouted to the empty street, then he turned towards the house and, for the second time that night, he remembered Beth.

Livvy ran all the way from Rubislaw Terrace to Holburn Road and her own house, the tears of frustration and anger streaming down her face, and arrived out of breath, her cheeks flushed, and soaking wet. She opened the front door, literally fell inside and leaned back against the wall letting the sobs take her over and uncaring whether Mrs P heard her or not. Seconds later, Mrs P's door was flung open and Mitch rushed out into the hall.

'Christ! Livvy! What on earth's the matter?' He took hold of her and pulled her to him. 'Ssssh. Please, stop crying, please.' He glanced over his shoulder at Mrs P and they exchanged confused and helpless looks, but he continued to hug Livvy until after a few minutes she eventually calmed down. He patted her hair, not knowing quite what to do, and mumbled what he thought were soothing words.

Suddenly Livvy pulled away and said, 'Oh, do shut up, Mitch!' and she started to laugh. 'What a load of old cobblers!' He stared at her and then he too started to laugh.

'I'm sorry,' he said. 'I'm just not used to women sobbing on my shoulder.'

'Good thing too,' Livvy answered, wiping her face on her sleeve. 'Fat lot of good you'd be!' She squeezed his arm. 'Thanks anyway.'

He shrugged.

'What are you doing here?' Livvy glanced across at Mrs P, who was watching the scene with great relish.

'I thought we'd celebrate the arrival of your telephone, but you weren't in and Mrs P asked me in for a wee tot to wait until you came back. She said you wouldn't be long.'

Livvy rolled her eyes at him, knowing his charm, and he grinned. 'May I get my bottle out of the fridge, Mrs P?'

'Och, of course. I'm so glad yae waited, I told yae she wouldna be long.'

She held the door wide for him and he disappeared, coming back seconds later with a bottle of champagne.

'Ooh, lovely,' Livvy exclaimed, 'that's just what I need.' Sod Fraser Stewart, she thought, that was his very last chance! 'Come on up and let's open it before it gets warm.'

Mitch followed her towards the stairs.

'Would you like to come up, Mrs P?' Livvy asked.

'No, thank you, Livvy dear, yae two just get on with it.' And much to Mitch's surprise, Mrs P winked at him as he turned and made his way after Livvy up the stairs.

Inside the flat, Livvy lit the gas fire and shivered, realising in the sudden warmth that she was frozen.

'I ought to get out of these clothes,' she said to Mitch, as he opened the champagne. 'They're sopping.'

He turned to look at her; even wet through she was sexy, he thought. He stared for a moment and then she moved to avoid his gaze. 'The glasses are in the cupboard above the sink, by the way,' she called, walking into the bedroom.

'Shall I bring you one?' He popped the cork, missed her answer and poured the wine into two whisky tumblers. He decided to do it anyway and picked the glasses up, wandering after her into the bedroom. In the doorway he stopped dead.

Livvy had peeled off the wet layers of clothes and stood in her underwear, a white cotton body, high cut on her thighs and low cut with lace around her bust. It clung, slightly damp, to the shape of her and she bent, unaware of Mitch, to take some clean dry clothes from the bottom drawer of her chest, the cotton moving up to reveal the rounded curve of her buttocks. Instantly hard, Mitch put the glasses down on the table by the door and, unable to stop himself, walked across to her.

'Livvy.' He placed his hands gently on her hips and she started. Running them down over her thighs, he bent and kissed the back of her neck. She straightened but didn't turn round. He let his hands move up to her breasts, his fingers caressing her nipples, and she sighed, a tiny, almost noiseless sigh. Mitch gently bit her ear.

I don't know why I'm doing this, she thought, and I really don't care. It felt good, relaxing and gently erotic. She let her shoulders drop down and she placed her hands behind her, feeling for Mitch, pleased when she heard him moan at her touch.

Suddenly there was a loud banging on the door and they both jumped.

'Livvy!' The knocking increased in violence. 'Livvy, I

know you're in there!' Fraser shouted. 'For God's sake, answer me! I've got to talk to you.'

The front door of the house had been open and he'd run in and straight up to the top floor without stopping. Now his chest heaved as he struggled to regain his breath. 'Livvy! Christ, Livvy, it wasn't what it seemed! Please, just open the door.'

Up until that moment Livvy and Mitch had stood motionless but as Fraser continued to shout Livvy's anger came flooding back and she jerked away from Mitch, striding in her underwear to the front door of the flat.

'Go away!' she shouted through the wood. 'I don't care what it was. Just go back to Beth and leave me alone.' She could feel the tears again in the back of her throat and that made her even more angry. 'Go on,' she screamed, 'go!'

But Fraser wouldn't budge. 'No!' he shouted back. 'I'm not going until you at least hear me out.'

Suddenly Livvy flung the door open and stood before him half naked, her face flushed with anger. 'I will not listen to you, Fraser,' she shouted. 'I'm in the middle of something myself!' She stared furiously at him, her eyes blazing. 'Now go away!'

Fraser shook his head, incredulous. 'I don't believe you,' he said.

'Oh? Don't you?' She widened the door and pointed to the champagne and Mitch's jacket, a fifties American baseball jacket. Fraser took in both items and then looked back at Livvy again. His face changed.

'Well, that's great!' he snarled. 'I should have known that you'd . . .'

'That I'd what?' Livvy's voice suddenly broke as she

snapped back at him and a sob rose in her throat. She turned away.

'That . . . Oh shit!' Fraser kicked the banister in frustration. Then he dug his hands in his pockets and without looking at Livvy again, he started down the stairs, half running, jumping one every now and then, desperate to get away. Livvy gripped the door for support, heard him jump down the final step to the ground and slam the front door of the house behind him. Silently crying, she went back into the flat and closed the door.

'What was all that about?' Mitch stood in the doorway to the bedroom and looked at her. 'Why didn't you tell me you had a thing with the boss?' He was angry, and he'd felt a fool, standing in the bedroom, listening to the turmoil of emotion on the landing and not being able to do anything.

'Because I haven't,' Livvy answered. She had stopped crying and had found a tea towel to dry her face on. 'And it's far too complicated to explain,' she said wearily. She went to the sofa and slumped down on it, pulling one of the tartan rugs around her. Mitch wasn't sure what to do.

'Shall I go?' he asked. Livvy nodded. Picking up his jacket, he crossed to the sofa and bent down in front of her.

'Are you sure there's nothing between you and Fraser?' He took both of her hands in his and looked at her face.

'Yes, I'm sure,' she replied. He kissed her hands.

'Then, d'you mind if I don't give up?'

'Give up what?'

Mitch smiled. 'The quest to get Livvy Davis into bed!'

She smiled back. 'No, I don't mind. Is that what it is, a quest?'

'Oh yes,' Mitch answered, standing and adjusting his

jeans to accommodate the effect she had on him. 'It's an age-old thing going after something you know you can't have!'

He blew her a kiss as he headed for the door. 'Ring me if you want,' he said, glancing back over his shoulder at her and she nodded. 'Night, Livvy.'

'Goodnight, Mitch,' she called gently and moments later she was alone.

Chapter Twenty-Eight

Paul Robson sat on a bench in Finsbury Circus and watched the bowls. It was the first fine day in March, spring was in the air and a pretty girl in a lawn dress and cardigan was playing with her boyfriend on the perfect, smooth green. She was rubbish but the boyfriend didn't mind; every time she did it wrong he had the chance to come behind her and show her again how to aim the bowling ball by gently lifting the arm and he had to hold her hips with both hands to keep her steady. She laughed up at him in a carefree, uncomplicated way and Robson thought, Lucky bastard. His stomach churned.

He moved his gaze away, wary of staring, and glanced down at his sandwich, half eaten in his hand. He dropped it back into the bag and put the bag on the ground by his feet. He wasn't really hungry. He wondered why he bothered to go through the pretence of buying lunch each day when he knew damn well he wouldn't eat it; he'd hardly eaten anything for weeks. He leaned forward on the bench, putting his head down between his knees, and tried to concentrate on the ground. The nausea and acid in his gut eased slightly and he took a deep breath. What was he doing? He was thirty-two years old and he was frightened, every minute of every day. He was scared out of his wits.

He wished he'd never seen that disk. He wished, as he had done continuously for the past two weeks, that he could forget it, that he could put it into perspective, dis-associate himself from it, but it was all in vain. Paul Robson wasn't that type of bloke. He couldn't switch off from the job; that was why he'd always done so well.

Howard Underwriting was a company that had been set up to launder drug money and that was a fact he just couldn't get away from. The chief names in the syndicate, all of the names as far as he knew, were suspected drug felons, criminals, according to Loman's investigations. They were Colombians, Brazilians, legitimate businessmen in the eyes of Lloyd's, all with bona fide backgrounds and all with sufficient collateral to meet the requirements. How on earth had it happened? How had Hugh set it all up?

Robson took another deep breath, his stomach giving him hell again, and glanced up at the park. That was another thing he'd started doing, looking over his shoulder, checking there was no one behind him. That and going to bed late, waiting until Annie was asleep so that he didn't have to make love to her, so that she wouldn't notice how long he lay awake in the dark just trying to think things through.

Of course he knew how Hugh had set it up and in some ways he understood why as well. The rationale was obvious. Make a fortune, then get out at, say, thirty-five, and go somewhere warm with enough stashed in the bank to last a lifetime. South American business was a huge, corrupt, enticing market and Hugh was bright, too bright and too ambitious to make it up the ladder the hard way. Robson didn't blame him – maybe he'd have done the same if the opportunity had ever arisen – but he did hate him. Howard was a bastard and he couldn't help thinking that there was more going on than even he knew; perhaps that was why he was so scared? The drug business was dangerous; he was under no heroic illusions there. It was highly dangerous, as Loman had already found out.

Looking up, Robson saw that the girl and her boyfriend had gone and that the sun had disappeared behind a thick grey cloud. He must have been sitting there for ages; he'd lost track of time. Standing, he bent and picked up his discarded lunch, dropping it in the bin on his way out of the park, another fiver wasted. Then he dug his hands in his pockets, looked behind him again and started on his way back to Lloyd's.

It was after two when Paul Robson walked into the office. Normally he would have been down at Lloyd's in the box but he had gone straight there only to be told that Hugh wanted to see him in private. Now. He had been sweating all the way over from St Mary Axe.

'Hugh?' He stood in the doorway of Hugh's office. 'You wanted to see me?'

Hugh looked up. 'Yes, come in and sit down, Paul.'

Robson did as he was asked.

'I've had Derek Dorsey on the phone. He wants you to call him back.'

Robson felt the tension in his chest ease. He took a deep breath. No Loman, no disk, no questions he couldn't answer. The relief spread through him like heat. 'I'll do it right away,' he said and went to stand.

'Just a moment. I haven't finished.' Hugh kept his face

impassive but he was edgy. 'What is this all about?' he asked. 'Why is Dorsey so uptight?'

Robson sat down again. He had no intention of being frank with Hugh. IMACO were being routinely investigated but it was highly unlikely that anything would be found; they'd donated far too much money to Conservative Party funds for that to happen and they were lobbying every MP conceivable. Howard Underwriting had made good profit on that business, marvellous profit, in fact. After the initial scare several months ago Robson had looked into it and then left it alone. He hadn't had time to think about it if he was honest, but he didn't reckon there was much to worry about. Besides, Hugh had an excellent level of reinsurance. All right, they'd taken a huge line, but they were well covered for it; Hugh had arranged it himself.

'IMACO have had the MAFF looking into one of their fertilisers,' Robson answered. 'There has been some worry about one or two of the chemicals used in production but that's all it is, "some worry". It's very unlikely that it'll go any further than the stage of investigation. It's routine procedure as far as I can see.'

'Then *why* was Dorsey so uptight?'

Robson shrugged. 'As far as I know there's no reason for him to be. I've been following this right from the beginning and it looks pretty harmless.'

Hugh tapped his pen against his teeth and the sound of the metal on enamel set Robson on edge. 'How much insurance did they buy?' he asked.

Robson was taken aback. Hugh knew that already; he'd reinsured it himself. 'Fifteen million,' he answered warily. 'But you . . .'

'Yes, I know, I'd forgotten,' Hugh snapped. It was weeks

ago, in the middle of the deal with Manuello, and Hugh wasn't sure now if he'd made the right decision. He knew he certainly hadn't reinsured the cover, but there was no need to tell Robson that. If things were under control then Howard Underwriting had nothing to worry about, nothing to lose. They could reinsure at a later date. 'I can't be expected to know every damned figure in the company!' he said aggressively; Robson's puzzled stare irritated him.

It was hardly just another 'damned figure', Robson thought; it was their biggest percentage of business, but he kept quiet. In the back of his head the tiny piercing ring of an alarm bell went off. 'Was there anything else, Hugh?' he asked.

'No. Except keep me informed, will you? I want to know every move that IMACO are making from now on. All right?'

Robson shrugged again. It was hardly necessary but if that was what Hugh wanted . . . The alarm bell was beginning to sound louder as he stood and scraped the chair back under the desk. 'I'll catch you later, Hugh. I'm off back to the market.'

'Right.' Hugh nodded and Robson turned to go. 'Let me know what Dorsey wanted,' Hugh called after him, 'as soon as you ring him.'

'Yeah, sure.' Hugh's sudden interest in IMACO unnerved him – didn't he have enough to worry about?

He headed down the corridor to reception thinking that the call to Derek Dorsey could wait. He was already late for an appointment with a broker down in the market and he was beggared if he was going to jump every time Hugh told him to.

*

Fraser made a note, underlined it and then flipped the computer file on to the next page, looking up at the information in front of him. It was late, he had been working on this since the close of business at the paper, and his eyes hurt from the glare of the computer screen. He looked away for a few minutes, took his glasses off and rubbed his hands wearily over his face before putting them on again and going back to work. He had to find a connection; he was sure it was there. A gut feeling told him that IMACO were beginning to panic and there had to be something for them to panic about. He put the heading McCreedy on his pad and started to go through the case, carefully listing the main points and trying desperately to see some kind of link with the other cases he'd brought against IMACO. He wasn't able to.

In all the lawsuits he'd brought against the company over the years, Fraser had never been able to argue a direct cause that linked them all together and that could be traced back to the fertiliser, although he was sure it was responsible. Skin complaints and severe respiratory problems, a cot death – they could all have been the result of the same toxin but there was no way to connect them. All the claimants came from different backgrounds. They had a connection with IMACO, granted – they were all employees or married to employees – but not necessarily with the fertiliser, except for McCreedy with his emphysema. He was a waste handler for the chemicals but he also smoked eighty a day and there was no way medically they could argue his case.

Fraser made the last point in his neat handwriting and drew a line across the page; he'd had enough. He stood, stretched his hands behind his back and dropped his head forward to ease the tension in his neck. He leaned over to the computer, saved the file and switched the machine off, taking the disk out and putting it back in its plastic case. It was well after nine and he was tired; he'd do the rest in the morning. He went to clear his papers away when he heard the doors to the main office bang shut and he looked across the empty desks to see Beth standing in the half light just inside the room.

He stiffened, unsure of what her reaction to him would be after last night when he'd bundled her, hurriedly dressed, out into the night, apologising lamely and anxious to get rid of her so that he could go after Livvy. He expected an outraged scene and it was no more than he deserved. Walking to the door of his office, he pulled it open and called across to her, 'Beth? Come on over.' She nodded and made her way across.

Beth had thought long and hard on how to handle this one. Normally, without Dorsey's threats, she would have ignored the whole thing last night and simply dropped Fraser from her memory. Gone! Not another thought wasted on him. She was good at that – she never lamented her mistakes, she just wiped them clean and started again. But Dorsey frightened her. He had something on her and she knew he wasn't playing games. If he went down then he would take Beth with him and she wasn't about to let that happen, not under any circumstances. So she was here to salvage the wreckage, despite what she would have liked to do. She was here to get what she wanted this time.

Letting Fraser kiss her cheek, Beth walked past him into his office and sat herself behind his desk. She looked at him and smiled.

'Beth, listen.' Fraser was embarrassed, unable to look her in the eye. 'I just want to say how sorry . . .'

'Forget it,' she said quickly, cutting him short. 'Let's just say it was a massive misunderstanding.' She waited for him to meet her gaze. 'All right?'

He flushed, remembering the sight of her. 'All right,' he said, not convinced. 'I completely understand if you never want to see me again.'

Beth laughed lightly and waved her hand in the air to dismiss his comment. 'Oh, Fraser, don't be so melodramatic! We were operating at cross purposes, that's all. There's no harm done, and no offence, certainly not on my part.' She slipped her coat off her shoulders. 'I'm sorry for upsetting Livvy, though.' She arched her eyebrow. 'She took it rather badly, I thought.'

Fraser prickled at the mention of Livvy's name. He was incensed by her behaviour and there had been an arctic silence between them all day. 'Don't worry about Livvy,' he said coldly, 'she's a big girl.'

Beth shrugged and looked down at the desk.

'So what are you working on so late in the office?' she asked, fingering the page of his notebook. 'IMACO? Good lord, Fraser!' She glanced up at him. 'Why on earth are you making notes on past IMACO cases?'

Fraser moved forward to take the notebook from her and then changed his mind, thinking it would make him look edgy. 'I was tidying things up,' he answered, 'sorting through some files to dump them.'

Beth looked questioningly at him and then down at the page. She read out the title of the case. 'McCreedy. Now there's a case I worked on. I remember it well. What's all this about, Fraser? Can I help?'

Fraser sighed and came to sit on the edge of the desk. There was no harm in telling Beth, he could do with someone to talk to. 'To be honest, Beth, I'm not really sure what it's about.' He picked up the pad and glanced down the page. 'I've heard through the grapevine that the fertiliser IMACO produce up here is being investigated by MAFF. I've thought for a long time now that there's something wrong with it but I've not been able to prove it. I've just been going through my files to see if there's anything I may have overlooked, anything at all, no matter how tenuous, that will link the various cases together and ultimately relate back to the chemicals in the fertiliser.' He shrugged. 'No go, I'm afraid; I'm no clearer at all.'

'But even though some of the symptoms were linked, as far as I can remember, none of the parties involved had had the same contact with the chemicals,' Beth protested. 'Some of them didn't even work anywhere near the processing part of the plant. Is there some reason why you've come to this conclusion?'

Fraser shook his head. 'Not really. Apart from the fact that MAFF are investigating it I've nothing to go on. It's gut feeling, nothing more.' He smiled. 'I'm like a highland terrier – once I get my teeth into something I won't let it go!'

Beth laughed. 'I can just see you as a West Highland White,' she said, 'in a little tartan coat!' They both smiled. 'Anyway, didn't IMACO settle out of court on all of these?'

'Yes. But that in itself was suspicious, wouldn't you say? If they had nothing to hide, why bother?'

'To keep interfering newspaper men off their backs, I'd guess,' Beth answered. 'Good will, not wanting to upset the local press, staff morale. There're loads of reasons, Fraser.'

'Whose side are you on?' He smiled.

'Nobody's. I examined the patients and I gave evidence

based on my medical opinion. I couldn't see anything unto-ward and I still don't.'

Fraser looked at her. She was a good doctor, well respected, and she was a reasonable woman, she thought things through. Perhaps he had always been too emotion-ally involved; perhaps he was looking for something that wasn't there. 'No, maybe it's just me,' he said. 'Anyway, I've finished for today. Can I buy you a drink, Beth?'

She looked at him for a moment as if making up her mind and then she shook her head. She'd got what she had come for; no point in wasting time tonight. 'Thanks, Fraser, but no. I've an early start tomorrow and I really just came here to sort things out.'

He stood. 'Thank you, Beth, I appreciate it . . .' He paused. 'And I'm sorry.'

Beth pulled on her coat, came round to his side of the desk and reached up to kiss him on the cheek. 'No prob-lem,' she said. He put his hand on the back of her head and held her for a moment, then he leaned forward and kissed her long and hard on the mouth.

'Beth?'

'Hmmm.' She opened her eyes. 'Will there be another . . .'

She put her hand over his mouth and eased her body away from his. 'Yes,' she said quietly, 'I'm sure there will.' And turning away, she smiled over her shoulder at him and walked out of the office. Derek would be pleased; she'd ring him straight away

Chapter Twenty-Nine

Livvy stood on the pavement outside 22 Holburn Road and glanced back again at Mrs P, who was watching her avidly from the window. Mrs P knocked lightly on the glass and waved, and Livvy waved back. Mitch was late and for the past twenty minutes this little manoeuvre had been going on every five minutes or so; Livvy wondered just how long Mrs P was going to keep it up. Didn't she have Tilly to feed or something? She turned back to stare down the street, tucked her hands deeper into her pockets and wished Mitch would bloody well hurry up.

It was a brilliantly clear, sunny day for the end of March but it was still bitterly cold. She wore the new coat she had bought to combat the Scottish weather, a fleece-lined, heavy plaid jacket with a big collar and pockets that went on forever. She wore a wool beret pulled down over her ears, two pairs of leggings, the underneath pair thermal, and her Timberlands boots with a pair of mighty grey arctic socks rolled down over the top. She was still cold.

Stamping her feet on the ground, she finally saw Mitch's black jeep come tearing down the street, radio blaring through the open roof, and she breathed a sigh of relief. She turned to wave at Mrs P for the last time and stepped forward to meet the car as he screeched to a halt.

'Good lord, Olivia! Is it really necessary to wear all that kit?' Mitch exclaimed, jumping out of the jeep. 'We're going in a helicopter, not on a mountaineering expedition!'

'I'm cold,' she said, 'and we'll have to get out of the helicopter at some point, won't we? It's bound to be freezing out there in the wilds of Aberdeenshire!'

Mitch laughed. 'You big soft Southerner!' He opened the door for her and helped her inside, dumping her bag in the back, then said, 'Hang on a minute.' He ran across to the house where Mrs P was still watching and tapped on the window which, after a bit of fumbling, she managed to unfasten and open.

'Och, Mitch! How are yae?'

'Fine, fine.' He leaned through the window and kissed her hairy cheek. 'All the better for seeing you, Mrs P!' And with a little gallant backward wave, he leapt athletically over the small furze bush in the garden, caught his foot, very nearly fell flat on his face and a little more soberly climbed back into the jeep. As they drove off towards Aberdeen airport, Livvy was literally bent double with laughter.

Mitch had been planning this helicopter trip with Livvy for the past few days; it was the one thing he was sure would impress her. After the disaster several nights earlier, halfway into bed and thwarted at the last minute, he had been consumed with sexual frustration, desperate to finish what they'd started. It wasn't so much that Livvy Davis was the only woman for him; no, Mitch McDonald didn't believe in love, excepting the love he had for his mum and his

Hassleblad camera. It was more a case of not really wanting a pudding, then seeing the trolley, deciding on a wonderful strawberry cream pavlova and being told that the last piece had been reserved for someone else. He wanted that pudding now and he could hardly think for wanting it!

By the time they arrived at the airport, Livvy had stopped laughing and was going over the sort of aerial shots they needed for the lead piece in the LIFE section. She had decided to do their main article in the first issue on tourism in Aberdeenshire, which was how Mitch had managed to suggest a day in the helicopter in the first place. It was a piece on the wealth and diversity of the area, a sort of celebration of the city and all its outlying areas, the coast, the lowlands, the Grampian Mountains and the Spey Valley with its history of the finest Malt. And for that Livvy required some really good shots. She wanted this to be the sort of pull-out section that people kept, for it to look so good that the advertisers would be falling over themselves to get a slot. It was the opening pages of a new venture and it was imperative that she show just how good that venture was going to be.

Mitch slung the jeep into a free space in the car park of the airport, switched the engine off and looked expectantly at Livvy.

'Excited?' he asked.

Livvy glanced up from her notepad. 'Hmmm?'

'Are you excited?' He drummed out a rhythm with his hands on the steering wheel. 'About going up in a helicopter?'

Livvy shrugged. She was about to say, 'Hardly, after spending a week making a programme with the Paras!' but something in Mitch's face, a sort of boyish, eager anticipation, stopped her. 'Oh yes,' she answered. 'Absolutely.'

'Good. I think you'll enjoy it!'

She smiled and watched him as he climbed out and began putting the roof up. He clipped all the bits into place while Livvy took his two cameras, her rucksack and a bag of film, spare lenses, sandwiches and a thermos from the back seat and piled them on the ground. Minutes later they were ready.

'Right, Livvy Davis, let's go and get some pictures!' Mitch could barely contain his enthusiasm as he picked up his bags and headed off towards the terminal. 'This is something that'll really impress you!' he called over his shoulder.

'I can't wait,' Livvy called back and held down the urge to giggle.

Strapped into her seat, Livvy sat back and waited for the pilot to adjust his headset and start the engines. She was so familiar with the procedure that she closed her eyes and relaxed, looking forward to the surge of power as the copter was lifted into the air. She switched her mind off from the chat between Mitch and the pilot, a friend of his who flew for one of the oil companies, and thought about the sort of photographs she wanted. A few moments later, she felt a reassuring squeeze on her thigh.

'There's no need to be nervous,' Mitch said quietly. 'These things are really very safe.' His tone was nauseatingly infused with patronising sympathy.

Livvy opened her eyes and frowned. He was beginning to get on her nerves and she very nearly snapped at him. Instead, she just smiled and removed his hand. 'I'm not nervous,' she replied coolly. 'Really, Mitch.'

He nodded but his look indicated that she didn't need to pretend, not with him. She took a breath, ready to make a sharp retort, and was saved seconds later by the roar of the engines as they were propelled off the ground. Within minutes, they had been lifted high into the air and were turning, making their ascent across the airport, away from the coast and inland, to the heart of Aberdeenshire.

Livvy was enthralled by the beauty of the landscape. They had flown over Aberdeen so that Mitch could take some grainy black-and-white shots of the Granite City, its steely grey buildings austere against the forbidding slate of the North Sea, the brilliant sky and pale March sun doing little to lighten the grimness; and then they had turned west, inland and towards the mountains.

The helicopter took them along the River Dee, high above the expansive beauty of the valley, past the village of Aboyne and into the rougher edges of the Highlands. It was breathtaking. They then flew up over the Grampian Mountains towards the Spey, over more castles, both standing and in ruins, than Livvy had ever seen in her life, over the heartland of Aberdeenshire and the town of Huntly. Livvy stared out and made notes on the scenes, while Mitch snapped in a frenzy of creativity, asking the pilot to hover over certain spots where he wanted to change lenses, get a different angle, leaning left, right, and all the time capturing the essence of the region against a backdrop of pale, clear blue sky and brilliant spring sunshine.

Finally they flew out towards the Correen Hills to put down for lunch, some walking and some shots from the ground. It was a beautiful, wild area, popular with walkers and picnickers from the city, scattered with streams and springs of fresh, ice-cold, bubbling water that came up from the ground, ran for a time and then seemed to disappear again, down into the rocks.

Mitch had already decided on a spot with the pilot and agreed to a couple of hours on their own while his mate went over to an estate in the Don Valley to pick up a businessman and deliver him back to Aberdeen. It was that job that had got them a day in the helicopter so Mitch wasn't about to complain, even though two hours wandering over the Correen Hills was hardly his idea of fun. Livvy had far too many clothes on for a passionate scene in the open air and the ground was cold and damp. Still, he thought as they prepared to set down, you never know when you might come across a nice, warm, cosy barn.

They had been walking for some time before they came across a spot sheltered enough to sit down and eat in. Mitch dumped the bags and slumped on to a large mossy stone overlooking the stream. He dug around for the sandwiches and coffee, pulling both out and handing them to Livvy, then he picked up his camera and took several shots of her as she sat, her collar turned up and her hat pulled tightly down over her head. She looked about seventeen, concentrating on the lunch packet, and Mitch, unable to stop himself, reached over and kissed her.

'Oh! What was that for?'

'I don't know. You looked as if you needed it.'

She smiled. 'I need this more. Here, I can't get the bloody thing open!'

Mitch took the packet from her and put it up to his mouth, cutting the plastic with the edge of his teeth. He ripped the film off, screwed it up into a little ball, and was about to throw it behind him into the stream when he saw the look of astonishment on Livvy's face and stuffed it quickly into his pocket instead.

'You wouldn't be the first, I shouldn't think,' Livvy said, standing and looking across at the stream. She stepped past Mitch and bent to pick up a very old crisp packet from the edge of the water. 'See!' She inched closer to the edge of the stream and peered into the water.

'Hey, Mitch. Come here a minute, will you?'

He looked over his shoulder. 'You're not going to throw me in, are you?'

'Don't be ridiculous!' She stayed where she was, peering into the water. 'No really, come here a minute. I want to show you something.'

Mitch stood up. The last thing he needed was a bloody lesson in stream life. He moved in behind Livvy and followed her gaze.

'What? What is it?'

'There!'

'Where?'

She turned to look at him. 'For God's sake, Mitch! Have you ever seen a stream bed that's bright yellow?'

He bent closer. 'That's not yellow,' he said. Then he got down on to his stomach and, rolling his sleeve up, dropped his arm into the icy water and picked out a small stone from the stream bed. He held it up for them to inspect. 'Christ!' he exclaimed. 'It *is* yellow.' He bent his face to the water and sniffed. 'Smells like good, clean spring water though,' he said, and he cupped a little in his hands, drinking it down in one go.

'Mitch, don't!'

He dropped his hands down and looked round. 'Livvy,

you're being paranoid,' he said, and rubbed his hands on his jacket to dry them. He got to his feet.

'I shouldn't think it's anything to worry about,' he said. 'There must be loads of mineral deposits under this rock; it could be any number of things.' He aimed the stone at the water and threw it in. They both watched it splash heavily into the stream and sink to the bottom.

'Come on, Livvy, let's eat. We can follow the stream up after lunch if you want, see if we can find any more colours in it!'

Livvy cuffed him on the arm. 'All right, I bow to your judgement as you know the area but I'm sure it doesn't look quite right, mineral deposits or not.' She bent and picked up the sandwiches. 'Anyway, cheese or cheese?'

'Hmmm, cheese, please.'

They laughed and she handed him a sandwich. Sitting down on a rock, they were silent as they started to eat.

After lunch they walked several miles but they lost the stream and Livvy, overwhelmed by the scenery, had forgotten all about the yellow stones.

'I envy you, having all this wild beauty within your reach,' she told Mitch. She stood looking at the scene, her mind not really on it and thought about Fraser. For the last few days she had hardly thought of anything else. 'I'm not surprised Fraser came back to Scotland,' she said, thinking aloud. 'I don't think I could have left all this to settle in London.'

'Oh, that's not the reason he came back,' Mitch said. 'I was talking to Carol a few days ago about it, after that conversation we had about him.'

'Oh yes?' Livvy had instinctively tensed. She didn't want to hear what Mitch had to say about Fraser; she regretted even mentioning his name now. It was completely and utterly ridiculous, thinking about him the whole time! She had no right to do it, not with the terrible prospect of her court case hanging over her head. How could she even consider Fraser in her life? In a few months' time it might not be hers to share.

'According to Carol, his father didn't die of natural causes but she doesn't know the exact details,' Mitch continued, hardly noticing Livvy's depression. 'Fraser's family, the Stewarts, owned a huge amount of land in Aberdeenshire until the oil industry started to decline in the early eighties. Apparently the British Government, seeing the slump coming, were trying to introduce other industry into the area in order to stave off a massive unemployment disaster.'

Suddenly Livvy was riveted, despite her mood, and she began to listen intently.

'Petrochemicals was one of those industries and IMACO had plans to develop a processing plant up here, only they couldn't get the land. They were in negotiations with Robby Stewart when the Government stepped in and issued a compulsory purchase order on the area needed. It was a bribe, of course – IMACO had several members of the cabinet in its pocket – but Robby Stewart was done over. He lost most of his land for a pittance and subsequently started a vicious campaign in the paper against the company. Now the next bit is more Carol's imagination than anything else, I'd say, but she reckons that the company retaliated with minor threats, and Stewart, 'his heart broken', and that's Carol's line there, started drinking, pills, and all that rubbish. Within a year he was dead.'

Livvy stopped in her tracks. She stared at Mitch. 'D'you think this is all true?'

He shrugged. He realised that he had just unwittingly transferred her attention from himself to Fraser in one swift move, and heartily regretted bringing the subject up. 'I honestly don't know,' he answered sullenly, 'but I guess it would explain the boss's preoccupation with IMACO, wouldn't it?'

Livvy glanced away. It would explain a hell of a lot really, she thought: flushing the pills down the toilet, telling her to face up to things and get on with it . . . Evidently an awful lot of him ran far deeper than she had ever imagined. She was silent for a few minutes, just thinking. Perhaps she wasn't the only one with a burden to carry?

Mitch took her hand. 'What's in your head?' he asked.

She shrugged. 'I suppose I was thinking what an awful thing to happen.'

Mitch frowned. 'Yeah, it is,' he answered and dropped her hand. He'd done it now; she was way off his scent. He looked at his watch and said, 'I think we should head back to our pick-up point.'

'OK.' Livvy smiled at him. 'Thanks for telling me that.' It had made a difference to her.

He really wished he hadn't but it would be churlish to admit it. 'That's all right.' He paused and added, 'If it's true of course.'

She smiled as they headed off to meet the helicopter; Mitch was useless at covering his pique. 'Yes,' she answered, 'if it's true.'

Back in the air, forty minutes later, Mitch forgot everything except the job in hand as he scanned the views below him for decent shots. He kept his camera up to his eye and worked silently, deep in concentration, while Livvy let the landscape roll beneath her and left him to it. They were flying over the place they had stopped for lunch and Livvy took the binoculars from her bag and peered down at where they had walked. She saw the rock they had sat on and the stream, then she zoomed in closer with the lenses and suddenly said, 'Mitch? Take a picture of where we had lunch, will you?'

He put his camera down for a moment and looked at her. 'Sentimental, eh?'

She ignored his tone of voice and kept her vision pinned firmly to the ground. 'Not at all,' she answered, busy adjusting the lens again. 'Take that stream, would you?'

He dropped his camera on to his lap, tapped his mate on the shoulder, which was the sign to hover, and expertly changed the lens to an eighty/two hundred zoom. He focused and then removed the camera from his face a second time. 'I'm sure it's only mineral deposits, Livvy.' She glanced up at him and raised an eyebrow. 'But it is a funny colour,' he finished, starting to snap, 'I'll grant you that.'

After a couple of minutes, he had what he wanted and tapped the pilot again to move on. 'I think we should head along to the Don Valley,' he called to Livvy. 'Maybe take a few aerial shots of the IMACO plant?'

'Yes, all right.' She was deep in concentration, scanning the ground below. The stream they had tried to follow after lunch disappeared underground several miles up and she made a note of where it was on the map, and marked the spot where they had had lunch. It puzzled her. She didn't for one minute believe Mitch's theory on mineral deposits but she couldn't see anything along the line of the stream that might be polluting it. She put the binoculars down and watched the land as they moved on towards the Don Valley and the IMACO plant.

'What was that huge area of land back there?' she asked the pilot as they flew in towards Inverurie.

'Garioch,' he replied. 'It belongs to IMACO. They were planning to redevelop it but they faced too much local opposition and had to give it up. I don't know what they use it for now but it's closed to the public.'

'Mitch, could you just take a couple of shots of that?'

'What? Garioch?'

'Yes, please.'

He snapped as directed and finally they were above IMACO, a huge chemical processing plant, twenty or so miles from the city. They circled it a few times so that Mitch could get some decent pictures and after five minutes, with as much as he needed, they turned in the direction of Aberdeen, flew over Kintore and home to the airport.

'What a marvellous day!' Livvy said, as Mitch began to pack up his cameras. 'Thank you, I really think we got some brilliant ideas.'

Mitch finished zipping his zoom lens into its case and looked at her. Despite the bad mood he was in after mentioning Fraser Stewart, he grinned. 'You did?'

'Yes. Thanks to you!'

Mitch pulled his shoulders up. 'I thought you'd enjoy it,' he answered smugly and they landed with him feeling as pleased with himself as he had done when they'd taken off.

Livvy had managed to wriggle out of dinner with Mitch.

She felt guilty about it all evening as he worked late to produce the photographs for her while she made copious notes for the article, or she did until Carol called across to him that she was going out with some mates and would he like to come. He was packed up and ready before Livvy had even looked up.

'Can't turn a pretty girl down,' he said, leaning over her desk, and, laughing at him, Livvy gave him a shove. 'Go on, go! You fickle man, you!'

He left with Carol, full of the day in the helicopter, practising his best lines on her to see what she found amusing and then storing them up before he got on to the serious business of impressing her mates.

After he had left, only Livvy and Gordon remained in the office, both working in silence, both at opposite ends, and Livvy lost track of time, going over the final details for the LIFESTYLE section, due on Gordon's desk by the end of the week. She was also waiting for the contact sheets to dry in the darkroom, eager to have a quick look at the day's work and get a rough idea of what they had before she went home.

She looked up as she heard Gordon leaving and waved to him across the office.

'Don't work too hard, Livvy!' he called.

'I won't.' But they both knew she would. It was Livvy's escape, the work on the paper, and she channelled everything she had into it. 'I promise!'

Gordon smiled in the rather grim way he had and, pulling his coat on as he went, he left the office without saying another word. Livvy watched the doors bang shut and listened to his footsteps on the stairs. Within minutes, she was completely alone.

She worked on for another hour and then suddenly tiredness hit her. She sat back in her chair, rubbed her back, which had started to ache terribly from sitting in one position, and then stretched. It was ten-thirty and she thought she really ought to be getting home.

Packing her things away, she reached for her jacket and then remembered the photographs. She left everything on her desk, went through to the darkroom and switched on the light. The contact sheets were hanging up over a drip tray so she unclipped them, stacked them and took the pile back to her desk. Tired as she was, she couldn't resist having a glance through them. She found Mitch's magnifying glass, sat down and cast her eye over each sheet with its thirty odd small prints. They were good; in fact, she thought, coming to the last one, they were absolutely brilliant!

Then she stopped. She peered in closer at the tiny print of their picnic spot and narrowed her eyes. Yes, she could see it. The stream bed was showing up a strange yellowish colour, as if someone had altered the tint of the film. She took the contact sheet back into the darkroom, switched on the spotlight and checked it once more. The colour was definitely there.

Running her gaze down the other shots on the sheet, she stopped at the three or four of Garioch, IMACO's wasteland and peered at each of them in turn. She didn't have a clue what she was looking for, but she knew it was something; her curiosity had been aroused. In the last one, just as they were turning right in the helicopter back towards Aberdeen, Mitch had captured what looked like an IMACO lorry heading up through the open land – a lorry that was surely out of place. What would an IMACO lorry be doing off the main road?

Livvy found the magnifying glass again and tried to increase the visibility of the shot but it was too blurred, too far away. She gave up after several minutes of squinting and switched the spot off. Taking the contact sheet and the roll of negatives, she closed the darkroom up and went back to her desk, tucking them safely away in her bag. For some instinctive reason, and she had no idea what, she didn't want anyone else to know about this. All the things she had learned as a researcher, about connecting the most tenuous of links, about building up a picture, suddenly came back to her. What with Fraser's almost unnatural interest in IMACO and his history, if it was true, there could well be something here and Livvy couldn't leave it alone, despite the good sense part of her that kept saying, don't get involved. Regardless of what else she had on her mind, she just had to find out what it was.

Standing where she was for a moment Livvy looked across the big open-plan workspace at Fraser's small glass-fronted office and saw that he'd left his desk lamp on. The light seemed to draw her forward. Picking up her bag and quickly tidying her own desk, she walked over, opened the door and went inside, thinking that she'd turn the lamp off before she went home. But glancing down at his desk, she saw the small box of disks he had been working on for the past few days and the word IMACO. She moved her hand over to the box, slowly opened it and took out the first disk. There was no going back.

Hurriedly, she sat down at his screen, switched the PC on and inserted the disk. She took out her notepad and a pen, went into the file and quickly, with the speed and dexterity of an experienced thief, she began to copy down all the information she thought she might need to know, going through disk after disk to give her a good clear picture of what was going on.

At midnight Livvy finally left the office. She said good-night to the security man on reception, pulled her gloves on and walked down to North Anderson Drive to find a taxi. She was no longer tired, she was buzzing with professional excitement. Hopping into the first one in the queue of waiting cars, Livvy gave Mitch's address and sat back in the seat as the cab wove its way through the lighted streets of Aberdeen to his flat. She climbed out at Bon Accord Street, paid the driver and stood in the light of the entrance to ring the bell. After quite some time, Mitch's sleepy voice came over the intercom.

'Mitch? It's Livvy.'

'Livvy! Jesus! What are you doing here?'

'I need a favour, can I come in?'

There was a silence and Mitch seemed to disappear. Livvy hugged her arms around her in the cold, dark street.

'Listen, Livvy.' A few minutes later he was back again. 'Er, it's a bit, er, embarrassing at the moment . . . I . . .'

Livvy smiled. 'It's all right, Mitch, I won't cramp your style. Look, I want to borrow your car tomorrow, would that be OK?'

'My car?' He sounded a bit disorientated. 'Er, yeah, sure. What for?'

'I want to see someone and I can't get there by bus.'

'OK. Can you wait a minute?'

The intercom went dead again and Livvy looked up at the building hoping to see a light. It was pitch black.

'Livvy? I'll let you into the hall and chuck my keys down to you.'

Livvy started to laugh. 'She can't be that ugly, Mitch!'

'Very funny!'

The buzzer sounded for the lock release and Livvy pushed the door open. She walked into the hall and pressed the light switch.

'Here.'

She looked up the flight of stairs and saw a dishevelled Mitch, half naked with a blanket pulled round the vital bits. He threw her a set of keys. 'Catch!'

'Great! Thanks, Mitch, I really appreciate . . .'

But he had gone before she finished her sentence. 'Blimey! That was brief,' she muttered to herself, heading back to the door just as the light went off. But it didn't bother her. And letting herself out into the street, she was more surprised by that fact than by anything else.

Chapter Thirty

Livvy was up early the following morning and the first thing she did was to ring Jenna, her assistant on the LIFESTYLE section, at home, and tell her that she was going to be late in; very late in. The next thing she did was jog down to the garage to buy one of their road map books. She brought it back to the flat and opened it out on the little table while she ate her Weetabix, looking up the addresses she wanted in the back and then marking out the best route to them with her fluorescent pen. By eight-thirty she was ready to go.

Packing everything she needed into her rucksack, Livvy pulled on her jacket and zipped it up. She found the keys to the jeep, switched the lights off and left the flat, locking the door behind her. She tiptoed down the stairs, anxious not to bring Mrs P out into the hall, and prised the front door open, stepped out and quietly clicked it shut. Hurrying down the street to where she'd parked the car, she unlocked it, threw her bag on to the passenger seat and climbed in. Her first stop was a small village off the B977, heading up towards Kintore, a cottage called Guthrie and a young woman named Myra Hadden.

Forty minutes later, Livvy pulled the jeep into a grassy

parking area at the side of a long, double-fronted stone cottage, peered at the sign on the gate to check she was in the right place and climbed out of the car. It had begun to rain, a slow, cold drizzle, and a chilly north-easterly breeze blew across the fields at the back of the house. She shivered, reached for her bag and went up to the front door.

Livvy was nervous. She knew the case history and hoped she was doing the right thing. She hadn't ever given much thought to the people she'd interviewed before – they had been part of the story, simple as that. But now, standing in the dank drizzle, she was apprehensive. She knocked, waited and then braced herself as she saw a tall thin figure approach the glass panel of the door.

'Hello,' she called out. 'I wonder if I might be able to talk to Myra Hadden?' The door slowly opened and a young woman looked out.

'Yes? Who are you?'

'Myra? My name is Livvy Davis, I work for the *Angus Press*.' The door started to close. 'Wait! Myra! Could you just spare me a few minutes, please? I won't take up much of your time and it's not for a news story, I promise.' Livvy saw the young woman hesitate, then the door opened wider and Myra Hadden stared at her.

'What do you want?' she said coldly.

Livvy took a breath. 'It's about the case against IMACO last year. I think I may have come up with something in connection with it and I just wanted to ask you a few questions . . .' Livvy stopped. She saw that the young woman's face had drained and a flicker of pain crossed her eyes.

'I've got nothing to say about it!' Myra Hadden snapped.

'Yes, I understand that,' Livvy answered. 'Please, can I just ask you a few questions? It's really important.'

Finally, after what seemed like ages in the freezing, whipping wind, Myra Hadden changed her mind and opened the door wider. 'You'd better come in,' she said and Livvy nodded.

'Thank you.' She stepped inside the warmth of the house and saw that Myra was pregnant.

Myra went across to her chair by the gas fire and sat down. She was heavy, probably about seven and a half months into her pregnancy, and she looked tired, strained with the effort of carrying a baby. She folded her arms across her stomach and looked up at Livvy, waiting for her to speak. But Livvy had momentarily lost her nerve; on the television set in the corner of the room she saw a large framed photograph of a small baby. Myra followed her gaze and said, 'I still miss him. Every day.'

Livvy bit her lip. 'I'm sure,' she answered quietly.

'I'm having another one, for my husband really, not because I want to. It won't be the same, you see, I'll always be frightened.'

Livvy moved over to the chair opposite Myra and sat down. 'I'm sorry,' she said. 'It must be a terrible thing to happen.'

Myra looked at her for a moment, unsure of her, but she saw only sympathy and feeling. 'Yes,' she replied simply, 'it is.'

They were silent for a few minutes and then Livvy said, 'Myra, I know this is very hard, but could you tell me what happened? The details of the day Alistair died.'

Myra didn't answer.

'Please?'

Myra shook her head and said, 'We've been through it so many times, I don't honestly know why we have to keep going over and over it!' Her voice was thick with tears.

Livvy looked away. 'I'm sorry, I understand.' She stood to leave. A few months ago she wouldn't have been able to let it go but now she couldn't bear the thought of putting someone through unnecessary pain. She turned towards the front door.

'Myra,' she said, glancing over her shoulder, 'can I ask you one thing before I go?'

The young woman shrugged.

'Do you ever go up to the Correen Hills, for picnics or walking?'

Myra closed her eyes. 'I've not been there since the day Ali died,' she replied. 'I just couldn't face it. It was the last place we took him, just the day before.'

Livvy felt a shiver run down her spine. For a second she was desperate to ask more but she knew Myra couldn't take it. She walked to the door, opened it and then said, 'Good luck with the baby, Myra.'

The young woman opened her eyes and smiled; for the first time since Livvy had arrived, there was a glimmer of hope in her face. 'Thanks,' she answered. Silently, Livvy let herself out and walked back to the jeep.

Heading towards Kintore, Livvy aimed to pick up the main A road towards Garioch; McCreedy lived in a small settlement out that way. The drizzle had turned to full-blown sleet and it pelted against the windscreen as she drove, the wipers splashing back and forth in a frenzy to keep the screen clear. The jeep held the road well but she was still nervous. The roads were high and deserted and she kept thinking that if she had an accident then no one would know for hours. She was excited about what she was doing, but she was also a little bit scared by it; she was well aware of the danger. What she was beginning to piece together in her mind was one hell of a big story; more than that, it was something that could change lives and she had every reason to believe that the people at IMACO were not going to like it, not one little bit.

McCreedy's cottage was out from the village, isolated on a road that led up towards the IMACO land. It was a desolate-looking stone house, battered by the rain and winds that came up off the sweep of the land behind it. There was no garden, just the rusting remains of a car in the back and a couple of sheds that housed McCreedy's dogs.

Livvy parked the jeep on the road and climbed out as a gust of wind blew full force across the hills and the road, knocking her back slightly. She held on to the car door to steady herself. Finding her bag, she slammed the door shut and made her way over the road to the house, the icy wind hurting her face as it lashed against her skin. Seeing a single light on in the front downstairs room, she walked to the door at the side, knocked and waited for someone to answer.

McCreedy wasn't long in coming. He pulled the door open and, looking behind him, said, ''Boot bloody time too! I called yae an hour ago!' He turned and his face darkened on seeing Livvy. He was small and thin, in his late sixties, a weatherbeaten Highlands man, mean and fierce-looking. 'Who're yae?' he growled, closing the door slightly. 'Yae're not the usual vet!'

'No, I'm not. May I come in?'

He huffed and glancing behind him again, opened the door to allow her to pass. 'I suppose Doctor Broden told yae?' Livvy nodded. Inside, the room smelled heavily of camphor and menthol. It was bare and shabby but it was warm. In front of a roaring fire a Border Collie lay in its basket, shivering and struggling for breath.

'What's happened?' Livvy moved closer to the dog.

'Shae were oot on the hills yesterday. Came back alreet but last night shae started all this. Shae canna seem ta breathe.' McCreedy's own breath was short and rasping as he spoke. 'I blame meeself, I should naer have let her go, not there.' He shook his head and looked across at Livvy. 'Where's yaer bag?'

Livvy let her rucksack drop off her shoulder but McCreedy's eyes narrowed. 'Was it the Correen Hills she was up on?' she asked quickly.

'Aye, that's them.'

Livvy bent to the dog. 'It's all right,' she began but she stopped at a loud knocking on the door. Standing quickly, she moved across the room. 'I'll get it,' she said. Pulling the door open, she nodded at a man whom she supposed was the vet, let him in and darted past him out of the cottage.

McCreedy was at the door after her and shouted across to her, 'Who the bloody hell are yae?' His face was black with rage and he held his stick up in the air. 'Coming inta ma hoose! I'll report yae to tha police!'

Livvy stood by the car. 'I'm from the paper,' she called back. 'I'm sorry, no offence meant.' And hurrying to unlock the door, she jumped into the jeep and started the engine. Shifting the gears, she moved forward and pulled off into the road. She didn't dare look back; McCreedy terrified her.

An hour later, Livvy was back in Aberdeen. There were several more people she had marked out to see but the morning had moved on and she needed to get to the office before anyone started asking questions. The rest of the interviews could wait. Dropping her things off at the flat, she left Mitch's jeep parked outside and took the bus to the paper. It was lunch time and she reckoned she could slip in without much trouble. Reporters coming and going on the paper wasn't at all unusual but keeping their stories to themselves was and Livvy didn't want anyone to know about this.

Calling hello to the girls on reception, she asked if Mitch was in and was told no, he hadn't been in all day. She breathed a sigh of relief and went up the two flights of stairs to the office. She walked in, dumped her bag on the desk and took her jacket off, glancing round. She saw Carol straight away, long-faced and making her way grimly over.

'Morning, Carol,' Livvy smiled. 'You all right?'

'Fraser wants to see you,' she said. 'He is absolutely steaming about something and I think it's connected to you.' Carol pulled a face. 'Be careful,' she advised as Livvy picked up her bag, 'he's in the executive meeting room downstairs.' That was a bad sign, everyone knew. When Fraser's office was too open for discussion, he went down into the meeting room; it was more private in there.

Livvy tried to smile but failed. 'Thanks,' she answered and slinging her bag over her shoulder, she grabbed her jacket, just in case, and made her way back to the stairs.

The executive meeting room was next to reception. Livvy stood outside with her ear to the door and listened for any conversation inside, then she stood straight and knocked. 'Come in, Livvy!'

She opened the door and stepped inside. Fraser was sitting on the edge of the table, looking through a file and waiting for her.

'Hello!' she said brightly.

Fraser dropped the file on to the table and glared at her. 'I suppose you already know the contents of the file I was looking at,' he said. 'Did you find it interesting?'

Livvy's mouth dropped open.

'I had a phone call from Beth Broden about forty minutes ago,' he went on. 'She was furious. Apparently a young woman with an English accent had been out to Bildare village this morning to see one of her patients, a Mr McCreedy? He rang her to complain, said she entered his house under false pretences and was snooping around . . .'

'I wasn't snooping!'

'But you were there?'

Livvy nodded and saw Fraser's eyes harden.

'What the hell do you think you're playing at? You've been through my files, presumably?'

Again she nodded, then looked down at the floor.

'Jesus Christ, Livvy!' She jumped at the roar of his voice. 'This is highly confidential information! What gives you the right to . . .?'

The realisation of what he'd just said suddenly hit Livvy. 'Beth Broden?' she interrupted. Fraser stopped.

'I beg your pardon?' he snapped.

'Beth Broden,' Livvy had moved into the room. 'She rang you?'

His nostrils flared as he tried to control his anger. 'I really don't see what this . . .'

'But Beth gave all the medical evidence on the cases for IMACO, didn't she?'

He sat silent and stony-faced.

'McCreedy asked me if Doctor Broden had sent me; he thought I was the vet. And he seemed to know what was wrong with the dog, said he blamed himself, he should never have let her go up to the Correen Hills. Christ, Fraser!' She was pacing as she spoke, completely unaware that she was doing it. Then she stopped and stared at him. 'Why didn't I think of it at the time?'

'Think of what?' Fraser roared and again she jumped. 'What is going on?'

'That Beth is involved somehow!' She had begun to pace again and suddenly Fraser jumped down from the desk and grabbed her, holding her still.

'Now you had better explain what is going on, Livvy, before I really lose my temper!' he shouted. She glared up at him and he dropped his hands, quickly releasing her. 'I mean it,' he warned.

Livvy took a deep breath, not really sure how much of it made sense yet, then began to explain. 'I think that there is some kind of water pollution up on the Correen Hills and I think it's coming from IMACO. I don't know how yet but I also think it's connected to some of the cases that you've represented over the past few years. I think this pollution causes some kind of respiratory problem.' She stopped and looked at Fraser's face, waiting for his reaction. He said nothing for quite some time, then he looked at her. He had forgotten his anger; he was too fascinated by what she was saying to let his emotion get in the way.

'Facts?' he asked.

She shook her head. 'I don't have any, at least not yet.'

'Then how . . .?'

She interrupted him. 'Mitch and I were up on the Correen Hills yesterday,' she said. 'We had lunch by one of the small becks up there and I noticed that the stream bed was an odd colour; it was yellow. Mitch noticed it too. When we flew over the area later, he took a shot of it and late last night, looking at the prints, I saw it again. I also saw something else pretty odd. That area of land, up past the Don Valley, where McCreedy lives? Well, it belongs to IMACO, it's closed to the public, but in one of the aerial shots Mitch took there's a lorry heading out there. A lorry! What for? They apparently don't use the land!'

She broke off, a little out of breath from talking so quickly, and swallowed hard. 'Fraser,' she said quietly, 'Myra Hadden took her baby up to the Correen Hills the day before he died of a cot death; McCreedy has emphysema, he lives up there, and he seems to know something about the area. His Collie was up there yesterday, and today the dog was fighting for breath. McCreedy said he blamed himself for letting her go there.'

'But these are only two out of God knows how many cases, Livvy, only two!' Fraser held up his hands. 'And how do you connect the areas up? I just can't see it.'

Livvy hesitated before she explained the next part of her theory. 'What if, and this is just a supposition,' she said, 'what if IMACO are using that land to dump chemicals, bury them for instance, and some of the toxins are seeping down into an underground water supply? Some sort of Artesian basin?' She paused. 'I don't know much about geology but the Correen Hills are scattered with streams that come up out of the ground, run for yards, half a mile or so, and then disappear back underground. Springs of water in the rock. The one we photographed was exactly like that.'

Fraser was thinking hard. 'D'you have the prints?'

'Yes, they're back at my flat. I didn't want Mitch to know what I was thinking.'

Fraser raised an eyebrow.

'I didn't want anyone to know,' Livvy said quickly. 'I get the oddest feeling that this could be quite scary.'

Fraser shrugged. 'You may be right.' He walked over to the window and stood silently for a moment, then he glanced over his shoulder at her and said, 'Do you think you could take me to the beck, the one you photographed? I'd like to see it for myself.'

'Yes, I . . .'

'Good!' He turned. 'If I get my coat, we could leave right away. I've got my car parked up the road.'

'I need to get the map and some other things from my flat. And we could do with a camera, do you have one?'

'No, I'll borrow one from photographic.' Fraser returned to the table and picked up the files. 'I'll meet you at my car. Here.' He dug in his pockets and pulled out the key. 'I'll be about ten minutes, all right?'

Livvy nodded and followed him to the door.

'Livvy.' He glanced back at her. 'If there is something in what you're saying then this is as far as you go. Do you understand that? I don't want you getting involved.'

'Why? Because of Beth?' she answered sharply.

'No, not because of Beth.' He hesitated, then said, 'Because of you. I don't want you to be in any danger.'

A part of her was relieved that he still cared enough to say that but the rest of her bridled angrily at his words. What did he think she had to lose? After what she'd been through the past few months this was child's play! 'Thanks, Fraser,' she answered coolly, 'but I can look after myself. Isn't that what you told me to do a few weeks ago?'

He stared at her for a moment, hurt by her coldness, then he shrugged it off. 'Whatever you want,' he murmured.

And walking out of the room, he left her while he went up to collect his coat.

They drove out to the hills in silence. The rain lashed against the windscreen, and the landscape, as they drove up, was bleak and forbidding. Livvy sat with her jacket over her knees and looked at the road map, trying to follow where they were going. She had the ordnance survey map in her bag, the one she had marked to show the spot by the stream where she and Mitch had picnicked, and as they approached the area, she dug it out and began to look for the roads closest to where they wanted. She directed Fraser to Coldwell's Croft and told him she thought that they should park somewhere round there. He did as she said and finally pulled up into the entrance of a field, switched the engine off and reached over for the map.

'That's where it is,' Livvy said, pointing to her mark. It was about two miles from where they were parked.

'Right.' Fraser climbed out of the car and went round to the boot, opening it up and taking out his walking boots, a bag of kit and his Barbour. He sat on the back seat of the car to get ready, pulling on socks, a thick sweater, a plaid sleeveless undercoat and finally his Barbour.

'You going like that?'

Livvy nodded. She had put on her Timberlands boots for walking but she had no hat, scarf or gloves.

'Here.' Fraser threw a cap and gloves over to her in the front seat. 'Zip your jacket up to your chin,' he said. 'The wind can be dangerously cold when it's like this.'

Livvy nodded and felt stupid. It annoyed her that he always managed to make her feel that way. She did herself up, pulled on the cap and gloves and climbed out of the car.

Fraser was already outside, clipping the map into a plastic holder.

'Ready?'

'Yes.'

Without saying anything else to her, he set off and she followed him, having to stride much faster than she normally would to keep up. They walked headlong into the sleeting wind, silent, grim, and both wanting to chat but far too stubborn to do so.

They made it to the beck twenty minutes later. Livvy had started to shiver, despite the pace of the walk; her jacket wasn't waterproof and she was soaked through. When they got there, Fraser stood on the same rock that she had the day before and looked down into the water.

'It's yellow all right,' he called to her. 'Come and have a look.' He held out his hand and pulled her up alongside him. 'The water looks quite clear but the bed seems to be stained.'

She nodded.

Jumping down, Fraser went up to the water's edge and took out the sample bottle he'd put in his pocket. He bent, immersed it in the water and filled it, trying not to get his hands too wet. 'Did you notice if any of the other streams or springs were this colour?' he called.

Livvy shook her head. 'We weren't really looking,' she shouted back, 'but we did follow this one up and it starts about half a mile along.' She jumped down after him, her voice strained at having to shout into the wind. 'There wasn't anything noticeable about the source,' she said, standing close. He tucked the bottle away.

'OK. Come on. I've seen what I need to.' He began walking but Livvy stood where she was. Several yards on he stopped and looked round. 'Livvy?'

'Is that it?' she shouted. 'All the way up here, no thanks, no discussion, just collect a sample and trudge back to the car!' She was angry; he was treating her as if she didn't exist, as if she hadn't done anything. He wouldn't even have known about this if it wasn't for her!

'What do you want, Livvy? A big pat on the back, heaps of adulation?' He shook his head, suddenly exasperated. He just couldn't understand her, she was impossible! 'This is just the beginning,' he called across the wind. 'One little sample, that's all.'

Livvy marched up to him. 'Well, it may be all but you wouldn't have had a clue without me.'

'Jesus, you're an arrogant bitch!' he suddenly shouted. 'The whole world has to constantly fall around you, doesn't it? You and your enormous bloody ego!'

The slap hit him right where his cheek was coldest and it stung like crazy. 'You . . .!'

But Livvy had stormed off.

'Come here, Livvy!' He ran after her and caught her, yanking her round to face him. 'What did you do that for?' he shouted as she struggled to free herself.

'Get off me!' she screamed back but he gripped her arms tightly so she couldn't move away. She went to kick him and he dodged it, shaking her, his eyes blazing. 'Don't you . . .!'

In the next instant he had pulled her hard towards him and was kissing her, his whole mouth over hers, his grip painful on her arms. It was the closeness, the sudden touching of her that did it; he couldn't stop himself. She fought against him, clamping her mouth shut, but he held her even tighter. It seemed endless, the few seconds that she was fighting against him, against herself but that was all it was, just a few seconds. Until her body responded in a way she had no control over and she almost fell towards him, desperate to be held, to be kissed, opening her mouth, letting his tongue in, as the freezing rain poured down over her face and cooled the burning that had started all over her.

'Oh God, Livvy . . .' He moved his mouth across her face, down to her neck, his fingers tearing at her jacket to uncover her skin. 'Livvy . . . I . . .'

She tangled her fingers in his hair, soaking, wet hair, and pulled his head down to her, closing her eyes and crying out as his lips touched the skin of her neck, the warmth of them followed by the iciness of the rain. She began to moan, lost to everything but him and then . . . then she felt nothing. She opened her eyes. Nothing.

'Fraser?'

He had moved away from her, only inches but it might as well have been half the world. She suddenly felt cold, bitterly cold and the dull ache of despair started in the pit of her stomach. 'Fraser, what . . .?' She couldn't speak, she didn't know what to do.

'Livvy, I'm sorry, I can't, I just don't know . . .' He broke off as he saw her face and wanted to run, as far away from her as he could. He was terrified, terrified that every time he was close to her he simply couldn't control his feelings, that they overwhelmed him, suffocated him and she had no idea how he felt. He just couldn't explain it but he knew he had to stop, to stop it all now before he found himself in the same pitiful mess as he had done in the past. He moved back to her and pulled her jacket together, covering the now frozen skin.

'Come on, Livvy,' he said, 'I think we should go home.'

She nodded, biting her lip to force back the tears. She was too proud to ask him what had happened; she couldn't face the thought that he might tell her it was because of Beth. She miserably watched his fingers, zipping up her coat as if she was a child, and then she stood back from him and looked down towards the car.

'I don't think I'll go back to the office,' she said in a tiny voice. 'Could you take me straight home?'

'Yes, of course,' he answered. He wanted to say something else but he didn't know how. 'Whatever you want,' he finished. And silently they started back down the two-mile stretch to the car.

Chapter Thirty-One

Fraser leaned back in his chair and stretched. It was still dark outside. The winter dawn took a long time to break through the night and he wished for some light, some changing in the sky. It was five-thirty a.m. and he had worked round the clock.

Closing his file, he placed his pen on top of it and stood up, crossing to the window to look out at the city of Aberdeen, a city he might never have come back to if it hadn't been for IMACO, for his father's death, for the paper. He loved it, he couldn't deny that, but he wondered what might have been if the love he had for Livvy Davis had been less hopeless. If he had been around her when they left Oxford, if he'd had the chance to step in when she grew out of James, as he was always sure she would, he wondered if it might have developed and grown, grown in a way he knew it never could now. He rubbed his hands wearily over his face. Turning back to his desk, he started as he saw Livvy standing in the doorway of his office watching him.

'Livvy!'

'Sorry, I didn't mean to make you jump. Alec on reception said you were up here. I came for some work.'

'He's still awake then? He has a tendency to drop off around five. Some of the reporters have had to wake him up if they're in early.'

Livvy looked at the shadows around his eyes. 'You look tired,' she said.

He met her gaze. 'So do you.'

They smiled.

'Do you want a coffee?'

'Hmmm, OK.' She walked into the office and dropped her bag down on the desk. She wanted to say something about yesterday, anything, just to clear the air, but she didn't. She had been awake all night thinking about it, that was why she was here, only now she had seen him she'd lost her nerve.

Fraser picked up his file, opened it and put it down in front of her. 'I've been working all night,' he said. 'Have a look through this and tell me what you think.' He went to move past her. 'White no sugar?'

She nodded. 'Fraser?' He stopped and turned. 'I thought you didn't want me to get involved.'

'I didn't.' He shrugged. 'I thought that you had enough on your plate and I reckoned that you should be doing something for yourself, not wasting time on this.'

'But?' How could she tell him that she couldn't even bear to think about her trial? That she was desperate to think of anything other than herself?

'But I guess that you're the best judge of that, aren't you?'

'Yes, I am.'

'Besides, you were right, Livvy, I wouldn't have found this without you.' He touched her shoulder. 'I'd like your help.'

Livvy looked down. She had no idea how close Fraser was to caressing her cheek with his fingers, to touching her lips, tracing the outline of them; she had no idea how close he was to forgetting everything he had told himself yesterday. If she had looked up at him then he would have been lost. 'Thanks,' she murmured.

He dropped his hand and walked on to the door. 'I won't be a minute,' he said, and disappeared, leaving her to read.

An hour or so later, the main office had begun to stir. Several of the journalists working on the first edition of the paper had come in and one of the photographers was in the darkroom, printing up. Livvy had managed to ignore the numerous comings and goings in Fraser's office and had finished what he had given her to read, making some notes of her own. Glancing up at him, she waited for him to finish his conversation with Barbara, the chief sub, and then said, 'I think we should talk about this.'

He nodded. 'You're right. Let's go down to the meeting room, I don't want any more interruptions.' Standing, he took his notepad and a couple of the files he had been working on. 'Come on, before anyone else catches me.'

She smiled and got to her feet.

'Hang on, I forgot these.' Reaching into his drawer, Fraser took out a plastic folder containing three large photographic prints and slipped it in between his files. 'OK. Let's go.' He held the door for her and followed her out.

'If it's urgent I'm down in the meeting room,' he said to Barbara on his way out. 'But only if it's urgent.'

She waved to acknowledge his comment but didn't look up; she was already hard at work on her layout.

In the meeting room, Fraser spread out the files and the information they already had, along with the photographs which Livvy immediately peered at.

'So it is an IMACO lorry,' she said, glancing up. He nodded. 'Who developed these for you?'

'I did them myself,' he answered. Then, seeing her surprise, he explained, 'Gordon was in charge of my training when I took the paper over; he's very thorough. "Yae're bloody wet behind tha ears, Stewart",' he impersonated, ' "but I think we can do something about that".' Livvy laughed.

'I used to be able to run the presses as well, before everything went highly technological. Oh, and I can operate the switchboard!' He reached forward and picked up one of the prints. 'An IMACO lorry travelling up to Garioch with some kind of load. Suspicious?'

Livvy nodded. She glanced away for a moment, then said, 'There's something else I find suspicious as well.' She faced him. 'Beth Broden.'

'Ah.'

'Do you?'

'Talk me through it.'

Livvy picked up the notes. 'Well, for starters, in many of these cases the claimant has had some kind of respiratory problem. Yes?'

He nodded.

'Didn't you make the connection? But more importantly, wouldn't you have been looking for similar symptoms if you were a doctor asked to investigate these cases?'

'They were all different.'

'Yes! But . . .' Livvy held her notes up to read. 'Chest pains, difficulty breathing, lung congestion, upper back pains. These things crop up time and time again whether the claim is for sick leave, early retirement or illness from direct contact with the chemicals.'

Livvy hesitated, then went on, 'Take Myra Hadden's husband Mike – he was sacked, and then he claimed for unfair dismissal, didn't he? Beth Broden, working for IMACO, diagnosed severe stress, owing to the cot death of his first child: "An inability to continue in a managerial position". She lists his symptoms . . . er . . . "lack of clear decision-making even on a local level", blah, blah, blah . . . ah, here we are, "psoriasis, depression, difficulty breathing"!' Livvy stared at Fraser for a moment. 'Panic attacks? It might have been; or was it lung congestion? Certainly IMACO settled out of court, pretty bloody quick as well!'

Fraser held up his hand to stop her. 'Wait! Let's get something straight here. What are you suggesting? That Beth Broden isn't very good at her job? Or are you implying a much more serious accusation?'

Livvy dropped the notes down on the table. 'I don't know, Fraser,' she answered. 'An awful lot depends on whether any of these seven people we've listed here had any connection with that area of land up near Garioch.'

'And if they did?'

'If they did, then my guess is that the symptoms were spotted, recognised, looked for even, then carefully played down, ignored.'

'You mean Beth is lying?'

Livvy raised an eyebrow.

'I don't think it's that,' Fraser said. 'I just don't think she's capable of it.'

Livvy was silent for a minute or so. 'How well do you know Beth Broden?' she asked quietly.

Fraser thought for a moment, understanding the meaning of what she was trying to say. 'Hardly at all, I suppose. I met her on the plane coming back from London several weeks ago. But that doesn't mean that I haven't been able to properly judge her character, Livvy.'

'No.'

They were silent for a few minutes.

'What would she gain by working for IMACO?' Fraser suddenly asked. 'She'd be risking her whole career.'

'I don't know. Some sort of big pay-off? I would imagine that losing a plant like the one up here would involve losing an awful lot of money with it. Maybe one or two big careers as well?'

Fraser was silent. He massaged his temples with his fist for a while, then he sat up straight, took a deep breath, exhaled slowly and glanced down at his watch.

'I think we should go and see some of these people we've listed down here. All of them actually. Then we can really start trying to make some sense of it all.'

Livvy watched him as he stood up, his energy almost instantly rejuvenated. He must have been exhausted, she thought; he looked it but he certainly didn't show it.

He smiled at her face. 'Robots don't need sleep,' he said.

She smiled back. 'Do they need showers, clean clothes?'

He lifted his arm and pretended to sniff his armpit. 'It'll do for another day,' he answered and she laughed. 'I could murder some breakfast though. Come on, Livvy, I'll buy you eggs and bacon down at Regent Quay and a giant mug of tea.'

'OK. You're on!' she said, and stood, collected up the files and stuffed them into her bag for safekeeping.

Hugh had begun to sweat. Heavily. His heart hammered in his chest and the receiver was hot and clammy in his hands. He looked at the clock and waited, each second agonising.

'Come on, Manuello . . .' he murmured under his breath. 'Come on . . .'

Manuello had called him. At seven-thirty a.m. a voice had said, 'Hold the line, Señor Manuello would like to speak to you.' It was now seven thirty-five and he was still holding.

'Hugh?' Manuello's voice was smooth, with only the trace of an accent.

He started. 'Yes? Señor Manuello? Good morning, I . . .'

Manuello interrupted him. 'It is not a good morning, Hugh. Is there anything further since we last spoke?'

Hugh swallowed hard. 'No, not yet . . . but I'm working on it.' Manuello had wanted the drugs traced, but Hugh hadn't even attempted it; it was far too risky.

'I see.' There was a silence and Hugh fumbled in his pocket for his handkerchief to wipe his hand. 'I am concerned about my investment in the insurance market, Hugh,' Manuello went on. 'I am not sure how safe it is as a name with Howard Underwriting.'

'Oh?'

'Put it this way, I am not sure how much we can trust you.'

Again Hugh swallowed; his throat had tightened painfully. 'But there's no reason for you to worry, I . . .' IMACO. Christ, he hoped Dorsey was worrying about nothing.

'You had better make sure that there isn't.' The smoothness had gone. 'I said I would give you a month to trace my goods and you let me down on that, Hugh, and I'm not happy.' There was another silence, then: 'Just ensure that it doesn't happen again.'

Hugh took a breath to speak but the line went dead. He

listened to the empty silence for a few seconds and then carefully replaced the receiver.

Paul Robson was late in. There was a good reason for it: the tube had been stuck in the tunnel at Bank and he'd stood on a sweating, heaving train, in the middle of a dark, hot tunnel under London for more than forty minutes. But good reason or not, he knew as soon as he walked in that Hugh was in a foul mood. His secretary told him that Hugh was waiting for him in his office.

'Morning, Hugh.'

'Paul.'

Robson walked in and sat down. Hugh dropped a British Airways travel folder in front of him and Robson picked it up.

'Aberdeen, tomorrow morning,' Hugh said. 'You leave on the first flight and I want you back by the close of day.'

'IMACO?'

Hugh nodded. 'I want you to find out what's going on up there, sniff around, see if there's anyone who's edgy at the plant. Then I want you to go and see the *Aberdeen Angus Press*, the local rag. One of the reporters there apparently thinks he's on to something with IMACO. I want you to find out what.'

Paul Robson smiled. 'A bit of insurance detective work?'

Hugh remained stony-faced; since that morning he had begun to panic. If IMACO went down then it took Howard Underwriting and all its names with it. If Howard Underwriting went down then Hugh reckoned he'd be lucky to see the summer. He kept his voice level: 'You could call it that.'

'Why? I told you I'd speak to Derek Dorsey. What's the problem?'

'Dorsey rang again last night. You didn't speak to him; I did. He was asking questions about their cover, said it was a routine call, but he's worried about something up there and I want to know what.'

'Shouldn't we be talking to our reinsurers about this?'

Hugh shrugged. 'Later, when I know what's going on,' he said.

'But . . .'

'But nothing! I said later, when I know the full story.'

Robson stood up. Hugh had been bloody odd over the past few months but this was just plain stupid! 'Can't someone else go?' he asked.

'No they can't!' Hugh snapped.

Robson moved to the door. He had given up being offended by Hugh's manner; the bloke was a bastard, simple as that. 'I'll be in the market if you need me.' He turned, chucked the BA folder on his desk as he went past and left the office. He was still angry when he got to Lloyd's, ten minutes later.

Beth Broden strode into the reception of the *Aberdeen Angus Press* and took off her leather gloves as she crossed to the desk.

'Good morning, girls!' She had an officious manner with secretaries, shop assistants and sales girls, the sort of manner that commanded respect, she thought, but which in fact irritated everyone she dealt with and resulted very often in a sharp tittering behind her back.

'I'd like to see Fraser Stewart,' she said. 'Now, please.'

Both the girls looked up at her, then briefly at each other. Rhona, the chief receptionist, stepped in smoothly.

'I'm afraid he's not available right now,' she said. 'Can I take a message?'

'I don't think so. Could you ring up and tell him that Doctor Beth Broden is in reception?'

'No, I'm sorry, I can't do that. You can leave a message.'

'Perhaps then I could ring him myself, if you'll just give me his extension number.' Beth reached for the phone on the desk.

Rhona shrugged. This woman really put her back up. 'You could,' she said. 'But you'd be better off leaving a message with me.'

Beth's finger stopped on the dial. She replaced the receiver. 'Is Mr Stewart not in?'

'No.'

'I see. Can you tell me when he'll be back?'

'No, I'm sorry, I can't.'

Beth was beginning to lose patience. 'I see. Is he out for the day?'

'I really couldn't say. He's gone out with one of our reporters.' The other girl on reception covered a smile with the back of her hand as Beth's nostrils flared unattractively.

'Would that be Livvy Davis?'

'I think so,' Rhona answered and Beth clenched her jaw.

'Right, thank you! I won't leave a message, you've been quite helpful enough already,' Beth said sarcastically. She slapped her leather gloves against the palm of her hand and stormed out of reception. Both Rhona and the other girl burst into a fit of giggles.

'If we've put that one off we've saved him from a fate worse than death,' Rhona spluttered and they both dissolved into hysterics once again.

Ten minutes later, Beth walked into the hotel on Summerhill Road, three blocks down, and asked for the telephones. She left her credit card on reception and went to one of a line of small booths opposite the bar. She found McCreedy's number in her address book and rang him first. They spoke for only two minutes, then she hung up and directly rang Derek Dorsey.

'Hello, Derek?'

There was no greeting, no warmth. Dorsey was anxious; all he wanted was answers. 'Beth. What have you got for me?'

'Fraser Stewart is out of the office this morning. He's gone out with Livvy Davis, the girl who was up at McCreedy's yesterday.'

'Do you know where they've gone?'

'No, I'm sorry, I don't.'

Dorsey swore on the other end. 'Can't you keep a closer tab on this Stewart? He is the last thing we fucking need right now!'

'I'll try. I was up at the office at nine this morning, he must have left . . .'

'Save it, Beth. Don't whine.' Dorsey sighed. 'Is McCreedy any problem?'

'No. He won't talk.' Beth was nervous – this was all getting a little beyond her. 'What are you going to do?' she asked.

Dorsey hesitated. 'For the moment, nothing. If things get out of hand, then I don't know, but I'll handle it.'

Beth felt an icy fear trickle down her spine. 'What d'you mean, you'll handle it?'

'Exactly that!'

'But you won't do . . .'

'Christ, Beth, shut up!' Dorsey lost his temper. 'This isn't a fucking game! If we lose this plant then . . .' He broke off.

A few moments later he spoke again: 'Let me know where they went, by this afternoon.' His voice was calm again, ice-cold. 'I'll ring you at the surgery at six.' And with that he hung up.

Beth stared at the wall of the phone booth for a minute or so, then she shook herself and replaced the receiver. She should have seen it coming. She'd known about the tests up at the plant; she'd known the risks; but she liked the money and she'd been obsessed with Dorsey. Still was, if she was honest, she thought, walking back to reception. That was the trouble – Dorsey was right; this wasn't a game. For Beth it was much, much more than that. She couldn't survive without the excitement of Dorsey, and she wasn't even about to try.

Chapter Thirty-Two

They had established themselves in Fraser's sitting room at Rubislaw Terrace. Livvy sat on the floor, cross-legged, her chin in her hands, staring at a mass of papers spread out over the entire space of the carpet. Fraser knelt on the opposite side of the room and did the same. It was nine-thirty a.m. and this was his second night with very little sleep. It had taken them nearly twelve hours to get this far.

The papers they had amassed were a collection of news cuttings, everything on IMACO they could find, some pieces even going back eight or nine years. There were financial reports that Livvy had asked Lucy Deacon to courier up from London – brokers' reports and the company's Annual Reports for shareholders. Then there were notes on the cases Fraser had brought against IMACO, on some of the cases he hadn't, and finally the interviews they had got yesterday, seven statements from the seven people they had seen.

The room looked like a World War II Ops room, with the map and the photographs in the centre, small red dots marking where people might have come into contact with polluted water, and all the information spread out around the edge.

Fraser was the first to speak; they had been silent for quite some time.

'Livvy, what if, and this is a big if, Benzotytrin is actually dangerous and IMACO know about its dangers? Why are they still producing it? Why haven't they researched an alternative? That's what I don't understand – why take the risks?'

Livvy lifted her head from her hands and reached forward to a small pile of financial reports. She took the top three and opened them on the pages she had marked. 'Pretax profits up 11.5 per cent, gross income from the fertiliser Benzotytrin, 19.2 million pounds,' she read from the first. 'Chairman's statement, two years ago in the middle of a mighty recession, where is it . . . er . . . here . . . "I am delighted to announce that the annual shareholder dividend for 1991 is up by 7 per cent to 3.5 pence", and here, there's a cutting from the *FT* that Lucy's sent. "City backs IMACO rights issue to finance new fertiliser plant in Eastern Europe".' She dropped the reports and looked at Fraser. 'This is monumental business, Fraser. The manufacture of Benzotytrin is keeping IMACO afloat; it's worth billions! And it's still growing, moving into Eastern Europe. What if they can't find an alternative? It's a hell of a lot to lose, isn't it?'

Fraser sighed heavily. 'All right, let's look at it a different way. If they know for certain that the waste products of Benzotytrin are toxic, if not the actual chemical, then why not dispose of the waste properly, with a specialist in that field? There are loads of companies dealing in that kind of thing, aren't there?'

Livvy shrugged. 'Maybe,' she said. 'Perhaps not as many as we think, and one thing's for sure, it would be bloody expensive! Toxic waste disposal does not come cheap. Also, it would mean that they'd have to come clean on it, admit to the waste being toxic, and that could lead to all sorts of complications. I know the MAFF is looking into the fertiliser now but it's a routine thing – they're not looking for anything in particular, are they? Chances are, they'll dismiss it with the minimum of tests, especially if IMACO has gone the traditional route and lined a few pockets along the way.'

Fraser suddenly smiled. 'Have you always been this cynical?'

'Yes, no.' She rolled her eyes. 'Oh, I don't know! Perhaps.'

'Well, I think . . .' Fraser stopped, interrupted by the telephone. 'I think I'd better answer that,' he finished and stood, his legs stiff from kneeling in the same position. 'I'll be back in a minute.'

Livvy watched him as he moved across the room, managing to tread on the papers without making a mess of them. She listened to him answering the call, heard his reaction and thought it must be the paper. Then she too stood, went to the window and looked out at the garden in the dull March light, shivering and suddenly realising how tired she was. Tired, cold and hungry, she thought, but oddly content. Another thing she realised, standing and looking at the daffodils, was that she hadn't thought about herself for days. Not about her life, or James, or the terrible drugs mess. She had thought about nothing but the paper, the LIFESTYLE section and now this, IMACO. Nothing else seemed important, except righting the wrongs with Fraser, and doing it before she was no longer able to.

'That was Gordon,' Fraser said, coming back into the room. 'Apparently there's someone to see me in reception, from London; he flew up this morning.' He crossed to Livvy.

'Livvy? Are you all right? You look terribly sad all of a sudden.'

She turned to him and attempted to smile. 'I'm fine,' she answered. 'Just tired, that's all.' She wanted to explain but she was reluctant to spoil the moment. It was so nice being close to him, sharing this, feeling that she was doing something worthwhile, something not just for herself.

'Who's this person? Did Gordon say?'

'He's an insurance man, an underwriter from a company called Howard Underwriting. Never heard of them, but I suppose it'd be rude not to go in.'

Livvy shook her head. 'Of course you've heard of them! It's Hugh Howard's company. He underwrites a lot of business for IMACO; it was through them that I got the interview with Lenny Duce . . .' She stopped suddenly, that name reminding her of all the pain she'd experienced. Then she said, 'He's sent this bloke up here to find out what's going on, I bet you. Hugh is always one step ahead.'

Fraser looked at her. 'But how the hell does he know anything about this? The only two people that know are you and me.'

'Are you sure?'

'Of course I'm sure!' Fraser snapped, unnerved by what Livvy had just said. How the hell could Hugh Howard in London know . . .? Then suddenly he clapped his hand to his forehead. 'Beth Broden,' he said, 'IMACO.' He closed his eyes for a second and sighed. 'Beth was interested in what I was doing with all my IMACO files out the other evening when she called into the office to see me. It was Beth who rang me about your visit to McCreedy, and she called into reception yesterday morning after we'd gone.'

'So Beth is keeping track of the whole thing.' Livvy

turned away from the window. 'If she *is* on IMACO's payroll and she knows the risk of Benzotytrin, then Doctor Broden has a hell of a lot to lose.' An idea suddenly struck Livvy, something that had been trying to take hold for several hours. 'Fraser?'

He turned.

'What if IMACO are more than aware of the dangers of Benzo? What if they've tested it themselves and have never disclosed the results? They'd have to have done some tests, wouldn't they, even right at the beginning?'

'Yes, but . . .' Fraser stopped for a moment. 'Look, Livvy, I know what you're thinking and it's out of the question!'

'Really? What am I thinking?'

'That if we had that information we would be able to wrap this thing up overnight.'

'Exactly!'

'No, not exactly at all.' He shook his head. 'There is no way that we can get hold of that information, no way! Do I make myself clear?'

She shrugged. 'You'll make yourself sick if you keep getting wound up like that.' She sat on the edge of the sofa and looked at the piles of papers. 'Fraser, listen. It would be a simple case of removing what we have a right to see.' She kept her head down, knowing that he was staring at her. 'We find out where the lab results are kept, and in broad daylight, under some sort of cover, we go in, take the appropriate file and disappear.' She leaned forward to pick up a press cutting on the IMACO plant. 'Easy,' she said, 'very little risk.'

'Easy!' he replied, imitating her. 'Until you get caught!' He stepped closer to her and she looked up. 'No way, I said, Livvy, no way at all am I getting involved in something like that.'

'But you *are* involved!' she cried, 'You've been involved for years, Fraser. Why not finish it now, while there's a chance that you're able to do so?'

'Tell me, exactly what sort of "cover" had you in mind?' he asked sarcastically. 'Go in as cleaners? Oh, I'm sure we wouldn't be spotted; we both look the part after all!'

Livvy ignored his derision. Mocking her or not, he'd stopped ruling the idea out completely. She was quiet for some time while he gazed out of the window, then she decided to go for it. 'Fraser?' she called. He turned back.

'How long do you suppose that what we found out yesterday is going to stay confidential? If Beth is following our steps then she'll know who we saw by, what? the end of tomorrow night, if she's bloody good; or maybe the next day? The day after? My guess is that even if she isn't Sherlock Holmes, she'll have pieced together a list of who we saw; and, remember, she already knows what's been going on, if our supposition is right.' She saw the look in his eyes and went on. 'Once it's out, there are an awful lot of people who'll want to keep us off the scent and I've no doubt they'll succeed. The whole thing will have disappeared before you know it.' She smiled. 'So might we!'

Fraser scowled. 'That's not funny!' He stood there thinking, then said, 'I'm not going to put you in any danger, Livvy, I simply won't do it.'

She let out a long, exasperated sigh. 'You're putting me in more danger if we don't find out what's going on. If we have some real information then at least there's something to bargain with.'

'Christ, you're tenacious!' He strode out of the room and she heard him rummaging in his study. Minutes later he came back. 'All right!' he snapped. 'I tell you what I'll agree to. I'm going to ring Pete Hines, the technician who's testing that water for me, and ask him to hurry the results along so that we've got them this afternoon. If, *only* if, mind, it comes up positive then I'll think about what you're saying. But only then, understood? Until then you'll forget it. I will not go about breaking the law and putting you, us, in grave danger for just one more bit of information that won't do us any good at all. OK?'

Livvy wanted to smile but she didn't dare. 'OK,' she said meekly, then, more briskly, 'I think we ought to get to the paper now and see the bloke Hugh's sent up.'

'*We?*'

'You asked for my help, remember?' Livvy squatted on the floor and began to stack the information they had scattered.

Fraser knelt beside her. 'How could I ever forget?' he asked and at last they both smiled.

Paul Robson looked up from the copy of the *Angus Press* he was reading as Fraser came into reception, followed by a tall blonde who looked vaguely familiar to him. He saw the girls on reception nod in his direction and he got to his feet.

'Fraser Stewart?' he asked, holding out his hand. 'I'm Paul Robson, from Howard Underwriting in London.' He whisked a card out of his pocket and handed it across.

'Paul, this is my colleague, Livvy Davis.' Livvy shook hands. 'Now, what can I do for you?'

'Well, my company underwrites insurance for IMACO petrochemicals and we've recently heard that your paper is investigating some sort of story about them. I really just came to find out what you'd got, and to see if there was anything for us, as their insurers, to be worried about.'

Fraser raised an eyebrow. 'You came all the way up to Aberdeen for that? That's not usual, is it? We're a local newspaper, surely you can't be worried about what we print?'

Robson shrugged; his sentiments exactly. 'To be frank, no, it's not usual but my boss, Hugh Howard, thinks in this case that it's important. Probably because of this MAFF investigation into Benzotytrin.'

'Ah, I see.' Fraser glanced at Livvy. 'Would you like to come through to the meeting room and I'll endeavour to explain what there is.'

Robson nodded. 'Thanks.'

'Coffee?'

'Yes, please. I had an early start.'

Fraser called across to Rhona for a pot of coffee and led Robson towards the meeting room. 'Go on in with Livvy, will you? I just want to call up to my editor and check everything is all right.'

Robson nodded. The blonde really did look familiar and he was sure he knew the name. It was beginning to bug him; he'd probably remember just as he got back on the flight for London. Livvy held the door open for him and he followed her into the meeting room. They sat silently for a couple of minutes after Livvy had enquired about his flight and Fraser joined them just as the silence became uncomfortable.

'So, Paul.' Fraser put a tray of coffee down and began to pour. 'I'm afraid you've had a wasted journey.' He handed Robson a cup. Livvy reached for her own and watched him as he went on. 'Being a good newspaper man, even if I had had a story on IMACO, which I can assure you I don't, there's no way I'd have told you about it.' He smiled. 'We tend to keep these things firmly under wraps; it's all to do with exclusivity.' He sat down. 'The only thing I can tell you is what you already know, which is that the MAFF are carrying out a routine investigation into the production of Benzotytrin.' He shrugged. 'Sorry, but that's all we know.'

Paul Robson put down his coffee cup. 'Well, thanks for your honesty,' he said, not without humour, and Fraser smiled. 'Obviously I'll take a drive up to the plant and see a few people there, find out if there is anything we should be looking out for.'

'Obviously.'

Robson sat for a few moments and then said, 'Look, I hope you don't mind me saying this, Livvy, but you look very familiar. Is there any way we might have met before? Have you ever lived in London?' Much to his amazement, the blonde stood up, walked across to the window and ignored him. He flushed. 'Er, look, I'm sorry, I, em . . . hope I haven't offended—'

'No!' Livvy turned. 'No, of course not.' She glanced down at the floor. 'I used to work for City Television until I was arrested on a drug-smuggling charge. It was about, er . . .' She broke off and looked at Fraser for support. He felt all the humiliation and distress for her.

'It was about five weeks ago,' he finished. 'You probably saw it in the press: it was, it is, a very traumatic experience.'

Robson wished the ground would open up. 'Oh God,' he said, 'I do apologise, I had no idea . . .'

Livvy came back to the table. She looked somehow less imposing than before, as if she'd lost her confidence in the space of minutes. 'Please, don't worry,' she said. 'I should have realised that you'd recognise me, what with my connection to Hugh and IMACO. I guess it was inevitable.' She shrugged and then said, as if trying to convince herself more than anyone else, 'I expect the man on the street has probably forgotten all about it by . . .'

She stopped as Paul Robson touched her arm. The colour had suddenly drained from his face. 'Your connection with Hugh and IMACO?' he asked. The shock in his voice was apparent and Livvy looked at him, surprised.

'Yes! It was Hugh who set up the programme on Lenny Duce, the programme that I went to Brazil to make. He had connections with Duce through IMACO's South American division.'

'But IMACO don't have a South American division,' Robson said. 'We do a lot of business with Brazil but not for IMACO.'

Now Livvy was shocked. She looked from Robson to Fraser and then to Robson again. She felt as if the ground had suddenly started moving underneath her and she was momentarily dizzy, disorientated. 'But I spoke to someone from IMACO,' she murmured. 'On the phone, he set it up . . .' Her voice trailed away. Suddenly she stood up. 'Jesus! I should have seen it myself, Fraser.' She was close to tears. 'I read the financial reports this morning. Why didn't I see that there weren't any operations in South America?' She put her hands up to her face. 'Oh my God!'

Fraser stood and went to move across to her but she dropped her hands and faced him. 'What does this mean?' she asked helplessly.

'I don't know, Livvy,' he answered, 'I just don't know.' He turned to Robson. 'I'm sorry, what you've just said has shocked us both.'

Robson just nodded; he was still trying to work out his own response. He had no idea what was going on. As far as he could figure it, Livvy Davis somehow knew Hugh

Howard. She had been involved in smuggling a huge quantity of drugs into the country. Hugh had all the connections to the drug world in Brazil, and he operated for several big drugs runners here, according to Loman's file. Was Hugh involved in the smuggling? Robson swallowed hard and said, 'Look, I know it's none of my business, but could you tell me how you know Hugh Howard?'

'You're right,' Fraser snapped. 'It is none of your business!'

'Fraser! Please.' Livvy slumped down on to a chair. 'Hugh and I were at Oxford together,' she said. There was no reason to tell this man anything but she just felt the need to. 'As was Fraser, but I hadn't seen Hugh for years, not until a few months back when we met up at a wedding. He used to be great friends at college with the man I was living with, James Ward, and apparently they struck up the friendship again. I only saw Hugh a couple of times after the wedding, but he did come to dinner and it was then that he mentioned he had a connection to Lenny Duce through IMACO.'

She stopped and rubbed her hands over her face before going on. 'He said that IMACO had been involved with Duce in some kind of deal on land they owned in the Amazon Basin, land for redevelopment, and that he could trace Duce for me if I wanted to make a programme on him. The day he came to dinner, I'd just had an interview for a new series of very high-profile programmes at City and they wanted some really hot ideas from me in order to consider me for the job. Hugh mentioned Duce over dinner and I jumped at it. Duce was perfect; he secured me the job.' She shook her head. 'Fat lot of good it did me, eh? Still, I got the first interview he had given in nearly ten years, quite an achievement, along with the prospect of fifteen years in Holloway.'

Fraser flinched at her last words and looked away.

'You think you were set up?' Robson felt sick. His stomach was producing so much acid he thought it was going to choke him.

Livvy smiled cynically but there was defeat in her eyes. 'I think I must have been the perfect dupe,' she said. 'I had absolutely no idea.'

'Shit.' Robson looked at her face. He'd had the eeriest feeling about this whole thing, even when he'd seen it on the television all those weeks back. Why would someone like Livvy Davis take that kind of risk when she was so well known, had so much to lose? He'd always found that hard to understand. Now, he just couldn't believe it. He looked down, silent for a few minutes.

At last he said, 'I think I'd better go.'

'Yes,' Fraser answered, and stood instantly.

Robson picked up his case and overcoat. 'Thanks for your time,' he said. 'I'm sorry if I've said anything to . . .'

'No! You haven't.' Livvy looked up at him and he thought briefly how incredibly beautiful she was, and how painfully sad. He held out his hand and they shook. 'Goodbye,' he said, 'and good luck. With everything.'

She nodded and he turned to follow Fraser out of the door. He couldn't think about anything except her face – her face and Loman's tape. He shook hands briefly with Fraser, eager to get away. He needed some time to think.

'I hope I didn't cause any offence,' he said.

Fraser shrugged and pulled open the double glass doors. 'Listen, Paul,' he said. 'May I ask you a question before you go? You don't have to answer it if you don't want to.'

'Go ahead.'

'Do you like Hugh Howard?'

Robson hesitated before he replied, but only for a few seconds. 'No,' he said, 'the man's a bastard.'

'Thanks,' Fraser answered.

'For my honesty,' Robson added as he went out into the street. And they both knew that for the second time that morning there was an awful lot that had been left unsaid.

Livvy was standing by the window when Fraser walked back into the meeting room. She looked over her shoulder and watched him walk across to her.

'Livvy,' he said, 'I want you to take the next train down to London. You have to sort this out. There's something here that we don't understand and you've got to . . .'

'No,' she interrupted. 'Save it, Fraser, because I'm not going!'

He touched her arm. 'Livvy, please, listen to me for once. You must go down and confront Hugh; you have to find out why he lied to you.'

Livvy put her hand over his. 'We will find out what's going on at IMACO first. We'll finish what we started.'

'No, Livvy!'

'Yes. If Hugh is worried then there is something to be worried about. We owe it to your father to find out what it is.' She spoke with a new strength and conviction. In the few minutes she had been alone in the room she had realised that for the first time since her own father's death she was doing something for someone else, not just for herself, and that it had been this that had brought her alive the past few days.

'I might never be able to prove anything about Hugh,' she

said, 'but I think we *can* prove this. I think we can make sure that at least the people in Aberdeenshire have some justice.'

Fraser held her shoulders and turned her towards him. He had the strongest feeling that there was more to it; that it might have something to do with him. 'Is that the only reason?' He held his breath.

But Livvy looked away. In that one moment she was so close to telling him no, that she was doing it for him, that she . . . But she broke off, stopped her mind from reeling with the impossible and stared down at the ground. The feeling passed. What was the point anyway?

They were silent for a minute, Fraser crushed by disappointment. Then he pulled himself together. She was right, they should finish it, once and for all, then maybe she'd leave him and he would finally have some peace. 'OK. We'll ring Peter Hines. We need to know what's in that water before we start doing any Bonny and Clyde act.' He dropped his hands and crossed the room, putting as much space as he could between them.

'Come on, Livvy,' he said sadly. 'Let's go.'

Hugh was waiting for Paul Robson. He had called the office to say he'd be back mid-afternoon, that there had been a slight change of plan and he wasn't going to bother going up to the IMACO plant. Hugh was seething; the little toerag couldn't be trusted with anything. As Robson walked in, Hugh went out to reception and met him.

'My office,' he said, 'Now.'

Robson kept his face impassive and followed him. He had decided on the plane on the way back from Aberdeen that he was through with Howard Underwriting, but he needed legal advice. He was locked tight into a contract and he was in one hell of a vulnerable position.

Walking across to Hugh's desk, Robson stood while Hugh sat. He kept his overcoat on; he didn't plan to stay and listen to any bullshit.

'What did you find out at the newspaper?' Hugh asked. 'And I thought I asked you to visit the plant as well.'

'There wasn't much point. There's nothing going on up there.' Robson watched Hugh closely as he said the next bit. 'The paper's run by an old friend of yours, did you know?'

'Oh yes? Who?'

'Fraser Stewart.' Robson was disappointed; there was no reaction. Hugh was highly skilled in the art of deception and he was half prepared for it – he already knew that Fraser ran a paper in Aberdeen, so this piece of information came as no big surprise.

'I knew him at college,' Hugh said.

'Yes, he told me. I met another friend of yours from college as well. Livvy Davis? They're working together.'

This time Hugh did react. A sudden flicker of shock passed over his face and Robson noticed before he had time to cover it. 'What's she doing up there?' Hugh asked. His voice was tense. 'Does she know anything about this IMACO story?'

Robson shrugged. 'Neither of them do.'

Hugh snorted derisively. 'You believed that?'

'Yes, why not?' He put his case down on the desk. 'What the hell is all this about, Hugh? Why the paranoia about IMACO? You've never been this concerned before and we're well covered. What's the problem?'

Hugh felt the sudden urge to get up and smack Robson in the face and his anger was so quick and so irrational that it took his breath away. He clenched his fists and his lip curled. He'd wipe the smug expression off that bastard's face!

'We're not covered,' Hugh answered coolly. 'I've never reinsured the IMACO business. It's primary and it's all with us.'

Robson gripped his case. For a moment he thought Hugh was going to laugh suddenly, tell him it was a big joke. The next instant he knew, more surely than he had ever known anything before, that Hugh was insane. He looked at his boss. 'Are you telling me that we have fifteen million pounds' worth of primary insurance risk on IMACO and no reinsurance?'

Hugh leaned back in his chair. He'd certainly wiped the smug look off Robson's face. 'You know, Paul,' he said, 'you're smarter than I gave you credit for.'

Suddenly Robson lunged across the desk, knocking his case over, and grabbed Hugh's tie. He yanked him forward by it. 'If there's anything at all in this fucking IMACO thing then the whole of Howard Underwriting is going to go under, isn't it?'

Hugh was choking; he struggled violently against Robson's grip.

'Isn't it?' Robson shouted. He let go and Hugh dropped back like a puppet. Hugh fought for breath.

'That's why you're so scared about it all, isn't it, Hugh?'

Hugh managed to nod.

'All these jobs . . . My partnership . . .' Robson broke off. He bent and picked his case up off the floor. 'Jesus!' He cracked it down hard on the desk and Hugh flinched. 'You bastard, Hugh!' he shouted. 'I'm liable, aren't I?' He felt a moment of pure panic, as if his heart had stopped beating, and he thought, quite rationally: I am going to kill him. He lunged across the desk again and went for Hugh's throat but his hands froze mid-air. What am I doing? he thought suddenly. How did I come to this? He dropped his arms limply by his sides, clenched his fists and turned away.

'Too much of a coward to hit me, eh, Robson?' Hugh taunted.

Robson looked back and saw the momentary sexual excitement in Hugh's eyes. It sickened him.

'Oh, I'll hit you all right, Hugh,' he snarled. 'Only this type of hit you're not going to enjoy!' And he walked out of the office.

On the corner by Bevis Marks, Robson hailed a cab, climbed inside and said, 'Euston Station, mate.' He leaned back against the seat and closed his eyes.

He should have gone to the police in the first place, he knew that; he should have handed the whole thing over right back in the beginning. Now it was too late – he was far too involved and there'd be questions he just couldn't answer. There was only one way out. They would know what to do with the information. And, if he was quick, he could courier the disk up to Aberdeen and have it there by tonight. If he was quick, it would all be over before he knew it.

Hugh put both hands up to his throat and massaged the red, sore skin where Robson had grabbed him. He swallowed several times to try and ease the pain in his throat, then he picked up the phone. He dialled James at the Foreign Office and was put straight through.

'James.'

'Hello, Hugh.' They spoke on the phone several times a week but James still felt a jolt of physical excitement at hearing Hugh's voice. 'You all right?'

'No I'm fucking not!' Hugh snapped. He stopped, took a breath, then said, 'James, Livvy has got herself involved in something with Fraser Stewart up in Aberdeen. I want her out.' He stopped, finding talking difficult.

'Livvy?' James recoiled at the sound of her name.

'Yes, Livvy! Remember her? The woman you shared the past – what? – eight years with!'

'All right, all right! Calm down, Hugh.' James was shocked; Hugh was losing control.

'I won't calm down, James, not until you get on the next plane and get her out of Aberdeen. Tonight! Do I make myself clear?'

There was a momentary silence. 'I'm sorry, Hugh,' James said tightly, 'but it's just not convenient to do that. I can't just . . .'

'You can do as I fucking well say, James!' Hugh's voice broke and he coughed painfully for several seconds before carrying on in a hoarse whisper: 'Livvy could be in the process of causing me, and you, an awful lot of damage. I don't care how you do it but I want her back in London, tonight!' He stopped again. 'Don't fuck me about, James,' he warned. 'You know what's at stake.'

And, unable to speak further, he hung up.

Chapter Thirty-Three

It was nearly three and the afternoon light was beginning to fade. As Paul Robson made his way across London in a black cab, in Aberdeen, Fraser brought the meeting with his editor to a close.

'Well, that just about wraps it up,' he said, glancing at his watch. They had been waiting since Robson had departed for the results from the lab and he was eager to get on the phone again, to find out if there was any news.

Gordon nodded. 'Reet yae are.' He turned to Livvy. 'Yae think Jenna's happy wi' what she's supposed ta be doing, do yae?' he asked, referring to the LIFESTYLE section.

'Yes, I think so. We went through it earlier this morning. She's got all the work there, it's just a question of sorting it out. Mitch knows what's going on anyway.'

'Aye, Mitch,' Gordon said and left the name hanging. This was the second day Mitch had called in sick and no one had seen him since the helicopter trip. Gordon wasn't impressed; in his book you had to be dying to take a day off work.

'I think I'd better ring him,' Livvy said quickly. In all honesty she hadn't given Mitch a thought in twenty-four hours. She had been so preoccupied with the IMACO thing and then the Paul Robson visit that she wasn't thinking straight; her whole mind seemed in turmoil. 'I'll do it now,' she murmured, standing and picking up her filofax. 'I won't be long.'

She disappeared out of the office and Fraser watched her through the glass as she strode over to her desk in the big open-plan workspace and sat down at the phone.

'I hope yae know what yaer doin', Fraser,' Gordon said. He didn't know the full story but he had a pretty good idea of what was going on.

Surprised, Fraser tore his gaze away from Livvy and looked at Gordon.

'IMACO's a big company. They won't like interference. I've seen it before, remember?'

Fraser's face darkened. 'Yes, I remember,' he said. His voice hardened. 'Only this time they're not going to get away with it.'

Gordon raised an eyebrow. 'Be careful,' he warned, 'that's all I'm sayin'. Watch yaer back.'

Fraser suddenly smiled. He could see that Gordon cared; he was grateful for that. 'Thanks,' he answered. 'I'll . . .'

They were interrupted by a knock on the glass door.

'Er, excuse me? Fraser, may I have a word?' Andy Roberts stood half in, half out of the office. He was obviously nervous.

'Sure, Andy. Come in.'

Gordon nodded to Fraser and stood up. 'I'll speak to yae later then.' And he walked out with the briefest of smiles in the direction of the junior reporter.

Andy Roberts came into the room and perched anxiously on the edge of the chair in front of Fraser's desk. Fraser waited for him to speak.

'Fraser, I owe you an apology,' he began. Fraser kept quiet, he had a pretty good idea of what was coming. 'I'm afraid that my interest in IMACO didn't end the day we spoke,' Andy went on. 'I've . . . er . . . been talking to my contact and keeping an eye on the situation.' The junior reporter was obviously embarrassed. He paused, glanced down at his feet, then continued. 'The thing is that I think I've come across something pretty serious and I need some advice.'

Fraser remained silent. He had anticipated that a junior reporter wouldn't be able to leave a good story alone but he hadn't been expecting any results.

'I think, or rather, I've got reason to believe that there's some kind of problem with Benzotytrin, something that MAFF know nothing about. My suspicions are that IMACO have been testing the chemical up at the plant for quite some time now and that the tests are being kept well under wraps.'

Fraser sat forward. 'What kind of tests?' he asked.

Andy shrugged. 'I don't know exactly. I'm not even a hundred per cent sure this is happening, but I will be, once my contact comes back to me. He's er . . .' He hesitated. 'He's looking into it today, that's why I need some advice. If my suspicions are confirmed, then I'll need to get some proof for this story to work and . . . well, I thought that I'd better come to you.'

'You thought right,' Fraser said. 'You've got yourself involved in a very serious business.'

Andy Roberts blinked rapidly several times but otherwise gave no sign of nerves.

'How much has your contact charged you for the information?' Fraser asked.

'I haven't paid him yet,' Andy answered.

'How much is he asking?'

'Somewhere in the region of a couple of thousand pounds. If the information comes up.'

Fraser tapped his pen on the desk and narrowed his eyes. 'And you think he's bona fide? There's no chance he's been giving you a duff line?'

'No, no chance.'

'OK. If the information comes up, I'll arrange for the money to be given to you in whatever form it's wanted.'

Andy Roberts was stunned. He was expecting a bollocking at the least, the sack at the worst. 'But I thought . . .'

'No, you didn't really think, Andy, not at all,' Fraser interrupted. 'But as it happens you've come up with the information at exactly the right time. You were lucky.' He dropped his pen on to the desk and leaned down to pull some files out of his drawer. 'This isn't just a story, Andy, not any more. There's an awful lot at stake here. When will you hear from your contact?'

'Any time this afternoon.'

'Good. And if tests *are* being carried out, how had you planned to get proof of this fact?'

'My contact was going to set it up for me.' Andy hesitated again, then said, 'He had constructed some sort of plan for getting me in and out of the labs up there.'

'Breaking and entering?'

'Yes, er . . . I suppose so . . . sort of.' Andy flushed and glanced away.

Fraser laid the pile of files across the desk, in front of him. 'This is what we've come up with on IMACO so far. I want you to have a look at them and at what we think is happening. I'm waiting for a call from a friend over at the water authorities who's testing a water sample for me, from the Correen Hills. Then we'd planned to somehow find a way into IMACO to see what's going on there.'

Andy picked up the first file and flicked through it. 'Who's "we"?'

'Livvy Davis and myself. Livvy put a lot of this information together.'

Andy nodded and looked up. 'You don't need to tell me all this, do you?'

'No, I don't.' Fraser had started tapping the pen again; he couldn't keep his hands still. 'But I don't want to take any chances on this going wrong. It's better that you work with me, know what's going on, than against me.' He stopped tapping for a moment, the pen held in the air. 'When I said this was a serious business Andy, it wasn't dramatisation. IMACO stand to lose a great deal if their fertiliser plant is closed down and the chemicals are withdrawn from production. They won't be into discussing things civilly, in my opinion.'

Andy nodded and went to stand up.

'And you read the files *here*,' Fraser said. 'They stay in my office or in Livvy's possession. All right?'

Andy sat down again.

'I'll let you get on with it, then.' Fraser stood up and stretched. 'I'll tell Livvy what's going on.' He walked across to the door. 'I want to wrap this up by tonight. Is there anyone you need to call?'

'No, I don't think so.'

'Well if there is, I suggest you do it.' Fraser glanced over towards Livvy and then back to Andy. 'Because I have a feeling that it's going to be one hell of a long night.'

*

Livvy was talking on the phone and writing at the same time when Fraser came over and sat on the edge of her desk. She looked up, gave him a worried frown and then carried on talking. He bent to read her scrawl. A few moments later, he tapped her on the arm and she said, 'Mitch? Can you stay there for a few minutes? I'll ring back, OK?' She waited for the answer. It seemed to take ages for Mitch to reply. 'All right,' she said, 'just keep warm.' And with that she hung up.

'What's all this?' Fraser held up the scribbled note. 'Temperature, shivering, difficulty breathing, feels like an elastic band tightening over the chest . . .?' He was worried. 'Livvy? What's going on?'

'It's Mitch,' she answered. 'He's not well. I think . . .' She stopped and thought for a moment. 'I think it's something to do with the water on the Correen Hills,' she finished. 'I can't be sure, but he drank some water from the stream there and he's been ill since we got back, unable to get out of bed.' Her voice faltered a little and Fraser put his hand over hers. 'I feel so guilty, Fraser!' she cried. 'I've hardly thought about Mitch. And all this time he's been really ill.' She looked at her note. 'I'll have to try and find him a doctor. He's not even registered with anyone, says he's never bloody ill!' She shook her head. 'It'd have to be a clinic in his part of the city, wouldn't it? Or they won't come out.'

Fraser didn't answer her; he was deep in thought.

'Fraser? Did you hear me?'

He turned and looked at her. 'Ring Beth,' he said.

'*What*? Are you mad?'

'No. Ring Beth.' He picked up the piece of paper. 'Difficulty breathing,' he read, 'a tightening over the chest . . Listen, Livvy, ring Beth first, tell her Mitch isn't registered and you didn't know who else to call. Let's get her round there, let's find out if she really does know anything about this water business. Mitch could tape the examination for us then we'd . . .'

'That's it! I think you've gone off your head!' Livvy exclaimed. 'Mitch is seriously ill and you're asking me to get a mickey mouse consultation from a doctor who we have good reason to suspect will do nothing for him. God, Fraser! You really are the limit!' She went to stand up but he held her arm.

'No! Listen, Livvy, let me finish.'

She glared at him.

'Look, start with Beth, find out what she says and the moment she's gone, get Mitch's local GP round there. That way not only is Mitch not in any danger, but also we have verification of Beth's diagnosis.' He held his grip. 'Please, Livvy, Mitch won't come to any harm, I promise you!'

She looked down at his hand on her arm, then up at his face. She trusted him. 'All right. Give me Beth's number, then I'll call Mitch and tell him what's going on.'

Fraser released her. 'Thank you.' He reached over to the other phone on her desk. 'I'll start ringing round to find out what clinic Mitch should be registered at. And don't let me forget to tell you about Andy Roberts.'

'Andy Roberts?'

'Yes, I'll explain later.' He jotted down Beth's number for Livvy, then dialled directory enquiries for the number of the Local Health Authority. He waited for someone to answer and heard Livvy back on the line to Mitch. He glanced at her and smiled. God, he loved her, he thought sadly, but then his call was answered and he put it out of his mind. He had more pressing things to think about.

*

Peter stood in his office with his back to Moira and stared out of the window at the small square of green sandwiched in between the Inns of Court; the only hint of nature in amongst the labyrinth of cold, grey buildings. Anxiously he waited for the fax from Rio.

As he did so, he went over and over the story he had begun to piece together in his mind, starting with the call that morning from Phil, Livvy's cameraman on the Duce documentary, then his meeting with Seb Petrie, and now the call to the Rio Palace Hotel and their reply, in writing. He turned after several minutes of silent thought and said to Moira: 'I just don't know if we should tell her yet. It's not as if we have any real proof.'

'Proof!' Moira unclasped her hands and reached for her cigarettes; a long-abandoned habit that had taken root again. 'I think what we have is quite enough, don't you?' She lit up and inhaled deeply, watching him. 'Come on, Peter! You can't seriously doubt it after what we've found out today?'

'Of course I can, Moira!' he snapped. 'Innocent until proved guilty, remember?'

'But Peter, look!' She leaned forward. 'What if James packed for Livvy? He's done it before, she told me so. Phil said this morning that all the luggage was collected from their rooms and that none of them handled their own bags again until Heathrow. If James had planted the drugs in Livvy's bag, she would have had no idea, none whatsoever; then there's the man Livvy thought was following her. Seb Petrie said that a drug ring wouldn't take the risk of sending that quantity with an innocent unless they kept an eye on things, he said . . .'

'I know what he said, Moira!' Peter interrupted. 'But all this is supposition.'

'Well, the calls from James to Hugh Howard aren't, are they? Why would James call this friend twice, eh? Once on the day Livvy was due back in the UK and then again two days later? I'll tell you why, Peter! He'd set her up, that's why. He rang to check that she'd arrived back with the drugs, found out she'd been caught and then rang a couple of days later to see if it was safe to come home.'

'Moira, stop it! Please. We can't possibly . . .'

Peter stopped as the fax machine rang. Both he and Moira listened to it click on then Moira stood up and walked across to it. She stared down at the paper as a copy of James Ward's hotel bill came through, with his two calls listed, then she looked up at Peter and said, 'We must find out if James packed Livvy's case, Peter, we *must*!' She glanced down at the fax and then back to Peter. 'Livvy should know all this. It's only fair. We must give her the chance to decide whether it means anything or not.'

He remained silent.

'She might remember something, you know, something important that we've missed.' The machine stopped and Moira tore the fax off the roll, holding it up. 'We must find out, Peter, and we must tell her now, before it's too late to do anything about it.'

Finally he nodded and picked up the telephone. 'All right. But if you really want to say all this, then you must say it to her face, Moira.' He glanced down at his book and punched in a number. 'Otherwise I'm afraid I think you'd be wasting your breath.' He waited for the line to be answered, all the time not in the least sure that they were doing the right thing. Then he spoke into the phone: 'I'd like a seat on the next available flight from London Heathrow to

Aberdeen, please.' And he smiled half-heartedly across at his wife.

Beth Broden rang on the buzzer, spoke into the panel announcing her arrival and waited for the door release to go. She walked into the hall of Mitch's apartment building and located the light switch. It was four-thirty, the street was dark outside and she was itching to get home. The surgery had finished early, this wasn't one of her days for home visits and she'd been out all morning trying to find out what Fraser was up to yesterday. She was tired. It was only the fact that Livvy Davis had mentioned the Correen Hills that had prompted her to agree to seeing the photographer at all. It was probably only a chill but Beth was feeling distinctly edgy and she wasn't about to take any risks. He wasn't registered, and, if by some chance there was any connection to Benzotytrin that she could detect, then she could treat him and keep it entirely to herself. She was playing safe, but that did nothing to ease her irritation.

She climbed the stairs and found the front door of the flat open. A weak voice from the bedroom responded to her call and she walked straight through to find Mitch in bed, with a couple of blankets on top of the duvet, an electric heater on, and still shivering with a chill.

'Hello, I'm Doctor Broden,' she said. She took off her gloves and coat and crossed to the bed. Unclipping her bag, she put her hand to Mitch's forehead.

'Right. Your colleague said that she thinks you caught a chill up on the Correen Hills in the rain the other day. How long have you been in bed?' She said all this as she took a thermometer out and shook it a couple of times.

'About two days,' Mitch rasped. He felt lousy, worse than

he had ever felt in his life before. He could hardly breathe and speaking was hell.

'Open your mouth, please.' Beth slipped the thermometer under his tongue. 'Close. Thank you.' She glanced at her watch and looked around the bedroom in silence for a couple of minutes. Then she took the thermometer out and looked at it. 'Your temperature is up,' she said. 'A hundred and one.' It was actually a hundred and three but she didn't want to alarm him. She wiped the thermometer and placed it back in her bag. Taking out a stethoscope, she said, 'Lean forward, please.' Mitch did as she asked and she checked his breathing. 'You finding it difficult to breathe?' she asked, folding the stethoscope and putting it back.

'Very,' Mitch croaked.

'Any pain in the chest, or back?'

'Yes, it's like an elastic band on my lungs, it keeps getting tighter and tighter.' He stopped, out of breath.

Beth was silent for a minute or so. Then she took out a needle in its packet, a syringe and a small bottle of liquid. 'I'm going to give you a shot of antibiotic,' she said, 'You've caught a very nasty chill.'

Mitch nodded, resting back on the pillows. 'What about my chest?' he asked.

Beth hesitated, then said, 'That's normal with a chill.' She filled the syringe. 'Could you roll over on to your side and pull down your pyjamas bottoms, please.'

With quite a bit of effort Mitch did as she said. He flinched as she injected him and then rubbed the sore spot with his hand as she turned away to dispose of the needle and syringe. He lay back and looked at her.

'I'd like you to sit up,' she said. 'Have you any more pillows?'

He shook his head.

'Cushions?'

'Yes . . .' He pointed to the sitting room and Beth walked out to collect them.

She came back, propped them behind Mitch and helped him into an upright position. 'I want you to try and stay like that. Sleep like that if you can and I'll call in again later tonight to see how you are.'

He nodded weakly and Beth closed her bag, clicking it shut. 'I'll probably be back around seven, or eight. I have to see someone at the hospital then so I'll call in on my way home.' She poured him a glass of water from the jug on the floor. 'Try and get some rest, OK?'

'Yes, thanks.'

She crossed to the chest, took up her coat and pulled it on, all the time looking at Mitch. She was anxious but trying not to show it. 'See you later then,' she said. He nodded and she walked out of the room and quietly left the flat. Minutes later she was out in the street. She stood in the orange light of the street lamp and wondered whether to call Dorsey. She was worried: this was the water, she knew it was. But glancing at her watch she decided not to alert him for the time being. If the antibiotic didn't work in the next couple of hours then maybe she'd call. Until then she didn't need Dorsey's aggression; she had enough to worry about without that.

Mitch climbed out of bed, pulled the blanket around him and knelt on the floor. He heaved the cassette recorder out from under the bed and switched off the record button. Then he rewound the tape, took it out of the machine and put it next to the jug of water. Weak and trembling, he got back into bed and closed his eyes. He'd ring Livvy in a minute, he thought, he just needed to get his breath back first. But he never made it out of bed again to the phone.

He slumped back against the pillows and within seconds he was asleep.

James Ward landed at Aberdeen Airport at five minutes past five. He walked off the plane and towards the airport terminal carrying only an overnight bag. He had no intention of staying but he had brought it just in case. He wanted Livvy out of Aberdeen with him that night but he wasn't taking any chances. If she couldn't be persuaded straight away then he'd stay the night and work on her for as long as it took.

Striding through the internal arrivals gate, he came out into the bustle of the main airport concourse and crossed to the car rental desk to pick up his car. There was no way that James was going to rely on a timetable to get Livvy home. Once he had made up her mind for her, she'd be in the car and off down the motorway to London before she knew what was happening. He wasn't going to risk giving her the time to think things over.

Doctor Chris Goodall stood in the entrance of the Elmhill Hospital waiting for the woman from the *Angus Press*. He had a small brown envelope in his hand and shuffled from foot to foot, glancing at his watch every twenty seconds or so, wondering where the devil she had got to. He'd phoned twenty minutes ago, just after they'd admitted Mitchell McDonald. The things he did for his patients, he thought – at times it really did go beyond the call of duty!

He waved as a familiar figure came into view and pulled the doors open for her. Beth Broden came in from the cold.

Aberdeen was a small place for the medical profession; they all knew each other.

'Hello, Beth. Who've you got here, then?'

'Hello, Chris. I'm visiting a patient with a hip operation. She had it done this morning so I thought I'd come in and check on her.' Beth shook hands with Goodall. 'You?'

'I was called out to an emergency tonight. One of the photographers on the local rag. Lung failure, he was admitted right away.'

Beth's face didn't change but her breath caught in the back of her throat. She coughed lightly. 'Is he all right?'

'Yes, he had a jab of antibiotics from another GP, couldn't remember who, but I'm surprised whoever it was didn't think the lung congestion was serious!' Goodall shook his head. 'Ah!' He looked over Beth's shoulder. 'This must be my journalist.' Moving towards the doors, he held one open as Livvy hurried across the car park towards the hospital entrance.

'You looking for me? Doctor Goodall?'

'Yes. Livvy Davis, from the *Angus Press*.' They shook hands then Goodall handed over the envelope. 'The things I do for patients!' he said and smiled. 'You can't see Mitch, I'm afraid, he's not allowed visitors.'

'He's all right though?'

Goodall nodded. 'And he's in good hands.'

'Tell him thanks for this.' Livvy tucked the envelope containing the tape into her bag. 'And to get well for me.' She pulled open the door. 'By the way, was that Dr Broden I saw you with a minute ago?'

'Yes, she's over . . .' Goodall turned but Beth had disappeared. 'Correction, she *was* over by reception,' he finished and shrugged. 'Obviously in a hurry.'

'Obviously,' Livvy answered. And turning to leave, she reckoned she knew the reason why.

Beth stood by the phone in the corridor next to reception and waited for it to ring. She had called Dorsey and he'd said he'd ring her straight back: She was sweating and her hands were trembling. Seconds later the phone rang and she snatched up the receiver.

'Derek?'

'What's going on, Beth? I told you not to ring me at home during the week.' His voice was cold.

Beth forced down her fear and anger. 'I'm sorry,' she said, 'but it's important.'

'What is it?'

'I think Fraser Stewart is on to something, about the water up at Correen.'

'How much does he know?'

'I'm not sure but . . .' Beth stopped. She suddenly had an urge to cry and she had to hold her breath to stop it. 'I think he's on to me, I think he knows . . .'

'Stop snivelling, Beth!' Dorsey snapped. He thought for a moment. 'Where does he keep all his files? At home or in the office?'

'In the office,' she answered. 'Derek, what are you going to . . .'

'Shut up, Beth!' Dorsey was getting tired of Beth; she was pathetic under pressure. 'I'll do what is necessary,' he said. 'Just go home and forget all about it. Leave it to me.'

Beth had started to cry now, she was unable to stop herself. 'But what . . .'

'Oh for Christ's sake, Beth! Pull yourself together.' Dorsey took a breath then continued more calmly, 'Just do as I say, all right? Just go home, have a drink and forget it. I'll handle it, understood? And keep your mouth shut!' He looked at his watch; he didn't have any more time to waste.

'Goodbye, Beth,' he said, and with that he hung up.

Fraser and Andy Roberts sat in Fraser's office. It was five-thirty and the tension was high. They were sorting through their information and they were waiting. Waiting for one phone call in order to complete the jigsaw.

In the past hour they had finally begun to piece it all together, the whole story, from the dumped chemical waste right through to the incidence of contamination. The tests Pete Hines had run were positive: the water was contaminated with two toxic chemicals, the result of buried chemical waste seeping into the underground water supply. Just how toxic the chemicals were or what sort of damage they were capable of wasn't yet clear, but what they had come up with so far was the groundwork. Now they had to prove that IMACO knew the dangers, knew them long before anyone else. If they did that, then they had a case.

'It's a bloody twist of nature!' Fraser said, holding up a geological map for Andy. 'See here – it's just like Pete Hines said. The only overlying limestone in the area is here.' He pointed to the map. 'And the waste is buried here, at Garioch, right next to it. That's how the whole thing happened. If there hadn't been an underground water supply, then the rivers would have been contaminated and the River Authorities would have picked it up in a flash. This way it went unnoticed, in the small streams and springs that flowed back underground and eventually out to the sea.'

'I wonder how long it's been going on?' Andy said.

'I have a feeling that if your bloke rings, we could very

well find out.' Fraser glanced at his watch. 'I wish he'd get on with it, though, I'm beginning to feel pretty edgy.' He suddenly stood up and stretched. 'I'm going to get another coffee. D'you want one?'

Andy shook his head, but just as Fraser crossed the room the phone went. Fraser reached back to his desk and picked it up. 'Hello?' He put his hand over the mouthpiece. 'It's probably Livvy,' he mouthed. 'I'd wondered where she'd got to.' Then there was a silence. He nodded and said, 'Oh, I see.' His face changed; he stared gloomily out of the window for a few moments and Andy saw a hardness in his eyes. 'All right, Alec, ask him to wait there, will you? I don't know how long she'll be but that's his problem, isn't it?' He hung up.

'Problems?' Andy attempted to clear the air but Fraser didn't answer; he continued to stare out of the window. James Ward was in reception. The information had hit him like a physical blow.

'Fraser?'

He started. Then he took a breath and looked over. 'No, no problem, Andy,' he answered. 'Or at least not one that I can do anything about.'

Moira stood in a phone booth at Aberdeen Airport and searched in her bag for her diary. Finding it, she looked up both of Livvy's numbers and decided to call the office first. She had caught the last plane out and it was getting late but she reckoned Livvy would still be in the office; she nearly always was. She held her coins ready, dialled the number and waited for the line to connect.

'Hello? Yes, may I speak to Livvy Davis, please . . .' She heard a click and then the ringing tone of another line. It rang on for some time and she wondered if perhaps Livvy had gone home, then finally someone picked it up.

'Hello? . . . Oh, Fraser! Yes, it's Moira Marshall. Hello, oh, I see . . . Will she be back tonight or has she gone home? . . Oh, right. Yes, if you could, could you tell her that I'm at the airport? . . Yes, I know, I decided to come on the spur of the moment. What I'll do, Fraser, is wait here for her, if you don't think she'll be very long, that is . . . Oh, right, good! OK. Yes, of course, I won't keep you any longer then. Thank you!' She quickly replaced the receiver.

Fraser sounded odd, she thought, rather edgy and abrupt – waiting for an urgent call, he'd said. Oh well, she guessed these things happened in the news world. She sighed, dropped the diary back into her bag and made her way towards the bar to wait for Livvy.

James was standing with his back to the doors, looking at the framed copies of the paper on the wall, when Livvy hurried into reception. He'd been there for ages, well over an hour and a half. He heard her before he saw her and waited for the right moment to turn. Glancing over his shoulder, he did a double-take at her boyish short-cropped hair and then stood practising his smile as the man on reception stopped her and pointed him out. He wasn't expecting her reaction.

Livvy was worried about Mitch, she was tired and beginning to feel confused as a result. On the way back from the hospital she had stopped at the flat to make a couple of copies of the tape, for safekeeping, but sitting around had only made her more tense. All her emotions were churning up inside her and all the time she tried to concentrate on IMACO, her ideas and thoughts were punctuated by feelings of panic, a panic that threatened to rise up any moment and swamp her.

Scurrying past the desk, she called out hello to Alec, the night security man, and went to dash up to the office. Alec called her back and told her there was a man waiting for her across reception. Livvy turned, puzzled, to see who it could be. Suddenly her face drained of colour and the smile on her lips died. She stood completely still and just stared, her heart hammering in her chest.

'Aren't you going to say hello?' James moved forward but he noticed that Livvy took an involuntary pace back. 'Livvy?'

His voice, his smile, his face, everything about him was so familiar and yet so unreal, so strange. She took in the immaculate line of his suit, his hair, beautifully cut and groomed, his shoes, polished, not a mark on them, and the intense memory of him startled her.

'Livvy? Are you all right?'

She pinched her arm behind her back. It was James, he was here in Aberdeen! She felt disorientated for a few moments longer then she managed to answer him. 'Yes, I'm fine, James,' she said and moved forward. 'How are you?'

'Fine.'

He leaned forward to embrace her, lightly kissing her cheeks. They had greeted each other in this way for many years and it ended her shock. She relaxed slightly.

'What on earth—?'

'Am I doing in Aberdeen?' he interrupted. His face took on its smile again but he changed it to a sad smile this time, a humble smile. 'Do you really have to ask me that, Livvy?' He shook his head and sighed. 'I came to take you home,' he said quietly. 'I've missed you, I don't want to be without you any more.' He went to touch her but Livvy stiffened angrily.

'It's taken rather a long time to come to that decision, hasn't it?' she said.

James took her hand and held it so that she couldn't pull away. She grudgingly let him lead her over to one of the seats. 'Sit down, Livvy. I think we need to talk.' His smile had vanished and as she sat he put his hand round her wrist, measuring the thinness of it. She pulled it away, embarrassed, and he decided to change tack.

'Livvy, had you forgotten that you're due to appear in court in ten days' time?'

She gazed down at the ground. She had forgotten, she had forgotten everything in the past two weeks; everything!

'You do realise the seriousness of that, don't you?'

He was patronising her and she jerked her head up. 'Of course I do!' she snapped. 'I'm not an idiot!'

James shrugged. 'No, maybe not, but you have been a bit foolish, haven't you? Running off to Scotland, burying your head in the sand.'

'How the hell would you know what I've been doing?' she answered angrily. 'It's not as if you tried to find out at all, is it?'

James pursed his lips. 'Actually I've known exactly what you've been doing, every step of the way.' This was a blatant lie but he needed to say it.

'Oh yes?'

'Yes! I've been in touch with Peter.'

'Oh.'

It was another lie but James reckoned Livvy would never know that: she hated Peter; she never rang home.

Livvy sat silent for a few moments. She felt suddenly

very confused and she put her hand up to her temple to try and ease the ache that had started there.

'Livvy, listen to me.' James touched her gently on the arm. 'I've put off and put off coming up here to see you but I decided today that I couldn't delay it any longer. You have a very serious situation on your hands at home and you have to come back and face it. You have to come back *now*, Livvy!' He held her by the elbows and turned her to face him. 'When was the last time you spoke to David Jacobs? Asked him for any developments on the case?'

Livvy shook her head helplessly. 'I don't know . . .' she murmured.

'Exactly. Look, Livvy, I need you, and I think you need me too.' He slipped one hand down to her fingers, taking them and holding them. 'One thing is for sure, Liv, and that is that you need to get on with your life.' He squeezed her fingers. 'Look, why don't you come back with me now, tonight? Hmmm? Seize the moment!'

She pulled her hand away. 'No!' she said tensely. 'Not tonight.'

'But, Livvy!' James sighed, exasperated, and stood up. 'What's keeping you here? What's more important than your own life, your own freedom?'

She looked up at him. 'I couldn't even begin to explain,' she said. 'Not to you.'

'All right then,' James retorted. 'Let's put it this way.' He faced her, still standing. 'You can go on ignoring this whole thing, ignoring it and not facing up to it, living up here in Scotland, and then one day it's going to be there, in all its horrific glory! You'll be tried, convicted and you'll go to prison, for how many years? Ten, fifteen? You won't be able to ignore it then, will you?' He stopped suddenly, knowing exactly the way to play it. After the aggression and fear comes the soft touch. Psychological manipulation had always been his strong point.

'Livvy, think about it, please.' His voice had softened; it was coaxing, persuasive. 'If you came with me now and at least found out what was going on, got involved, then you could come back to Aberdeen after the committal hearing.' He squatted down in front of her, their faces level. Frankly he didn't care what she did once he'd got her back to London; it was getting her there that he cared about. She was silent, staring at the ground; it was a good sign.

'Livvy, I love you,' he said gently, another lie. 'I don't want to lose you. You might have a chance if you came home, but you won't if you stay here, hoping that it will all go away. That chance is like a lifeline to me.'

She lifted her head. His face was earnest, his eyes pleaded with her. She was suddenly filled with a longing for the familiarity of him, for the comfort of someone she had known for so long. All the adrenalin went out of her; the buzz of the past few days stopped. He was right, she had to think of herself, she had to save herself before she saved anyone else. Fraser didn't need her, not really. If he loved her it might have been different but he *didn't* love her, he had made that quite clear. She struggled with her thoughts for a while longer then said, 'Do I have to come now?'

'Yes. It's now or never, isn't it, Livvy?'

She looked away for some time and then finally she nodded.

'I'll get my things,' she said and, not noticing James's fleeting look of triumph, she stood and silently walked out of reception.

*

Fraser looked up as Livvy came into the office but he didn't say anything. The sight of her and the thought of James in reception rendered him speechless. They stared at each other for a few moments, both ignoring the presence of Andy Roberts, and then she said, 'I've got the tape.' She took it out of her bag and placed it, with the two copies she'd made, on the desk. Fraser caught her arm as she did so.

She turned her face away. 'James is in reception,' she said. 'He's come to take me home.' If she hadn't been looking out at the rain over Aberdeen city then she might have seen the terrible look of shock and pain on Fraser's face. It was there for only a moment but it would have convinced her not to go. She would never have been able to leave him had she seen it. But by the time she turned back to him he had somehow managed to veil his eyes, to change his face, and he just looked at her, blank and distant.

'You're going?'

She nodded. 'I have to,' she said. 'I have to go to court next week. I have to sort this thing out, or at least try.'

Fraser's hand was still on her arm, frozen there. He looked down at it and removed it, almost as if it didn't belong to him. Livvy walked over to her chair and picked up her bag. Now she had said it, she was desperate to go, to get out of that tiny office and away from him. He watched her silently as she collected up her coat and scarf. He'd forgotten all about Moira at the airport.

'How long . . .?'

'I don't know,' she answered quickly. She couldn't bear to look at him. 'Goodbye, Andy,' she said. 'Good luck.'

'Yeah, er . . . Bye, Livvy.' Andy Roberts was embarrassed. He didn't know what the hell was going on but whatever it was, it was bloody heavy.

'Goodbye, Fraser,' Livvy murmured, but Fraser had turned his back on her. He stared out of the window, his mind numb and blank, and ignored her. By the time he turned round she had gone.

Minutes later, after a painful, still silence, Fraser looked up at Andy Roberts. 'D'you think this bloke of yours is ever going to—' He was interrupted by the phone. He picked it up and handed it instantly over to Andy. He listened hard and in the next few moments the pain of Livvy's departure gently eased. He forgot everything except IMACO and all that it meant to him. Andy replaced the receiver.

'We're on,' he said. 'We've got one hour, fifty minutes exactly.' He looked at his watch and stood up. 'Come on, Fraser, let's finish IMACO once and for all.'

And grabbing his coat, and the small bag they'd already prepared, Andy led the way out of the office with Fraser close on his tail.

Chapter Thirty-Four

Alec looked up from his crossword book as the door leading into reception opened for the third time in about ten minutes. He couldn't keep up with events tonight; they were coming and going in all directions. A bloke in uniform walked in and crossed to reception holding a small brown package.

'DHL,' he announced. 'Package for Olivia Davis.'

'She's just left.'

'Can yae sign for it, Jimmy?'

Alec put down his book and unclipped the pen he kept hooked inside the pocket of his shirt. He glanced out into the street as he did so. 'Och, hang on a minute!' he said, catching sight of Livvy climbing into a car across the road. 'I think I might catch her.' Jumping up, he hurried round the desk to the doors and looked out into the wet night.

'Och! Missy?' he shouted, waving his arm. 'Livvy Davis!' He stood for a minute straining his eyes but the engine started and the car drove off. He realised he hadn't been heard and turned back inside.

'Here.' The bloke held out a form. 'Sign on the line, will you?' Alec returned to his seat. He didn't like signing for other people's deliveries, it made him nervous. He clicked down the ballpoint of his pen and leaned on the counter just as Fraser and Andy Roberts came hurrying out into reception.

'Oh, Mr Stewart?' He looked up at the welcome interruption. 'There's a package here for Livvy Davis.'

Fraser was at the door before he turned. 'Can you take care of it, Alec? She's gone away for a few days and I'm in a bit of a rush.' He shrugged helplessly.

'Right, Mr Stewart.'

'Could you leave it on my desk when you've signed for it?'

'Aye.'

'Thanks, Alec.' Fraser didn't have time to say any more. He held up his hand and followed Andy out of the door, running down the steps and catching him up further along the street.

Alec underlined the place he had to sign with his little finger and scribbled his signature. 'Where's it from, this package?' he asked.

'London,' the DHL man answered, folding the form and tucking it back inside his jacket. 'Must have been important to send it DHL, seems a bit of a waste of money as she's not here.' He rolled his eyes and zipped his jacket up again. 'Oh well. Cheerio,' he called over his shoulder as he strode to the door. He stepped out into the pouring rain, unlocked the door of his van and climbed inside.

Alec watched the red and white vehicle drive off and then went back to his crossword puzzle. He'd lost track of it now; bloody interruptions! He'd seen more action tonight than he usually saw in a week. He hoped it wasn't a bad omen.

Livvy sat and stared silently out of the car window as the lighted city of Aberdeen passed before her eyes. They were on South Anderson Drive, heading out towards the A92, the coast road down to Perth and, as the rain poured, the orange street lights blurred in her vision. She put her arm up and silently wiped the wet off her cheeks with the back of her hand. She didn't know why she was crying but she couldn't stop herself. All she kept thinking, as the tears streamed silently down her face, was that maybe she should have stayed, that one more day in Aberdeen shouldn't have made any difference to James.

That morning she had determined to do something for someone else for a change and now here she was, running out on Fraser and thinking only of herself. She was miserable, confused and she wished she'd had the time to think it all over.

As he slowed the car for the traffic lights at the Bridge of Dee, she reached behind her for her bag. She had packed it in less than ten minutes, James standing uneasily just inside the door of her attic flat with his overcoat on, a barely covered look of distaste on his face. She pulled out a handkerchief and blew her nose. Then she looked at his profile and to make conversation said, 'So how did you get the new number of Peter's chambers? Mum said it was . . .' She stopped, noticing a tightening of his jaw as she spoke, an involuntary muscle spasm in the side of his face, and she watched it for a few seconds. He kept his eyes on the road and stayed silent, pretending he hadn't heard her.

'James?'

'Hmmm?' He took his hand off the steering wheel and patted her leg. 'I'm trying to concentrate, Livvy darling. I don't want us to end up in Aberdeen docks!' He smiled, a small, tight, little smile and she thought how false it was. She wondered why she'd never noticed it before.

'James, I asked you how you got hold of the new number for Peter's chambers?' she said again, this time staring openly at his face. Something was beginning to feel odd. A feeling of wariness took hold. 'Mummy would have told me if you'd rung home.'

James edged the car forward but the lights changed before he had time to drive off. He ignored the question for the second time and concentrated on inching the car forward.

'James?'

'Directory enquiries,' he answered at last. 'Good old BT.'

Livvy saw the muscle twitch again. 'But how did you know the name of the new chambers? He's not listed under Marshall.'

Suddenly James stopped the car. He was irritated by her pointless questions. 'Livvy, what is this? The third degree?' He looked at her with a mixture of distaste and exasperation. 'I just knew, all right? Now let's forget it!'

Livvy stared at him. It hit her like a thunderbolt; he was so transparent, she could see right through him. 'No,' she said, shaking her head, 'it's not all right and I won't forget it! You didn't know, did you, James?' Why hadn't it occurred to her to ask him earlier? 'Because you've never spoken to Peter!'

He faced her. 'For God's sake, Livvy! Grow up! What the hell does it matter anyway?' He went to touch her but she pulled away.

'You didn't know and you lied to me.' Her voice was hard. 'That matters!'

He looked away and his nostrils flared angrily. He wondered how he could ever have stomached living with her and it showed in his face.

'My God!' she suddenly cried. 'Why are you here?'

'Well, it's not from bloody personal choice!' James shouted back angrily. He hated pushy women, pushy snivelling women! He turned back towards her and for an instant he really hated her. Then he got a grip on his emotions and calmed himself. 'Look, Livvy. What is all . . .'

But it was too late. Livvy had seen his face.

'You bastard!' she cried and lunging behind her for her bag, she dragged it over into the front seat and began to open the door.

'NO YOU DON'T!' James grabbed her arm and tried to force her back as she struggled with the door.

'Let go of . . .!'

He yanked her in and put his foot down on the accelerator, shooting the car forward and wrenching her shoulder. Without thinking, Livvy bent and sank her teeth into his arm just as he slammed on the brakes, narrowly missing the car in front.

'Jesus! You bitch . . .!' In an instant James had hit her. He swiped his palm across her face and smacked her head back against the window. It knocked the wind out of her for a few seconds and then she tasted blood in her mouth. It incensed her. Struggling frantically, she forced the car door open and jumped out into the rain. Her knees buckled momentarily from the shock and then the cold air hit her. Clutching her bag, the icy rain stinging the gash on her cheek, she started to run across the road, darting between the cars and away before James had a chance to realise what was happening.

Seconds later the lights changed and the two cars in front of him moved off.

'Livvy!' He jumped out of the car after her and left the engine ticking over, the door open, running across the road after her. 'Livvy, come back here!' he screamed at her. 'You stupid bitch! What are you doing?'

He spun round just as the Ford Escort 3i, speeding up the inside lane to dodge the traffic at the lights, failed to see his stationary car and hit it, at forty miles an hour.

The noise was phenomenal.

'Oh my God!' he shouted, then spun back to see Livvy urgently flagging down a black cab across the road and hurriedly climbing inside. 'Livvy! Come back here!' he screamed again, but it was a waste of breath. The cab moved off into the traffic and she was gone. He put his head in his hands and shut his eyes as a crowd began to form around the accident and someone ran for an ambulance. He heard shouts in his direction and, trembling violently, made his way back to what was left of the car.

Alec finished the last clue of his crossword and sat back in his chair, reasonably contented. It wasn't a personal best – it had taken twenty minutes longer than normal, but that was only to be expected with all the interruptions he'd had. He replaced his ballpoint pen in his top pocket and put his feet up on the desk. It was nearing eight now and things looked to have settled down a bit for the night. He closed his eyes, relaxed for a few minutes and in barely any time at all reception was silent except for the gently wheezing sound of his snoring.

*

The front man was in a suit with a black anorak over the top. It was easier to work that way; it saved questions, looking like a businessman. He walked silently into reception with his colleague out of sight behind him and stopped, just inside the double doors. He could hardly believe his luck. The night security guard was asleep.

Taking out the small, blunt leather-covered truncheon he kept in his pocket, he walked across to Alec, his footsteps noiseless on the carpet, and stepped neatly behind the desk. At just the right point on the back of Alec's head he brought the truncheon down with a swift, hefty blow and Alec's body fell sideways, unconscious. He caught him, dragged him off the chair and motioned to his colleague.

They laid Alec behind the desk out of sight and then went back out to the car parked in front of the building. It took only minutes to carry in the four litre cans of petrol and lock up reception after them. Then they made their way up the stairs to the main office to do the job.

Pouring the petrol freely, they covered most of the surfaces in the main office and left a trail to the front door. They were quick and efficient, experienced. The man in the suit walked into the two editorial offices at the far end but couldn't see anything lying around. His brief was the main office.

'Yae got any left?' he called across to his colleague. The other man shook his head. 'Naer mind, this'll go up in a flash anyways.' He walked back out into the main office, looked everything over and took up his two empty cans.

'Come on, let's go.'

He emptied the waste paper from two bins on to a desk and while his colleague held the fire door open, he struck a match and put it to the small pile of rubbish.

'Goodbye, *Aberdeen Angus Press*,' he said as a flame took hold. And darting out on to the staircase, he hurried down after his colleague, unlocked the doors of reception and they both disappeared out into the night.

Livvy leaned forward on the seat of the cab and tapped the glass impatiently behind the driver's head. He glanced behind him and slid it open.

'Can you get there any quicker?' she asked.

'It's tha traffic,' he said. 'Not up to me, henny.'

She nodded and looked nervously out of the window. They were stuck in a jam at the roundabout on North Anderson Drive, just past King's Gate; the road was up and it was a mess. Opening her bag, she took out her purse and leaned forward again. 'How much is it so far?'

'Two fifty-five,' he answered, looking at her in the mirror.

'Fine.' She emptied the change into her hand, found three pound coins and passed them across. 'Sorry,' she said quickly, 'but I'll walk. I'm in a terrible hurry!' She yanked open the door and jumped out. 'Keep the change,' she called to him as she ran along the street, 'I really can't wait!'

She ran all the way up Summerhill Road, her heart pounding and the rain whipping against her face. She was soaked within seconds but she didn't care; all she wanted to do was get back to Fraser. Sprinting down Lang Mastrick Drive she hared round the corner into White Myres Avenue and the *Angus Press* building was suddenly in front of her, about four hundred yards up on the left. She had never been so pleased to see a neon sign in her life. Not letting up, she ran harder towards the entrance, slowed just as she got there and jogged up the steps into reception, pulling the doors open and dashing inside.

'Alec?' She hurried past the desk. 'Alec?' She glanced behind her as she pulled open the doors to the staircase and it was that that probably saved her life. She narrowly missed a cloud of thick, black, choking smoke billowing out and hitting her full in the face.

'Jesus!' Putting her arm up immediately over her mouth she staggered back. 'My God! Alec!' She saw the body under the desk and kneeled down to check his pulse. 'Alec? Alec, can you hear me?' She saw his eyelids flutter. 'Alec! . . . Alec! Is there anyone else in the building? Alec!' She stopped as his eyes opened momentarily and bent her ear to his mouth. 'Come on, Alec . . . please . . .' She had started to shake. 'Alec . . . Is there anyone else in the building?'

He managed to indicate that there was no one. 'Oh, thank God!' she breathed; the relief almost overwhelming. Fraser was safe. Seconds later she acted.

Getting up into a squat position, she put her body weight under Alec and held him beneath the arms. With a massive effort, she dragged him, half standing, her knees unsteady with the weight, out from under the desk and away from the doors. Her face was throbbing painfully from the blood that pumped round her body and she was panting hard, but she managed to get him to the glass doors. Heaving him forward, she shoved the door with her leg and hauled him out on to the steps. Then she let him drop, the rain coming down on to his face, and stood with her hands up to her head, dizzy and sick with the pain of the effort.

After that, instinct took over. She ran down the steps, took off her jacket and dumped it into a muddy puddle by the gutter. She did the same with her scarf, then she bent her face to the water, splashed her head, her jeans, all over, with as much water as she could, wetting her handkerchief through, and wringing it out. She stood, put the sodden jacket back on again and held the handkerchief. Running back into the building, she stopped at the phone, dialled 999, gave the address, then put the wet square of cotton up to her face and tied it round the back of her head, covering her nose and mouth. She tied the wet scarf around her head and pulled on her gloves.

She was ready.

Taking a huge gulp of air down into her lungs, she held it there, opened the door to the staircase and ran up on to the stairs. She had only a matter of minutes.

The smoke was blinding. Her eyes streamed but she knew her way up and she managed it almost without sight. At the first floor, the air in her lungs had started to expand and she felt the overwhelming urge to gasp. She fought it down and clamped her mouth shut, opening the door to the main office. In a smog of toxic smoke, she staggered in and wiped her streaming eyes to try and see. The flames were fierce and high but the fire followed the line of the petrol; it hadn't taken hold of the whole area yet. She had seconds.

Darting along the side wall where it looked safest, she ran to Fraser's office, her lungs burning now, the sweat pouring down from her forehead, rewetting the handkerchief that had started to burn on her face. She picked up a heavy stapler and hurled it at the window, smashing the glass and lunging forward to the gush of fresh air. She gulped painfully, taking several deep breaths and coughing as she did so. Then she took one final breath and turned in to the office. She picked up the rubbish bin, emptied it on the floor, grabbed the plastic bag from it and swept the papers, the tapes, the package, everything on the desk, into the bin liner. She stuffed it down inside her jacket and started for the door.

But the air coming through the smashed window had fuelled the fire. The flames spread up across the office and licked the walls. Already parts of the ceiling were alight, thick, foul smoke from the burning of the tiles pouring into the room. A sob of panic rose in Livvy's throat as she watched for a couple of seconds. But there was no time to think. She ran out, back the way she came, along the side of the office, the heat knocking her back several times and forcing her to change direction.

She made it to the door but she didn't see part of a ceiling tile as it crashed down in flames and caught her on the back of the shoulder. She screamed with the pain and seconds later her arm was alight. Staggering forward, she clutched her arm, all hope of holding her breath gone. She made it to the staircase, smashed her arm violently against the concrete wall to try and put out the flames and took in gulps of thick black smoke. She started to cough as she fell forward towards the stairs. Her whole body felt on fire – her lungs, her face, her arms. Then she lost her footing and plummeted. The black smoke enveloped her and that was the last thing she knew.

Fraser was silent as he drove Andy Roberts home towards Aberdeen. He kept glancing anxiously at Roberts as he looked through the files they had stolen from IMACO, files he'd just risked his reputation for. He knew they were full of undisclosed tests on Benzotytrin but Roberts was looking for results; it was the results that they needed. He wondered why he didn't feel better about it, why it somehow didn't make much sense any more. This was his life, it was what he had been trying to achieve since the day he had come back to Aberdeen, but now, after all the fear and the adrenalin, there was nothing inside him, no sense of justice or triumph, just an ugly taste of disappointment that he had no one to share it with.

They were on the outskirts of the city when Roberts found what they were looking for.

'Here it is! It's here, Fraser.' He glanced across. 'Pull over and have a look at this. I think we've done it!'

Fraser slowed the car and indicated, pulling into a lay-by. He switched the engine off and Roberts handed him a file.

'There's more,' he said excitedly. 'Here're test results on the fertiliser . . . from five years ago.' He began to quickly flick through the rest of the files. 'And here . . . and here . . . Bloody hell, Fraser! These files date back six years – they started testing Benzotytrin back in '87.'

Fraser had begun to look through his file. It was dated April '91 and it contained pages and pages of statistics on the level of certain chemicals in hundreds of water samples. He briefly scanned the columns, leafed through the papers and then closed the file. He switched the engine back on and Roberts looked up.

'I want to get these back, copied and into the safe,' Fraser said. 'Then I've got to get across to the airport.' He'd forgotten all about Moira in his haste to get to IMACO. He felt guilty; he had to go and explain about Livvy, apologise to Moira. 'Can I leave this to you?'

Roberts nodded. He closed his own file and glanced up at the sky up ahead. 'Jesus! Looks like a bloody great fire in the city somewhere.'

Fraser followed his gaze. 'Yeah, it does. I hope we've got it covered.'

Andy smiled. It was the first time Fraser had sounded

normal since Livvy had left. 'It looks as if it's in our part of town,' he answered. 'I'd be surprised if we hadn't.'

They drove on, watching the orange glow of the sky, and all the time they headed towards it. Neither of them spoke again but the closer they got to the city, the more a sense of unease began to creep into the car.

'Fraser? D'you think . . .?' Andy glanced across at his boss.

'I don't know,' Fraser said quickly, 'but for some strange reason I'm beginning to feel concerned.'

They were on North Anderson Drive now and Fraser took the turning off towards Mastrick. He drove down Lang Stracht and turned into Fernhill Drive. As they approached White Myres Avenue to turn they were forced to slow; the whole area was cordoned off. A police officer came up to the car and Andy wound down the window.

'What's happened?' he asked.

'The *Angus Press*,' the young officer answered. 'It's gone up in smoke . . .' He stood up quickly as Fraser jumped out of the car. 'Hey! Where're you . . .?'

Fraser had started to run, under the plastic tape and along White Myres towards his paper. Andy jumped out after him. 'Oi, Fraser! Wait!' He turned to the policeman. 'He owns the paper,' he explained. 'I'd better . . .' He started to move off after Fraser.

'Hey, you!' the officer shouted. 'Move this car!' Roberts stopped and turned. 'NOW!' He hesitated momentarily, then walked back towards the car. By the time he glanced back, Fraser had sprinted away.

Fraser stopped behind a crowd, his chest hurting like hell from running, and bent his body double while he tried to get his breath. He didn't have the energy to push through for a few minutes.

'Och, tha poor lass! I dunnae believe it, some people are sooo brave.' Two old women in front of him stood ogling the flames and discussing the situation.

'Shae dragged him, I hearrd, tha security guard, I dunnae know how she got tha strength.'

Both tutted and Fraser began to feel uneasy. He listened hard.

'D'you know who shae was?'

'Och no, just a journalist, I hearrd. Shae'd come back for something . . . Hey! . . . D'you mind, sonny! There's other people here afore yae.'

Fraser didn't stay to hear any more. He elbowed his way through the crowd, mumbling his apologies, an icy fear inside him. Making it to the front, he saw the chaos of the fire, the engines, the hoses, two ambulances and the police trying to hold back a nosey, insistent crowd. He began to run.

'Hey! You! . . . You can't go near there.' Shouts started up all around him and he felt someone try to grab him but he was oblivious to it all. He ran on, almost blind with panic. On the pavement on the opposite side of the road from the building he caught sight of Alec, sitting on the kerb, a red blanket round him. He shouted out and ran across. 'Alec . . .' He could hardly speak, his lungs burned. 'Alec . . . what . . . happened?'

'Oh God! Mr Stewart!' Alec was trembling. 'They wanted me in the van but I told them no, not yet, I couldn't, not until I saw you . . .' He shook his head and put his hands up to his face. 'Oh God . . . That poor girl, Livvy . . . I . . .' He was near to tears with the shock. 'Thank God you're here, Mr Stewart . . . I . . .'

But Fraser didn't hear him. He had started to run back across the road towards the building, pushing and shoving his way violently past the firemen to get closer to it, to find Livvy. He had no idea what he was doing; he couldn't see or hear anything.

Suddenly someone tackled him from behind. He cried out and hit the ground face down, cracking his shoulder, the weight of the fireman on top of him. He struggled for a moment despite the pain and then moments later lay still, his face in the grimy wet tarmac. All the fight had gone out of him and he closed his eyes.

The man roughly pulled him up. 'What the hell do you think you're doing?' He held Fraser by the shoulders and shook him.

'I . . .' Fraser dragged his mind back to reality. 'A young woman,' he said. 'She was in the building.'

The man's face changed. 'You know her?'

Fraser started. 'Know her? Jesus!' He caught his breath. 'Where is she? Is she all right? Where . . .?'

The fireman nodded towards the ambulance. 'They're just pulling out now . . . You'd . . .' He didn't finish his sentence.

Livvy was strapped on to the stretcher. She had an oxygen mask over her face and a medic sat by her side, monitoring her pulse, as they positioned her ready for the ambulance to move off. The driver came round the back of the van to close the doors just as Fraser got there.

'Wait!' he cried. 'It's . . .' he broke off. 'It's my girlfriend,' he said and the driver let go of the doors. He climbed inside.

'Livvy?' Bending towards her face he whispered, 'Livvy?

Can you hear me?' Her eyelids fluttered, then she opened them. He could see her try to smile beneath the mask and he choked back the tears.

'Don't make me cry,' he said, gently touching her scorched hair. 'Boys don't cry.' He put his hand up and wiped his face.

She nodded, down towards her chest.

'What?' He bent closer. 'What is it, Livvy?' He glanced up at the medic. 'What's she trying to say?'

'She had something in her jacket,' he answered. 'She wouldn't let us get at it. A bag, I think. Full of files? Papers?' The medic shrugged. 'Perhaps you'd better come to the hospital, take it off her there.'

Fraser looked at her eyes, a clear intense blue, and saw the relief in them. 'Yes, I'll come to the hospital,' he said. Then he lifted his face to hers and kissed the oxygen mask. She tried to smile once more and her eyelids gently closed. 'I won't let this woman leave me again,' he whispered, close to her face. 'I love her, you see.' He stopped and swallowed hard. 'Besides, look at the terrible mess she gets herself into without me.'

Aberdeen, October 1993

Livvy sat at the table in the large untidy kitchen of Fraser's house, correcting the article she'd written for the paper's LIFESTYLE section that morning. She should really have been in the office but she'd taken the morning off. For the first time in years, Livvy Davis had finally slowed down and work had ceased to be the focal point of her life. She was happier than she could remember ever being.

Glancing up at the clock, she saw the time and stood, crossing to the radio. She switched it on to hear the news and went back to her work, tucking her legs up under her on the chair and resting her head in her hands to read. Seconds later the headlines came over the air and her whole body froze.

'The two Oxford graduates convicted of smuggling five kilos of high-grade cocaine into the country earlier this year were sentenced today in the Crown Court. Hugh Howard of Howard Underwriting pleaded guilty to all charges and was sentenced to fifteen years imprisonment; James Ward, a former senior secretary with the Foreign Office, pleaded not guilty but was convicted and sentenced to five years.

'In his summing up, Mr Justice Ottorman commented on

the ruthlessness of the operation which involved the wrongful arrest of Livvy Davis, back in February this year. Miss Davis, a former City Television presenter . . .'

Livvy was still sitting at the table an hour later when Fraser came home. The Archers were on in the background but she heard nothing. She just stared out of the window, blind to the windswept, high white clouds in the pale blue October sky. Her face was wet but she had no idea she was crying.

Fraser took his jacket off and walked straight through to the kitchen. He stopped in the doorway and stood looking at Livvy for a moment. He often did that, just looked at her, unable to believe that she was here, in Aberdeen, with him. He saw that she was perfectly still and he crossed to her, bending to sweep back her hair and kiss the side of her face, the side that bore an ugly red burn scar. She started.

'Oh, Fraser! . . . I . . .' She turned towards him.

'Livvy? Hey.' He sat down quickly next to her. 'What is it?' She shrugged.

Taking her hand, he kissed the palm. He knew why she was crying; that was why he'd come home for lunch. He'd seen it on the Press Association screen an hour earlier. He kept hold of her hand and said, 'D'you want to talk about it?'

Again she shrugged and they stayed silent for some time.

After a while, she turned to him. 'Is it over, d'you think?' she asked.

Fraser squeezed her hand. 'Yes, I reckon it is. For you, anyway.'

'What will happen to Hugh?'

He thought for a moment. 'I don't really know. The whole Lloyd's business is still under investigation, thanks to

Robson, and if it's what they think it is then he'll have some pretty heavy people after him.'

'Is that why he confessed, d'you think?'

Fraser shrugged. 'Maybe. Certainly I should think that he's safer in prison, Livvy.'

She looked away and shuddered. A few minutes later she began to say, 'What about . . .?' but Fraser silenced her by putting his fingers to her lips.

'You asked me if it was over and it is,' he said gently. 'But we aren't.' He leaned forward, his face just inches away from hers. 'We are just beginning,' he said, and pulling her towards him, he kissed her.

Maria Barrett

ELLE

She has nothing but a name and a dream of revenge . . .

Ruled by a tangled and violent past, Elle shuts her heart to love in a ruthless search to find her mother's murderer.

Glamorous, brilliant and rich, poised at the pinnacle of her career as the young head of a prestigious banking company – she must risk losing the key to her past and the love of her life as she engages her enemy.

ELLE
introduces an exciting new writer destined to catch your imagination and sweep into the bestseller lists.
A story of one woman's lonely fight that grips the reader from beginning to end.

General Fiction

Maria Barrett

DANGEROUS OBSESSION

From the day of her mother's death to her husband's murder, Francesca has known only hatred, violence and jealousy. Until, fleeing her past to forge a new life in England, Francesca at last finds kindness – and with Patrick Devlin, true passionate love . . .

But a peasant girl from Italy is no asset to an aspiring politician, and Patrick ends their affair, leaving Francesca to rebuild her world a second time. Yet, as she gradually makes her name as a fashion designer and he is promoted to the cabinet, neither can forget what they once shared.

And Francesca's past is never far behind . . .

General Fiction

Nicole McGehee

REGRET NOT A MOMENT

'A sparkling story, a luscious setting, a memorable heroine. Wonderful' *Janet Dailey*

The year is 1930. Beautiful, spirited and independent, Devon Richmond is the daughter of a prominent Virginia family. Though many men have asked for her hand, none has captured her heart – until John Alexander, a dynamic business tycoon, walks into her life and Devon knows that the love will never stop flowing between them.

Their electrifying passion is celebrated in marriage and a fairy-tale future seems preordained. But Devon can foresee neither the terrible tragedy that will blight their union, nor the conflicts that will drive deep divisions between them.

From the dizzying sophistication of New York to the thrilling bazaars of Cairo, *Regret Not A Moment* spans the unforgettable life of a breathtaking woman. Devon Richmond.

General Fiction

Warner now offers an exciting range of quality titles by both established and new authors. All of the books in this series are available from:
Little, Brown and Company (UK),
P.O. Box 11,
Falmouth,
Cornwall TR10 9EN.

Alternatively you may fax your order to the above address. Fax No. 0326 376423.

Payments can be made as follows: Cheque, postal order (payable to Little, Brown and Company) or by credit cards, Visa/Access. Do not send cash or currency. UK customers: and B.F.P.O.: please send a cheque or postal order (no currency) and allow £1.00 for postage and packing for the first book, plus 50p for the second book, plus 30p for each additional book up to a maximum charge of £3.00 (7 books plus).

Overseas customers including Ireland, please allow £2.00 for postage and packing for the first book, plus £1.00 for the second book, plus 50p for each additional book.

NAME (Block Letters) ....

ADDRESS..

....

☐ I enclose my remittance for _____

☐ I wish to pay by Access/Visa Card

Number ☐☐☐☐☐☐☐.☐☐☐☐☐☐☐☐

Card Expiry Date ☐☐☐☐